HOW LONG IS *Exile?*

BOOK II
Out of the Ruins of Germany

Astrida Barbins-Stahnke

HOW LONG
IS *Exile?*

To order additional copies of this book, contact:
Xlibris
1-888-795-4274
www.Xlibris.com
Orders@Xlibris.com
726791

CONTENTS

Foreword xi

Acknowledgment xiii

PART I 1

The Ruins of Germany

Winter 1945 5

Arriving in Oeslau 7

Learning the German Language 10

Holy Week 12

Easter Sunday, April 1, 1945 18

After the Holidays 22

Herr Niert 26

Mildchen and *Mutti* 35

As the World Crumbles 38

Defying Age 44

Treasures in the Attic 47

The Way the Big War Ended 49

The Swallows 53

Walpurgis Night 58

May Day 63

In Sickness and. 65

The Egg Hunt 68

Blood 72

Capitulation 77

All that Jazz 80

Milda Makes a Move 86

Summer 1945 90

Reconstruction 94

Milda finds Juris 96

Milda and Gert 98

Open Borders 103

On the Road Again 104

Rest Stop in Nurnberg 108

Searching for a Destination 113

PART II 117

A Place for the Displaced

Esslingen 117

Lido 126

Next Door Neighbors 129

The Gymnasium (high school) 132

The Theater 134

Establishing a *Latvian* Esslingen 136

Autumn 1946 142

Saulcerīte (Hopeful for the Sun) and Zelta Zirgs
(The Golden Steed) 144

After the Performance 148

Christmas Eve Celebration 149

1947 152

Miss Exile Latvia 153

Entertaining the Veterans 157

The First Song Festival of Free Latvians in Free Germany 161

The First Wave of Emigration 163

New Arrivals Next Door 168

The Reverend Gramzda family 171

Impressing Americans 184

New Parts to Play for Milda and Alma 187

1948 196

At an Art Exhibit.. 205

Migration of Displaced Persons 212

Stairway to America...217

Above the Vineyard..221

Kārlis Arājs 230

Neighbors Can Help 241

Milda Prepares for America.. 243

Milda and Kārlis.. 247

Alma takes Control of Milda... 249

1949 251

Kārlis Departs for America.. 252

Separation and Anxiety... 256

Roses on Ice...261

Alma takes on another Role 267

Christmas 1949.. 268

New Year's Eve.. 270

The Marriage Proposal.. 272

The Engagement...274

Mrs. Gramzda Gives Advice... 279

A Package from America 289

Under Watchful Eyes... 292

Confirmation 296

Dinner with the Gramzdas 299

The poem *Daugava* 304

A Letter in the Night 313

St. John's Eve...314

Sin, Guilt, and Expectations..321

Screening and Inoculations for America......................... 327

A Scolding Letter 331

Milda Obeys Kārlis's Order...332

Under the Pink Rose Bush..333

The Aftermath..339

Milda's Trial 344

Jealousy 347

Freedom of Choices... 348

A Trip to the Alps...352

Summary Glimpses of Germany.. 354

Last Week at Lido...355

Departure...357

The Last Train Ride.. 363

Last Screening and Benediction.. 380

Dedication

In loving memory of my parents,
who brought us out of the ruins of Germany

FOREWORD

Out of the Ruins of Germany is the second book in the *How Long is Exile?* trilogy. This book, in turn, is divided in two parts: Part I covers the last half a year of World War II, roughly from October 1944 to May 1945. In this part, Alma Kaija, the main character's Milda Bērziņš-Arājs-Hawkins aunt, takes center stage, as she became her thirteen year old niece's guardian. Together they fled through the ruins of Germany until spring, when they found refuge in a remote town in Thüringen. There they lived until the war ended and American troops arrived.

Part II depicts their lives after the war in devastated Germany. After a year of uncertainty, in the autumn of 1946, they arrived in Esslingen, a picturesque town in Württemberg, in the American Zone. There, in the care of the United Nations Relief and Rehabilitation Administration (UNRRA) Americans had set up the largest all-Latvian displaced persons (DP) camp where approximately 6000 lived on both sides of the River Neckar. When in September 1946, Alma and Milda got off the train in the Esslingen station, they went looking for the UNRRA headquarters. They were welcomed and assigned an attic room in Lido, the fine arts six story building. There, they spent the next five years, until August 1950, when they separated. Alma emigrated to Sweden and Milda to the United States of America.

During those five years, each had found her place and resumed a more or less normal life. Alma continued her acting career in the theater, and Milda went on with her education and other activities. There she met Kārlis Arājs and Pēteris Vanags. There she matured into an independent, free-thinking woman, ready to make the important choices of her life. The book ends with Milda's waiting for a ship to take her to America.

ACKNOWLEDGMENT

In Book I, I paid my respects to my brothers. In this Book II, I want to pay equal respect to my two sisters, Miranda (1928-2000) and Ruta (1938—). From the autumn of 1944 and the winter of 1945, until the end of the war, our family as refugees trudged the ruins together. Needless to say, this time for us (and thousands more) was most traumatic and full of uncertainty. Fear, hunger, homelessness, and uncertainty plagued us daily, yet, as long as we were together, we felt safe. With my sisters, on either side, the cold and dark days also held sunshine and joy. Together we explored the outdoors, hunted for food and coal, attended churches, schools, and worried whenever one of us was sick. Although our father was strong and seemed fearless, he depended on us to do the daily chores and watch over our mother. In the end we came out of the war alive and enriched, with our family ties strong and binding. I cannot imagine that time without my sisters and the love that carried us through and forward.

I also want to thank and acknowledge the German Christian families that took us in, giving up a room to shelter our family of six. They gave us food and clothing, when all was rationed and the local people like we were or soon became homeless and hungry. To mind comes the Reverend Grüber family. He was pastor of a small Baptist congregation in Marienburg. I don't know how and who worked things out so that when our family left the farm where we labored for a while we took the train to Marienburg, Prussia. (It must have been late in November.) Mr. Grüber met us and took us in. Everyone of his six member family was kind. We ate at their table, *Frau* Grüber found clothing for us, and Rev. Grüber opened his wardrobe and let our father choose any garment he needed. He even invited father to share his pulpit, while his children quickly became our friends. Together with the congregation we celebrated an unforgettable Christmas. But the candles had hardly burned, when the Reverend was called into the army. He was killed in battle. As Prussia fell into Russian hands, his widow and children became refugees like we. Many years later, after we were settled in America and its doors opened wider so that German refugees also were allowed into the United States, father repaid the kindness by finding sponsors for the Grübers and other German refugees.

There were more kind people whom we met on our journey westward who opened their hearts and doors to our family. Perhaps they like my parents, brother and sister, no longer walk the earth, but their help and generous spirits are not forgotten. Certain people came to my mind as I wrote this book. Through my memory and imagination they turned into various characters, who live in these pages. And to them—the positive and negative—I am indebted and eternally grateful.

Thank you all!

Sincerely,
Astrida

Meditation

Whenever Milda Arajs looked back at her life that surprisingly, incredibly stretched over half a century, the time from the autumn of 1944 to the summer of 1945—such a little time!—stood out as one separate, colossal era ruled entirely by the forces of war. "It was a complete act in the drama of my life," she explained to her children, Ilga and Gatis. That era, like a well-made play, had a beginning, middle, and end. In the transition from childhood to early teens, the war had not allowed her to go through normal patterns of growth. Between her late thirteen and early fourteen years, she had experienced things that did not belong in the course of a *normal* child's upbringing— according to the high school sociology and psychology text books. Wanting to be normal instead of foreign and strange, she tried to blend in, but no matter how hard she tried she could not erase her accent, her manners, and her particular outlook on people and things around her. In time, living in America, she had to accept the fact that she was *different,* even interesting to many and that she lived and moved in an exclusive place and state of being called *exile.* There she belonged—there World War II had placed her and sealed its borders.

As detailed in Book I *(The Song and Dance Festivals of Free Latvians)*, she had entered that state when she, on October 8, 1944, holding her Aunt Alma's hand had walked up the ramp onto the ship in the harbor of Liepāja (Liebau), Latvia. The ship was heavy with refugees who, like she and Alma, had suddenly been expulsed from their apartments, houses, and country estates and, within hardly a day, had become refugees—homeless, confused, and unwanted. Some had escaped the onslaught of war by fishing boats across the Baltic Sea to Sweden; others left in caravans of horse-drawn wagons over land, going south through Kurzeme (Courland), on through Lithuania to Germany; still others boarded ships sailing to Germany.

"Our exile won't be long," Milda heard people say to each other that October day, as the ship rocked on the calm, dark waters of the Baltic Sea, its helm cutting the path towards Danzig. "The war will soon be over . . . . England and America will come to the rescue," so went the talks. She smiled cynically as she remembered those talks and knew better how governments worked and how political promises could be made and never carried out. The winter of 1944-45 was long and cold, and no one came to the rescue.

Many decades later, imbedded in her *State of Exile*, living in peaceful Grand Rapids, Michigan, her thoughts wandered back across lands and seas to locked up Latvia, which, she feared, as the years rolled on, would slowly, imperceptibly lose its contours, like once beloved faces were losing their features and turning into bland orbs. Yet, at night, when she looked at the sky with a full moon, her body would feel a pull like at high tide. Still, she could not imagine herself actually going home and being on any concrete road with her feet on the ground. Meditating, she would remind herself that she must accept the fact that not only she but her whole family lived in a separate state that only her countrymen and women inhabited. She also knew that consciously or subconsciously they too tried to escape from the feeling of exile by building dream bridges across the seas and skies. They sang songs, read the old classics, demonstrated for freedom, organized festivals, and, most of all held onto the language, just in case. . . And they all knew that they would never be whole until all the war-split parts would be united, as in one glorious song and dance festival.

For all that alienation, longing, and pain Milda blamed the war. She cursed it and swore at it in inaudible sighs and gasps. She called World War II as the most brutal, devastating of all the wars in history. But when she exclaimed too loudly, she was put down, especially by those smart people who had not felt its bombs and scars. She heard rebuttals about how this war seemed so momentous to her and loomed matchless in its terror and destruction only because she happened to be living through it and happened to be born in an insignificant, in-the-way-of-everybody country such as Latvia, which stubbornly would not admit (for its own good, some argued) to being a part of Russia and make the best of it.

"Oh, can't your forget it? Drop it!" people would say soothingly at first, but irritably after a quarter of a century of the same. And Milda then would withdraw to the side or corner and in long internal dialogues, shout back, saying that she cannot forget or drop anything. How could she ever forget her sister and what happened to her family? She would state that even the United States government has not forgotten. It had not yet recognized the 1945 (She wasn't sure of the date.) incorporation of Latvia into Russia and *that*, though it did not mean much to others and did not seem to affect present-day foreign policy, still counted for something. "Who knows?" she heard a wise man say, "Some day that might be the decisive trump in the card game of history."

"Yes. So we must hold on and forget nothing," she said.

She looked up facts in the library and knew that the 1939 Non-aggression Pact was a *Treaty of Shame* between two brute forces, namely Communist Russia and Nazi Germany, and this knowledge fed the often expressed belief that one day Latvia would again be free. That belief was sacred. For that she and Kārlis Arājs had married. For that they lived and raised their children.

It was comforting to know that all exile communities of the Eastern Block, communist-ruled nations, living throughout the world and guided by firmly committed leaders, believed that it was their highest duty and moral obligation to tell the free world the truth about communist oppression and never forget their imprisoned brothers and sisters.

As the years turned, Milda grew weary of discussing her feelings with "foreigners." She didn't like to meet new people because she would have to explain herself over and over and then spell her name: "Aa-r-aa-ys… It means plowman." Her husband made things more difficult by stubbornly holding on to his Latvian grammatically correct masculine ending with an *s* in the masculine Nominative and an *a* in the feminine; that is, Kārlis Arāj*s* and Milda Arāj*a*. She argued that she would be all right with the masculine ending, that it was no big deal, and she was tired of being questioned why her and her husband's names were not spelled the same. She said she was tired of people looking at her as if she didn't know her own name.

It took some years before Kārlis let her have her way. While at it, she dropped other diacritical marks and simply went with *Arajs*. She took that liberty the next time she applied for her drivers' license. Eventually Kārlis Arājs also dropped the *ā* lines, but not the *is* ending. Among Latvians, of course, they retained the names' correct spelling, as set down by old grammarians and their faithful disciples, who, not only took upon themselves to reprimand their countrymen and women for lacking national pride and Americanizing their names but also transcribed American places and names according to their own ideas of spelling and pronunciation. Ilga raged: "Why can't you all leave the names of people as they are—like in the phone book or on the cover of a book? A name is everyone's private, intellectual property, so how do you dare mess with it?"

Kārlis, as usual, had no answer but said something about order and uniformity, which Ilga dismissed with an, "Oh, give me a break!" In the end nobody gave in and the back-and-forth arguments about how to write one's own name became a part of the DP or alien culture, ending in the cliché *nothing can be done about it.*

"The war blasts names," Milda would say softly to her husband, and to her mind would come the associated meanings of their own names so common and easily pronounced by any Latvian. *Bērziņa=B-ee-r-z-i-ņ* (like in *knew*) *–a* = a sapling birch, with a feminine ending. A little girl tree, in a white bark gown and a shimmering pale green cape. . . Immediately at any laborious spelling, the associations would swarm her. She would see the groves, the *birstaliņas,* of white birch, glowing in the sun, their bright green whisks sweeping the sky and the clouds. She would hear the starlings singing and be her little self at the foot of the white trunks, picking strawberries and mushrooms or just lying there with cousin Anna, looking up dreaming, talking, giggling. She, too, transformed herself into a little birch tree, afraid to be broken by storms and gently holding nests with precious eggs, like a cradle rocking in the wind.

And *Arājs,* the plowman. A strong man, turning the soil. She would see Uncle Imants holding the handles of the plow, urging the horses, himself as heavy as his native clay and as hard and promising: there would be bread and peace and warmth during the harsh winters of snow and ice. She would see rich fields of green and gold, sprinkled with cornflowers, like the blue eyes of fairies, always watching, always smiling and winking

She often mused how she evolved from one name into the next and how her life carried their meanings and how a woman always took on the man's name and became a part of him.

"Beautiful and rich are our names, deeply rooted in the earth that's ours since the beginning of time," she would tell her children, who complained about their names because the kids at school teased them. The teachers could not pronounce them. So, until they learned, they would keep asking the blushing boy and girl to repeat their names clearly and slowly. As if that was not enough, the teachers sometimes went off their subjects and asked questions they didn't know how to answer. Some asked if they had nicknames, while others wanted to know what the names meant in English. Ilga then would pinch her lips and say nothing, but Gatis wished the floor would cave in.

"Yes, I understand. Outside of one's country, any name disintegrates into unpronounceable, irritating letters and syllables without meaning, without associations. I'm sorry," Milda said, feeling guilty.

"Look at the Germans, the Irish, the English!" Kārlis' colleague provoked him at a cocktail party. "They all broke with their old countries and made homes here, so why can't you?"

Milda tried to defend him and her people. "Excuse me. We have made a home here and we are happy, but it's different," she said. "My country was torn in half. We didn't leave it because we didn't like the weather, or our parents were poor and we wanted to be rich. Oh no!"

Kārlis added: "It's different when people leave of their own free will instead of being pushed out, as we were, as all of us were, without settling things, without making proper arrangements, without telling our sisters and brothers that we would go away and not meet them at the train station or wherever." Seeing blank expressions, Milda stopped explaining and turned inward, seeing it all over again, seeing Zelda at the station, waiting, the white handkerchief fluttering against a black train. "It's getting late," she touched her husband's sleeve. "We better go home."

Of course, in Milda's general daily life, things stayed in the background; the past was safely covered by the present until, suddenly, some clerk or a new mail carrier would disturb her again with the innocent, yet overbearing question, "Where're you from? … You got an accent." Sometimes she would say as casually as she could, "Latvia." But that would be no answer, for the next question would be, "Where's that at?" Then she would try to draw a map with her finger in the air or on some counter and explain again, only to be asked, "Why can't you go back? Why can't your sister come and live over here?" And then her heart would start pounding, the anger and sadness come over her, and her whole being would rail at the injustice, the frustration and alienation. And so it would go in circles, all the time, until her hair turned gray and she started coloring it.

Naturally, Milda understood that others had it worse. The globe was full of totally wiped out nations and civilizations, full of mummies, castle ruins, grave yards, archaeology sites. Her friend Helga Williams told her that she lived close to once-sacred Indian mounds that had become the playground where children scampered about and university students painlessly, scientifically dug looking for fossils. When they discovered the remains of a chief with sacrificed virgins on either side, the mounds became a national preserve. No one knew exactly how that ancient, once-powerful civilization met its end, for it did not cease to be because white men smote them.

Yes, Milda understood all this very well and realized that she and her people were lucky. They were not wiped out; there was a remnant— herself included—that would live on. Still, the ever-present sense of foreignness remained, and she could not help but interpret history out of her own center and squint at life with her own sadly expressive blue eyes.

When she contemplated World War II, she compared and contrasted it with other wars. She thought about the idea of war in general, and in her glances and readings through popular history and historical novels, she felt the tragedy of all wars, as well as all the major and minor uprisings and revolutions. She spared no tears for the heroes and heroines who rushed through flames saving lives and bent over dying lovers. Still, the wars seemed to be where they belonged, where they made sense and where their causes seemed clear and just, where the arguments stood beside and in front of the people like the crosses on the shields of crusaders. Even World War I, as far as she was able to judge, had seemed necessary. So much music and poetry had come out of it, precluded by revolutionary excitement and hope for a bright future. And when it ended, so many nations had sprung out of the trenches—like turtles crawling out of buried eggs and rushing for the sea, the great blue shimmering mirage of freedom.

The First World War had changed much. Women were released from their insufferable girdles and long, awkward dresses. They rode bicycles and cars, attended universities and voted. They cut their hair and smoked cigarettes (even her mother!) but best of all, the Latvia of her grandparents, free and independent of Russia and Germany, was suddenly blooming like a poppy in a field of wheat. Riga, with her proud and ancient steeples, had risen up and charmed the modern world as one of the most beautiful capitals of Europe, yet having its own beat and glamour. Some called it the Paris on the Baltic, only it was not French, but Latvian! This had happened as a result of World War I. So, Milda reasoned, the sacrifices were worth it all. A golden age had indeed dawned for all Europe, said the speakers on memorial days. The bright rays of a new sun had spread over Latvian towns and meadows. Even she had felt the joy and euphoria!

"We had this time, this wonderful time of freedom and prosperity," she impressed on Ilga and Gatis. "And you must honor it, study and respect the time and the people who made it all possible."

"Yes, Mother."

But World War II, with its swastika on one side and the hammer and sickle on the other, had cut the new nations up and down. It had diced and sliced up the painfully constructed lives of millions and hung an iron curtain across all Europe, fencing them in and making might seem right. Now it bulged, churning up the millions who had lived as if buried alive for fifty years. They were rising and speaking up. The poets spoke for those had been afraid to talk to their friends and even members of their own families, but all listened to the static Voice of America. They heard their counterparts on the free side feeding the Voice with their assurances and sighs.

Milda saw the whole world, as she had seen in some cartoon, caught up in a duel between Stalin and Hitler, whose boots were bigger than the lands they stomped. Those boots trampled over her country's cities and countryside. They kicked away bridges and borders. They smashed towns and murdered the innocent and the guilty with equal, indifferent, blasphemous swings and blows, eventually replacing beauty with ugliness of square, concrete, massive building where people were boxed in and stacked up. The powerful had no fear of God or Satan, neither did they fear thunder and lightning and nature's inevitable revenge. *Ah, what can I do?*

So she was often quiet, meditative, thinking and pondering. Once, on a snowy December day, after her husband had returned home from a conference in Los Angeles and was in a good mood, telling the family about the exciting time he had had and how well the conference went and that he believed that communism would drop like a rotten apple off a warped tree, he turned to Milda and asked her what she thought. Startled, she had not listened attentively and looked at him with a blank expression, covered with a vague, distant smile.

How could she admit that as he talked about sunny California, she was with Aunt Alma back in beautiful, snow-flurried Marienburg, Germany. It was December 1944, late in the day. They had gotten off the train and gone exploring the pretty Christmas-card-like town on the edge of the wide, frozen river. Standing high on the shore, out of the castle's shadow, they had watched skaters—children and grown-ups sliding with and without skates and a cluster of young men racing with devilish speed, their silhouettes black against a red sky. She and Alma had been so cold that they did not even feel their feet anymore. When she cried out, Alma pulled her down the bank. They stepped on to the glassy ice and slid around until the sun set, turning the ice orange, then red. Their feet burned in pain. . .

When Kārlis repeated his question and asked why she would not talk to him, she gave him a wide-eyed look and said, "I had a very difficult childhood."

PART I

The Ruins of Germany

When the ship set anchor in the Danzig harbor, *Mildiņa*, too small for her thirteen years, holding her Aunt Alma's hand, walked down the ramp into Germany. From there they were directed to board a train. From the window they watched in tired resignation the landscape slide by, for they did not know where they were taken, nor what would happen to them at the end of the ride.

When the train stopped in Marienburg, Alma grabbed *Mildiņa's* hand and their things and jumped off. Others followed and escaped into the strange streets of this ancient town. Somehow Alma found the Red Cross or some other helping organization that seemed to welcome refugees. After hours of waiting, they were guided into a large building, a school or warehouse, with boarded off areas like large stalls. Men and women were ordered into separate rooms lined with straw mattresses and topped with gray horse blankets. Alma took everything in at a glance and, again taking Milda's hand, headed for a far corner and set down their belongings, then hurried across the room, where large, serious women dished out soup and handed each a hard brown bun. Still feeling hungry and cold, they huddled together, pulling the blankets over their heads, and went to sleep. The war seemed far away.

Milda, with other refugee children, was placed in a school, where she had to learn how to read and write in the Gothic script. She wrote with a dip pen that had a split tip and tore holes in her notebooks. Every morning the children had to hold their arms up and say "Heil Hitler!" One day she saw her teacher hit a boy's hands with a ruler because he had not saluted. The boy cried, and she was scared. From then on, she made her arm stiff and lifted it high. The teacher noticed that and nodded approvingly. When in a good mood, the teacher praised her for trying hard and learning diligently. Still she was afraid. What Aunt Alma did during those days, and what chores she had to perform, Milda did not know. Alma was always tired and her hands were red. In her memory all the days blurred in common grayness until the Advent. Then it lit up suddenly, and the snow sparkled under her feet. One day the teacher opened the door and in came *Christ Kind,* wearing shining robes, followed by two angels who sang beautiful carols and gave each child a piece of candy.

On Christmas Eve, she and Alma explored the old town, which they entered through a fir-garlanded stone arch. Enchanted, they wandered through the narrow streets, so much like Old Riga, looking at gingerbread houses and winter scenes in sugar-iced shop windows. Milda remembered Hansel and Gretel and the cunning old witch with a crooked nose and a mean finger leaning over the children who were lost in candy and sugar frosting woods. She remembered being so terribly hungry that she would be ready to jump into any oven for just one cookie. But Alma pulled her away, past windows with elves, trains, nutcrackers, and choirs of angels to the end of the street, where loomed the huge castle, dark and foreboding. Alma stopped, pulling Milda close beside her. Taking a deep breath, she explained that back in the Middle Ages the Zemgale tribal chieftain Namejs with his soldiers had fought the Crusaders, right there, perhaps on the spot where they were standing. She said, that he was trying to hold back the black knights from pushing into Zemgale, which then was a separate kingdom that only much later became a part of Latvia. "Just so you know and remember where you've been,"

"Yes," Milda said, looking up at the castle and down, where the frozen river lay still in the castle's shadow. Not knowing where to turn, they did not wanting to go back to their shelter and sit on a straw mattress. So they walked on. On the other side of the castle they saw a church whose dim light beams seemed to invite them in. Alma went boldly up the steps and opened the large door. The vespers were in progress, and they tiptoed inside the sanctuary, which was warm and beautifully decorated. It looked exactly like the Riga Dom, making *Mildiņa* confused, as if she had been winged back into some lost and forgotten dream. Coming towards her, through the candle-lit darkness, were her parents, grandparents, and sister as they had been on their last Christmas Eve all together before the war in the heart of Riga. The angel chorus up front even sang the same carols.

The vision faded, when Alma guided her to an empty space next to the aisle. They sat down in the narrow space and smiled, feeling good to be off their frozen feet. Milda hid her face in Alma's frosted fox fur until it hurt and tingled. When she pushed the dead animal aside, she saw children in white robes standing around a huge, candle-lighted fir tree singing more familiar carols and again hid her face in the fox's tail. Alma nudged her and told her to stop sniveling and look. A parade of more angels in shining robes and golden crowns were coming from the rear of the sanctuary and walking up the aisle past them, their wings spread out. One wing, like her mother's gentle stroke, brushed her shoulder. . . .

And there were shepherds carrying real lambs in their arms, and three wise boys in brightly striped cloaks, carrying gifts. They knelt at the open barn, where a woman held a doll, wearing a halo. And then the minister began the Christmas story: *Es begab sich aber zu der Zeit...* Mildiņa listened and saw that Alma also gloried in the sound, in the whole scene, and, when at last they stood together to sing *Stille Nacht,* Alma's thawed face glowed.

But all too soon the bells began to ring, and the vespers ended. While the children gathered around the tree to receive presents from *Christ Kind,* Alma took Milda's hand and pulled her toward the large door. Again they were out in the slippery street, in the star-sprinkled night that had turned much colder. Alma squeezed Milda's mittened hand harder, making her run and glide until they came up against the gloomy building, their temporary home. Startled, they saw newly arrived refugees crowd around the door that opened and closed, their hands reaching as if trying to grasp the light inside.

Alma pushed through the crowd with all her might until they were inside. A harsh voice ordered everybody to move on, but Alma made a path toward the potbelly stove with its large cauldron of soup. Wearily, she and Milda received their portions and took them to their assigned corner. They ate greedily, snatching up more hard buns that kind, warm hands passed around because it was Christmas Eve.

Then a man in a black overcoat entered the room and read from the Bible about the escape of the Holy Family into Egypt and, having closed the Book, preached to them in German. The sermon was followed by uncertain singing with one of the refugee women stepping forward and sitting down at the piano. She played beautifully, calming down the crowd and herself, perhaps imagining herself in some other better time and place. When the lights dimmed, the people, lying on their mattresses, talked among themselves, telling each other where they had come from and confessing that they didn't know where they were going. In whispers, escaped strange words that carried frightful meanings: *Waisenhaus* (orphanage) and *Arbeitsdienst* (labor service/forced labor?)

When Milda asked Alma what those words meant, she stroked the girl's head and held her close against her warm body. "I will never let them take you away," she whispered, "so let's go to sleep."

Many years later Milda told her children that once, on Christmas Eve, she too had slept on straw.

Winter 1945

Hardly had the year 1945 started, when all hell broke loose. Overnight Marienburg had turned into a war zone. People fled however and wherever they could. The railway station was jammed; trains, with people lying flat on the roofs and holding on to iced-up iron bars, passed through without slowing down. *Mildiņa* cried, and Alma yelled at her to shut her mouth. After another train rolled past them, she desperately, irrationally started pulling the girl across slippery tracks to some distant row of wagons. Others followed. When the conductor told them that the train should be allowed to move on soon, the people climbed aboard, packing themselves in. Alma held *Mildiņa* on her lap. Hours later, the train did start chugging out of the station. People cheered as it crossed the iron bridge over the Vistula River, glad it wasn't blown up, leaving them trapped on the wrong side. In slow motion and making many stops, the train carried them toward Berlin. The day turned into night, night into day. And so it went for exactly how long, Milda could not remember. All that mattered then was that they were on the safer side of the war and that they must keep on going—by train, by foot, by farm carts, always moving, going West.

Silently, always hungry, they trudged like that through bleak Germany. "Now is the winter of our discontent. . ." Alma recited, resting her head against some hard board or worn out upholstery.

Their arms seemed stretched out form the weight of their suitcases, which they dragged from city to town, from train to streetcar, shifting their grip to relieve the pain and the pull. However, as long as they held the suitcases, they felt at least secure, like children holding on to a ragged blanket. Those suitcases still connected them to their lost homes and reminded them that they were not sleepwalkers but real travelers. The suitcases were the storage bins for all they owned and also served as tables, chairs, pillows, foot stools, also scratched up and bruised by the war. Their shining firm dark brown leather became dull and limp. The handles hung dangerously loose, the locks rusted. Yet they survived the beating as they carriers pushed, pulled, kicked them in and out of stations and bomb shelters. They disappeared only when the building blew up.

It happened in Chemnitz, when, Milda, Alma, and many other people hid in a cellar during an air-raid. Dressed in their winter coats, everyone sat stiffly pressed against the damp, cold walls for uncounted hours. They heard the whistling of bombs and the explosions, one following the other. And then there was a silence—a long, still silence—and inside that silence *Mildiņa* said, "I am thirsty." Without a word, Alma rose, allowing the child to take her hand and lead her into a dark passage. Two little girls followed them, whispering in the Latvian. But Milda didn't stop; she only turned her head slightly and glanced at their faces. She did not say any words because her lips hurt from frostbite and lack of water. Holding her screams inside, Milda pulled her aunt, as they raced for the barrel of water toward the far end of the cellar. Barely had they dipped into the barrel, when the whole half of the building exploded. The next instant they found themselves spewed out under an open night sky. Fire leaped all around, threatening to block their path. Blindly holding on to each other, they came out into what had been a street but was becoming a narrow smoldering crack in the earth. They saw the airplanes fly away, lightly, without a backward glance, their noses cleaving the sky, leaving a bitter stench behind. Alma shook her fists at the bombers and then laughed a mad, crazy laugh and said, "We lost our suitcases." She laughed louder, wrapping her coat and the fox collar tightly around her, tucking her scarf around Milda, glaring around, crying, "Where's the blanket? Where did you put it? Where are we?" She trembled, saying over and over again, "We've lost everything.... *Meine Ruhe ist hin, mein Herz ist schwer....* Yet how light it is!" She tried to lift up the loose bricks, tried to burrow again into the ground, but Milda pulled her away from the ruins, on toward where she thought the sun had set.

They walked, crawled, dodged until the war was over, until the army of American Negroes rode into Oeslau, the small borough where they had stopped to rest.

Arriving in Oeslau

They had come upon this quiet small town by chance. It was late in the evening, in the middle of March, right after the Ides of March, immediately after Alma's 29th birthday. Their stockings had holes, their shoes were worn through, their heels red and blistered. They were famished and exhausted, and so they had leaned against an iron gate. On the other side stood a two-story, red-roofed house, the color of whipping cream. The stately home was not touched by any splinters of war. To the refugees it seemed to have risen out of the ground and stood before them like a mirage, a haven of welcoming respite.

Soon a slightly stooped, graying woman came out from the large door. She trotted down the stone path and opened the gate. She greeted the strangers and introduced herself as *Frau* Lutz. After listening to a short explanation from Alma, she invited them into her house. Without further ceremony, she showed them where to wash up while she set out some food. Luxuriously clean, Alma and Milda sat down at a round table covered with a starched white cloth with cross-stitched deer running all along its edge. *Frau* Lutz pulled the wax seal off a jar of jam and excused herself for not having butter. Spinning between the table and the pantry, talking the whole time, she set out a huge loaf of brown bread but not much else. She poured apple cider into three mugs, and the feasting began. *Mildiņa* made up for all the days and nights of hunger. She ate one slice of bread after another, as did Alma, until their bellies swelled. Lightheaded *Mildiņa* barely heard *Frau* Lutz talking about her *Mann* and *Kinder* and blowing her nose. Then, very dizzy, she got up from the table and stumbled up some stairs. She felt hands lifting her in bed and covering her with a dawn comforter. Alma lay down next to her and together they sweated, kicking the comforter off, then feeling chilled, they pulled it back up over their heads until the sweat rolled over them, and they sunk into deep sleep. The next morning Alma told Milda that she had offered herself as cleaning woman in exchange for the attic room where they were sitting. "We'll stay here as long as we can or must," Alma said and quickly explained *Frau* Lutz's situation: Her husband, a surgeon, was—the last *Frau* Lutz heard—in Vienna. Her two daughters, both nurses, worked behind the trenches in Belgium. They had written that they were well and hoped to be home soon, by Easter, God willing. They assured their mother that the war would soon be over.

Alma went on, sarcastically telling Milda that *Frau* Lutz had called them a God-sent because there was much cleaning to be done before Easter and before the family would be reunited, and, *Gott-im Himmel*, she could not do it all alone. God knows and sees her needs, she had said, for He answered her plea for help as soon as she opened her eyes and looked out the window. "There, she saw us standing at the gate," Alma said, "and so here we are, led through hell, so that we can clean this pitiful woman's house. It is truly mysterious, isn't it, how God works!" Alma scoffed. "It's just this kind of nonsense that makes me be an atheist. It's what I couldn't stand about my sister Matilde, always God this, God that, followed by I prayed. Oh, well," she plopped into the stuffed chair, sending a cloud of dust up toward the light. "It's all right. What do I care? I will play the game as long as I need to or as long as I can take it. You'll have to help me."

"Yes, Aunty."

Alma stood up and stretched and said, "Look!" Milda looked and saw a calendar hanging on an ornate hook on the dull, flowery wall paper. Time had stopped in this room in September 1944. Laughing, Alma pulled it off the wall and started tearing off one month after the other until they came to March. "Only two weeks left before Easter," Alma said. "So we better go down and start the spring cleaning, as Lutz instructed, or we'll be out on the street."

They heard the outside door close. "Lutz said she would run out to tell her neighbors of her fortune," Alma said laughing loudly now that they were alone in the large house. They went down the stairs and into the parlor, where the furniture was covered with dull, dust-laden sheets. They opened the windows and looked out. The day was balmy, with soft, warm winds blowing fresh air through the room. Down below in the garden bloomed many colored crocuses. Birds sang in the budding trees. "It's a beautiful morning, aunty, don't you think?" Milda asked and started pulling the sheets off the rosewood furniture, letting it breathe. In spite of herself, Alma also caught the spirit and went to work. It will be all right," she said and seemed happy and full of energy as Milda remembered her before the war.

In the afternoon, having done her share of scrubbing and while Alma rested, Milda tiptoed around the garden admiring the flowers. Presently, as she walked along the fence, she saw a girl about her own age and size, looking at her from across budding tulip beds. For some seconds they eyed each other, long enough for Milda to notice the freckles on the girl's face and the redness of her tightly braided hair. The girl smiled and stepped closer. Reaching her hand through the iron bars, said, *"Ich bin Gisela Niert"* and opened the gate. Milda knew she was meeting a friend.

Gisela's brothers, the twins Wilfred and Alfred, suddenly sprung up from behind a bush and jumped at them, pointing their fingers and shouting, "boom, boom!" They were no more than four or five years old and funny in every way, making Milda laugh and grab them by their hands. As she did, she realized that she had not touched children's hands since she had held her little cousin Lilia. The only hand she had held all winter was Alma's, which she had learned to read, day-by-day, mood-by-mood. Sometimes it was warm and welcoming, other times cold and stiff, like a false limb. The boy's little hands felt warm and good so that she and didn't want to let go, didn't want her hands to twist and ring each other.

Learning the German Language

The next day, Gisela, with *Frau* Lutz's approval, took Milda to school and presented her to her teacher, a large woman with very red cheeks and hair tightly pulled in an ashen bun. She wore a gray suit buttoned tightly over a stiff white blouse. Startled, the *Lehrerin* looked at the girls through wire-rim spectacles and finally said, *Also.* She naturally mispronounced *Bērziņš* and, having learned its meaning, introduced her new student as Milda Birke. "It will be easier that way," she said kindly and, seeing her accept the direct translation and show relief, arranged the seating so that she could sit next to Gisela at the double desk. Then the class said "Heil Hitler!" and went to work. They turned to the poems of Schiller, reading them aloud. Milda loved the rhythm and sound of the poetry and tried to gather its meaning but could not.

When school was over and everyone was noisily walking or running home, Milda realized that the German language was not the same in the street as in the classroom. Outside, the children spoke in, what she guessed, was the local dialect or some odd language mixture typical of border lands. But whatever it was, she knew she had to learn that too in order to belong and not appear *dum.*

As Milda's first school week went on and because she could not say things correctly, other children became overly familiar; they whispered among themselves and laughed at her mispronounced words and funny phrases, embarrassing her to tears. Some went further, calling her *Pole* (a Polish person) and cursing, calling her a *damned foreigner,* until Gisela put a stop to it by getting the older boys to beat up on the obnoxious bullies. After a good fight the bad boys left the girls alone, while the older boys watched them with special interest, whistling as they walked past and around them. Gisela pretended not to notice such compliments, but Milda enjoyed the attention. Still, in the class room, there were moments when she wished the bombs would fall and she would not have to stand up and speak with every eye turned on her and the teacher's nods punctuating her slow, laborious phrasing. Luckily, after only one week of this, began the two week Easter recess. On Friday, much to her delight, the dark-haired, handsome Gert, an upper classman, followed her and Gisela as far as the Nierts' house and then gallantly wished them happy holidays. They curtsied. Lifting her eyes, Milda saw Gert looking at her intensely, as if trying to see inside her or say something clever. For an instant their eyes met and a shiver went through her. She blushed, saying *danke,* as Gisela quickly opened the gate. Gert turned and walked away, but Milda went on slowly, lifting her eyes to the heavens, her heart beating in strange, wonderful rhythms. *Oh, the world is beautiful after all*, her heart sung. She spun around, wishing to see Gert close behind her, but he wasn't there. Slowly, in a daze, she walked up the stairs to the attic room. Alma was there, waking up from her afternoon nap.

"What are you grinning about?" she asked irritably. "And why are you late?"

Milda set her books down and tied her apron. Like a slap, Alma's voice cut across the room, hitting Milda's heart. "I was with my new friends. The school will be closed for two weeks. It's Easter time." She watched her aunt get out of bed and stand looking at the calendar.

"April one!" Alma said and laughed. "Ha! Easter is on April one! All fools day.... *April, April, April!*" In her laughter the *r's* rolled as if she were gargling her throat with salt water. Milda could not stand the sound and sight and dashed down the stairs and out of the house, past *Frau* Lutz. She found Gisela in the playhouse and told her that she thought her Aunt was not right. But Gisela only smiled sympathetically, and Milda realized that no one could understand Alma, no one could help her. She and Alma were foreigners.

Holy Week

On Monday of Holy Week, spring-cleaning began. It was as if some invisible hand had raised a baton and all the women came together with buckets, rags, brushes in hand, to begin their drumming of carpets, swishing of brooms, squeaking of glass, and on and on until the last specks of dust were caught in rags and the last spots of dirt washed away. Even the birds helped by quickly swooping up the feathers that fell from the *Betten* shaken out of wide open windows. The wind also helped. It blew the clouds of dust over the hills, fields, and woods, leaving the air clear and blue, the windows brightly mirroring the sun and the clouds. By the middle of the week the town sparkled, and the women smiled in victorious satisfaction, as they filled their vases with earliest flowers and leafing branches.

After a brief silence that marked Mundey Eve, the next morning dawned with another wave of the invisible hand and ordered the next movement: the women began their baking. All at once the whole town was fragrant from freshly baked bread, cakes, and cookies. *Frau* Lutz baked only one pound cake, and Alma lazily twisted some *zaķausis* (rabbit ears) and fried them golden brown in the lard she had scraped up. "It would not be Easter without them," she said cheerfully, but Milda didn't miss the deep sadness in her eyes. "There's no powdered sugar," Alma complained. "Not right, these bits of memory," she mumbled, tasting one and giving another to Milda. Both servants knew that *Frau* Lutz kept her private sugar bowl under a lock in the cupboard, wondering how to get at it. At that thought, as if conjured, *Frau* Lutz startled them. She appeared in the doorway, saying that she will let Easter pass quietly because her family would not be home and that she was going to visit her sister. She hoped that she could trust them to take care of the house. Alma said of course and, giving her a taste of a rabbit ear, asked if they may have a bit of sugar. Chewing and showing approval, the woman kindly unlocked the cupboard and scooped out some teaspoonfuls fulls from the sugar bowl and then locked up the cupboard, slipping the key into her apron pocket. Alma sprinkled the sugar on the cookies, wrapped up half a dozen and gave them to *Frau Lutz.* "A greeting to your sister," Alma said. The mistress nodded and left the kitchen.

"That takes care of that," Alma said when she and Milda were alone, cleaned up. The work finished, Milda ran over to *Frau* Niert. There, in her kitchen, every large bowl was full of dough, either rising or waiting to be rolled, kneaded, and twisted into all sorts of delicious forms. Milda rolled up her sleeves and sunk her hands deeply into the dough. She watched Gisela make the Easter *Kranz*—a braided wreath tinted yellow with saffron. In the oven it would turn bronze and double in size. The trick, instructed *Frau* Niert, was not to let the strands split and puff out unevenly and to baste them with an egg and cream mixture so that there would be no pale spots. The *Kranz* was treated with reverence. It symbolized Christ's crown of thorns and was *Frau* Niert's own creation. Milda watched and memorized the steps so that she would know how to make it later—when she grew up.

When all the pans were filled but a bit of dough was left over, still rising Milda remembered Aunt Matilde and her *piragi.* She scraped up the leftovers and asked for a little bacon, a bit of onion, a sprinkle of pepper. Expertly, as if she had done it countless times, she diced the bacon and onion, added the pepper and a spoonful of mustard and cream for the filling. She pressed out the dough in thin circles and spooned the filling in the middle and carefully sealed the edges, forming fat little crescents, which she lined on a cookie sheet. She basted them with the left-over egg and cream mixture and gently pricked them with a fork to let the air out. Nervously, she pushed them into the oven and then helped to clean up. A different aroma filled the kitchen and drew everyone around the oven door, when Milda pulled out her work of art. Not even one was split open!

"Be careful not to make your *piradziņi* laugh at you," Matilde had taught her. "Turn the seams under and let the air out on top." Milda closed her eyes to keep the tears inside as she remembered and missed her dear Aunt and the whole family. *Do they think of me too?* she wondered as her senses bathed in the fragrance and memories of other, very far away Holy Weeks. Unable to keep these things inside her, she slumped into a chair and cried like a little girl who is hurting. She had no words to explain anything, but *Frau* Niert understood and offered her bosom. "*Ach, Kindchen,*" she said stroking the girl's hair with her flowery hands. "Life is sometimes very hard." She talked on, saying words Milda had not yet learned, but words that soothed and made her rise out of the apron dry-eyed and calm. When she opened her eyes, there was Gisela packing a basket with the things they had baked.

"In the afternoon of Holy Thursday we always make our spring walk in the woods," *Frau* Niert explained. "Go and tell your Aunt and *Frau* Lutz that we are ready."

HOW LONG IS EXILE?

*

Milda Arajs would never forget this outing. It was another bright day that blotted out the many gray ones. She never would forget how once inside the deep woods, the women became like young girls. They sang, played games with the children, and gathered tiny flowers and large leafing branches. Alma sang some Latvian songs, softly and sadly at first, but then louder so the notes trilled and echoed, and passers-by stopped to listen. They walked on, deeper through pine woods, until they came out on the other side, where the grass was soft, sprinkled with violets. Tired out, they sat down under a tall oak tree and drew in the sweet, cool air, feeling healed and hungry. They spread a tablecloth over the grass, set out their food and drink and ate heartily. When satisfied, the women put the food away and reclined against the huge tree trunk, enjoying the bird songs and gentle breezes. The twins played games until they had enough and then challenged the girls to a race. When they would not give in, the boys attacked their mother, talking silly and pulling the hairpins out her bun. Milda watched *Frau* Niert's thick rust colored twists unravel and fall in waves halfway down her back. The boys played with the hair, peaking through it, giggling, and pelting it with dandelion and violet blossoms. *Mutti* laughed and tickled them, having fun. Only *Frau* Lutz looked at her neighbor scornfully and checked the pins of her bun, pushing the loose ones back into her head. *Frau* Niert ignored the scowls and suddenly, scaring the boys, jumped up and raced with them down to a far sunny spot and back again. *Frau* Lutz rose in indignation and watched. Frida Niert, her hair blown back, was in front, running like a deer. When she hit the tree three Alfred declared her the winner. "And you are the loser," he said to *Frau* Lutz, who rose, saying *for shame*, and went home alone.

"A cloud has passed over us," Frida said lightheartedly, as Gisela put a garland on her head and named her Flora—the Queen of Spring.

When the sun's rays turned orange and the shadows became longer than the trees, they wound their way home, tired and happy. With sidelong glances, Milda wondered what Alma was thinking and feeling as she let each twin take a hand and lead her out of the woods.

"I feel as if I were inside a fairy tale," Milda said and challenged everyone to race down the green slope.

*

On Good Friday it drizzled. "As it should," said *Frau* Niert as she walked with *Herr* Niert under one umbrella, her hand in the crook of his arm, a little gray woman, made smaller by a black hat.

"The Savior's sorrow rains down on us," said Gisela solemnly from under her umbrella she shared with *Mildchen*. They, as part of a procession, walked up the hill to the Evangelical Church. The bells rang heavily.

Alma was wrapped in her own gray silence, her eyes tear-glazed. She took her niece's hand, something she had not done quite that strongly since their flight from bomb-burning Chemnitz. She squeezed it, playing with Milda's fingers, sending her signals of love and warmth. Milda looked up at her face for some promise that this offer of love would not be snatched away, but as soon as they entered the gray, cold cathedral, Alma pulled her hand away. She fixed her eyes on the crucified Christ hanging above the altar. Together with the congregation, they kneeled and rose automatically, saying the prescribed words and singing the hymns. *Oh, Sacred Head now wounded.* Milda's tears fell on the open book; Alma wiped hers. The whole congregation wept and sighed, undoubtedly more for their own lost and sacrificed loved ones than the Savior's sacrifice for a sin-sick world.

Was there ever such sorrow?

*

On Holy Saturday, Milda was again at the Niert's house coloring eggs and helping in the preparations for Easter Sunday. She watched *Frau* Niert make a dessert with gelatin, preserved raspberries and whipping cream. Again she memorized the recipe so that, when she grew up, she would know how to make this wonderful Bavarian crème. Seeing Milda's curious eyes and the dark windows across the yard, *Frau* Niert invited her to join them for supper. Feeling guilty and knowing that her aunt was left alone, Milda still yielded and lingered on even after the dishes were washed.

Late into the night, she entered a very quiet house and went up to her room. Alma sat in the corner, illuminated only by the moon. She was sousing her chapped hands with glycerin and rosewater. Not saying anything, she offering Milda the surplus. That done, she turned on the light, opened her book of Goethe's dramas and started mumbling some lines and passages from *Faust,* as if she were preparing for some audition. Milda listened puzzled, but said nothing, waiting, as was her habit, for some words of explanation. As she waited, she thought about what to wear in the morning and decided to lower the hem of her pleated skirt (which she had saved through the bombing by wearing it as a slip). She turned on the lamp and started pulling out the old threads and then threaded her needle. Suddenly Alma's loud voice startled her. "Unbelievable! Here I am so close to where Goethe lived and wrote *Faust*!" Excited and rising to her feet, she read some lines out loud. "Can you hear how the poetry fits here, in these parts, in these streets?"

"I guess so," Milda answered and stitched on.

"We'll take the train to Weimar tomorrow morning. Only you and I. We'll have our own Easter walk where Faust walked!"

Easter Sunday, April 1, 1945

And so it happened that in the dawning light and to the loud pealing of church bells, Alma dragged her sleepy niece by the hand, hurrying her so they could catch the early morning train. It drizzled and rained the whole day.

Milda remembered little of the excursion, except that she wished she were with the Nierts. She had imagined that the sun would shine in their garden and through the clean windows, and she wondered how she would explain to the Nierts her sudden disappearance, when she had promised that they would go to church together. She was afraid of spoiling her friendship with Gisela and tried to reason with Alma, but she didn't care. Alma sat inside her own world.

In Weimar, angry Milda trudged along, again pulled by Alma's cold hand. She listened to the excited actress, like some tour guide, going on about Goethe, pointing out the markers in the streets and on houses. They stopped at the statue of Schiller and Goethe, where the poets stood high on a pedestal close together. "The world's guiding lights," Alma said and, having paid homage, they walked on, toward their houses. "They had actually lived here!" Alma said, sounding surprised. They passed the closed Schiller house and went on to Goethe's. But the doors and gates were bolted. It was Sunday—Easter Sunday. Nothing but church doors stood open.

Under a common umbrella, as if expecting someone to open the gate, aunt and niece stood at the high fence of Goethe's house, looking in. They saw the budding apple trees dripping and swaying in the wind and starlings sitting in the branches whistling indifferently. Rejected, they turned away and followed an upward path leading to the cathedral. "That must be the church," Alma pointed and started going up the stairs. They went inside. The church was full; a choir sang. "Here's where Margareta prayed," Alma whispered. Milda admired the altar carvings and the paintings, which were not at all gloomy. The carved altar seemed glazed with honey; the stained glass windows were amazingly colorful and not at all like the gray woodcuts in Alma's *Faust*. "No wonder Mephisto came here to tempt and provoke Faust," Alma whispered, kneeling with the congregation and, when on her knees, softly recited Margareta's prayer:

Hilf! Rette mich von Schmach und Tod!

(Help! Save me from disgrace and want)

Ach, neige, du Schmerzenreiche,

(Oh, incline, thou grieving one,)

Dein Antlitz gnadig meiner Not!

(Thy gracious face onto my need!)

"The words feel right here," Alma said when they were outside. 'But there is so much more we must see," she said, mindful that time was running away much too fast. They hastened down the rain-soaked hill, over the bridge toward Goethe's garden house, then on past the graveyard and through the valley along the river, where silently floated a white swan. They paused to take a photo and then went on, up the incline. "Here is List's house," Alma pointed, nearly out of breath. "Goethe, Schiller, List, Herder, the queens and kings—the court—is all here. Or was. Don't you see how they all come together? This is it—the very heart of our western culture! Classicism, romanticism, sin and redemption, Greeks and Egyptians. God and Nature. All, everything! These men turned it all into most magnificent art so we too could partake. Oh, it's beyond our understanding!"

"But they're dead and gone. They aren't *here*!" Milda said spitefully.

"Oh, be quiet, what do you know!" Alma snapped.

"I know that Germans started the war and killed millions of Jewish people, and they wanted to take away our country," Milda lashed back.

"Who told you that?"

"Gert. . . and. . . and. . . everybody knows it." She was hungry. Her feet hurt.

Alma said nothing.

*

Late in the afternoon, in the train, they looked at each other with cold distant eyes. Except for Alma's cookies, they had not eaten all day, for no restaurant or café was open. Their feet were wet and blistered. Slowly Alma's eyes filled with cold, salty tears. "It never is what you imagine," she said. "You are right. They are not here and the living should not bother marking the streets and houses because poets have so little to do with time and place. They live only in their works, if they live at all. We carry them. We are condemned to live and die inside their words—over and over. If *he* were with me," she said looking at the drizzle, "perhaps it would be different, but I didn't see any poodles, did you?"

"Not without a leash."

"Ah, you see! No Mephisto, even in disguise."

Alma was exhausted. She kept her feet out of her wet shoes. Milda saw the blisters, the turned in toes. "Easter 1945. April Fools' Day. I shall never forget it," Alma croaked bitterly.

"I will never forget it either," Milda confirmed. "I wonder how many days there are in a lifetime that we should never forget."

"That depends on how you live."

"Or how others make you live."

"Yes. You're smart—and growing up to be very pretty." Alma smiled a sad, resigned smile, while Milda looked out the window at the gray sprouting landscape. Unable to keep her eyes open, she cushioned her head against Alma's padded shoulder and dozed off.

"I am sorry we didn't have a nicer day," Alma said. "It was selfish of me to take you away from your friends, but, you understand, I had to do it. I had to find his footsteps. Had to see it so I could be a better actress."

"I know."

"What's strange," Alma talked on, her voice sounding, far, far away, "is that I am not sure anymore if I really like the play. I hate something about it now, after what you told me, and after living in Germany. Maybe I don't like the German side of it. The feeling of being constantly cramped, pushed together between houses and people so that when you finally break out, it has to be all the way. You suddenly are turned into something very different—well, like Faust. He was condemned from the start just because he wanted to get out of his stuffy room! But he could not simply go out and come back in. It was all or nothing, right or wrong. Faust was forced to change—with or without Mephisto. And here it's still that way." Alma stopped talking and stared at the fields. "I do understand her now," she said.

"Whom?" Milda asked yawning.

"Margareta, of course. She was a fool, but I understand. I'd also do anything for one kiss from my Viktors, my Mephisto." As she spoke, fresh tears filled her eyes, and she let them splatter without bothering to wipe her face. Milda sat up and stared at her, blinking nervously.

"I wonder where he is now and what he's doing," Alma sniffled. She had never talked so openly about the man she had kissed before boarding the ship. Innocent *Mildiņa* hadn't realized that he had been always with them, between them, calling her, the way Zelda called her, the way she always felt her parents' absent shadows.

"I feel," Alma went on, "that I must memorize the lines for him so that when this separation is over, we can again work together—only on bigger and brighter stages. Maybe in Berlin or Hamburg. So, I haven't much time because everyone says the war will be over any day." She leaned her head back and closed her eyes, smiling. "Soon we will be going home, my child."

"*April, April, April,*" Milda muttered.

"What did you say?" Alma demanded angrily.

"*April, April, April,*" she repeated.

Then Alma laughed in that uncertain voice Milda hated and feared. She could not wait to get out of the train, to end this ride, to get off the wrong tracks.

After the Holidays

Milda Birke was glad and relieved when the heavy holidays ended. When she and Gisela walked to school on Tuesday morning, she still had a cold, but she felt as free as a bird who had escaped from a closed-in room. She skipped with other youngsters and greeted her classmates, who joined them. They chatted and giggled as though there were no foreigner among them. At the school gate, she almost bumped into Gert, who apologized, smiled, and held the gate open. When she glanced back at him, she caught the light in his eye. She thought it winked, but maybe only the sun was shining on him; maybe the sun winked. The blood rose to her face and her heart stormed. In the classroom, the teacher also seemed overly friendly and asked about everyone's vacation. From Milda's easy answers she knew that she had not been idle in venturing deeper into the German language and nodded approvingly.

Still, Milda was not satisfied. She knew that the struggle with the German language had only begun and realized that it would never end. She knew she had to learn new words so that she could answer any question, so that she would not wish to die or slump under her desk when called upon to recite. And she would have died or slumped many times in a single day had not Gisela been beside her. At times Gisela pressed her hand, at times she nodded and always watched her with her quiet green eyes, as peaceful as still grass. Those eyes buoyed her up, forcing her to speak the words and make phrases the way Gisela had instructed when they worked on their homework.

"You know the answers, even better then any of us," Gisela would keep assuring her. "You only need the right words."

And so, in the evenings and late into the nights, Milda and Alma, too, would go over long lists of words which *Mildchen* had gathered from all her day's reading and living. Superstitiously she would tuck the lists under her pillow so the words would press into her head while she slept. It seemed to work. The daffodils had hardly let the tulips take over, when the German language she had known only by snappy shouts, scared whispers, multiple dialects, and chopped phrases started coming together more clearly, interestingly, and beautifully. Excited, she began memorizing poetry and recited it aloud, with proper expression, as Alma insisted.

"No, don't overdo it! Just know what the words mean. Understand and feel them," Alma would advise, adding: "You don't have to hang your head like that! You are smarter and prettier than what I see around us in this scrubby *Dorf.* Think of yourself as standing out like an amber gem among pebbles and that those around you are jealous and..."

"Don't be so..."

"So, so what?" Alma cut in. "Just don't you dare become a pebble! I didn't save you for that."

"I know, but..."

"But nothing! Always remember you're a Latvian girl, that's all." Having said that, Alma dismissed her with an irritated wave of the hand.

Milda shrunk from Alma's tone. She didn't like her sickly similes but said nothing, because it was easier to let things drop of their own than to provoke Alma to a higher pitch by arguing with her, so she learned to listen but not hear, accepting or rejecting her aunt's opinions as she pleased. She was afraid to tell her that she was terribly embarrassed about being different and about coming from a country that hardly anyone had heard of. Gratefully, however, she did accept Alma's advice on how to interpret poetry and learned how to recite long passages of Goethe's and Schiller's masterworks. It pleased her when the classroom became quiet as soon as she stood up to recite and how the silence followed her until she sat down, until she heard a loud applause the teacher had started.

But that was not enough. She was not satisfied and felt overwhelmed by all she did not understand. She was like a swimmer safe only in shallow, sure waters, while longing to spring-dive into fathomless depths. In public and around her school mates, generally, she was too embarrassed and unsure to let the words carry her where they would; only with Gisela she could measure the depth and height of the impossible German language. Only with Gisela she was not afraid to fumble and laugh at herself and let go of the hard rules she had memorized and venture into the art of free expression. Daily, as the weather became warmer and after her cleaning chores, Milda tried to express more complex thoughts and sentences to her friend. She concentrated on high German, letting the local dialect come out as it would or not at all, for it didn't matter. She knew that one day she would be leaving this peaceful valley. She and Alma would walk on, move into other old kingdoms whose languages had disintegrated into mere dialects and accents. She knew that if her speech was correct by formal standards, she would be rich even if she had nothing in her hands.

"Talk, talk, talk," Alma urged her, and Milda was so glad that Gisela listened and helped. Also, she was becoming much freer with

Frau Niert, who was always there, like her garden and her house. As she grew less timid, she asked more questions, forcing herself to use the interrogative mode. Then she would listen to Gisela's natural construction of the answers. She tried re-telling her friend what she had read, carefully placing the verbs at the end of the sentences, splitting them in half, feeling the sense of them. And finally—what joy! —they were conversing! About themselves, people they knew, the flowers in the garden and even the events of the world. Then Milda was at last able to tell her protectors about her lost homeland, her father who was deported and her mother whom, in a cloud of steam, she had left weeping on a gray platform in the train station of Riga. She told them about a free and happy Latvia and how, when the communists took over and the Red Army surrounded Liepāja, she and Aunt Alma had to leave everything—without even locking the door. "It was a beautiful Sunday morning," she said and broke down exhausted. "It wasn't my fault that I couldn't let my sister know I couldn't get back and meet her at the train station, as I promised."

It was after the re-telling of the escape that the Niert family surprised her with a book of stories entitled *Das Fremde Kind* (The Strange Child) and a most beautiful doll, so large that she came up to her waist. Milda, of course, felt too grown-up for dolls, but accepted the gifts with a curtsy and a kiss on *Frau* Niert's hand. She named the doll Zelda (who did not at all look like her sister) and seated it in the children's garden house on a velvet-covered footstool. Gisela's old dolls paled as they slouched against the parlor wall.

"I am happy you came to us," Gisela assured her, as they tidied up the miniature storybook house hidden, like the nests of birds, deeply inside sprouting, bursting shrubs. "Before you came I lived like my dolls in this house. Silent and dumb. I thought the world ended at the Thüringen Wald and the Bavarian borders, but now I can imagine it going on and on, circling and never ending, only circling and changing—like spring into summer, summer into fall."

"And fall into winter."

"Yes," Gisela said. "Like that… I wish the war would end. I don't want Germany to win and spread all over."

"I don't want any country to spread over another, especially Russia. I don't want it to spread at all, to come near me." Milda paused, hugging her doll. "I wonder if we will ever go home. My Aunt is sick for home. She will die if we can't go back." She said nothing more about Alma's moods, because she was afraid that Alma might hear and punish her by leaving her alone in this strange, enchanting garden.

"I should miss you," Gisela said kindly, but I would understand. I could never leave my home—especially this old house and our woods."

The more they talked, Milda thought, the more Gisela seemed to take on the blame for her homelessness. "You are too small for the burden that life," Gisela talked motherly and reached out for her friend's hand. "… and what our dear country has done to you. But the war will soon be over. Papa also thinks we are finished. He keeps waiting for Dr. Lutz to return so they can play cards. But, really, he is scared for any of us to get sick because there is no good doctor in town."

"Why?"

"Because our doctor was a Jew."

Herr Niert

Herr Niert was the director of the doll factory at the end of *Hauptstrasse*. Most townspeople worked there, behind the closed iron gate, making a good living in spite of the war. Punctually, at twelve o'clock the whistle blew and, ten minutes later, *Herr* Niert entered the house for his dinner. He walked straight and superior, and, after nodding and saying *Heil Hitler* to his wife and children, he removed his hat, and set his umbrella in the stand. He combed down his thin, gray-streaked hair, went into the washroom and then on to the dining room. Only after he sat down could the children take their places; *Frau* Niert served them all. Everyone watched the *Herr* tuck his large white napkin over his starched shirt and bow tie. Then he and the children folded their hands, bowed their heads and listened to his never-changing words of grace that fell in his lap. When he picked up his knife and fork, only then the meal could begin. He ate heartily, hardly saying a word and only rarely glancing nervously over his silver-rim spectacles, as if afraid to be caught at something or other.

Milda thought he looked like a rabbit she had seen in one jerky children's film. His face bulged out, coming to a point in his small dark Hitler mustache. His teeth bucked, and he had only a bulge where his chin should be. Milda wondered if he ever kissed *Frau* Niert and whether she was happy then—the way she had been in the Easter woods. In her husband's presence she appeared small; her movements cautiously self-conscious. At times she seemed to be trembling like a shadow or a leaf. Milda felt sorry for her, anxious that she might drop or spill things. She wondered if Gisela, too, pitied her mother, but then Gisela also was not herself at the dinner table. She ate silently with downcast eyes and rose when it was time to clear the table. Wilfred and Alfred shoveled their food into their mouths with great seriousness and relaxed only when the plates were empty. Often, especially when there was spinach or leeks, Wilfred would not swallow the last bite. He would wait until past one o'clock, when his father was out the door. Then he would spit the cud out. *Frau* Niert pretended not to notice.

Milda did not like to dine with the family. The good meals were always ladled with tension that caused her stomachaches. Once she choked on a tough asparagus stalk, while everyone stared silently. She felt she had done something awful, shameful and blamed herself and not the wooden vegetable, but she could never refuse Gisela's invitation, and so she sat with the family frequently, looking at them with her outsider's eyes. She felt guilty about her wicked thoughts, about wanting to know what *Herr* and *Frau* Niert were like when the lights went out at night and they had put on their long nightgowns. Did she then, too, tremble like a leaf caught on a warped branch? And what did his children really think of him? She did not understand why the noon-hour perfection of the household made her so afraid, nor why the relief was so complete when, through the opaque glass, they saw the master's back disappear, suddenly causing everyone to breathe easier and talk loudly.

She could not understand how the Nierts could live that way. It was the exact opposite of how Milda remembered her home—before the communists. Her house was happiest when papa's form stood behind the laced glass door and his hand turned the key. *Oh, may God help me, if this kind of life awaits me! But no... I would marry only for love and would always run into the arms of my husband like mamma did and the way Alma wants to.*

The contrasts between what she saw and what she imagined were too mysterious to comprehend. Trying to find some easy explanation, she began to suspect evil in the *Herr*, who carried his authority like he carried his briefcase, which no one was allowed to touch.

"They are all afraid," she told Alma. "They are afraid to speak because he frowns at whatever they say. It's like they cannot find the right words. His presence makes us all feel separate and stupid."

"German authoritarianism begins at home," Alma said. "But who cares? His mustache is so puny."

"It's not that, it's the tone, the words."

"Oh, leave me alone," Alma said irritably and leaned out the window.

WORDS. . .

Milda pondered as she wrote the assigned essay: *Words are like mortar that seals people. They bring people together. They make feelings strong and important. All emotions become better when they can be sorted out into words. Love becomes sweeter with words and hate more bitter. But hate can also be dissolved through words. Anger can become less frightening. Even war, when put into words, somehow does not seem so dreadful. Embarrassing moments can be cleared up with words. For example, at a dinner table, the girl should have been free not to eat a wooden asparagus and the little boy should have been allowed to let his father know that he does not like leeks. Maybe then all would have laughed and swallowed more easily. However, the father gives a stern look, and all the words choke inside everyone like that wooden asparagus.—*

She crumpled up the paper. She could never risk Gisela reading *her* words.

Milda sensed that her rising antipathy toward this man who, with his cold, haughty silence killed so much goodness in his own family, was becoming noticeable. To overcome that she pitied him, thinking how he was missing so much and how he must feel lonesome like the lone oak tree in the corner of his garden. She also saw how people only nodded politely whenever they met him in the street. She saw no one stopping to talk to him, no one asking him how his day was, nor saying that it was a good morning. From her window, she saw him walking to work, looking nervously over and through his neighbors' fences. She wondered if he was afraid of people or if his neighbors were afraid of him. She hated that cramped up feeling, and that was why she laughed in the dollhouse. It was a way of killing the poisonous silence. She didn't blame the twins either. They were only silly little boys.

It all had begun innocently. The children were in the dollhouse having a snack. The day was beautiful and unusually warm. Hot with spring fever, the twins began their games. Wilfred, mimicking his father, sat down at the head of the table and started eating some snacks off their luncheon plate. Everyone laughed, and the more they laughed the more he clowned. At last, he picked out a carrot and, wiggling his nose, chewed it with his front teeth, which also bucked like a bunny's. Milda started laughing, uncontrollably, doubling up and nearly crying. She didn't see Gisela's shocked face.

Meanwhile, Alfred, at the other end of the table, tried to mimic his brother, but no one laughed with him. Bored, he got up, straightening himself like his father and, walking up to Gisela's old doll, which slumped on a bed, said, "Come to me, my *Frau, comme her!*" he whispered coarsely, commanding, pulling the doll to him by her stiff, outstretched arms. "You must come, when I call you," he scolded, lowering his mean voice and looking around as though he wore glasses. At that Wilfred dropped his carrot and giggled; Milda went on laughing, not noticing Gisela turning pale when Alfred laid the doll on the toy bed. He slobbered all over her, smacking his lips, and then lay on her imitating movements he must have seen in some dark night. Milda threw her head back and Wilfred jumped on her, tickling her under her arms and neck. She tickled him back and kept on laughing.

Suddenly Gisela upset the dolls and the dishes and burst into tears, crying, "Stop, stop it!" She pulled Alfred up by his collar and grabbed Wilfred by the hand. She smacked them both on the backs of their heads and set them down at the table. Milda choked up in shame and tried to apologize, but Gisela didn't even look at her. "Poor, poor Papa," she said through her sobs, turning herself to the wall. Milda put her hand on her friend's shaking shoulders and stroked her red braids. At last Gisela brushed her face with the corner of her white apron and turned slowly, looking down on her brothers who chewed on their carrots, looking with each nibble more and more like scared twin rabbits.

"You ought to be ashamed of yourselves!" Gisela scolded. The twins only looked at each other and started giggling again. The girls waited the way patient mothers wait for temper tantrums to die down.

"Most children in our whole town don't even have fathers," Gisela said quietly. "They are either lost or fallen or. . ."

". . . deported," Milda completed the sentence.

"Yes," Gisela said, looking at Milda shyly, forgivingly. The twins sunk into a pouting silence, swallowing hiccups and giggles, and glaring with accusing eyes at Milda's pale face. The game was over.

"My father is dead," Milda said.

Only after the words had crossed her lips, she realized their full meaning. She somehow knew, assumed that her father had perished with thousands of others in the mysterious horrors of Siberia, but she had never put that into words, into four little words—in one complete German sentence. Strangely, it did not hurt. Nor did she care that the twins scrambled out the low door and escaped into the garden or that Gisela, like many women cornered by sad news, hid herself in housework. She picked up the dirty little dishes and said she had to go help *Mutti*.

Tired and ashamed, Milda, left uncomfortably alone, lingered in the sunny garden. She stooped down and picked violets. She picked carefully, right down to the earth, laying each blossom close to the other, putting in the heart of every flower a thought about her father, whom she remembered only as in clipped photographs. She wept because she did not even have one photo of her parents; she had nothing to keep them from bleaching out of her mind.

When her hand was so full that the violets, all in a mass, looked like a ripe purple mushroom, she picked enough leaves to form a wreath all around it. She stroked the earth as if it were a grave and then stood up.

She carried the bouquet into the house, up the stairs to her attic room, where Alma sat memorizing *Faust*. She put the violets in a glass and placed it in the middle of their round table.

"Lovely," Alma said. She bent over the bouquet, inhaling deeply. "They have no fragrance."

"No, not like the dark purple violets in the sunny spots of our country," Milda said. "I was so little when we all rolled down the slopes of *Herr* Reltof's valley, getting dirty. The whole ravine was purple and so fragrant! I've almost forgotten that sweet fragrance and other smells and sensations of our country. But they look the same," she said, tidying the heart-shape leaves.

"Ah, yes," Alma sighed. "Nothing smells the same here, and these are such deceptive little things and so clever at getting us all weepy and sentimental." She fingered the blossoms lightly. "Oh, I shouldn't be mean to the poor flowers. It's not their fault, and maybe they too are sad and ashamed. What flower wouldn't wish to make the world dizzy?" Impulsively Alma put her arm around Milda's shoulders and pulled her so tightly against her that they felt their hearts beating as one.

Milda said, "I picked the flowers for my father's grave."

"Stop that!" Alma pushed her away. "What right do you have to bury him alive? We haven't gotten any news, no black-edged letter or telegram."

"Still…"

"Still, nothing! Go down and start pealing potatoes! Lutz wants dumplings and lots of them."

"*Jawohl.*"

Letters

But one letter was brought to *Frau* Lutz's door a few days later. It was dated December 25, 1944.

We light candles on this night. Fighting is all around and many fall. The snow is red. I'm so afraid. Where are you? I waited for the train but it did not come. Forgive me. Where is Juris? Where is Papa? We all kiss you. Z.

Feeling faint, Milda turned the letter over, searching for more news, then focusing on the envelope that held the address of the farm.

"So," Alma said, "They are still at home. That means they're not starving, so let's be glad!"

The letter had traveled for months and how it finally reached Milda Birke, no one could guess. Perhaps it was through the Red Cross or perhaps there were spying agencies that kept lists of those who escaped, who were labeled *traitors of the fatherland*. Whose were the invisible hands that wrote down even changed names and temporary addresses of the escapees? And what strange eyes were reading every word of however camouflaged, coded notes people wrote? They all were curt, inadequate notes, carrying abbreviated, eclipsed news that left everyone crazy and anxious, with visions of Stalin beating innocent people with his wilted arm and fist—even while little girls picked violets in sunny gardens. Hidden from the spying eyes of the rest of the world, his arm grew in power and evil. Like a roaring, thunderous anvil cloud it hovered over humanity and forced all the smaller arms and fists to bear down on starved, broken, scared people—even small children.

"I am so thankful to God for letting us escape," Milda told Gisela. But she and all those who had been lucky enough to get away still were terrorized. Milda feared the huge hand. Alma dreaded it, not only for herself, but mostly for him, her betrothed, her Viktors. She also feared for her sisters, Matilde and Katarina, and the actors left on dark stages—everyone—her whole nation.

Impatiently, Alma snatched the dirty envelope out of Milda's hand and stared at it. She put it against the window and searched for some hidden note but found nothing. She paced the room, twisting her handkerchief, blotting her eyes, looking out the window. "I must write," she said, "today."

She set herself to the task. That spring she wrote many letters to Latvia, slanting her hand this way and that, signing names from characters in plays. She sent quizzing notes to Ella, who, she was certain, would not be hurt by the communists. "And if the Reds get her, I don't care. One traitor less," she said, licking the envelopes addressed to Liepāja. "I'm sure she's a spy, but so what? What could she find out that everyone doesn't know already? We're all the same—those who got out and those who are trapped. We're cut in half, or in thirds, counting Siberia. But we'd all rather die than not know what's become of the other half, isn't that right?"

"Yes," Milda said unconvinced, because she knew that she would rather live than know. She could wait and see. She had so much homework, and Gert smiled at her.

"What are you grinning for?" Alma asked. "Are you laughing at me? Do you think I'm crazy, you selfish girl?"

"No, no, I wasn't laughing, not now, I'm only thinking how . . ."

". . . happy he will be to hear from me," Alma broke in. "Yes! My letters will bring light into his darkness. They will light up the stage, bring joy and hope."

"Maybe. But what if they bring deportation and death?"

"It's the chance I'll take. All life is a gamble. Besides, all Stalin wants is for everyone to sit paralyzed in fear. We must not give in."

But most refugees would not dare to take such chances. They were afraid that the slightest note might send their loved ones directly to Siberia or put their names on black lists kept in dark cellars. And so a silence, frightful and iron, ruled both sides of the iron curtain. It grew and separated brother from brother and sister form sister; parent from child, and lover from lover—one half of the nation from the other. Meanwhile, the world seethed and turned during these years; the atoms of humanity split and shattered in millions of molecules all over the globe—until the Atom Bomb exploded over Hiroshima. Only then the silence of death or peace set in. It was an uneasy, painful peace, like the peace behind locked prison doors and gates. For some the torments had just begun, as the hot war gave way to the cold war. Millions enlisted in the Cold War. It did not hurt so much, especially if one was lucky enough to live in America.

At the time Milda received Zelda's letter in the winter of 1949, announcing the death of their father, she had already turned her back on Latvia. She was preparing to leave for America, where communists would not reach her. She was engaged. She was full of life and excitement. She wrote a short letter to Zelda, telling her that she would soon sail across the Atlantic and that Juris had fallen in Berlin. She promised not to forget her and poor Latvia. She did not confess that every one, including Zelda, was turning into bland outlines with no faces. Her mind's eyes could not see any of them. She could not draw them either, and that's why in all her art classes she drew only people's backs or vague, blurry profiles. Never the faces. Shadows are faceless. But— all that happened months and years later. Meanwhile. . .

Mildchen and *Mutti*

After the episode in the garden playhouse, *Mildchen* was drawing ever closer to *Frau* Niert with the kind of forbidden longing only orphans feel toward real live mothers. Her chores and homework finished, she would linger about the Niert house, impatient for Gisela also to be free. Then they would go for their daily one hour walks, taking the twins up wooded, fern and wild-flower edged paths, where they would climb rocks and play games in a castle ruin. She noticed, somewhat alarmed, that after such outings, she would be impatient to get back to the Niert house so she could tell *Frau* Niert what they had seen and done and how the woods felt. She never failed to bring back some treasure—flowers, egg shells, a gem-like pebble. She would anticipate *Frau* Niert's needs and wishes and run errands for her before her own children had a chance. Yet she dared not get too close, because she did not want to wedge herself between the mother and her children. Painfully aware of her place and station, she learned to restrain, like the stepdaughters of fairy tales. Only *Frau* Niert was more like a fairy godmother who never tired of doing good and speaking comforting words. Milda learned the tone and the words that averted cries and tantrums and changed tears to laughter. She thought that if *Frau* Niert were an actress, she would be a prettier, more natural Margareta than Alma. Or—with touches of Alma's make-up, *Frau* Niert might have made a good model for some master of religious art.

Frau Niert loved to embroider. She also made all her children's clothes and knitted her husband's sweaters. She herself had four dress-up dresses, one for each season, but she had a full drawer of aprons and wore them all in turn. Gray workday aprons displayed faded cross-stitched borders, while white Sunday and holiday ones showed off the satin stitch, tatting, and appliqués.

Once Milda had become aware of an inner and outer *Frau* Niert and had guessed about her troubled marriage, she studied the aprons with special curiosity. It was in them, Milda believed that the young, beautiful, suppressed part of *Frau* Niert seemed to hide and live. Only in the truest symbol of domesticity this *Hausfrau* dared to be ornamental and free—like the crusader at the museum in his decorated metal shield. Milda tried to read the embroidery the way her grandmother, whom she remembered only vaguely, had taught her to read some of the old Latvian designs woven in long sashes and stitched in linen shirts. Fascinated, she tried to read in the hieroglyphics of the aprons *Frau* Niert's moods, pleasures, sorrows. She imagined that *Frau* Niert, as she worked on the intricate pull-out patterns, had discarded all the unpleasantness of her days and let sheer beauty take over. As she stitched the deer, the rabbits, the birds and garlands of flowers, Milda sensed a kind of excitement and freedom. She was certain that whenever *Frau* Niert walked inside the circle of the woodland animals and bright flowers bordering her ankles, she was happy, as though she were dancing even through gray days. She then wondered if the good woman felt safely bordered from *Herr* Niert's cold, gray, critical over-the-spectacles scans, while he would not have a clue of her guarded mystery because he never looked down at her hemlines. Mystified, she doubted if the *Herr* ever saw things that went on below his own tight belt.

"*Mildchen*, you may call me *Mutti*, if you wish," *Frau* Niert said one Sunday afternoon as she played with the twins. Surprised, Milda tried to read Gisela's eyes, but they did not meet hers.

"*Mutti?*" Milda tried to say that word wondering if it sounded at all like *māmiņa* or *mammīte*. Of course, she would never call another woman by those sacred names, but the German endearment did not feel the same on her lips as the Latvian. Keeping her tears back, she kissed *Frau* Niert's hand and thanked her. She knew that she would not overuse the word. It would be a Sunday word, like the bright white aprons, to be handled reverently and worn only on special occasions. She would not say it when the real children were present, for she would not want to steal anything from the rightful heirs and risk their jealousy. And, of course, she said nothing about the changing scales of this delicate relationship to Alma.

Mutti worked like a magical key. It allowed Milda to enter the white stucco house whenever she was free. She could ask the substitute mother for help and advice and sit and embroider with her and learn the smooth satin stitch.

While they stitched, sitting by a window in the afternoon sun, the twins resting from their walk and Gisela softly practicing on the piano, *Frau* Niert told many happy and sad tales of old Bavaria and the surrounding kingdoms and woods and her own childhood. Sometimes she would sing softly. Her voice was ordinary, often falling out of tune, and, to cover up, she would ask Gisela to play and the others to sing along. In such manner, Milda learned many regional songs and became aware of the pleasant sound of her own voice. Soon, with Gisela's help, she resumed her piano playing that had ended after her father's disappearance. In the Nierts' parlor the nearly forgotten notes came back surer and stronger as soon as her fingers touched the keyboard. That made her so happy that she would forget to retreat to her attic room until Alma called and welcomed her with a scolding: "You're wasting time over there!" When nervously Milda showed her the embroidered doilies, Alma smirked: "How many hours have you been sitting at the silly woman's feet?"

"I haven't counted."

A slap singed the warm cheek. "Don't be like the child of a cuckoo that sits in another's nest," Alma nagged. "You still have a mother and a homeland somewhere, remember that! And we will go home, when all this is over, so don't get too cozy!"

"Yes," Milda said, guilty for having been happy, for letting her lips play with the word *Mutti,* a word like no other. But she, hearing the cuckoo clock strike, smiled and put away the doilies on which *Frau* Niert had outlined various stitches and patterns for her to follow. It was not long before she was making up her own designs and choosing her own threads.

As the World Crumbles

Meanwhile Alma became extremely restless and much more moody than during their escape, when everyone—even the whole world—whirled in constant motion. In the dull stillness of the large empty clean house, she tilted her head and listened for some whistle to blow or a particular voice to command: "Go home!"

She squinted, looking for signs and signals and put her things in order. Often she sat bent over the radio, trying to hear the words through constant static. She would turn the dial back and forth, trying to gather the right news on which to lay her hopes, but the words would not congeal, would not hold together and lend nothing for her hopes to grab onto.

"Americans and the Brits have slashed half-way across Germany," she heard and repeated the news to her niece.

"The Russians are advancing westward." She echoed the radio in a shocked whisper, as though trying to delete the statement. Often she would stare at her niece, shouting for her to be quiet, to stop scratching her pen over papers or clicking her needle against her thimble.

"Roosevelt is dead," Alma announced one day, adding uncertainly, that someone named Harry was the new President of America." Her laughter was deep and bitter. And then she said, "It's good that he is gone. He drank wine with Stalin, and he sold us all out in Yalta. Maybe for a knife's tip of caviar. So maybe now there will come help from this Harry. Maybe he will understand what communism is all about. And it's our duty to tell him the truth." She slapped at the dust in the air which the sun suddenly illuminated. "We must tell the truth to the Americans and the British. Oh, Churchill is smart, he knows Europe. They will push the Russians back, you'll see, and we'll go home! Won't it be wonderful?"

"Yes."

But nothing wonderful was happening, except the days were wonderful, stormy and calm, throwing out new colors and warmth every morning. The birds chirped and sang, calling each other, yanking the worms out of the earth and stuffing them down their babies' open beaks that popped out of their nests hidden in pink and white blossoms, garnished with light green leaves. The women, wearing men's clothes, worked in the fields and gardens. They talked loudly, hopefully, telling one another in their local dialect that their husbands and sons will soon come home and pick up the shovels and hoes. The school children too were excited and helped to set the houses and fields in order. Yes, spring in the Thüringen hills was as it should be, as it always had been and will be.

"*Wien ist gefallen*," Alma repeated what she heard on the radio.

But for Milda the fall of Vienna was far away, in another country. Besides, she was studying very hard so that she would have the highest marks in her class, and, at the same time, she tried to push away a certain feeling that threw her off-balance every time Gert's brown eyes caught hers. She heard *Frau* Lutz moan and saw her clasp her hands desperately to her heart. "*Ach, mein Mann*... and here I stand and cannot go to him." She had recently received broken news about her husband being wounded and in a hospital. Nothing more. The radio said that the street fighting in Vienna was bitter. *Frau* Lutz wept, and Alma reached out and tried to comfort the confused, scared woman, saying that Americans will come to "save us all."

But within days or hours—Milda could not remember the lines of time—the worst news hit them like lightning from a clear sky. Alma screamed out in real terror, pulling her head away from the radio with such force that she hit it against the headboard's brass scrolls. Then she cried the way children cry because it hurt. The urgent voice on the radio announced: "The Russians have charged into Berlin...Street fighting is fierce.... The *Führer* will address the nation at any moment"

Milda stopped stitching. The nation held its breath as it waited and listened in doomed silence. Hitler said nothing.

HOW LONG IS EXILE?

*

Thereafter, Oeslau felt as if it were poked from all sides at once like those huge anthills in the woods. And, like upset ants, people rushed head on, aimlessly, this way and that, through and about the streets and winding roads. After capitulation, trained by habit and constant regimentation, some arms went up, hands, fingers extending in the *Heil Hitler*! salute without hesitation, without giving in at the elbows. Other arms rose a bit and sunk down as in pain; some fearfully slid into pockets for safe keeping. Still other people let their arms hang down their sides like wooden limbs. The women clutched their string bags and worked their hands so hard that there was no desire to either raise or hold them back. Their hands always knew what to do. Only in the doll factory's turret, the siren blew every morning, noon, and evening, and *Herr* Niert remained punctual. *Frau* Niert treated him with special care, offering him second helpings of pudding.

Milda stayed close to Alma, chopping her afternoon hours into quarters, sorting them around her duties and her pleasures. She watched Alma, who acted more and more strangely. She wiped the sweat off her forehead. Sometimes she hid the radio, but then Alma would yell at her, telling her that she was waiting for Hitler to speak. She was waiting for history to speak, she shouted, and took the radio to bed with her.

But he did not speak. They did not hear him.

On one of those Sundays the cathedral was full, the organ loud.

I lift my eyes onto the hills from whence commeth my help.

My help commeth from the Lord who made heaven and earth.

Milda listened to the clear voice of the aged minister say the same words in the German as Uncle Imants, in his troubled hour, had said in the Latvian. Yes, God is one, and He rules the world, Milda tried to believe. *One God. One Faith. One Baptism...* She tried to lift her eyes to the hills that leafed and bloomed all around. She tried to believe the minister that there would be help and solace. Everyone did. Everyone looked up to the light that streamed through stained glass windows.

Only Alma did not look up. She did not care for the Sunday calms and false peace. She was glad for the day to be done. She hated *Frau* Lutz's starched aprons and mock kindness served up in overcooked, over-salted meals she, in her anxiety, suddenly insisted on sharing. Alma belonged to the nights and workdays. And on some of those late April days, early in the mornings, she would impulsively pull Milda out of bed to tell her about something that had kept her awake or to take her somewhere far out of town. She would urge the sleepy girl to hurry because they had to catch a certain train to some uncertain place. It did not matter that school would be missed. Milda knew that Alma would kick away all obstacles to reach whatever destination she had in mind, and so she never argued but went along lamb-like. People saw them from their windows and talked about them over the fences. *Did you see? —Can you imagines? —For God's sake*! But no one dared to stop them, for they were, after all, foreigners whose ways and speech were strange. The people merely shrugged their shoulders as the two refugees rushed past their houses to the train station.

Once they reached the assorted, nameless places, Alma would hold her niece fast, digging her fingernails into her hand until it hurt. She would pull her toward some wall or post glued with sheets of papers filled with names of men wounded, missing, or killed. As Alma pored over the lists, her eyes large and glassy, Milda read the names also. Many names were not German. They were strange names, names she could not decipher, let alone pronounce. Always surprised to find Latvian names, she stared at them, easing up only when she did not know any of the men who hung before her eyes by mere letters. She did not see the name *Juris* and, closing her eyes, breathed her thanks to the Almighty. When she opened them, they watered as columns of print ran together in blurred, black streamers while she waited patiently for Alma, too, to sigh in relief. Then slowly they pulled away from the post and let other women squeeze into the spot, like changing guards. Sometimes they hurried, at other times they strolled back to the station to catch the train to the town they wearily called home. On some of those mornings Milda would go from the station straight to school, but on others, there would be no reason to disturb the class and draw needless attention to herself. Then she would follow in Alma's shadow to their attic room. On such days, when they closed the door behind them, they were again reminded that they were travelers in a strange land, where they had only paused to rest.

"He lives," Alma would say looking up in the blue or cloudy skies. "I know he lives."

"Mamma and Zelda also live, don't they?"

"Yes, of course. But they wouldn't be listed. We wouldn't know. They don't list civilians, only soldiers. But we cannot give up hope. So, yes, certainly, they live. Latvians are a strong people. We've survived centuries. I would bet that more of us get killed than die naturally— except for the very old and the children. Our people have lived through many wars and famines and genocides, and they still aren't wiped away. Isn't that marvelous?"

"Yes. Marvelous." Milda echoed. She found reason for joy in that and put her hand in Alma's. "You are so wise," she said. "Thank you for watching over me."

Then, sitting with their sides glued together, they would break the hard rolls in half, put jam on them and eat, while drinking herb tea. Warmed, they would talk about people they knew and loved—people who were very far away and who waited for them. They talked softly in words others would not understand, believing that as long as they mentioned the names of their loved ones they would not die. During such times, Milda would feel their common blood and heartbeats and know that they would be bound together forever. She also knew that only she could help Alma in her mad displacement because only she— though she often feared and hated her—loved her beyond words. They were each other's duty, each other's reflection and salvation. "Yes," Alma mused, "every one of them—and us—is a story."

Defying Age

One day, one windy April day, when Milda returned from school, she caught Alma in front of the mirror coloring her lips red with a piece of crepe paper and penciling her eyebrows black. That done, she plucked from her head single gray hairs, rolled them between her fingers and set them on fire. From outside the half open door, she watched her aunt's hair curl up and burn out. It was a weird sight in the middle of a hot day, when the sun shone through the open window. The small flame rose as high as it could, trying to meet the sun, and then went out, not leaving behind even a pinch of ashes, only a bit of gray dust. Spewing out a short, high-pitched laugh, Alma blew the dust away and stood up examining her figure she had clothed in a tight flowery dress *Frau* Lutz had ceremoniously presented to her on Holy Week. Irritated, on Good Friday Alma had shoved the *rag* in the bottom of the nearly empty wardrobe.

"I'll never wear it," she had said. "It stinks like her armpits." Milda had seen her throwing a dead rat away in the same disgusting manner.

But spring had turned hotter, and Alma did not have any summer clothes. Even if the suitcase had not been blown up, she still would not have had one single dress; she had not planned to stay away that long.

All the shops were empty, and she had no means of getting things *under the table*. And so, the heat had melted her pride and forced her to wriggle inside the fermented and wrinkled crepe garment.

"Oh, Auntie, you are beautiful again!" Milda rushed forward, but Alma, taken by surprise, hissed at her, "Don't lie to me! Don't flatter! There is no *again* for me. You saw me go up in smoke, didn't you?"

"Only your hair," Milda admitted. "There's more to you than that."

Alma laughed. "When you see the first leaves turn, you know that winter isn't far away."

Milda turned to leave her alone, but Alma ordered her to come to her. She stood her up in front of the mirror. Feeling naked, the girl stared at her awkward reflection flanked against Alma's sturdy pose. Her blue skirt was much too short and miserably faded. Her blouse pulled open at the buttons.

"You need new clothes," Alma said. She drew her own stomach in, pushed her chest out, and quickly shifted her mood from bitterness to solicitous caring. "I'm getting old, and you are no longer a child," she said. "I didn't even notice that you have almost turned into a woman. We could pass for sisters."

"People here think you're my mother," Milda said carelessly, but her words struck Alma so hard that she slumped down into the stuffed chair that filled a corner.

"Your blouse is shamefully tight, and that old skirt. . . Pitch it!"

"But what do I wear?"

"How should I know?" Alma shrugged her shoulders. "Ask your friends! You're there all the time. Doesn't that gray mouse of a woman ever look at you?"

Milda turned and left the room. For the next few days she kept to herself, covering her front with an apron and trying to lose herself in books. She didn't raise her hand in class and refused to go to the blackboard, saying she knew nothing. She looked down on her miserable shoes every time Gert was nearby. Gisela, of course, saw that something was wrong and would not leave her friend alone until she confessed her shame and distress. Then Gisela led her to her mother.

"*Ach, mein Kindchen!*" *Frau* Niert embraced her. "I saw it all along but was afraid to say anything. I didn't want to offend you. Can you forgive me?"

That same evening, while Gisela cleaned up the kitchen, the kind woman rummaged for scraps of materials, measured and re-measured *das liebes Mildchen*, and the next day a dress was ready. "But that is not enough," *Mutti* said, cutting patterns out of newspapers. Milda worked with her, designing and sewing her first seams on a treadle sewing machine. By the end of the week a spring wardrobe was put together. On Sunday morning there was no little girl, no *Mildchen*, who walked out of the house, but a lovely maiden, transformed. "You bloom with the daffodils," *Frau* Niert said smiling, herself sporting a new dress she had stitched up while the sewing machine was out. Later, in the afternoon, in the garden, Milda whirled the twins in full circles, watching her skirt flare out and aware of her tender breasts nicely filling the bodice edged with lace.

Inside the playhouse, with Gisela's help, she parted her hair in the middle and coiled her braids over her ears, making spit waves that softly framed her face. "You're so beautiful," Gisela said, standing back and staring at her as if seeing her for the first time. The twins giggled but wouldn't attack her with jumps and playful slaps. When *Herr* Niert came home, he wasn't sure he was seeing the same girl and adjusted his glasses, but *Frau* Niert looked on smiling, checking the hem, the wideness of the belt, and made various tucks here and there. Only Alma mocked, saying. "You look like a patched up Bavarian peasant. The people in Riga will mock you. They will laugh."

"Mamma won't laugh," Milda said. "You're cruel."

Next day Milda went back to *Mutti*, who looked at the transformation she had made with such pleasure that she too became younger and more beautiful. "How nicely your figure shows up!" she said. "But watch out that the young men don't carry you off!"

Milda blushed. She remembered Juris, who already had carried her, and thought about the way she felt when Gert looked at her. Oh, how she wished that he would carry her away, somewhere far, far away, where pain and mean words would not reach her, like princes carried wronged princesses to castles where roses bloomed! But there was no time to remember and wish. *Frau* Niert was holding out a pair of scissors and laying out material for another skirt.

Throughout the days that followed the sewing machine worked constantly. Dresses were also made for Gisela and matching outfits for the twins. Gisela, too, did not look like a girl anymore. She, too, had turned into a *Fräulein.*

Treasures in the Attic

Together the young ladies transformed the playhouse into a garden house—a house of many secrets. Except for a few dolls—all arranged around "Zelda"—they packed away the rest with other useless playthings and carried them to the attic. There they spent hours looking through magazines and faded novellas, setting the interesting ones aside. Shockingly Gisela came upon a whole stack of magazines, addressed to *Herr* Niert, with pictures full of naked women. Together they leafed through them, imagining *Herr* Niert doing the same, up here in the attic, all alone, while *Frau* Niert swept the house. The girls noticed that the magazines were not dusty like other things.

"*Ach*! So my Papa, my own father, sneaks up here to look at this!" Gisela whispered in shocked accents, her face burning with shame.

"*Mutti* must not find this trash," she said, and they carried the exciting filth down and burned it.

On their next trip up in the attic, they opened a large trunk. There *Frau* Niert had buried her wedding gown of white lace and chiffon and her bouquet of dry, white roses. The petals crumbled from Gisela's touch, but Milda carefully picked them up and wrapped the bouquet back in the old newspaper. "Lindberg crosses the Atlantic," said the faded headline.

They dug deeper into the trunk and discovered photo albums full of brown and black photographs: a young Franz Niert looks down on *Fräulein. Frida Metzger. Franz & Frida, 1928.* She smiles not. A wedding picture in brown tones. A drop waistline dress of lace with billows of chiffon and ribbons. She sits as in a cloud and sadly smiles down on her white roses. Her veil is low, covering her hair. Franz looks like a glazed Easter rabbit with his chin chewed off. He holds a serious pose. No mustache. Hair slick and parted, brown like the rest of the picture.

"It's all so very sad," Gisela said, brushing the dust off as though brushing back lost time. "She was so beautiful!"

"Yes. But she still is. Your mother is beautiful."

"You think so?"

"Yes, oh, yes! Like you will be one day. Here she looks just like you."

"Still, it is sad."

"Because everything changes?"

"Yes. And we can never go back in time."

"Yes, I know," Milda, sighed. "Still, nobody wants to change backwards, do they? No.— No butterflies want to go back and be cocoons; no flowers want to be buds." But in spite of her conscious, grown-up words, tears rose to her eyes, and she let them fall. She did not have to explain that she longed for her mother, longed that her mother would see her now, growing up, turning into a woman. She dreaded any change in Mamma, for how would she find her?

Gisela giggled. She held out a photo of herself balancing on her bare feet, holding onto a flower. The flowers bloom high over her head. There is a hand in the picture, a hand reaching for the baby, being there in case it might fall.

More pictures. A stack in an envelope. Someone didn't have time to arrange and anchor them in place. There are two babies, so unbelievably alike. Of course they are Wilfred and Alfred. There is a whole stack of them in black and white. Everybody is smiling or laughing. Both take turns being in *Mutti's*, then Papa's arms. In one photo the twins cry, their mouths wide open. Perhaps both had lost out in a scratching, hair pulling baby fight until the large hand in the corner settled things. It's a father's hand caught in time's wheel.

Silently the girls closed the trunk. They buried the dolls inside, knowing that one day, far in the future, these dolls will be raised again by yet unborn, eager hands. . .

The two friends then went down the narrow, winding stairs, carrying stacks of dusty romances. They will put them on the clean shelves of the playhouse—turned into a most charming teahouse—and read them secretly, after their hourly afternoon walks.

The Way the Big War Ended

Alma's restlessness and tension had become more and more alarming to Milda, who did not know what to do, nor how to respond to the shifting, unpredictable mood swings. During her working hours Alma, dreadfully bored with *Frau* Lutz's dust and talk, pushed the mops and rags in angry spite even as her mistress's Bavarian accent grated on her nerves. "How can anyone do this to the German language?" she railed.

She would mimic *Frau* Lutz, trying not to hear the twisted words and glancing at Milda for her reaction. But she only saw Alma's tight lips and bottled-up tension. She was upset that Alma made too much of little things that passed over as quickly as they came. But then, again, she knew that Alma was only acting a maid's role on some cluttered, imaginary stage, waiting for the curtain to fall. She could not understand how this woman, her beloved aunt, could be so many people during one single day, let alone throughout her lifetime. And she never knew from one day to the next what minor supporting role Alma's whims and moods would assign to her, forcing her also to act in peculiar ways. She was never consulted nor forewarned but had to be ready to catch whatever script was hurled at her unexpectedly. Her reflexes became quick and sharp, as she took her cues from Alma and forced herself to learn to be a puppet because it was the easy way out. She could never have learned that kind of acting, so useful in later life, had there not been real talk, laughter, and love next door in the Nierts' house—in spite of the master's foreboding silences and the collapse of Germany.

Even when the outside forces became increasingly overwhelming, *Frau* Niert held everyone together. She never slapped her children with rash hands or words, even when the news tore her heart. In fact, the opposite was true: *Frau* Niert continued to give her love and comfort freely to all who needed it. When everything was rationed, her love was not. Neither was such food and clothing as she could spare. Milda tasted this great, silent love in the food she was invited to share and saw it in the brightness of new embroidery and the flowers *Mutti* planted in the garden.

As the news of fighting on all fronts resounded over the radio, Alma paced about the rooms as if caged, going back and forth rapidly, then abruptly stopping, posing, and reciting long passages she kept memorizing from various drama books. She had discovered a set of gilded volumes on *Frau* Lutz's locked shelf. The books were brand new, with uncut pages. They were inscribed gifts to her daughters—Ursula and Magdalena—who, Alma jibed, must have cold scientific minds and hands that could only cut, bandage, and tie knots. "In the portraits on the wall the sisters look as stiff and starched as their nurses caps. "I bet they can amputate any arm or leg without blinking, don't your think?" she asked, turning to Milda, who only shrugged her shoulders and ran her dust rag over the oval wooden frames. "Their fingers would rub the gold off the pages of these great books," Alma said and, gently with her roughened hands pulled the books out of their jackets and stealthily carried them up the stairs to read late into the night.

Also, at night, Alma wrote letters, she usually addressed them to Ella, but Milda knew that they were meant for Viktors Vētra, her betrothed, her Mephistopheles of the classical Liepāja stage. In the dark, when Alma assumed that her charge was asleep, she repeatedly chanted, "*Mans mīļais* (my beloved), oh, how I miss you! How I need you, my darling, my love!"

From over the edge of her blanket, Milda saw her pause as if waiting to hear his voice. She saw her like that on many a night, staring out, waiting and listening, especially when the stars and moon were bright. Then Alma cried louder, trying to push her messages through on the night's short, uncluttered airwaves: "*Mīļais, ak, mans mīļais. . . . My peace is gone, my heart is heavy.*" And again she would fall to writing, page after page, furiously darting her pen into the bottle of black ink, never bothering to blot the pages when her tears hit them. Milda had no idea how long she stayed up because she would always fall asleep before Alma corked up the bottle of ink. In the morning Alma would wake up in a foul mood that hardly ever cleared up.

On some afternoons, when done with her housework and without any warning, Alma would pull Milda away from the Nierts and make her go with her for walks in the woods. The intense, fast walks scared her, but Alma would keep on walking. Alarmed, she noted that Alma always walked eastward, never westward, as if measuring the distance home, as if she planned to return to Latvia by the same route they had escaped.

On one such a walk—it must have been sometime between the fall of Vienna and Berlin—they had just passed the castle ruins, when, suddenly, in front of them they saw a body in full German uniform hanging from a tree. They screamed and stood still as the surrounding hills echoed their piercing cry. They ran back to town, Alma pulling Milda by the hand, straight to the police station, and in one breath told the chief what they had seen.

"These days we see such sights. I advise you not to go into the woods, not so deep inside. Stay at the edge, if you must walk at all," he lectured, leaning back in his hard chair and making a tent with his knobby fingers.

"*Ja, ja*," Alma said shaking, rubbing her hands like Lady Macbeth, standing there as if stapled to the floor. "When, oh, when will it all end?"

"Soon, I'm afraid, very soon. The battles, I mean. The real war will not be over for a long time. Wars never end, you know."

"Yes… I know," Alma said wearily, taking the vagueness as a confirmation of her idea that the Americans would come to save the world from communists. She nodded nervously rubbing her hands. The chief offered her a cigarette, and she grabbed for it and stuck it between her trembling lips. Milda watched her, biting her lips so hard they hurt.

"Our men are afraid and hang themselves," the chief said, striking a match. "The Jews, you understand," he lowering his voice. "It's already begun—the vengeance that will last for generations." He was holding Alma's hand as she sucked on the cigarette, letting the match burn all the way down before he blew it out. Alma gave him a *don't touch me* look and withdrew her hand that had felt the flame. The chief stared at her perspiring cleavage and wetted his full lips with the tip of his tongue, watching her smoke the cigarette down to the end.

Milda, left standing at the edge of a cluttered desk, felt the draft of the open window but understood little. To her the conversation was as cloudy as the room, smelling of congealed blood. That night she had nightmares about dogs barking at people who hung from trees like giant pods. In the morning, terribly exhausted, she said little before she escaped to school and her friends. She was now really afraid of her aunt. She was afraid of where Alma might lead her next.

The Swallows

"Wake up, Milda! Come here, my child! Look!" Alma calls, pulling the blankets away, pulling Milda with a hot hand. "The garden is full of swallow!" She whistles and calls the birds, reaching out, stretching her arms. She pulls the sleepy girl so close to her that she feels once again the full excited heat of her aunt's salty body with all its electricity that shocks and awakens her nerves.

"They are flying home! Spring has come to Latvia! The snow is melting in the fields, woods, and streets! I can see it all… the birches, the flowers, all! The grass is green at last, my love! I know you're looking out of some window, waiting for me. I can feel it in my poor heart and my tired blood." She presses Milda tighter to her, between her full, half-naked breasts, inside herself. She strokes her cheeks, kissing her, speaking softly, "I thought I heard him calling me, that's why I woke up—so suddenly—so very early. I swear I heard him call my name." She squeezes the shivering girl, breathing hard into her disheveled hair. "We must be patient, my darling, very patient. We must wait for all the evil men to hang themselves, the good men to clear the way, and then we'll be free! Free to fly home!"

Alma lets go of Milda, throwing her off. She stretches, growing taller, leaning forward and out, higher and higher, her arms turning into wings. She is flying out the window, her cheeks flushed, her eyes burning like night-lights. Milda, too, gets singed by the heat as she holds onto both ends of Alma's sash of an open robe. But the actress speaks on: "It's a wonderful morning! It's a sign—these swallows gathering right here. They are telling us something. They're telling us to be ready to fly home!"

Frightened, Milda sees the birds trampling through the spring branches. She is not sure they tell them anything. They don't even cock their heads to look up. Only, in their great rush, they keep swooping after mosquitoes and fluffing their wings, making a terrible racket. Across the gardens, on the other side of the sleeping Niert house, another woman looks out, shooing the birds away with her broom. *The mess, oh the mess they will leave behind! Those damned, careless migrants!* The woman keeps sweeping the air.

"Ah, I cannot wait!" Alma cries. "I wish I could hop on their backs, become small, like Thumbelina and fly, fly, fly!" She stretches out, almost touching the branches of the linden tree in Niert's garden. Milda pulls her back by the silken sash.

"But the communists. You wouldn't want to fly into their hands, would you?" Milda succeeds in turning her around. "Remember, there still are communists in Latvia, aren't there?"

"Yes, yes, for now, but the Americans will save Latvia. They would never let it fall, you'll see, you will see!" Alma speaks freeing herself, pulling the sash out of Milda's hands and tying it tightly around herself. She stands tall, as if on barricades. "The best part of the war has not even started. That's what the police chief said. Did you hear him? Did you listen, you stupid girl?" She is leaning over, pressing her against the ledge. "This war must end in victory for justice and goodness," speaks Joan of Arc. "Oh, how exciting it will be when all of us sail home again—all who were on that ship, do you remember? Do you remember the great big brave ship?" She asks sternly.

"How could I ever forget?" Milda shivers in the draft.

"Oh, my poor child, you are cold, but don't worry, soon you'll be home. With your Mamma and sister, and all this will be nothing but a bad nightmare." Alma again holds her tightly against her. "Oh, you poor, poor darling!"

"Back with Mamma and Zelda?" Milda asks uneasily. The names don't fit her tongue anymore. She feels no ground for the thought and keeps shivering in the chilling dawn-streaked darkness. "Will they really be there, when we come back?"

"Of course they will! Where else would they be? I've written to Katerina, I tell her to stop crying and wait for us. We'll come, I said, you'll see, just stop crying."

Milda was taken aback and stared at Alma with her large disbelieving eyes. "You wrote too Mamma? Do you suppose she got your letter?"

"I don't know, but we must trust. We haven't gotten any death notices, nothing with black edges. But I must write again… to all of them. Must write to him so he won't forget. Men do forget, you know. In all the tragedies men always forget—or remember too late, and then the women kill themselves." She puts her hand over her eyes, shielding them from the first morning sunrays. She probes far into the distance, watching the swallows rise from the trees and form flocks, chirping orders. Alma steps back from the window and gropes for a chair. "Child, get me my pen and paper! Come, quick, help me write!" She speaks rapidly, her face beaded with sweat. Like a blind woman, she keeps hitting the small cluttered table as she searches for a pen. Then, suddenly she veers and staggering, falls into bed. Her hair sticks to her forehead in wet strings. Her arms mill the air as she calls for pen, paper, glue. Stamps! Stamps with a Hitler head—green, purple, yellow! She gasps and is silent. Milda is afraid of the silence like death and screams.

Frau Lutz, still in her flannel nightgown, rushes into their room. With her thin veined hands, she checks for Alma's pulses, measures her temperature standing over her, then takes the thermometer out of the armpit and, holding it up to the window, reads the mercury that has climbed high over the red line. *Frau* Lutz clicks her tongue and leans over Alma, getting much too close. She pulls back the eyelids and peers into a pair of glassy eyes.

"*Grippe*," she pronounces and rushes from the room only to return with a bottle. She slaps Alma's cheeks, lifts her head in the crook of her arm, and pours a brown sticky liquid into a limp mouth. Alma rolls her eyes open and smiles stupidly, "*Mamma*?" she asks smiling. *Frau* Lutz lets her head sink onto the pillow. She packs the heavy down comforter around her so she will sweat good and hard. She tells Milda not to worry. "I am a nurse. I was very good, but then, you know, *die Familie... ach Gott!*" but she looks happy, turned on like a rusted spring, glad to be useful.

*

Frau Lutz nursed her servant with teas and thin soups, and, before the week was over, Alma put her feet on the reeling floor and staggered around a bit. But Milda saw her rise every night and walk in her sleep very close to the window. The moon was a bright, swollen eye during those nights. It winked and magnetized, coaxing her to walk straight as on stage and speak to her man.

During the afternoons of Alma's recovery, Milda sat quietly by her. She embroidered, read, and day dreamed about Gert, whom she missed. Just thinking about him caused her heart to skip several beats and her blood to tint her cheeks. And he? *Does he miss me*? She wondered as she stitch on—slowly, guiltily, for she was making a Mother's Day present for a woman who was not her mother. Alma did not ask her what she was doing and Milda did not care. Relaxed, she filled the corners and edges with brighter, more open flowers and hearts. When the half finished white, cotton cloth unrolled over her knees, she hardly heard Alma say, "It's nice—what you're making. It's pretty." The needle paused, and Milda listened. *Is Alma bending, giving in, honoring me*? She smiled and stitched on.

"Is there any news?" Alma asked wearily.

"No, nothing new, Aunty, except the fighting. Sometimes I think I can hear it."

"I hear it all the time. It bombards my head." With a weak hand Alma picked up the edge of the tea cloth. "You are good with hearts and borders," Alma said and let the cloth slide off her fingers. Then she turned on her side toward the wall and closed her eyes.

*

"*Achtung, Achtung!*" They hear the radio and sit up. It is another lovely day. The attic window is open, the birds sing close by. "*Radio Rome...* Italian partisans assassinate Benito Mussolini. Stand by!" Alma stands by and turns up the volume. All day, mixed with drawn-out symphonies and funeral marches, the announcements keep coming: The Italian-German front collapses. The bodies of Mussolini and his followers are taken to Milan and thrown in the street. Fascism falls.

"All the pillars of Europe are falling," Alma says. "What will happen to us?" She stares bewildered at her niece, who looks small and frightened. She keeps turning the dial crazily, searching for answers, but there aren't any. Disturbed, she thrashes around like a storm-rent branch.

The days pass slowly. Alma sleepwalks through the nights. She pushes away *Frau* Lutz's teas and soups. She yells at Milda to stop staring at her. She hugs the opened *Faust* to her half-bare, sweating breasts. She smells sour, but the day is sweet and boisterous. It ends with a burning sunset—red, purple, gold flames streak the skies, and Alma, too, burns in feverish excitement.

Walpurgis Night

"It's tonight."

"What is?" Milda asks as she dresses to go out to a school dance.

"Walpurgis Night! Don't you know? It's the night when Faust saw his Margareta, and Mephistopheles would not let him go to her—the devil! Here, listen!" Alma tries to find the right page, but Milda is in a hurry. She will meet Gert at the ball, and she is excited. Alma turns into a nervous blur.

"Don't leave me!" Alma calls, but Milda does not hear her. For once her ears turn deaf. "You'll be sorry!" Alma calls from the top of the stairs. Her warning rings through the house. But Milda rushes on, past *Frau* Lutz, who also tries to stop her, but cannot. She opens and closes the large door, leaving the madness behind and escapes into the blue darkness.

*

When Milda returned many hours later, the room was dark. Alma was gone. In a glance she caught the messed up drawers, the snippets of red, twisted threads, and the lace curtain pulled off its rod. She sees the large tooth comb, the red crepe paper and black pencil. She sees *Faust* open on *"Walpurgis Nacht"* and is afraid. Trembling, she reads the lines underlined in red, then races down the stairs, out the door and down the garden path, through the back gate. She runs up the narrow road leading to the woods. She is scared to death, sure that Alma has gone to hang herself or, maybe, to some secret masquerade.— She pauses. Had there been any kind of a celebration, others would have known about it, and there would have been talk. The town is small enough for any news and gossip to bounce quickly from house to house, from fence to fence. *Frau Lutz* certainly would have said something, but all is quiet.

"She's only scaring me, punishing me," Milda tells the shrubs and trees along the way. She runs faster, tripping over roots, seeing the wind in the branches. The huge full moon, weaves in and out of black and silver-streaked clouds lighting her way. She hears dogs barking but hurries on, knowing they would be inside their fences. This is Germany. She trudges straight toward the castle ruins; having taken the clues form the last two underlined lines of the open *Faust:*

> *When I find you on the rocky mountain*
>
> *That is good, then get yourselves o'er there."*

Alma had underlined those lines twice, as if setting clues for a treasure hunt.

When Milda sees the broken stone walls of the castle ruins and the giant boulders around it, she slows down and creeps in the shadows afraid of startling Alma, in case she is there. She knows that one should never wake up a lunatic, and she is not sure whether Alma is asleep or awake, dead or alive. For a second she stands still, listening to the night, hearing the night birds and the far-off rumbling of thunder. She watches the moon whitewash the castle wall, lighting it with silver and then blackening everything out. It is a strange night, a night she will never, ever forget.

And then she sees Alma dance. It is the only time she sees her dance like an enchanted ballerina. Her body is as luminous as the moon; her movements seem liquid. Milda feels wild excitement rousing every hidden, secret part of her body. She is ashamed, scared, thrilled—all in one breath, one heartbeat. She longs for Gert or Juris or any other man, for that matter, a stranger—Faust or Dracula—to draw her blood and mark her forever with four dots on her neck.

As Alma bends and twists, wrapped only in the sheer lace curtain, Milda stands still, terrified that Alma might slip and fall. She is afraid that she herself will fall if she makes even the slightest attempt to save her. Entranced, she watches the storm clouds gather above and inside her, until the dance comes to an abrupt end and a huge cloud covers the moon, leaving the rocky stage dark.

When the moon appears again, she sees Alma walking, gliding along the edge of a boulder, holding the curtain tightly around her. Milda thinks she can see the thin red threads *as narrow as a knife's blade* around Alma's neck and stands ready to catch the falling star. But Alma stands on a high ridge like a risen Venus. Milda creeps up. She slides between the rocks, glad she knows all the ups and downs, the turns and the sharp edges from having played there with the twins.

Another eclipse and darkness, and Alma is lost to her, perhaps floating away—silently on the wings of night birds—until she turns into a very soft voice, crying among the branches: "*Nehm mich mit. . .* Take me with you!"

Milda recognizes Margareta's plea and rushes forward. As the moon frees itself from the black cloud and gives all its light to illuminate the night, Milda sees Alma lying on the rock, her arms reaching to heaven. And again she hears the cry, only now it is not staged but honest and soft, heartbroken.

"Aunty," Milda speaks tenderly as to an infant.

Alma sits up and goes on with *Faust*: "What's going on?"

Milda springs to her side. She pulls the curtain off, exposing Alma's white nakedness. Venus has arisen. . . . The evening and the morning star shines low in the sky. But another cloud overtakes the moon and the star turns into a dark, dull, naked planet. Milda sees Alma's coat lying on the side of the boulder that was her stage and picks it up. She wraps it around her aunt's shoulders and the fox collar around her neck. The green eyes shine.

"Let's go home," Milda says and guides her down the stone steps.

"Home?" Alma echoes forlorn. "I have no home. There is no home without him."

"I know," Milda comforts. "Let's just go back to our room."

*

As soon as they slip inside the down comforters, Alma pulls her trembling niece close to her shivering body. Alma strokes and pets the girl as though she were a child, her child lost in the woods. Gretchen without her Hansel, oven ready. "These people don't even know how to celebrate their own holidays," Alma says and throws out a cynical laugh.

"But you do," Milda whispers, pressing Alma's cold hand to her lips.

"Yes, my darling, my little savior, my angel."

Comforted and warm, the angel pulls the end of the red thread—as narrow as knife's blade—that encircles Alma's neck and tosses it over the edge of the quilt. Then, with her arm around her neck, she falls asleep.

*

Confused, Milda sits up, yanked out of her dreams. Alma's side of the bed is empty. The moon shines through the bare window boldly, winking and grinning. Strange noises come from down below that separate into voices. She hears *Frau* Lutz's high pitches hitting the ceiling. They are matched by a man's low voice. She hears Alma's laugh, bitter and provocative, and a chorus of other voices, in indistinguishable, blurry accents. *Aufregung*. . . She glances at the alarm clock by her bedside. Its florescent hands are spread out on the night and morning sides of its Roman face. She jumps out of bed, slides into the hall and looks down the open stairway. The outside door is wide open, and she sees a crowd of people. Alma stands apart, laughing stupidly and hangs on to the chief-of-police who had lit her cigarette. She says gurgling, "But don't you know this is Walpurgis Night? The witches should be out—dancing, why don't they? Why don't you dance, *Frau* Lutz?" The chief holds her back from charging at the flustered woman. "Where are the witches of Oeslau?" she shouts, "I know they are all around me, so why don't they come out and dance? The moon is red and full." Alma becomes lyrical. She rests her head on the uniformed shoulder and smiles. "No one should sleep on such a night," she says and yawns.

Milda runs down the stairs—an angel in flight—and covers Alma with a blanket. She saves her from *Frau* Lutz and the chief-of-police, whose one arm is wrapped tightly around her, his fingers spread out and sunk in her breast. Milda is afraid of the mob that laughs, shouts, stretches this way and that like witches and goblins at a burning. To her horror, one shadow separates and comes forward. It turns into Gert, and Milda tries to shrink out of his sight. She is mindful of her ugly nightgown, furious that he had dared to break into their closed garden. *Why is he out anyway? . . . Hadn't he said good night at the gate hours ago?* Tears of fury and shame flood her eyes, but she has no time to self-indulge. She must pull Alma up the stairs. Her aunt, a lost Margareta, a faded ballerina, the best actress is heavy and foul. She throws out shrapnel screams, sour curses and laughs. From the top of the stairs she shouts down, "This is a night you, Nazis, will never forget!"

Milda shoves her inside their room and shuts the door. She doesn't scold her but eases her into bed and cools her burning face with wet sponges and rags. She cradles and kisses her, rocks her and lays her in bed and lies down beside her. She lies awake, making sure that Alma falls asleep. She weeps. *Oh, the shame, the shame!* Gert saw her. He saw the night side of Alma, the foreigner. She hates Alma so much that she would like to tie the red thread around her neck and pull hard at both ends. *How could she so carelessly dash my heart against all the gate posts in town, not caring, not caring at all what my classmates might think, what the Nierts might whisper among themselves, even the twins and dear, sweet Gisela.*

But the Nierts' house is dark. Decent people, they all sleep. Gisela sleeps. *Or does she? Was she looking out of her night window, seeing the nightmare? And Gert? What will he think of me now? What will he do?*

*

A note from Milda's carelessly kept journal: *On the night when Aunt Alma shamed me, on Walpurgis Night, April 30, 1945, in Berlin, a Russian soldier stuck the red flag on the Brandenburg Gate. Next to this great gate, through which the proudest armies of the world had marched, der Führer, Adolf Hitler, in his bunker, shot Eva Braun and himself.*

Der Führer had spoken his last. But it was a while before the people really heard him. Many didn't believe the news. The people of Oeslau went about their daily ways. It was a beautiful spring Unter den Linden, and there was work to be done. Only Alma had caught the thrill of the moment. 'Ah, he knew how to celebrate Walpurgis Night!—He understood high drama. He loved Wagner!'

That's how the war was lost: with a bang under the ground.

May Day

Alma awoke with a sore throat and in high fever. *Frau* Lutz diagnosed the mad night as a delirium and called a doctor from the next town.

Milda stayed in until noon, when Gisela came to look for her. She carried a picnic basket and sensitively invited her to go for a long walk. "Why not up to the castle?" Milda suggested. The twins jumped around at her side, happy to be out of school. Milda then remembered that it was May Day, and it was a holiday. No school! *Postponed humiliation,* she breathed in relief. At least for the day, she wouldn't have to face Gert, would not have to die in shame. Not yet. And she had a chance to escape from Alma! She decided to forget the nightmare—call it only that.

Among the rocks Milda found bits of lace and a small piece of red twist. She tied it around her neck, but the thread was too short. Instead, she made a tiny bow around her top button. Gisela said it looked nice with her white blouse. Gave it a spark. And *Mildchen* smiled. Nothing in Gisela's eyes showed any knowledge of the witch-night that had just passed. So, for the time being she was safe.

Lazily stretching, the girls lay down on the flat boulder to sun themselves, while the boys scampered around making, what they insisted were, scary noises. After a while, when the sun's rays began to burn, the *May maidens* slid down and picked bunches of flowers. Suddenly Milda stopped picking and stood still, listening. "I must go back to my sick aunt," she said, wrapping the bouquet of wild flowers with the piece of lace.

She opened the attic door with a "Happy May Day!"
Alma opened her eyes.
"You know, my dearest Margareta, people here don't know what to do on May Day either," Milda said brightly, seeing Alma's feverish grin. Alma stammered, saying that she had had nightmares, and then she turned away, inside the wallpaper. Watching the curved back, so calm, so white, Milda re-lived the nightmare, step by step, scene by scene. It all seemed very far away, as if on another planet, in another time. *It didn't happen, it could not have happened. . .* She rose and decided to go wash the lace curtain and repair the window before Alma awoke.

"I dreamed it," she told herself.

In Sickness and. . .

The days grew ever warmer, and the attic room became very hot. Alma's fever broke, but Milda caught her germs and was glad to be sick so she would not have to go to school, nor face the Nierts. The next town doctor instructed her to take half of Alma's medicine and rest, especially the nerves. *Frau* Lutz watched and guarded both. She kept the windows closed and the curtains pulled tightly together. The outside world came to the patients only via the old radio, which Alma had madly held on to in spite of *Frau* Lutz's hard pulls and admonitions. The radio carried constant news of German surrenders—to Denmark, the Netherlands, North, South, East, West. To the refugees whose throats hurt, it seemed that *Deutschland*, only a while ago so very high and mighty—*Over all in the world*—was being strangled, tied with a narrow red ribbon.

Milda tried to keep her neck warm, coughing up the phlegm, but Alma fell into a pained, choked silence. In that stultifying silence dropped a glue-smeared letter from *C.C.C.P.* From Liepāja. Alma rose and tore the envelope open with her teeth.

"He went to Riga. To the big stage. 'Tell her I have no time to write. The director won't let me. She'll know how it is.' Then he laughed and said that the devils do not use ink but the juice of life. He said you would understand, you would know what it is. I don't like riddles, and I don't have time for letters. He also wants you to know that he is glad to be away from Liepāja, where he never stops thinking of you. 'Tell her not to cry,' he said and his face was sad. 'She must study to be a better actress,' he says as if my lady was not the best already, and I say, 'go on, sir, she was the best.' And he says, 'the future stages will be large, much larger—like our new Motherland,' and then he goes, leaving me with my mouth open. I don't see him anymore. He is in Riga, but others go even farther East – to Moscow and still farther. But I stay here. I live with an officer's family and serve them. I also work in the wardrobe at

the theater. It is very dark here at times, but we are very happy since our liberation from the fascists. The future is full of sunshine, and we all wait for you and other wanderers to come home to our dear Motherland. I cannot understand how anyone could live under a capitalist sky. You should come home. Ella."

Alma passed the letter to Milda, who read it. She saw Alma gasp and afterwards clam herself up. She did not cry but for many days remained a forlorn, pale blank. Passively, on sunny days, she let *Frau* Lutz take her down into the garden, as the doctor ordered. There, wrapped in blankets, she lay in *Herr* Lutz's lawn chair and stared at the bees. Milda, feeling almost completely well, stitched her tea cloth, sitting impatiently by her aunt's silent side. She was afraid that Alma would never be well, even when her throat healed. She imagined herself walking on alone, going she knew not where, but she kept her fears to herself and the herbal tea warm. Together they watched the honeybees wade in spring blossoms, rise up and, heavy with pollen, fly home. She envied them: they were free, and they had hives of their own. She stitched bees on her tea-cloth flowers with fine satin threads as she observed Alma's every move. Mostly, her aunt kept her eyes shut tightly as she leaned back and let the sun burn her; only whenever a fly lit on her outstretched legs did she move quickly and precisely, catching and killing the bloodsuckers with hard dashes against the stone patio. These strong, well-aimed attacks somehow did not go with her sickness, and Milda finally, stealthily talked to *Frau* Niert about it.

"*Ach Mildchen*, your *Tante* is unhappy, not really sick," said the kind woman simply. "Sometimes people run away into the land of sickness because they are sad and afraid.

"*Fräulein* Alma is fleeing from life. The doctor said that many people nowadays are suddenly ill. It's the times. It's what war does to people and nations. We already lived through one war. My mother died after my father was killed."

Frau Niert then became very busy, but after trotting in useless circles, she took *Mildchen's* hand and, with eyes full of tears said in a broken voice, "*Herr* Niert is not feeling well either. He hardly speaks to me. Oh, it is not only the men who fall in wars, but the women also. We all fall together. But we must struggle on. We must not let anyone make us sick," she said, wiping her eyes, leaning closer to Milda's puzzled face. "You must not pamper her. Take care of her—yes, but not buckle under her. You have your own work to do and your own life to live. Your teacher told me that you are a brilliant pupil of many talents, the best she has ever had. *Also.* You must go back to school tomorrow. You are well now, I know, and it is duty and work that can make the body strong and, in time, heal also the soul. May God help you, *liebes Kindchen.*"

Milda pulled away gently from the comforting bosom and with a determined step went to face her aunt.

Frau Lutz looked at Milda scornfully when, the next morning, she closed the door with a slight bang. Thrown off her hinges, *Frau* Lutz fussed over Alma that much more, preparing special treats from such stuff as could be scrambled together in order to lure her back to life and work. The furniture needed polishing, the kitchen floor was sticky. But Alma would not lift a hand; she would not even turn her head while the doctor examined her, talking, talking, talking with his plump hand resting on her thigh.

Meanwhile all sorts of rumors spread about the whereabouts of Adolf Hitler. Some said he was whisked abroad; some believed he had escaped from the fires of Berlin; others hoped he was in the Alps pulling new troops together for one final battle with Stalin. Hardly anyone dared to say that he was dead, even though the death announcements were out—all over the air. People talked huddled in small groups, sitting on park benches, walking in gardens and wooded paths. *Herr* Niert said that there was a conspiracy to frighten the German nation. "The Allies want to destroy us, even with arsenic" he said at the dinner table, hiding behind the large white napkin covering his front. "And why?" he asked looking over his glasses. "What have we done?" The twins glanced at one another and slid down into their chairs.

"Boys, please sit up straight," said *Frau* Niert.

The noon hour dragged on unbearably. *Herr* Niert's hand shook, and Milda's stomach hurt as never before; she excused herself as soon as it was politely possible.

In the afternoon it rained, and Alma slept, her head covered with a sheet. In pain, Milda, too, fell asleep while doing her homework. That night they locked the door early. Milda felt the heaviness of the sky pushing down on her, as she had never experienced. Quietly she watched the birds fly past the window in swirling flocks. Her whole being was so terribly sad that the tears would not stop flowing until she fell asleep. Alma tossed about deliriously, kicking off the sheets and comforters, and calling, rising and calling—falling back and crying.

The Egg Hunt

But a new morning came and broke the night. *Frau* Lutz woke Milda up very early, while the dawn was barely tinting the sky a soft pink and before the trees had shaken off the night's rain. The high-pitched voice alarmed the girl's ears, urging her to hurry and go to Sommerfeld because word was out that there were eggs for sale at Fleischman's. "And nothing would be better for the *Fräulein* than good protein," she said and counted her money. "So, please hurry!"

Wordlessly, sleepily, Milda obeyed. Hunger pains cramped her stomach, but there was no time to eat. *Frau* Lutz spoke with greatest intensity, all the while circling around wasp-like. Minutes later Milda was on her way, a basket hooked on her arm. Except for the early birds, the silence of the night was still all around. In half darkness, she saw other female forms moving in the same direction, like phantoms sliding along the paths, their legs lost in the rising fog. By the time Milda reached the shop, around its locked door a group of women already huddled in a tight round hive, their bodies wrapped in shawls, their hands holding empty baskets. She, shyly, self-consciously, joined them and waited. At last, when the sun shone above the rooftops, the door opened. Stirred, the women pushed inside the shop, shouting, shoving each other and saying loud words in their dialects about there being too many foreigners now that the war was ended. And refugees were crossing the border, trying to escape from the east, they lamented. Who could feed them all? Where would they sleep?

Eyeing Milda maliciously, the female barricade blocked her from making even one forward step, as more women forced themselves inside through the narrow door, while others squeezed out cackling, holding their baskets over their heads. As the stampede intensified, Milda was being pushed farther back, away from the door, away from ever reaching the counter of diminishing eggs. Yet she waited.

At last, she watched how the women scattered in every direction, moaning as they vanished into the narrow streets. The door was left wide open and empty. Milda stepped over the threshold. She saw the empty shelves and counters and the shopkeeper's smooth blank face. Embarrassed to look at the poor man's shame, she curtseyed and, turning about, quickly left the pathetic shop. She had seen such sights too many times. She was used to going back to her temporary home empty-handed.

As she hurried back to Oeslau, she noticed that for the late morning hour, the streets were empty. She knew she should not be out either, but where would she hide? And so she walked on. She saw faces peering from behind half-drawn curtains and heard women calling their children to themselves. She walked on, out of the village and into the open road. She had to rush because she didn't want to be late for school. But then, for a moment, she stopped to listen. The whole landscape around her seemed to tremble. Black lights turned on and off inside her head. She thought she heard drumming in the distance and felt strange vibrations. The telephone wires overhead swayed in the wind. Scared, she slipped down into the ditch and crawled on, catlike against its rapidly flowing stream of muddy water. Faintly aware of thirst and hunger pains, she kept going, losing sense of time and distance. The drumming and vibrations drew closer and closer until the earth shook.

She saw an airplane almost raze the treetops, leaving behind a trail of silver strips and exhaust smoke. She saw another plane fly down low and then another and another. One by one, parachutes floated below the airplanes and landed in a bright green field. Then, as if rising out of the earth, she saw a farmer with a pitchfork charge at one of the parachutes, drive his fork into its stem and run off. She watched the huge umbrella fold over the stem—the man—and heard one single gunshot. She slumped deeper into the ditch, crawling on, faster, her feet sinking into the mud, her dress dragging over the wet grass.

When at last she saw red rooftops, she knew she was at the edge of Oeslau and not far from safety. She flattened herself and watched for a chance to slip across the street, which was full of ash-green tanks with white stars. They passed her in a long parade, leaving no gaps through which she could reach the other side. Cautiously she stood up. Everything around her reeled. As in snapshots, she saw black and dark brown men riding atop the tanks, their white smiles glistening in the sun, their arms waving. She rose out of the ditch. She saw children—several of her schoolmates—running beside the tanks and shouting, "*Ami! Ami!*" They caught the candy and oranges the Americans pitched to them, but others yelled for more.

"Hey, *Fräulein!*"

She looked for the voice and, suddenly, out of the sky fell an orange, large and round like the sun. She caught it as it almost knocked her over. And then there were sounds of bugles and drums, and she knew Oeslau was being occupied. She had heard the same tunes long, long ago—in another world, another life.

From her distance, across the full street, out of focus, she saw Alma behind the gate, waving, while *Frau* Lutz watched from around her blooming snowball bush. It appeared to Milda's dazed view that the tanks and men were sliding over the whole opposite side, over the women, over the row of white stucco, red-roofed houses. Those houses had always seemed so safely locked up inside their iron fences and bolted gates, over which children hardly dared to slide their fingers for fear of being scolded. Clean houses they were with shining, sparkling windows. Innocent houses, as in pretty paintings of the Middle Ages. Now she saw them cut, wrecked by the rolling tanks and open jeeps. She blinked hard, trying to erase the sight.

When at last the victory parade was over, she dashed across the street, steadily stretching out her arm, her hand holding the orange. But Alma was already peeling one, letting the juice run down her bare arms.

"Did you get the eggs?" *Frau* Lutz asked in a small, quivering voice.

"No," Milda called back. "There was nothing in the shop for foreigners." And she handed the empty basket to *Frau* Lutz..

"*Ach weh*," the woman groaned. "What can I make for *p* Alma? She must be cured."

"I think she's cured already and will take care of herself from now on," Milda answered. She didn't know why she said it like that and why Alma gave her an angry look and, holding her head, went to lie down in the sun. Milda was too tired and hurt to care. She went straight into the house. Her sides and stomach ached. It hurt that no one bothered to ask her where she had been and what she had seen. No one, not even Gisela, asked her how she felt. Gisela had stood like a stiff doll on the other side of the fence until *Frau* Niert had ushered all her children inside. *A mother hen with her chicks. A nest full of eggs.* But there were no eggs for sale, not for foreigners anyway. No one would have offered

Mildchen a poached egg, nor a glass of apple cider. What had happened to breakfast that morning, she wondered.

"Oh, I'm so tired, so tired of life and armies and occupations!" her soul cried out as she staggered alone up to her attic room, feeling more dizzy and chilled with each step. When she pushed the door open, the room slid out from under her, the bed came forward, and she fell on it. She tore off her messy clothes and threw them as far away from her as the walls allowed. She crawled into a flannel gown and pulled the sheet over her, but still she kept seeing silver streamers and white parachutes raining down from a clear blue sky. One, like a shroud, had wrapped the fallen man—poor victim of another man's crazy fury. She was sweating terribly; her body twitched as from the gun shot.

That shot in the green field marked for her the end of World War II. It had happened so quickly, so simply. All was at last finished, and she could sleep peacefully.

Blood

Milda awoke late in the afternoon. Gisela was standing beside the bed, her warm hand gently stroking her friend's limp, sweating shoulder. Slowly, heavily Milda sat up and pushed off the heavy comforter. The room tilted as a sharp pain stabbed through her. Gisela put a porcelain cup with warm tea in Milda's trembling hand. She drank all of it, and, feeling better, tried to rise, but she leaned back, her eyes fixed on Gisela. A warm liquid seeped out of her, between her legs. As if in shame, her head sunk slowly deeper onto the pillow

"You have started," Gisela said

In wide-eye horror Milda looked at the bloody sheets and her nightgown. "Where is my aunt?" she cried out.

"I don't know." Gisela shrugged her shoulders. "I'll help you," she said, sounding like a nurse. "Wait!"

She left the room and minutes later returned with a washbowl of warm water, soap, and a towel. She closed the door on *Frau* Lutz's alarmed face and then turned full attention on her friend. She washed the blood away, prepared the padding and helped Milda put on clean clothes. As she calmed herself with another cup of tea, Gisela cleaned up the room and gathered the sheets. She packed them into a pillowcase and told Milda to follow. She led her to *Mutti*.

Frau Niert was not surprised. She had expected this, she said, and then explained the reasons and intricacies of the female monthly cycle and proceeded to give instructions on what to do and how to behave. "Don't be afraid of being a woman," she said. "Every month the blood tells us that we are born to create life. Menstruation is not a sickness, only for some a little painful. But you are strong, born to be a mother." She paused, taking her hand. *"Ach, du armes Kindchen,"* she sighed. "Today was a bitter day for all of us. We all are bleeding, and God only knows what will happen tomorrow. All is in His hands."

"Na ja," *Mildchen* agreed wearily and glanced out the window, where apple trees budded against a bright blue sky, and all was quiet, except for the distant heavy rumbling as of thunder.

"The tanks have moved on the meadow across town. Braun's farm is occupied. All his work is trampled into mud," said *Frau* Niert, but then turned her caring eyes again on Milda. "But you must go about normally," she said. "No one needs to know what day of the month it is for you. Gisela knows. She started last fall, and she'll help you get used to your new self. Still, I'm a little surprised you knew nothing about it. Hadn't you seen your aunt? Didn't she tell you anything? Didn't Gisela? Didn't anyone warn you?"

"Nein," Milda answered and looked at Gisela as if she saw her for the first time and glanced all around in confusion. Indeed, the whole world seemed to be bleeding, but Gisela only smiled—a woman's smile.

*

"So, you see," *Frau* Niert put her arm around Milda's slumped shoulders. "Don't slouch. Hold your head up and know that you are a woman—the beautiful crown of God's creation. God made women just the way they are, and He makes all things good."

Later, when Alma saw the stripped bed and Milda sitting in her chair reading, she snapped. "So. Now you know what a curse is put upon us, what punishment it is to be a woman!"

"I am glad you feel well again, Aunty," Milda said, but Alma looked past her.

"I don't know how much you know about women's plight," she said almost apologetically. "But watch out for men, I'm warning you, especially now with the place full of soldiers." Her face held panic. "Stay away from the army camp and never go walking alone." She sat down on the stripped bed and spoke evenly: "Beware of men, I repeat, especially handsome ones. They are the first to deceive you. And I have no time for bastards, so keep your legs crossed and your shoes on!. . . You hear?" She spoke over Milda's head, looking past the chair, out the open window, over the little round table on which lay Ella's letter. "Gone East," it said.

"Riga is East of Liepāja, and the Far East is Russia. Siberia is the crater of hell," Alma had raged after reading the letter, as she paced the room, twisting her tear-soaked handkerchief. "Oh, he could be deported or sent to Moscow for propaganda reasons. He would never go there on his own, never in a million years. He loves freedom too much, loves acting—loves me. I know he'd die for Latvia before he'd choose to leave it. The East is an icy tomb, a sepulcher, a slaughterhouse of our people… It is over for us, all over for me."

Milda pictured the handsome, dashing Viktors Vētra; she recalled the stage and the enticing, sly movements of Mephisopheles. She remembered him in bed with Alma, doing she knew not what, but now she knew what it was. Now, merely thinking about it, she felt that strange excitement, like water crushing over rocks. She understood the heartbreaks on their last ride together and their black-gloved hands waving in the hazy Liepāja harbor.

"My dearest Aunt," she said, "I understand now how painful a woman's life can be. I think I know how a woman's heart beats and aches, but he's not dead. You must not give up hope." Not wanting to be crushed by more pain, she turned to leave the room.

"Don't run off," Alma blocked her way. "Listen to me! Look out that you don't fall—well, like some poor Margareta, like the hundreds of us. You understand? Do you hear me?" She was desperate and frightened, as if trying to find her *Mildiņa,* who was no more.

"Yes," said Milda pushing past her, leaving her behind, not hearing Alma's helpless sigh: "I saved a child, my sister's child, not a woman. — How do I live with a woman who has my blood but is not of my mind and body? Oh, God, if you're up there in those fluffy clouds, tell me how you want me to go on?" She gazed weeping at the silent, distant sky.

Milda knew that the old tie was broken between them. Her aunt would not call her *Mildiņa* anymore, nor would she lead her by the hand, but she would always watch her and hold her as on a leash. Milda dreaded that and knew that they would have to secure other, new ties that lay somewhere in confusing tangles. Hearing Alma cry behind the closing door, Milda re-entered the room. When she saw Alma lie on the bed, her face soaked in tears, she stroked her head, saying, "Please forgive me. I will be good, I promise. But now I really have to go and learn how to wash blood out of the sheets." Once outside she paused. The sky was red, full of rippling clouds. All around, the gardens seemed enchanted, so beautiful. She stepped off the path, hoping no one, not even Gisela, would see her. She wanted to talk to her own Mother, send her love to her over the bleeding earth and sky, on the brilliant light waves of the oncoming night. With her back turned to the Lutz house, Milda strolled about, touching, stroking the swelling buds and opening petals. She breathed deeply the potpourri of fragrance, hovering over and inside the intense brilliance of opening buds. At the end of the path, she remembered a sad folksong about an orphan who cried for her dead mother, who lay buried under a blooming apple tree: *white blossoms fall from the apple tree/sad tears fall from my eyes*. . . . She slipped beneath the branches and, hugging its rough trunk, wept like many other orphans the world over.

Purified, she looked up through the dome of pale pink blossoms at the splendid sky. She let the wind dry her face, as from deep inside her rose inexpressible relief and gratitude, she did not know for whom or for what. Perhaps her mother's and father's spirits hovered over, protecting and blessing. She whispered, "Thank you" and slipped out from under the tree.

The menstrual blood oozed peacefully. The cramps had stopped. The war was over, and she and Alma were alive and free. *That should be enough reason for me to be glad.* She wondered why she and Alma had escaped, when so many perished or, like Zelda, were left behind like in a prison. What was her destiny? Her mind could not comprehend the reasons and the turns of her fate but believed that there must be a reason for why Zelda was left behind, when she was here, in this strange and beautiful world.

She stumbled as she wove her way out of the garden, which was turning dark. She heard Gisela calling and hurried to meet her. *Wonderful Gisela, coming to rescue me, coming to help me!* Together they would rinse and wring out the sheets. And then she would go back to Alma. In the morning a new drama would begin.

Capitulation

Quickly and efficiently the American troops set up camp on the outskirts of Oeslau—on farmer Braun's land—and started leveling things. They cut down trees even while in bloom and pushed into the hills with their tanks and other machines no one had seen before and could not name them. Sprouting fields were buried under asphalt, and strange items littered the sidewalks. Children picked up chewing gum the soldiers spat out and stuck in their mouths and said *okei, okei!* Youths collected cigarette butts, broke them up, rolled the tobacco in whatever paper was on hand, and either smoked or sold them in dark alleys and behind flowering bushes. The young people picked up a slouching walk, with hands in their pockets, and dared to put their feet on tables. They aped the *Amis* in the most unpredictable ways, upsetting the mothers:

"What is to be done? Oh, in heaven's name, what can we do?" The women huddled together and discussed capitulation and occupation, while jeeps and trucks sped through the streets and up into the wooded silent and sacred areas, right over the grass, flowers, and vines. Gasoline fumes polluted the air, and living quarters were re-arranged. The people whose ancestors had nestled at the edge of the *Thüringen Wald* and tended the fields since forever felt as though they lived in a foreign land. Overnight, it seemed, they had become refugees in their own towns and villages.

The officers, the light-skinned Negroes, took over the finer homes. On *Hauptstrasse*, one by one, the houses fell to the conquerors. Their owners were squeezed into their own back rooms and became janitors and cleaning women of their houses, their homes. Some women, afraid of being molested or losing their houses altogether, tried to escape. They huddled with their bundles in the marketplace and around the small train station, in shame, waiting for the trains that would take them away. Other women cried and wrung their hands, but the men, such as were around, went down in their cider cellars for help. Often, in the evenings, they left their invaded homes and miserable women and went to sit in the *Beerstube* until a Military Policeman (men with MP bands around their arms) made the bartenders close up for early curfew. Then the darker troops would take over. Jazz and swing, in wild rhythms and beats, became part of the night sounds, lasting until early morning. Throughout the nights black and brown men danced with white, willing girls, trading lipstick-tainted kisses for candy, coffee, cigarettes, oranges—even for cans of green beans.

Meanwhile, almost daily, the missing wounded and defeated Germans returned and tried to find places where they might fit, where they could set down their crutches and hang their limbs. The dreaded black-edged messages also came. *Frau* Lutz received one in the middle of May. She let out a scream and fainted, but she had little time to mourn her husband because she was ordered to vacate the ground floor immediately. Alma also received another short note from Ella, telling her that "Meph" had a job on the Riga stage and didn't want to be bothered. "Perhaps later," he had relayed to Ella, whose message was clear: "*I do not have time to write letters. You wanted to leave, you betrayed the Motherland, you are gone. Why do you look back like Lot's wife?*"

Alma showed the dirty graph paper with its cruel words and innuendos to Milda. She read it, her hand over her mouth, and slowly, wordlessly, returned it to Alma, who tore it up in tiny bits and sunk it into the slop bucket. That night she drank herself into a stupor and vomited until, Milda feared, she would turn herself inside out. After that she changed. She threw away *Faust* and turned to surrealism. She changed characters and began another act.

Milda saw that act one afternoon in lilac time. A bouquet with fragrant, purple clusters in hand, she came suddenly upon Alma and saw her leaning on *Frau* Lutz's grand piano, tinkering with the keys and singing like Marlene Dietrich. It was not long before some officers arrived, paused, and said, "Hey!" They clapped their hands, and Alma smiled, her lips red like ripe cherries. A honey-colored officer came forward and offered her a cigarette and smiling she took it and put it between her bright red lips. Another officer closed the door. Milda went up to her room, past *Frau* Lutz's door, fell on her bed and stared at the ceiling.

What happened in the house throughout that spring and summer is best left alone. Milda saw the awesome shifting of relationships all around. The army turned the house into their headquarters; they ran the place, not only invading the ground floor but also messing up the order of time. The days ran into nights and nights into days. Meal times couldn't be set any more by the siren of the doll factory, nor by the church clock; confused, bereaved *Frau* Lutz trotted in and out, up and down, as if she were perpetually banging her head and losing consciousness. But the dizzier she appeared, the more she lost control and, before she knew what was happening, Alma had turned into the mistress of the house. She became the one to give orders. Quickly she was learning English—southern-American that is—and quit scrubbing and dusting. Instead, she hosted parties, allowing many men to crowd the parquet floors and slouch on the furniture, injuring it with cigarette burns. She installed herself in the upstairs master bedroom, which had been closed up since Dr. Lutz joined the army. Outraged, in their separate rooms, *Frau* Lutz and Milda crouched wide-awake and anxious. Throughout the evenings and late into the nights they heard the clanging of glasses and gasped from cigarette smoke until the break of dawn. When they heard the last banging of the outside door, holding their aching heads, both slid into their beds to catch a bit of sleep. Milda was ashamed and helpless and avoided her aunt and all those men who walked through the once-proud portals. Whenever she slipped, quiet as a mouse, in and out the back door, she heard *Frau* Lutz's moaning, *"Ach, mein Gott, mein lieber Gott…"*

All that Jazz

A day came when Milda could not hold out any longer. It was a hot and sticky day, following another swinging, jazzing party. Her head ached unbearably, and she could not concentrate on her studies for final examinations. Cautiously and bravely, she tiptoed down the stairs to the master bedroom, now Alma's boudoir. She was afraid to approach Alma, for they had not spoken for days, even weeks, and did not see one another at night. Noiselessly she pressed down the shiny brass handle and opened the door a tiny crack. Alma, clad in a pink satin robe Milda had never seen, sat brushing her hair. She hummed some *Schlager* and smoked. A half full glass of amber liquid glowed on the edge of the dresser. Milda opened the door wider. For some seconds she watched her aunt smear creams on her face and transform her eyes, lips, and cheeks as though she were making herself up for a premier circus performance. She saw Alma stretch, pose, push her chest out, her hips sideways, slide her hands, fingers extended, down her sides and her legs, and then laugh enticingly, but not from the heart, Milda noted. Only her clown face laughed. Suddenly Alma turned and jumped up. A glass crashed next to Milda's head. A sticky liquid splashed all over her. Like a wounded tigress, Alma charged, "So you're spying on me, you sly little fox! You and Lutz… Ganged up on me—always watching, nosing about, getting in my way!"

"You are bad, Aunt Alma," Milda said and opened the door all the way. She entered the messy room and closed the door. Behind her she heard *Frau* Lutz's moans and sighs, but Alma balanced herself awkwardly in the middle of the room and then slowly backed off.

"Bad, eh?" she spoke, throwing her head back and laughing synthetically.

Milda saw the gray of her molars and her long red fingernails. "Evil has made you ugly," Milda whispered and leaned against the wall, trusting it to hold her up.

"Bad!... Ugly..." Alma spewed. "So, my little angel, you really think I'm bad." She drew hard on her cigarette and let the fumes out slowly in blue, hazy rings. The silence between them was cleaved as with a sharp blade. Milda picked up the broken glass and wiped her face with shaking hands.

"Tell me, sweet maiden," Alma provoked, moving now toward her niece. "Was I bad when I saved you from communists? Was I bad when I let you eat the only stale pieces of bread I could find?" She stopped and looked at Milda with half-shut eyes, her mouth blowing smoke straight at her, fumigating her, measuring her words for poison. But Milda said nothing; she only stared at her aunt with her great, big nervously blinking eyes. She notices that they had become the same size. Their eyes spanned the same parallels.

"You gape at me like I'm crazy. Bad. Or ugly, eh?"

Alma staggered forward and took Milda's chin in her hand. "You're good, always good. A flower in a tight bud," she spoke into the frightened face. "A virgin princess, but so ready, so ready to pop open that you don't even know it. You don't see, my sweet little, tight rosebud, all the lusting princess tangled among the thorns, do you? Well, they hang about right at the gate and the fine white marble posts."

Alma pulled her hand away, as if the thorns were tearing it. "I was good too, like you," she said. "And I wanted to be perfect, but life did not let me." Her eyes were a dead sea. "Fate rules cruelly. The gods and goddesses don't like me either, my dear, so I'm forced to side with the devils and men of darker hues—also rejects." She faced the mirror and talked at their reflections.

"Bad... tell me, who brought you here and who feeds you now so you can live innocently and stand in judgment of me?"

Milda's reflection paled. Alma sucked again on the butt of her cigarette. "You are mum... Well, let me remind you, in case you don't remember anything, that it was not my fault that the communists cut my life in half and made me drag my broken pieces around the world. It was bearable as long as I could feel the winds of our sea, as long as I could feel him." With her mean, sharp forefinger, she pressed out the minute cigarette butt.

"But he is gone. Out of my reach forever. Changed. They break and mold men, step on them like turds. So what should I do? What should I save myself for? Here today and gone tomorrow, you know, life is a stage, said smart William Shakespeare."

She filled another glass and raised it high. "But, while the heart beats and the stomach growls, we all must eat, isn't that so?" She sipped slowly, then gulped. "Oh, he'll play his devil's role all right—with another, a Soviet Margareta—ugh—for—yes. There always will be dear innocents and devils and men. Yes, he'll fill his days and nights splendidly," she said, shutting her eyes, squeezing her tears through tight lashes. "The way I fill mine. We are making our own separate little hells, I'm sure of that!" She lit another cigarette. "Stalin's boys need all the devils they can find, and they have found my Viktors, my own personal Mephistopheles," she cried. "You know, actually, he was a little weak, a little evil, so he'll be OK. All men are, so why should he be any different? I know they will make him sign things in blood—in our poor Latvian blood, in women's and children's blood... My sisters Katerina's and Matilde's, your Zelda's."

"Don't!" Milda's reflection cried. "Please stop!"

"All right, all right, just don't you ever call me bad again or I'll show you what bad really is! Understood?"

"Yes."

"Now," Alma leaned back, her elbows resting on the cluttered dresser, a burning cigarette hanging between her red-nailed fingers. "Do you really want to know what I'm doing, how I'm earning an honest living?" She sounded sober, suddenly alert and calculating. "I want you to know so you don't need to sneak around and spy. I won't cover up and lie, or make you think I'm lying." She inhaled slowly, smiling like a clown. "Bad…evil," she exhaled.

"I know what you do."

"Oh, no you don't! How could you?" Alma took on again her tragic victim's role. "You haven't even soiled another pair of sheets, or have you? I cannot keep track. I bleed too, you know! —Well," she spoke in a low voice, coughing for punctuation. "I have a job and I work hard… I do the kind of work, my dearest child, that only women can do and have done ever since the Big Man kicked Eve out of her garden—after she had been weeding and trimming, sweating her ass off."

Alma turned so she would face Milda and spread out her sheer stocking-covered legs, letting the robe fall open. Milda saw pink panties with white lace. "You see? Here is my wealth, they pay me for it! Dangerous ammunition, more powerful than the bombs the men of the world—miserable queer scientists—have invented. Women power! Beauty is power, said our old Rainis; he didn't have guts to say sex is power. Aspazija would have gone after him—or the stupid censors who can't read. But that's what he was saying in those dry verses, only no one gets it. Oh, yes, Rainis had felt the power of sex, but couldn't wield it, so he called it pure love. Bah, poets! Old Goethe too, setting the whores up on pedestals, and when they can't stay up there, they call them fallen women in pitiful diminutives—like *Gretchen*, but it all turns on rejection; it's not they, the men or poets themselves that kill women, oh no! It's the rejection that drives us to madness and death."

She took a long drink. "So, what good would it do to waste all this? I saved it for him, but he'll never need it, so what do I care?" She crossed her legs, and Milda saw that they were beautiful. "Nice, eh?" Alma caught her gaze. "I like them in nylons, wouldn't you? And look what else I have!"

She pulled the robe wide open and displayed her breasts cupped in a pink brassiere, separated by a sheer butterfly. Milda felt her own home-made undergarments hang loosely and tightened her arms around herself. "America must be a wonderful place," Alma went on, "where women are beautifully dressed all the time—like actresses in French plays." She looked away dreamily and spoke as she used to in her sleep. "Imagine every woman as pretty as an actress... But I shouldn't want to live there. How would I sand out?" She pulled the robe around her, stood up, and slid across the floor in her stocking feet, reaching for Milda, who stretched out her arms full length in self-protection.

Alma stopped short when the dart of rejection hit her heart. "Afraid, eh?" she laughed. "Afraid I might dirty you, aren't you? … Sure, I see." She stepped back and reached for her cigarette, grabbing it, stabbing it between her lips, then pulling it out, holding it high, blowing smoke all the length and width of the room. "Well, let me assure you, let it be known! I swear to you and to this dumb, gray heaven that I will never again walk with blistered feet, and I will never wear stockings with holes!" She was dressing now in a new pink blouse and wriggling into a bright flowery cotton skirt. "How'd you like this?"

"It's pretty."

Milda did not know how to leave the room and stood, seeing herself in the elegant mirror, clumsy and unnecessary.

"Wait," Alma said, "I teach them world history. I teach them about us and what it was like only a few months ago, when they were in the air throwing bombs down on us. I tell them about what they have destroyed—the castles, the cities, the Western civilization. 'What cilzation,' they ask, and I tell them. I've even tried to explain Faust to them. 'He is the personification of modern man,' I say, but they only laugh and cannot pronounce Margareta. *Maagrt*, they say," Alma mocked. "I tell them what communism is, and they don't believe me. They have no idea. They tell me that Stalin is very popular in America; they call him Joe... Joe!" She lit another cigarette.

Milda was afraid of the red burning tip and wanted to yank it out of Alma's mouth, but she only blinked and bit her lips. Alma was clearly enjoying her performance. "I tell them a lot. I give them background, try to explain Marx, Engels, Lenin, but they only look down on me with their white eyes. Then I try to show them the difference between Hitler and Stalin. Hitler, I say, at lest was civilized, efficient, liked Wagner, but Stalin—a madman, a butcher, a sadistic boor, but they don't want to hear anything; they don't believe me, and I say, all right, don't believe me, but history will prove me right, you'll see, I say, that is, if you ever bother about history at all."

"I have to go."

"Wait! They teach me also. Do you know that in America I could never talk, eat, or sit on the same streetcar with Negroes like I can here if I want to? They tell me, 'In America, honey, the races are segrated. The Negroes and whites are separated.' That's too bad, I say, but I don't believe it's all bad. I think there should be lines and borders instead of mixes of people, like soup, but I tell them it's not right, not when you have to go to war and then have no rights in the country you live in. And then they say, 'That's right,' and they adore me. They call me their queen. Desdemona said a smarter one. It's a fine role I play now. I'm not always bad, not really, you must believe me."

The doors downstairs banged. *Frau* Lutz's steps started doing her rounds in the kitchen. Alma put out her cigarette and, perfectly sober, took up a pad of paper and a pen that wrote without having to be dipped in ink. She was making some list, writing names and numbers. "I almost forgot my assignment," she said. "I translate for them. Letters and things. Love letters, you would be surprised how many. I never knew there were so many hot women in these hills and valleys. Woe onto you, Sodom and Gomorrah!"

In her high heels, Alma towered. "Stop staring! For a good actress all life is a stage, and all action becomes material for drama. I'm learning English and so should you. It's the language of the future, and you might go to America, who knows?" Alma stepped forward, ready to go to work. Momentarily unguarded, her voice turned kind. She looked at her stunned niece with pity and said, "Don't worry, little one. It won't go on forever. We'll move on as soon as we know which way to go." She swept out of the room but turned back and said, "Clean up this mess you brought on, will you!"

Milda, left behind, blinked at her crazed image as her hands turned into tight fists. Her knees would not stoop to clean.

Milda Makes a Move

Unable to bear the guilt and shame alone, she told *Frau* Niert in toned-down excerpts, about the hell she was forced to live in. "Come live with us," urged *Mutti*. "So far our house is not occupied, but how long we can be safe—who knows?"

Throughout the town housing became tight, and people were moved about quickly, without sympathy or compensation. Besides the American soldiers and officers, others invaded not only Oeslau but the whole region. Refugees from the East came in caravans, settling wherever they found space to build a fire or a river to bathe and wash their clothes and lay them out in the sun to dry. Milda remembered how, only a short time ago, she and Alma had arrived and knocked on a strange iron gate. Now she was on the inside, looking out, fearing a stranger's knock and plea.

Late one evening she saw a woman pulling a miniature wagon stop to wipe her sweat. Tucked inside the cart were two little girls eager to jump out and run. The woman looked sadly through the iron bars of the fence. Milda ran into Niert's house and came out with Gisela. The girls had assembled a basket of food and were taking it to the refugees. The woman thanked tearfully, squeezing her hands before they took the basket. When she coaxed her little girls to say thank you, Milda heard Latvian words. Exclamations of surprise and joy ensued. The gates opened, and Mother Courage and her children came through and sat down at the garden table. The woman had walked, pulling the *Wagele* for 500 kilometers, resting as she traveled, waiting out the sicknesses of her four and five year-old girls, wherever she found kindness. She came from Saxony, barely having escaped the Dresden bombing. "Like my aunt and I," said Milda. "We also escaped. We watched that massive bombing from a dark train," she said. "So many died. When we pulled out of Dresden, the morning after the bombing, I saw doomsday."

The woman narrated slowly, dramatically, that she passed people who overnight had been turned into ash statues and seemed to watch her, with her bundles and children huddled in opposite ends of the wagon walk away. "We had passed the night in a cellar of a building that was miraculously saved. In the courtyard, covered with ashes, I saw this "chariot" as if put there by some angel of the dreadful night. I was so blessed, I cried from joy. Then I could save my babies and walk out of hell, over and past countless dead bodies, pulling this wagon." She paused. "My husband was arrested in Riga even before June 14, 1941. He disappeared. No one told me what happened. I was pregnant then. So, when the Russians came back last year, I took my girls and we left by ship from Liepāja. Anything, but not to be under communists!"

"I know," Milda said. After they compared their escapes, it turned out that they all had been on the same ship and the same train.

Frau Niert kept running back and forth, bringing more food and drink, and then offered the Mother and children her guest bedroom. The kindness was accepted. "Again God's angels are watching over us," the woman said, wiping her eyes.

That night Milda stayed with the woman and her cute, golden-haired girls. She and Gisela bathed them and tucked them into a clean bed and, softly singing, watched them fall asleep. Then Gisela left Milda and the guest alone, "so you can talk in your own language." And talk they did. They talked and talked until midnight. In the morning "Mother Courage" was up early, ready to go. Having breakfasted, she tucked her girls inside the wagon and harnessed herself. Clean and refreshed, thanking *Frau* Niert she went out the gate. Milda accompanied them to the edge of town and then said her sad farewell. She stood watching the brave woman pull her wagon with her precious cargo down the white, sun-bleached cart road, through blooming meadows beneath a cloudless sky until they vanished from sight. She felt that a part of her soul had walked out of her, for in that little wagon she saw her country moving, escaping from hell's flaming inferno. (Many years later Milda met the woman and her grown daughters at a song and dance festival in San Francisco.)

More refugees passed through Oeslau—from Sudetenland, Slovakia, Moldavia, Poland. Everyone moved West, only stopping to rest and tell about the near escapes from the brutalities of war and attendant communist threat. They were anxious to get on, saying how one never knew how far the Red Bear will stalk. But some stayed. They were too tired, too sad to walk on. The local people had to make room for them, and by the end of spring, the attics and cellars were packed, the empty shops emptier than ever. The Nierts were only too glad to take Milda in so their house would be full according to the newly issued stipulations. Alma didn't seem to care about her niece as long as she continued to do her share of cleaning. She was very busy. In the daytime she presided over a desk, but in the nights—well, the nights remained dark and mysterious.

Meanwhile, trouble visited the Nierts also. Right after the occupation, a scandal broke out concerning *Herr* Niert, but, fortunately for him, so many uprooting, scandalous things were happening that his shame received less notice than if a rat had run across *Hauptstrasse*. It was disclosed that his factory had been manufacturing arms, not dolls. The dolls were only made in one small part of the plant as a camouflage. The dolls were set in shop windows to guard the town, make it look quaint and frilly.

Milda heard about these revelations, possible penalties and trials, but no dates were fixed, nothing clearly stated. There were no newspapers that printed actual local news, and so no real interest was fired up. In those days people protected one another. *Do onto others as you would have them do onto you* or else they would get you. There were henchmen who knew how to get people and how to turn things inside out, but there were people who helped and kept quiet or spoke up, as was necessary. So it had been, and so it was then. Besides, *Herr* Niert had provided employment, and the people were used to being afraid of him. Also, they loved *Frau* Niert and her children and looked at them sympathetically, squeezing the good woman's hand comfortingly, bringing her small presents, for children had to be protected. And the youth was not to be corrupted; it was to be admonished, tended, guarded, especially now when all group activities, such as *Hitler Jugend* and other clubs that smacked of nationalism and eliminated fascism were banned.

For the time being, *Herr* Niert, wearing faded out dress shirts and trousers of old suits, potted around the garden from morning until evening, looking more and more like a trapped rabbit. He seemed to be hiding among the shrubs and young vegetables, mumbling to himself, always nervously popping up here and there. Gisela and the twins treated him politely whenever they came up against him, but they did not stay to chat, nor listen to his vague orders. At dinner, he didn't bother to put his white napkin over his shirt, but *Frau* Niert went about cheerfully.

She was more busy than ever and more nervous than ever, but the bows of her apron strings were always carefully tied. She cooked and baked her husband's favorite things, always aiming to please him, who hardly spoke to her. She did not fault him because he hardly reacted to anything around him. Only whenever the factory siren blew, he jerked himself straight up out of the shrubs and stood motionless until it stopped.

Summer 1945

In the summer, of course, school was in recess. Milda had received excellent marks, and when things were difficult and Alma unjust, she remembered her achievements and learned to depend on her pride for her inner peace and self esteem. Oh, how she would have liked to show her report card to her parents and her sister, even to all the uncles, aunts, and cousins, who would have celebrated the ending of a good school year with mountains of food and dancing in a decorated hall, as was done all over Latvia! But this was only a foolish fantasy. She was not in Latvia. Riga was fallen—fallen out of her life, and a hard line was drawn across it. She recognized the divide between home and exile that soon would be called the Iron Curtain. It was being forged at that very time.

The refugees, who passed through Oeslau, kept bringing constant news of terror. Everyone, they said, who had anything to do with the West would be charged with treason. "Enemies of the people," they said. Treason was a catchall. Everything was treasonous, even one's birth! A postcard with a foreign stamp could be enough evidence for attempts to overthrow the Soviet government; therefore, no one wrote to ones relatives and lost loves. Alma had stopped writing long ago. People fled, escaped, hung themselves every day, the refugees said, and their frightened faces and movements bore witness to the terrible truth. Such was the world becoming. . . .

Yet, people get used to everything. In Oeslau, as the warm, beautiful spring and summer days passed, they got used to the Americans also. The Germans learned the occupiers' rank by the shades of their skin. They learned their names: Charlie, Tom, Bill, Willie, Jim... Short, clipped names they were behind very broad, white smiles. The smiles invited girls and children to come closer. Curious, the children flocked around the army men, keeping a safe distance. Wilfred asked Alfred how come the black men had white palms, and Alfred answered that it was because of baseball. "The color rubs off, you stupid!" said Alfred and dared his brother to shake hands with Charlie next time he came to see *Fräulein* Alma. Wilfred accepted the challenge and, when the time of testing came, watched wide-eyed how his hand disappeared inside the huge black one. When he pulled it away, he quickly wiped it on his *Lederhosen,* but Charlie laughed and laughed and then picked him up and threw him in the air. When the black man set the screeching child down, he gave Wilfred and all the other children who had gathered around sticks of chewing gum and promised to teach them how to play baseball. The news of this spread with the speed of running feet, and before long all the kids in town pestered the soldiers, shaking hands with them, sitting on their laps, climbing up their legs. Regularly at sundown, lots of people gathered at the edge of a field to watch the Americans play this mysterious game called baseball. It made no sense to the adults, but it wasn't long before the bigger boys played with the soldiers, standing far out in the field, wearing huge leather gloves and reaching up for the little hard ball the size of an orange. Some of the German youths, chewing gum and walking with a new twist of muscle and sinew, said they were training to go to America and challenged others to follow them.

To the dismay of their parents, in no time the boys—big and small— formed their own baseball teams and churned up the soccer field. The parents and teachers had no way of stopping anything anymore. Where was the world going, they asked each other, over their fences.

One cloudy curfew evening, someone knocked on the Niert window, making everyone jump from fright and then sit still, as during bombings. After a while—again came the knocking and the banging. *Frau* Niert peered out through he curtains, pressing her hands together, her neck stretching into the darkness. She screamed and jumped back. Out of the jasmine bush rose two black, curly heads with white smiles that turned into gleeful, familiar laughs. "Charlie!" shouted Alfred. "Jimmy!" called Wilfred, leaning out the window.

"Here's something for being good baseball fans," Charlie said and with Jim's help pushed a big box through the window. It was a case of condensed milk. "Carnation," each can said, and there were a dozen. *Frau* Niert kept twisting her hands and saying, "Sank you, sank you, werry muuch."

"Oh, it's nothing," said Charlie, and another crate slipped through the open window. It was full of oranges, chocolate, coffee, powdered eggs.

"It isn't even Christmas," Gisela said, taking things out of the boxes.

"We can live on this until Christmas," *Frau* Niert said and stared at the things that had suddenly appeared on her kitchen table. "Sank you, sank you, Kinder, *sagt* sank you."

"Thank you!" they said and giggled.

"That's OK," the men said and slipped back into the night and vanished. Later *Herr* Niert looked at the goods suspiciously and adjusted his spectacles.

*

Gisela, Milda, and most of their classmates signed up for swimming lessons at the pool in Sonnenfeld. Everyone seemed to be there, and all the boys flirted with all the girls. Gert was an instructor. Milda watched him in awe, as he demonstrated the movements and strokes at the edge of the pool and in the water. She had no idea that he was such a fine swimmer and diver and an excellent teacher. She tried to follow his instructions with a cool head and did not mind to keep her eyes on his wonderful body, which had turned a light bronze—like Charlie's. *I'm in love. . .*

That possibility hit her like a bolt of lightning. She felt that all the girls watched her, especially when he held her knees from buckling when she was learning how to dive. After the lessons Gisela stuck to her closer than her own shadow— and would not let her out of sight for the rest of the day. *Why don't you find a love of your own?* Milda wanted to ask, but she dared not. Something in Gisela's green look scowled at her, signaling that she was a foreigner and should keep her hands off other people's property. But the boys hung around her, lying on her side of the blanket, boring her with their jokes and awkward seductions. Only Gert stayed at a distance, upright and professional, and she saw only his suntanned body and longed for his kisses.

At night, Milda lying in her bed next to Gisela, heard her softly crying, and there were whole days when Gisela never smiled. *Is she jealous? Does she love him also?*

Love—the lustful, ignoble kind—was out in the open everywhere. It was in the streets, the air, the wild areas. Not only Alma walked about shamelessly, her hand lost in an officer's large palm, but other young ladies also strolled with the soldiers and rode in their open jeeps, eating oranges and candy, drinking Coca-Cola and smoking cigarettes. It didn't matter what was whispered across the fences or that, from behind the shrubs, *Herr* Niert saw everything. The colored men ruled the town, and things were happening. The shops gradually filled with all kinds of goods, and, in time, the older women, too, stopped frowning. By the middle of summer, the factory opened again and the siren blew clearer than before. One day *Herr* Niert shaved off his mustache and announced that he is being called back to work.

Reconstruction.

And so, to the great joy and relief of *Frau* Niert, again precisely at noon her *Mann* sat at the head of the table, his huge white napkin over him, protecting his new tie. As time went on, he became friendlier and richer, and no one bothered about what was being manufactured as long as shipments went out and orders came in. *Frau* Niert cut her hair and became much younger. *Herr* Niert disapproved and blamed Alma, but nothing could be done. He saw the soldiers wave at the pretty redhead and was angry, but he could do nothing. He said nothing when Charlie brought her a box of lipstick, powder, rouge, nylons, toothpaste and brushes for all, and more chocolate and oranges. The twins shied away from their Mother, who took on a worldly look and a freer stride. Gisela seemed confused.

The café on the corner opened, and people sat under a striped awning and ate ice cream. It was all so delicious! The women started buying bread and vegetables. They carried money in their purses and, laughing nervously, guiltily, spent it on small, unnecessary luxuries.

Then a day came, when Alma called Milda and told her that the lists of those killed in Berlin and the East were in. "Why don't you run to Cobourg and see. I cannot go with you, you know," Alma said with a voice from the past. Milda's heart banged against her ribs. She felt her blood rise in warning. "Yes, Aunty, I'll go right away."

They glanced at each other and became one, as if nothing ugly and estranging had come between them. Milda left Alma gazing in the distance, shading her eyes from the sword-like rays of the bright morning sun.

*

Milda slipped out the back gate and took the path that cut through the fields. At first she went half crouching, not wanting anyone, especially Gisela, to see her and follow, but once a safe distance away, she walked straight. The meadows, full of blooming flowers, reached up to her waist. It was beautiful, so still and quiet. She enjoyed the peace and quiet, as always when she was alone in the fields and woodlands. She jogged, skipping freely, letting the wind blow her hair and her skirt. She had to hurry; she had to know!

But suddenly she stopped, almost falling forward, trying not to run into a ragged man in a wheelchair. She had not seen him inside the grasses, but he must have expected her because no sooner had they met, when he, too, stopped, blocking her way. He stretched his crutch across the path and shouted, "What right do you have to run?" He looked like death, but she leaped and jumped over the crutch and raced on. She heard the man shout ugly words after her, but she didn't look back. She trembled, imagining that he would grow terrible bat wings where his legs had been and fly after her, suck her up like she had seen in a film an octopus suck up a crab. When she stopped running and, turning around, saw no invalid form marring the landscape, she slowed down. Shaken to marrow, she sat down in the grass resting and thinking. She thought about the invalid and wondered if a man so wounded would not be better off dead. Then people would put flowers on his grave—or on the grave to the unknown soldier. His mother would remember him as he was when he ran toward her for the first time. And his girl friend, if he had one, would weep clutching his photograph to her heart. But now—oh, now! —What horror, what a fright! An apparition, a constant remainder... an eternal, unanswered question mark. . . .

Milda finds Juris

Cobourg, like most cities, had been terribly bombarded. Milda had to wade through paths of rubble before she found the town's square and the post with the list glued on it. It was an extra long and wide list, wrapping itself around the post, where women compressed in a tight circle slowly rotated. When Milda stood on the inside, she sought only Latvian names, all in alphabetical order. Many names were foreign, far away from Germany, far from their homes where mothers and widows waited. Trying to read the names and guess their countries, Milda slid her finger down, through the columns until and she found it: **Juris Kalnins, 17, Lette, 15. Div.**

Her body stiffened. *Oh, dear God. . .* She closed her eyes. She was back on the farm, watching Aunt Matilde run across the yard, pleading, crying and Uncle Imants picking up his ax. The ancient oak tree splits and Juris carriers her through the storm, carries her forever like that, even as the world ends. . . . Her hands are tight fists and beat against the ugly post, standing in the middle of a broken city. The sun burns on her back, but she keeps hitting the post, fighting the war until someone pulls her away. Other waiting, broken women yell, shout, cry German words, pushing against her, "You think you're the only one! You should be ashamed of yourself! Damned foreigners! *Ach, die Polen!* Go home, go back!"

In a daze she stumbles out of the ruins, out of town. She finds the path that had led her to the post of death. She backs away from it and heads towards the fields, where all is a blur. The poppies are splattered blood. She does not touch them. They are poison, opium. She is hot and sticky and dying of thirst, but here are no springs in the fields; they flow out of the woods, from on high, down into the ditches and rivers, and the rivers that meet other rivers and flow on to the sea—eternal and vast. She goes looking for a spring and takes the path that leads away from the Oeslau, makes a loop around the far end of town, the end where Gert lives, and then she climbs up the hill into the woods. She will go to where the spring starts, where life begins. She is afraid of death. The post has a long shadow that stretches over her body and soul. She hopes and does not hope that she will run into Gert; then she will know that she is alive, but he mustn't think that she has come looking for him. Nice girls don't look for nice boys.

She walks faster. It is late afternoon, and the straight path on which she met the invalid is crowding. The homebound people are shadows, longer than trees. She must get away from those shadows before they cover her. She walks faster, her hands pulling at the wild flowers. She picks flowers out of the sharp grass that cuts her hands. She gives the beautiful blue, white, red, pink flowers to Juris, and he tickles her face with a stalk of timothy. Laughing he falls into the hay on his father's wagon and pulls her down, tickling her gently. She giggles and tells him to stop. *First kiss me!* —*No!* He tickles harder, and she puckers up her lips. He gives her a noisy kiss and lets go. When the wagon stops, they slide off. He grabs her hand, and they run down the ravine to the river. She sees him dive into the green water. He disappears. . .

What did you remember, dearest cousin, when the bullets hit? How did you die? Did your head slump down slowly, my love, or did it hit a stone wall in Berlin? Did it hurt, my Jurīt, tell me, did it hurt?

She sees a small dell and weaves through the grass toward it. She wants to be all alone. She sits down and plays with the sand, making a mound, and then she makes a tiny wreath of white clover. She writes his name with a stick and makes a cross and puts the wreath on top of it. Such a tiny grave for so big a man! A field mouse would need a bigger grave for a proper burial. But his is very improper. She is kneeling, and then she tries to pray, to bless the spot. She talks to God as if He were sitting beside her in this sacred dell. She prays like Uncle Imants, in familiar tones, leaving all the horrors to Him because he could not understand His holy will, nor why things were this way or that. Her lips form a silent Amen, and then she rises. She takes the path up into the woods. So what if Gisela and *Frau* Niert worry? Let them, let them all worry! They are only temporary, not of her blood, not of Juris's either. Oh, they sympathize but do not, cannot understand. She doesn't care about anyone or anything. She needs to be alone in the woods. She loves the woods; the pines are like the pines of Kurzeme. They disinfect the air, cleanse the broken spirit.

What happened to Zibenis, his horse, she wonders. Did he die with Juris or did the war drive them apart? The horse had made a man of him. . . her dream man. . .

She climbs a rock and watches the sun go down. She stares into the red disk so hard that when she closes her eyes she sees green and red rings. Inside those rings she sees Juris in a blur, circling through the air, flying into the sun free and happy...

Milda and Gert

Startled, she is thrown back into the real world. Someone was coming toward her. Thinking it could be some wild creature, she sat still, hoping to be invisible. But, moments later, out of the thicket came Gert. Relieved, she slid off the boulder into his outstretched arms.

"*Mildchen,*" he said tenderly. "*Ach, mein Liebchen*! Where have you been all day? What happened to you? I saw you leave this morning and been on the lookout all day because people are in an uproar. I heard on the radio that Russian soldiers and other foreign men are out and about this area. I was so worried that they would pick you up and send you back to your country or—who knows?—put you on a train to Siberia." He held her close, and she rested her head on his shoulder. "Thank God, you are safe and here with me," he whispered, stroking her hair. "I love you so much!"

Slowly, unwillingly, she disengaged herself from his embrace and smiling shyly held him at arm's length. Leaning against the sun-warmed boulder and gazing into the slowly intensifying sunset, she told him about her adventures. She told him about her parents, her sister, aunt and uncle and their broken up lives. She told him about Juris, around whose wrist she had tied a blue ribbon and was on her way back from burying her memories of him and their love in a tiny grave. But she told it all calmly, tearlessly as if she were re-telling a story she had read or heard long ago, as though it were fiction, for so much could not ever have happened to anyone in such a short time. "It is finished, " she said. "So much has come to the end for me and my aunt this year."

"I am so sad about it," Gert said, gently wiping a tear from her face.

"Let's go on back to town," she said and put her hand in his.

Before they stepped out of the woods, Gert stopped and cautiously took her in his arms. Shyly and softly he asked if he may kiss her. She hesitated and lifted her eyes to meet his and presented her lips to him like a gift. His lips barely touched hers, but he smiled and, pressing her close to him, asked if she would like to be his best friend. He confessed that he had wished to be with her from the first day he saw. She nodded, and giving his had a warm squeeze said, *"Gute Nacht."*

The next day she told Gisela that Alma wanted her back in the house. She needed her, was all her explanation. She gathered her things, tidied the spot she had occupied, and, thanking Gisela for her kindness, left the cozy room. From then on, she and Gert met often. Together, hand in hand, they explored the deeper woods, where, one day, they came upon a small cave. Making sure that no bears or wolves lived there, Gert went in first and, finding no traces of any inhabitants, called her to follow. For a while they sat on a rock, cooling off, and then, awkwardly, not knowing what else to do, Gert started scraping together layers of moss. He carpeted a corner around a flat rock—*like Juris did so long ago, when I was a little shepherdess,* Milda recalled and went out to pick flowers. Back in the cave, she spread out a small table cloth she had embroidered and set their food basket on the rock. Like children playing house, they sat at their "table" and ate, glancing at each other, smiling and happy.

As they became more comfortable with each other, the cave became the destiny of their walks. There, inside the cool den, Gert, cuddled up to her as close as was proper, and she leaned against him, inside his arms. She liked it when his hands touched her skin and lifted her chin for kisses. She had never imagined that kisses would be so sweet, so wonderfully dizzying. But mostly they talked. Milda said endearing words in Latvian, but Gert told her about his visions of a new Germany and his plans for his own future. At times, overcome with suppressed emotions and feeling free to say what was on his mind, he apologized for all the suffering Germany had caused the world, especially people like her. He said he wanted to make up to those who suffered. In the new Germany there would be no destruction of other people. The new Germans, like he and his friends, would show mercy and welcome the wounded, homeless, and lonesome. Milda listened and smiled when he kissed her. He said that he was glad that Hitler was dead and had lost the war. He was ashamed that he had lifted up his arm in the *Sieg Heil* salute and that she too had to honor the man who killed millions. It's like kissing the paw of a lion which had devoured his own young. "But all that is now in the past, and we, who were too young to go to war—we, the men of the future, will build a new and fair Germany, a real democratic nation, like America."

After such and other declarations, he would take Milda in his arms and comfort her with kisses, their warm bodies pressed against each other. When she pulled him closer to her heart, he unbuttoned her blouse and slid his hand down inside her bodice. Caressed like that for the first time, she closed her eyes and leaning back, pressed her open lips to his and felt the thrill of their first deep kiss.

"Yes," he breathed and sunk down, his leg now pressing her skirt-covered thigh.

"So wonderful," she cooed writhing and held him closer, her face buried in his hair, waiting, forgetting Alma's threats and warnings, forgetting everything and wanting to stay in the cave forever. But sudden steps through the brush startled them. Aroused as from a dream, they quickly pulled apart and stepped deeper inside the cave. From the darkness they saw girls' skirts flutter by. "We must not, *Liebchen*," Gert spoke in her ear, holding her close. Quickly, she buttoned up her wrinkled blouse and pulled down her skirt.

At night, unable to sleep, she knew that things had turned. She wasn't sure that she would hold out and keep her promise to Alma. Gert too must have lain awake thinking because almost a week passed before they met again. Milda did not know what to do, how to take the cold silence and where to go or hide. Spitefully she did not go to the pool but spent hours looking for him down from her window. When she saw Gisela, she hid behind the curtain, her body flushed with anger and longing. But at last there he was standing below her window. As soon as she heard his low whistle she dashed down the stairs and into his arms.

Casually they walked out of the garden and impatiently hurried toward the cave. But once inside, Gert did not continue their interrupted pleasures. Awkwardly they sat quietly side by side, only their hands touching, and then he started talking, telling her where he had been. His father had taken him to Leipzig University and registered him for the fall semester. "I shall study where doctor Faust had his *Keller*," he announced all excited, telling her that he, too, wanted to study philosophy and was thinking about becoming a teacher, a man of influence and for the good of mankind. As if on a cloud, he held out to the surprised Milda a vision of their life together in a new Germany. He put his arms around her and said, "And then we could. . ."

A chill went through Milda, and she quickly slipped out of his embrace, saying that she had to go and help Alma.

After they separated, Gisela confronted her: "What are you and Gert doing when you go out alone?" Taken aback, Milda blushed but explaining nothing. *Let her worry and wonder and suffer pangs of jealousy! Let the whole town gossip!* She looked down and recognized Gisela's skirt and wanted to ask her who else was there, on that day spying and snooping but said nothing. Only their eyes met for a moment like crossing swords and then turned away. She longed to tell her friend, who stood before her strange and distant, that only for the moment Gert belonged to her. She wanted to tell her that he was protecting her from other boys and the soldiers and that they did nothing wrong. She wanted to tell her friend to be patient, for she knew that her time with Gert in their cave would soon be over and she and Alma would be on the road again. *But meanwhile, I am happy.* After a long pause and in as casual a tone as possible she said, "We read poems and like to talk about them." Although this was not quite true, it was neither a lie, for there were many hours, when leaning against each other, they read, what she thought, were the best poems of the German language.

She wanted to tell Gisela how beautiful their pure and wonderful love was next to Alma's—what? She had no name for the nights of jazz, smoke, and noise such as robbed her of sleep. She wanted to say that Gert respected, loved, and guarded her, but the words would not come out, because her soul guarded her lips.

As the days went on, Milda was so lost in the joy and pleasures of their love that she hardly noticed that *Frau* Lutz's daughters arrived and took their mother with her rosewood furniture away. A black man become the cook, and Alma was very busy. The parties became louder and longer, and the decent people turned their heads away when they passed the grand old house. Milda had paid no attention to what was happening all around and that they were seeing history in the middle of making. She didn't know that in Potsdam, not very far away, the four leaders of the world drew up the borders and zones of Germany and debated about what to do with all the refugees who would not go home. Alma was in an outrage because Latvia was put behind the iron curtain, as were other East European countries, and that the bombed, burned, devastated Berlin—the heart of Europe—was divided in four parts. The landscape, through which she and Alma had trudged, was firmly fixed behind the iron curtain. She told Milda that no help came from America. "My peace is gone, my heart is heavy." She spoke the lines of *Faust* and meant every word.

Open Borders

The day Milda dreaded with a kind of wishful, sad anticipation came suddenly. It was a hot day in July. Only for a very short time had she been in the cave with Gert, and they had only talked. She could not explain to Gert nor her own heart why she was impatient and turned her face away from his lips. When they separated, she walked an unusual distance through the woods, all the way to the castle ruins and came around directly above the Lutz house. She felt dirty and stopped at Nierts' garden pump to wash her face and feet, when she saw Gisela run out of her house. She was distraught, breathless, telling her that Miss Alma was looking for her and that the radio was full of bad news. Startled, Milda only squinted and blinked, shaking the water off her hands. "Must we leave?" she asked, knowing the answer.

"I think so," Gisela said sadly, but Milda saw her eyes dance. Suddenly everyone was with them. *Herr* Niert came with a hoe, *Frau* Niert was carrying dishes to the gazebo, and the twins raced around half naked, throwing a softball back and forth.

About the time they finished eating, Alma charged through the gate, not even apologizing, only calling Milda hysterically and talking in the Latvian. She said that they must move on and fast. Because of the borders, she said. They would go right through the *Thüringen Wald.* "That puts the Russians only about five kilometers from here. We are leaving in the morning," Alma said, her old self again. The Nierts tried to calm her, but she was eager to go, to move on. Her voice betrayed relief—like a release from bondage; or was Milda who felt the release?

"You understand," Alma talked to the Nierts. "We must go. You have been very kind, but we cannot stay. It is too dangerous for us. We don't know where exactly the borders are, as there are no barbed wires yet, and so, suddenly, the way we love the woods, we could step over the line and be in Russian territory. Oh, the Reds haven't given us up; we belong to them, they tell the world, and they would take us—catch and arrest us." She saw Milda blush. "My niece could be kidnapped and sent back all by herself," Alma said. "The Americans talk about returning refugees to their countries as part of the border arrangements... I wouldn't trust any white, black, or brown men with my life. I know them too well."

"We would rather die than live with communists," Milda said, eager to be talking about things that turned everyone's attention away from her burning face.

"We agree on that," Alma said, and they left the gazebo.

On the Road Again

The next morning, while it was still dark, a jeep waited at the gate. Alma and Milda had been packing late into the night. Two suitcases branded LUTZ were ready. Again they would travel lightly; they did not know where they would go, nor how far they would have to carry their added belongings.

It was a bit chilly in the half darkness. All the Nierts had crawled out of their beds, as did the nosy women from other houses, perhaps ready to help shoo Alma away. People blamed her for ruining the reputation of their town, and no one knew better than Alma herself that she, at this dark moment, was a symbol of what the world had become and of what happened when one was kind to strangers. The neighbors certainly will write to poor *Frau* Lutz, Alma knew. "Send our regards and thanks to *Frau* Lutz," she said loudly.

Herr Niert walked back and forth like a pondering judge, puffing on his cigar, and said what the others dared not: "You have taken advantage of our kindness. You were a bad influence on our youth." Alma controlled herself and stood tall, and then she said, "Is that so?" She walked up to him and lit a cigarette from his smoldering fire and straightened out his bow tie. She stepped back and repeated, "Is that so?" With a smirk she put her hand with the cigarette on his shoulders and kindly, as to a child, she said, "*Lieber Herr,* it was I who saved you from losing your home. It was I who ordered the supplies to be delivered at your window, I who insisted you be back at the factory." *Herr* Niert jerked back. He spewed and twisted in the cool air and then wordlessly walked back into the house, puffing on his cigar. In the shadows, the black men were shaking hands, slapping their palms against the twins' little hands, teasing and saying, "We'll miss you Miss Alma, oh, yes m'! We'll sure miss you!"

Frau Niert shrank from the men and turned to Alma saying, "You? You saved us?" She tried but could say nothing more. She handed Alma a net bag full of food and composing herself asked, "How did you do it?"

"Oh, it was nothing," Alma said sadly. "*Das ewig weiblich.*" She grinned as those who win the prize but lose the game. *Frau* Niert said *God bless you*, but Gisela pulled Milda aside and asked her, "What should I tell him?" Milda looked at her through the twilight. "Tell him that our love was the most wonderful thing on earth, but tell him also that all wonderful things must end. Tell him, I will never forget him and that I wish him good luck in his studies and that I hope and wish that he would marry you."

Gisela tried to find sincerity of this unexpected behest deep in her friend's eyes, but Milda didn't look up; she wiped her eyes and sniffed into her handkerchief. She tried not to imagine, not to picture what her words had just said. Gisela giggled nervously. To Milda's fogged vision, she looked small and already far away as she leaned against the iron fence, looking at the dawning day with dreamy eyes. Milda knew they would never meet again and captured the scene as it was, as it would be in an album of photographs, where the smiles never change, where Gert would always be handsome and Gisela shy and caring; the twins always five years old, sweet like Easter bunnies.

"Let's get goin' there, ladies!" a deep voice urged, and Milda felt herself being passed from one set of arms to another. She felt tears wetting her face from all sides. The horn honked. The motor was running. *Die Letten* climbed into the front seat of the jeep, and Charlie shifted into first gear. Minutes later Oeslau lay behind them. Looking back, Milda thought she saw Gert running after them, but she was not sure. There were other dots they were leaving far behind.

"Didn't he know we'd be leaving?" Alma asked.

"No."

Milda looked straight ahead, watching the trees become distant, the houses clear of fog. She was sad because she was losing a world, a strange, sad but a beautifully enchanting world, where she had lived and loved for only a short time.

But Alma laughed. "Of course people watched you and wondered. The woods whisper to the wind, and the wind carries even things that are hidden in the deepest caves," she said, smiling and put her hands over Milda's cold, clamped hands. "It was all so very interesting, like a story, a drama, but now the story has ended." Alma looked at her niece mockingly, victoriously. "You do have a sense of drama after all. That's good. That will save you in life. Some people make theater out of life, but we turn life into a play. At least I do. That helps. *All the world is a stage,* and we don't even have to worry about props and directors; it's all done for us. We simply play. No rehearsals, just one-act performances."

"Oh, stop it!" Milda cried. "Please stop. We didn't do anything bad or even wrong, and you and everybody can think what they want."

Alma squeezed her grown-up niece's hands. "It will be all right," she said tenderly. "Everything in life moves on, or we move away from everything, always putting untraceable distances between the moment and the recollection, sliding like a cable cart."

Charlie whistled as he roller-coasted through the fresh morning countryside, taking the curves sharply so that Alma would be thrown against him. He liked to hear her scream, and then he laughed a big white laugh. But Alma was in no laughing mood. She held on Milda's hand, and the hand trembled. "We both have our secrets," she went on in the Latvian. "And we will keep them where they belong. Right here in these hills. No confessions, you understand?"

"Yes."

"Gypsies and refugees have certain privileges, remember?" Alma spoke now in carefree tones. "They can revise their past with every re-telling. No one knows, especially in times like ours. The borders are sealed. We have many chances to start our lives over."

"Yes."

"You now know what love is like, don't you?"

"Yes, I think so, but not like you."

"Well, well," Alma studied Milda's profile. "I want you to believe me that I was actually happy for you, a bit jealous, yes, but mostly happy. He's a handsome boy and so smitten, so in love—not like the men I entertained. He'll wander about forlorn like a poet—for a while. Then he'll forget. You'll fade out of his mind and life, but it's all right. Such is life, it gives and it takes away."

Milda pulled her hands out of Alma's grasp.

"We'll see what happens next. What our next act will be," Alma mused.

"Yes."

Out on the open road, Charlie leaned back and sang:

Row, row, row your boat gently down the stream!

Merrily, merrily, merrily, merrily, life is but a dream. . ."

Alma, laughing, put her arm around the big, broad uniformed shoulder and, leaning her head close to his, joined in, taking her part, and pointing to Milda to pick up the next phrase. And so they rode away, over the hills and valleys, singing:

Merrily, merrily, merrily, merrily life is but a dream. . .

life is but ae dream. . .

ae drree-mmm…

Rest Stop in Nurnberg

The jeep reached Nurnberg around noon. The city was overcast and in ruins as far as they could see. Charlie had no idea where he should stop. There were no curbs. There was no map to guide Alma, since nothing on maps is bombed or barricaded. So they simply circled in narrow labyrinths of desolation. At one turn they broke out laughing, stupidly, hysterically. They found themselves in a dead-end street. A papered wall blocked the way; pretty paper it was with scrolls and flowers in little streamers going down, down, down. Attached to this wall, high in the air perched a toilet, its tank and chain shining in the pale sunlight. The whole drainpipe like an open vein, wig-wagged down into the debris. Charlie laughed, his head back, mouth wide open. "It says something, don' it?" But Alma slapped his face into a painful grimace.

"Sorry, honey," he said, bewildered. "We sure left a lot of mess behind us, didn't we?" He fumbled for more words, but Alma didn't hear them. With eyes full of horror, she saw it all. She saw the nights, her suitcase, a child leading her.—

"Get us out of here, get us out, pleez!" Alma called, and the man backed up and drove as fast as he could on a wide, cleared street to the outskirts of town.

A *Gasthaus* with a broken sign appeared on the side of an empty street or road, edged with debris. The jeep stopped. "This OK?" Charlie asked glumly. He gave every indication of wanting to drop his load off quickly. He'd had it!

Suddenly he women had become much too heavy and irrational. They didn't speak the language he could understand; they were of different color; their vocal chords produced different sounds with confused meanings. Awkwardly, as if to compensate for the strife, he offered Alma a carton of Lucky Strikes, and she took it eagerly. Milda was quiet. She was bleeding hard, afraid to stand up, but Charlie opened the door for her and gave her some candy and two oranges. "That should help you."

"Thank you," the *Fräuleins* said in unison. He smiled. "I'll check up on you soon," he said, grabbing for Alma's hand, but she jumped out of the jeep quickly, out of his reach. Standing at a strange gate, they watched the jeep drive away as long as they could see the white star, like fading hope.

Uncertainly, the women opened the gate and stepped up on the porch, dragging the suitcases LUTZ. The porch was a large one, all wrapped around the building. On it were round cabaret tables with chairs turned up-side-down on top of them. Overgrown roses and broken lattices spoke of past coziness. Soon a gaunt man came out of a door and greeted his guests. He complained bitterly about hard times until Alma gave him a package of Lucky Strikes. She lit one cigarette and gave it to him, and he immediately called out his wife. Within an hour a table was set, the others pushed aside. The tidy woman swept a corner guarded by the broken lattice. She cut a rose and, showing the travelers a pump, took it inside. Left alone, they rinsed off the dust and went to sit down at the table. The hostess brought back the rose in a slender crystal vase and set it down, then hurried to bring out the food. Potato dumplings, sausage, fresh tomatoes and, for dessert, strawberries.

"Ah, what a feast! We are so hungry! Thank you, *danke sehr*," Alma said delighted. Pleased, the woman stood for a while, wiping her hands on her apron and watched her guests savoring the simple meal.

*

The short pause in Nurnberg was blurred in Milda's memory. She remembered ruins upon ruins through which she and Alma climbed no doubt in search for food or lost civilization. They slept upstairs, in a musty bed and woke up not knowing where they were. Milda vaguely remembered, a bright day at the edge of the city, near an airfield. Small airplanes were lined up behind a wire fence through which daisies bloomed. There were tall pines and huge holes in the ground, tangled with thorny creepers. Further on, the fields bloomed with poppies, and she and Alma waded waist deep in those fields as in dreams. They plucked off the ripe heads, shook out the seeds on their palms and threw them in their hungry mouths. They napped in one of the bomb-holes because it was warm and calm there, like a grave. They slept until an American soldier shouted. Then they ran through the poppies—two frightened grouse—until they landed again on the big porch, which was full of soldiers—white soldiers—who grabbed at their skirts, whistled, and teased. In the evening, Alma impersonated Marlene Dietrich for them and collected cigarettes like tips, like gold, while Milda sat outside on the porch and wished for Gert, whose image she was losing too quickly, as though these men were slapping it away, the way they slapped uninvited flies. Annoyed, Milda went for a walk down the dark street. And then they were again on the road, traveling, shifting from one slow and crowded train onto another. They passed through towns of rubble, one after the other. "So many doomsdays in a row!" Alma remarked. The train rolled past a city which was nothing but a pile of bricks and mortar, only the cathedral was whole, its twin steeples, unharmed, pricking the sky. The twin rose windows reflected the sun, like bloodshot eyes of God.

Through the dirty train windows they saw many strange sights. But they also saw life picking itself up and moving forward. Men, carrying umbrellas, like *Herr* Niert, went into business buildings, or half buildings, while workers cleared the bricks and poured cement. They saw housewives lined up at shops; now there was clearly something to wait for. Counters were filling up, and the smell of baking bread often greeted them whenever the train stopped. They saw children running, skipping rope, balancing on stilts. At some of the stops musicians played the old folk songs, the men and women in traditional costumes beating drums and plucking mandolin strings. Milda had heard those tunes in Riga, when the soldiers mixed with the people and walked arm-in-arm with pretty young women. Then she had wished she'd be grown up and could walk like that, her dress blowing in the wind, her hand tucked inside a man's bent elbow. Now she was grown up. Her dress did blow in the wind, but there was no man to hold on to. She could not tuck her hand in memories.

It seemed so strange, she mused, so bizarre, the way tunes and movements turned and twisted and strangely connected themselves without making sense, without concerning themselves with propriety and order. Milda saw that occupations and conquests all looked alike, all sounded the same. She never forgot the sound, the smell and their dreary look.

It would be many years later when she would realize that they had traveled through a ruined civilization and a rising new world. She hoped that Gert was glad, seeing his visions take on tangible and visible shapes. Smiling, she wished him well. While enroute, they heard that important trials were about to begin at Nurnberg, but had no idea that many years later, in America, her children would read about them in history books, in the English language, and she would fill in the blanks for them in the Latvian. She peopled the pages of their books. She also told them that the trials were unjust, allowing Stalin's men to sit in judgment, not telling the world anything about the trains that carried their people—Ilga's and Gatis's grandfather among thousands of others—far away from the Baltic shore. Carried them all deep into Siberia—where they perished. She would repeat to Gatis and Ilga, when each was in junior high, saying, "I remember your great Aunt Alma shouting at the Americans, telling them, 'You'll see, you'll pay for it. Giving so much of Europe to the Russians and bombing so much culture and beauty out of our civilization! Why did you bomb Dresden? Why? Ha, you don't even know! You think you won the war, but you'll pay for it, you'll pay for not saving us!' And she was right, so right," Milda added. "Just look at the taxes we have to pay now. Look at how much the war they call *cold* now costs!"

"From Stettin in the Baltic to Trieste in the Adriatic an Iron Curtain has descended over the Continent," the children read in their text books.

The sentence was extracted from Sir Winston Churchill's famous iron curtain speech, but Milda could explain to anyone who would want to know the truth what it all felt like, chain by chain, link by link, herself envisioning Zelda trapped behind that iron curtain, crying to get out. "Long before the speech," Milda impress upon Ilga and Gatis so that they would never forget: "The iron curtain had become a fixture in my life. I never close my eyes but when I see it stretching across my Europe, mean and ugly, with prongs of barbed wire the size of telephone poles."

When her children said that she was exaggerating, she rose to her defense, saying that the iron curtain would become a fixture in every refugee's mind. It would put a clean line between then and now, between them and us. All sense of loss and exile would be summed up in that long hard line, and that same line would outline nearly all foreign policies and the battles of the cold war, for many years, perhaps forever, until such time when the iron would start to rust and crumble.

But in the summer of 1945, Milda only watched and felt Germany shake itself out of the war, eager to get on with life. She had felt the exuberance and joy of the living, the bereaved, yet miraculously saved.

Searching for a Destination

"We'll head for Stuttgart," Alma announced, smoking. "I know there was once a good theater, and I am a good actress." They milled around the timetable in a train station, looking at the chart of all the possible destinations and the times of arrivals and departures. They would not have to wait long for the Stuttgart train, and they were tired.

They arrived in bombed out Stuttgart the following morning. Alma left her niece watching their suitcases at a broken fountain while she went in search of shelter. By late afternoon she appeared, tired but in good spirits. She had found a dentist who needed a cleaning woman, and when he discovered that a kitchen maid would also be on hand, he was overjoyed. His wife, he said, was a lawyer and despised housework. And—there was an empty attic room. "Waiting for you," he assured Alma.

And so the travelers dragged their suitcases again up narrow stairs and settled down. The landlords were nice. Polite and sad—damaged as all Germans, as all Germany. There were no children; hence, for Milda, there would be no emotional attachments. She would do her work efficiently, the way she had learned from *Frau* Niert. There would be plenty of time to read, embroider, and dream. She decided not to enter school because no school was close by and, anyway, what would be the point? What would she need to learn in this damaged city? And how long would they be here and where would they go from here? This room, this house, would only be a stopover; that was their only certainty.

For wages, besides the room, the dentist agreed to repair their teeth, which had gone quite bad, and so both migrants submitted and underwent torturous drilling, some pulling without any medication, and the tedious filling of cavities. The dentist also provided brushes and tooth power. In time their smiles brightened.

As everything edible was rationed, there was very little food, but the dentist and lawyer were fair people who shared the little they had with the servants. Of course, they would eat their meals in the kitchen and only what was left over, but they knew very well that beggars cannot be choosers. Constantly hungry, aunt and niece glared at each other across a scrubbed oak table cluttered with empty dishes, often shivering from cold because coal was rationed.

And so it continued for several weeks until Alma looked hard at her hands, her figure, and her hair. She pulled out the gray strands, rolled them in a tight ball and pitched it a waste basked. She dressed up and went out. When she returned in the evening, her hair was carrot red, her lips a bright pink. They smiled victoriously: "I found a job at a cabaret!" She had found it through a pair of the American service men whom she met in the street. Or who met her. She wasn't sure. All she told Milda was, "We will eat well again, my darling. We will live!"

After that Alma did not scrub anymore. The attic room was constantly stuffy from cigarette smoke, and Milda again suffered from headaches, but Alma always wore a bright smile, even for the dentist, with whom she was very friendly, especially when the lawyer was at work litigating. Sometimes she assisted him, but in the evenings she went out, and many nights her bed in the attic was empty. Milda didn't question her. She knew, and she was glad because on those nights she slept better because the air was clean. Still, something was wrecking Alma's glamorous face. Under the mask, Milda saw the old fears and hopelessness crack through, and she notice that there was no talk of any future; they only recalled the past, their Latvian past, that is, if they talked at all. For them, there was only one day at a time. One by one. Day into night, night into day.

Milda dragged through that winter with constant, hacky colds, dull without fever and sweat. She had mumps and jaundice, but she went on working, afraid to lie down, afraid to burden Alma or die. In her sickness she often thought about Gert and mourned for him as though he were dead. At times she wondered if she should not have stayed in Oeslau and married him. She tried to see the Niert garden in bloom, with Gisela, the twins and dear *Mutti*. But no! She could not imagine herself in those houses and walking those streets with a basket full of potatoes and cabbages. She was sad that she had forgotten her beautiful doll. *I forgot Zelda for a second time*, she accused herself and was sad that she did not even have a lifeless object to love and hug. When she was well, she embroidered her gloom on scraps of cloth she later—much, much later in America-- turned into a quilt and hung on the wall in her basement. She named it *Misery*.

Thus she buried herself in the woods and caves of her memory. There was no place to walk now, except for some patches of green that used to be parks. She was afraid of the bombed-out buildings that glared at her with their blind, cavernous eyes and the stray dogs that went in and out of them like true owners. *Such has my life become! Why? Oh, why? It's not my fault, not Alma's either. It's the war, the cruel war. . .*

To keep her hopes from sinking further, she planted a bright pink cyclamen in a tin cup and set it on her narrow windowsill.

*

Only in the autumn of '46 came the release, when Alma burst into the room. She had changed her hair from carrot red to platinum blonde; her skirt flounced around her in big circles showing off her bare legs. "Surprise!" she called. She pulled Milda up from her seat by the window and squeezed her arms around her. She told her that they would be leaving the very next week for Esslingen, some fifty kilometers away, where a refugee camp was set up by the Americans as part of their effort to repair and rebuild Europe. She had telephoned the administrators and received their welcome.

"So, everything is in order," she announced days later and, catching her breath, went on. "Well, you see, the Americans have saved us after all! I'm happy that we can get into an all-Latvian settlement instead of the mixed ones. That means there will be a theater for me and a good school for you."

That same hour, they pulled the beat-up Lutz suitcases from under their beds and spent the night packing. In the morning, they thanked the doctor and the lawyer, who closed the door behind them.

PART II

A Place for the Displaced

Esslingen

Ah! Here is Esslingen! Alma (stage name *Kaija* [seagull] exclaimed.... *Esslingen am Neckar...* She holds a worn down map of Wurttemberg they found in a bomb-scarred antiquarian in Stuttgart.

The town sits in the heart of hilly Württemberg, less than a peace-time hour's train ride from Stuttgart. Its beginning goes back to 777 AD, when the St. Dennis Monastery was established in the Neckar valley and merchant roads started to connect the fledgling town with other towns and other parts of Europe. Yet, still in the early autumn of 1946, this medieval town seemed as remote from the modern world's destruction as those dark centuries when its first cornerstones were set. Painting pretty, it had not suffered even one bombardment on its antique face. The old church spires had never quit piercing the sky; the lovely stained glass windows had not stopped filtering sunshine into the cold and dark Gothic interiors. The Madonna had never lost her Child, and the saints around her never lost their heads, nor ever stood up like renaissance men, defiant and challenging. The terraces of swirling vineyards, warmed by the afternoon sun, kept on yielding all sorts of grapes from which juices and wines were pressed every year, all in due season. The orchards topping the vineyards had ripened their delicious apples for centuries. The townspeople carried the fruit down in baskets and cycled it through wooden presses, which turned it into cider and applesauce. The cider was marketed but also stored in home cellars in precise rows of scaled barrels, from keg to cask, depending on the size of a man's house and his orchard, where it fermented into *Most*. The Schwabs drank their *Most* from colorful S*teins* throughout their days and even into the nights.

The trains that stopped at the Esslingen station had kept their schedules. The large bridges over the Neckar and the quaint canal bridges had never ceased connecting. Only the Neckar was not as innocent as it once must have been. Like all grown-up rivers, it had become heavy with contamination as it flowed nonchalantly through the city, breaking only at the falls into splinters of foam and then flowing on and on, encased between mountainous strands, where acacia trees thrived and birds sang in their fragrant branches. Eventually it flows into the Rhine, which, in the Netherlands turns into the River Leek, which, in the end, tumbles into the North Sea.

The stone and wood castle, a relic of the old Wurttemberg kingdom, suns itself on top of the highest mountain, on the North side of Neckar. The townspeople love it, enjoy it, and leave it alone. They call it *Dornröschen* (briar rose), after the bewitched princess who sleeps for a hundred years and whom no prince as yet has awakened. So *Dornröschen* lies comfortably, though a bit disheveled, on the mountain top. The courtyard forms a square whose corners are marked by the main fat turret and three small ones that seem to stand guard like enchanted watchmen. Once supreme but now crumbling at the edges, *die Burg* receives the usual measure of nostalgia, respect, and attention. The courtyard, as in the past, is still a place for games and pageantry, for circus acrobatics, and Sunday afternoon strolls, when all is quiet and lovely. Its look-outs grant magnificent views of the whole city and snapshots of interred kingdoms, dating back to the Holy Roman Empire and the Württemberg dynasty.

A long enclosed stairway with look-out squares leads down from the courtyard to the heart of town, which is a large cobblestone square and also serves as the marketplace. Around the square stand antique houses—irregular, tight, tall row houses made of stucco and black beams. All year round their windows bloom with red geraniums and pink cyclamen. These houses lean against each other, as though self-conscious of storing too much *Most* in their foundations.

In the middle of the marketplace, set on a pedestal, like an inviting eye, winks the fountain. It marks the spring, the primeval well of pure, healing water that gave birth to the town. Baroque lion cubs ceaselessly spew pretty, clear, sparkling loops of water at the children and birds that hover around in all seasons.

The four seasons in Esslingen are rather normal for southern Germany: the spring is enchantingly warm, rich with the loveliest of blossoms; the summer is hot, a steaming bowl; the autumn cool and golden, full of chestnuts; the winter is mild with rare short snowfalls, like gifts from the Norse Queen, robed in veils and wearing thin ice slippers. People are out and about all year; they take their walks into the hills and vineyards and then rest on benches facing the fountain and one another. Chatting, they watch the world go by or come to them as it always, inevitably does. And if it does not—well, so much the better. They have their *Most* and their *Dornröschen* sleeping forever in tangles of briar roses.

On the eastern end of the marketplace stands the old *Rathaus*, also made of stucco and thick, black beams. Its roof scallops upward in layers, ending in a weathervane perched on a vertical bead of three balls. One clock takes up the center of the first layer of the façade, another—the second, and the *Glockenspiel* a third. Every quarter hour mythological figures emerge and proclaim the passing of time. Some play, some dance, but all remind those who look up and want to know what time it is that with each stroke of the clock they draw another step closer to death. The people pay attention to the clock. It has kept perfect time for centuries.

On the south side, in the very heart of town, is the two-towered St. Dionysus church. Its origins date beyond the 13th century, but, like everything else, it had suffered many times, and many times it had been rebuilt, reworked—like the faith it houses. Silently and with the ringing of its bells, it never lets people forget that God lives and rules the world. And the people remember to keep Sundays holy—at least until noon.

There are many churches in Esslingen. There are the Catholic St. Paul's and other cathedrals and the protestant churches, with no steeples at all, only plain crosses on white walls, their humble roofs slightly raised above the houses, like working hands whose fingers touch in prayer. The travelers would bypass these Baptist, Methodist and other unconventional places of worship. They turn their eyes on the most beautiful cathedral slightly uphill, at the edge of the vineyards. It is the *Frauenkirche* that the Schwabs built in the 14th century. It is an architectural wonder. From below, it seems as though the steeple were tatted or crocheted, so beautiful is this stone lacework, which like an altar cloth, lies on the sky. And then the bells. —Oh, the ringing of those bells, bells, bells, the bells that bombs did not blast into silence!

Stairways, bridges, and under paths, plain and ornate, antique and new, wide and narrow go up and down throughout the old town. These bear testimony of a lost time, when people respected the hills and mountains and built their macramé of passages accordingly, adapting themselves to the blueprint of nature, no matter how difficult it might be.

Esslingen evolved slowly. The trades developed gradually, almost imperceptibly. Industry, too, came slowly, by degrees, without upsetting the old town, nor tearing up the surrounding hills. The town along the northern-western bank of the Neckar grew following its contours, resulting in winding streets and canals. Not much in the old town is straight. The streets meet at odd angles, suddenly, and just as suddenly the names change, and the stranger is lost. He might as well go back to the railway station and start over; that is, if he can find his way. Or—he might wish to ride the streetcar to East Esslingen, farther out and enjoy the modern gardens, cafes, the cinema with American films (In the West are the factories and beyond them endless cabbage fields. No use going there.) Or—it's hard to understand—did he say he was looking for Esslingen—*Am Neckar* (at the Neckar)? There the streets are straight, and the so called block apartment buildings take up large squares. Those apartments housed temporary residents, such as, soldiers, guest workers, and now—refugees.

Die Letten (the Latvians) all go there. "From the station you get there by crossing the Plensau or Vogelsang bridges." The stranger tries to pronounce the names, but cannot get them quite right. He smiles at the latter because he understands the word—*birdsong*. It fits his mood and condition. It humors him, and, in a good mood, he whistles a folksy tune, as though he were calling other birds of his scattered flock. He wants to be where the birds sing or once sung; he wants to alight or take wing when the season is right. . . . He takes up his suitcase. *"Ja, ja., . Vogel-sang."* He says *danke* and starts toward it, up the ramp. Lighthearted, he swaggers like some dandy, his hat pushed back and his lips whistling. He is a bird. A migrant bird coming from the north, where bad boys tore up his nest and fed his family to the cats. Unbirdlike, his heels click on the *Trotuar*. He is aware of making too much noise in a strange land. People stare at him, and he, throwing a careless look at them, slows down and listens, but he does not notice the river and the town like native inhabitants. For him the bridge is blown up; the hills are heavy with uprooted trees and vanished nests. He stops for cars speeding by louder than loons, crosses the street and goes on, full of purpose. He goes to the UNRRA. He does not know what that word in capital letters means; he only hopes that in it lies protection and food. He is very hungry.

Ach, so many, foreigners, complains one Schwab to another. "When and how will it all end?" And distressed they pontificate about times past and the old kingdoms. They remark how the modern man is not like the old. He is too bold, too aggressive; he pushes himself impatiently through the narrow streets, regarding them as a nuisance. He, like a usurper king, climbs higher than the *Burg* and disrespectfully builds his villas above it, even on the next mountain. He does not have time to walk up and down the stairways, but he drives his car on the outer streets, making a terrible noise. But those avenues, so elegant and cascading with roses, are *something,* the folks admit. *Aber. . . s*till… Must man go quite so far, quite so fast? At least in June he might slow down and smell those roses. At least he might remember the holy days. Aren't there enough churches? Isn't there enough time for man to give God the honor due to His name? But—so it goes in life… Progress. *Modernisierung.* What's to be done? *"Aber die Ausländer, die verfluchte Ausländer!"* (The foreigners, the damned foreigners), spits a Schwab, sitting on a bench.

*

"This is an oasis!" Alma, the actress, exclaimed as she and her fourteen year old niece Milda Bērziņa hopped off the train at the quiet station, warm in the early September sun. She smiled with so much color and hope that Milda impulsively wrapped her arms around her. For a second they blended, surprised by their mutual joy, but immediately

Alma stiffened, throwing a familiar *leave me alone* chill between them. Milda understood what her aunt tried to establish or signal and stepped back, her heart injured. Alma paid no attention. She glowed as a holiday light bulb, swaying in the warm breeze. And, then, following directions, humming, they started walking up the long, hot concrete ramp, to the bridge crossing the Neckar River. She turned right and looked for the UNRRA. They found the school building with a billboard with the letters painted in black. Over the open double door cascaded the American and Latvian banners.

"At last together!" Alma said, adding in biting irony, that the Latvians had always hoped Americans would save them. "And here it is. Now we see it with our own eyes." She set down her suitcase and wiped the sweat off her face, smearing her makeup, which Milda, with a gentle hand corrected. Then, with all the just pride of poor and tired victims, they climbed the hot concrete steps. Inside the building, they followed the arrow under RELIEF to the basement. There, other Latvians milled around. All were displaced and seemed embarrassed as they looked for familiar faces or, people they lost along the way. But no one connected. All waited in lines for lodging, food stamps, and instructions. Alma and Milda queued up.

"One room still happens to be available," a clerk said, looking doubtfully at what she had assumed to be mother and daughter. "Would you mind living in the attic?" she asked.

"No, no! Oh, no!" Alma answered and signed on a pale line, grinning sideways at Milda, who winked. The clerk informed them that they would be in safe company. "Three Baptist clergymen and their families share the rest of the floor."

"I didn't know there were that many Baptists in all of Latvia," Alma remarked and took the key.

"I wonder who they are," she said as soon as they turned down at the train station and saw beyond the cluster of September chestnut trees the unmistakable Lido, which took up the whole corner of a large block. They walked faster toward their destined new home, and when they came to a small park they set down their suitcases.

"Baptists!" Alma said, as she collapsed on a bench under a golden tree. "I can't get away from them."

Milda stared at her sideways, sitting uneasily. "Uncle Imants and Aunt Matilde are Baptists, so why do you talk like that? And they are far away. I miss them. I loved their little church and the songs they sang," she went on, defending everyone, remembering all. Alma did not react.

"I'll never forget the storm and our Sunday school outing in Embute," Milda added softly. "That was my last happy day in Latvia."

"Oh, well, you were only a child then, not the fallen woman you are now," Alma snapped. "Just look out! They'll try to save your soul; they'll do anything to get close to you and then—you're down on your knees, crying and confessing, even to things you never thought of doing. You mark my words," Alma paused. "I know. Matilde tried to push into my life with her sausages and cheese. She insisted I was sinning— anyone connected with the theater, in their eyes, is a sinner. Going to the theater is one of their deadly sins."

Milda knew that, but it did not matter because for Matilde and Imants there was no time or interest in those worldly things. She did remember Uncle and Aunt talking about Alma, saying that she will come to no good unless she gave her life to Jesus. They had prayed for her and Katerina, anxiously on their knees. But Milda said nothing about that.

"I think she actually used the war to get to us," Alma continued. "But before it, to be honest, she was an embarrassment, so heavy, so different. No one would marry her, and so she decided to join the Baptists, who didn't look on the outward appearance but liked her voice, and so she started going to some off-the-track gospel church and singing in the choir. It traveled all over Latvia, and that is how she met Imants, the typical poor but honest farm boy. He sang base and she was a low soprano. Together they sang duets. They married secretly because the rest of us didn't approve her choice. Our father disowned her but mother cried. I remember my parents' fights and mother's tears. At last father gave in and allowed mom to visit her daughter, but he never welcomed Matilde back. When Imants inherited the house and farmland where you were, they moved down to Kurzeme. We talked how Matilde was the country mouse, and the rest of us the city mice and so we left each other alone. We got used to the marriage, the way people get used to any blight. Even Latvia was plenty big for all kinds of people. I must admit that they did well and even prospered. And then came the communists and the war and, as you know, there wasn't enough to eat in the cities. That's when Matilde started coming around to save us."

"I didn't know all that; you never told me," Milda said and remembered the hours she was sitting in a dark corner in her apartment in Riga crying and listening to her mother yelling at her for staying too long on the *stinking* farm. "Maybe you love Matilde more than your own mother," Katerina had shouted. "You should be ashamed of yourself, leaving me here alone." Filled with guilt, Milda had hugged her mother's knees and, begging forgiveness, had cried in her lap until she felt the limp hand push her off. *Like grandmother had pushed dear Matilde away from her and like I Aunt Matilde* had gone to her room and cried until she fell asleep. "Yes, I know how wars eat up all the food, but I didn't know it was like that between you all." Imagining the heartbreak, Milda could hardly speak. Her mouth was too dry. She was very hungry.

"There are many things you don't know," Alma said, looking at the red roof of Lido. "Oh, my father had a temper! Mother was quiet, and I think scared of him and his loud shouts and orders whenever he thought she stood in the way of his grand ambitions. I saw him strike her down once and ran away screaming."

"Oh, no!" Milda exclaimed. She turned toward her aunt. *So—it's inherited—Alma's stormy moods and violently shifting tempers that strike with a man's hand*, she thought and braced herself.

"My sister was Kate, your mamma," Alma continued. "Oh, how I envied her, how I wanted to be like her when I grew up! She was so beautiful, so very charming and had such good manners! When she married your father everyone was happy. Their pictures were in the newspapers. What a match! What promise, what hope for Latvia! Yes. . . Who could have ever foretold our tragedy? — Damned, damned, damned communists!" Alma swore. "They ruined everything, inside and out. I've lost myself and don't know if I can ever find me, and now they're raping my Viktors also, I'm sure, and all the other actors, one at a time. They are doing it right now, never stopping until we are done, finished forever. —I hope you will never have too much hatred for the communists!"

"How could I?" Milda's heart pounded against the Iron Curtain. The invoked images of their relatives seemed to float around, waving in every golden leaf, peeking from behind every cloud, playing checker games on the dappled pavement. "There are times when I want to die," she whispered, slumping inside the bench, bending over, not wanting to go on, catching Alma's mood like a bad germ. But Alma blew her nose and pulled up her heavy dependent. "Come on, let's go!"

They picked up the suitcases with **Lutz** burned into the leather. The name accused them and was heavy.

Lido

"It's nice here," Milda said, looking around with curious eyes. "Peaceful and separate. I would not want to be on the other side of the river, would you?"

"No! Baptists or no Baptists."

They set down the suitcases and reached for the double door. Two men in gray striped suits approached the same door. They stopped, bowed, and held the door open. They entered the DANCE STUDIO, exposing a polished golden floor and a woman playing the piano at the far end of the slick room. Alma, with Milda behind her, started climbing the stairs.

They smelled food. With each turn of the stairway, the vapors became stronger, as they floated down, making them sweat and salivate. When the stairs ran out, they stood in a dark foyer and counted the doors. Just then, one door opened a crack and a bead of little heads appears. Some hand quickly shut the door, while Alma pushed the key into their assigned key hole. They stepped inside. The room was a stuffy, dusty little rectangle, facing east.

"So—the sun sets on the other side. Thank God! That means the room won't heat up too much," Alma said and opened the small window as wide as possible and looked out. They were high up, higher than ever before. Milda, too, tried to fit inside the window frame, and for some minutes, squeezed together, they looked at the gathering twilight.

Unexpectedly a soft knock distracted them. Alma opened the door. A lady, rather pale and modest, greeted them and set a bowl of soup on the table. One little girl followed with slices of white bread and another put two apples and a cluster of golden grapes on the edge of the table. "My name is Emma Strals," the lady said. "This is my girl Daina and this—her friend Marta. We live across the hall. Please accept this. You must be very hungry and tired."

"Angels, you're angels," Alma chanted but thanked them reservedly, as if practicing a new act. "Thank you very much. But we shall manage in the future." The last words were too cold for Milda's ears. To cover up, she shook hands with everybody. The girls curtsied, giggled shyly, and backed into Mrs. Strals's flowery dress. The good Samaritans left and closed the door softly behind them.

"The angels have flown away, and the sinners may now dive into the manna from heaven," Alma said, taking up an aluminum spoon. They didn't say a word until the spoons hit bottom. Then they picked up their bowls and licked them clean.

"I don't want us to be involved and dependent," Alma said firmly, licking her lips, gray without lipstick. "It's all right now, but never again, do you hear? I don't want any entanglement. Next thing, we'll be going to their silly church and so on. Do you understand?"

"Yes, yes," Milda muttered irritably, as she looked around the room, wondering who and how should their new life be set up. In the corner, behind the door, stood a black pot-belly stove and some cookware and dishes. Along opposite walls were two narrow beds with folded sheets and gray blankets at the foot. The table, with two rickety chairs on either side, took up the middle. One stuffed chair crouched in the corner across from the stove. A wardrobe and a dresser leaned against a wall. A naked light bulb hung from the middle of the ceiling. Alma turned it on. Moths and mosquitoes also turned on and, with the cooling dusk, drifted toward the light and the intruders' sweaty skins. Alma closed the window. The women swatted and hit, creating dust storms, but at last gave up. For a while they sat on the squeaky beds, scratching, staring at each other, as they had done so often during their journey, their spirits and bodies leaning on each other.

Alma smoked and studied the instructions, maps, and food coupons. She calculated everything carefully. "I should stop smoking," she said and pressed out the stub. Milda was glad. "We'll sell them. Fortunately Stuttgart is close," she muttered, but Milda didn't hear her full meaning.

"Water," Milda said. "We need water." She wanted to wash the soup bowl, but there was no water, and it was almost dark. She took up the instruction sheet the UNRRA woman had handed out and studied the directions and the map of the building. Meanwhile Alma wiped herself with a crumpled handkerchief and took off her shoes. Without a word,

Milda picked up the bucket under the washstand and went out and down the dimly-lit stairs. In the courtyard, she spotted the curved handle of an iron pump of a well and went to fill the bucket. The partition for coal was against an outer wall. She picked up a couple of briquettes with some kindling twigs and carried all up the stairs.

"It's a start," she said, as she returned to the room, where Alma was lying down, her eyes closed.

And so their household order was established in small measures, by hard upward winding stairs—gyres of body and mind. Without any discussion it was clear that Milda should be the housekeeper and Alma the provider, and, as much as possible, they would leave each other alone; they would try to be independent.

Next Door Neighbors

Milda, though exhausted, was not sleepy; quietly she unpacked and tidied up her side of the room and then went to return the soup bowl. Little Marta opened the door, and Milda saw a table cloth covered table in a cozy nook, around which sat men, women, and children, as in some painting of still life. Disturbed, they welcomed their new neighbor, who stood confused in the doorway, an empty bowl in her outstretched hand. Once inside, her eyes, in a glance, took in the crowded kitchen, the people at the table, and behind them the bedroom with lines of cots like some ward. On one cot she saw a familiar blanket and, staring at it, stepped forward. One of the women caught her eye and followed her gaze.

"What is it?" she asked, "Do you want something else? Can we help you?"

"The blanket on the bed," Milda said, turning pale, as if it were alive or a ghost. "We had a blanket just like that one. We lost it in Chemnitz, in a bombing," she said and looked at the people closely. *Yes, I've seen these people somewhere; yes, for sure—the lady who just spoke. She was there, too, when the bombs fell.* The man, the large one, with a dimple in his chin, who, on that fateful day, had been sitting quietly in the corner listening to the children crying for food, had risen and gone out, saying he would take a chance. "Maybe I'll find a shop or bakery." Then she (Milda) had stood up and cried out for water, and she and Alma went to the other end of the building, where the barrel was located. The little girl (clearly Marta) with a bigger one had followed them. Yes, Milda now remembered a child talking and crying. *It's the same voice!* At that moment, little Marta pointed at Milda, chattering at her mother's side, pulling at her dress. Shaking her head in disbelief, the Mother stood up and went to pull the blanket off the bed.

"So then this belongs to you," she said. "Now I remember! How could I ever forget? The pretty young woman and her child, yes, yes, of course," she spoke nervously, remembering, perhaps seeing the cellar and her interment. "This blanket saved my life. It cushioned my head. It might have been my shroud." She leaned against the door post, closing her eyes, until her husband came to take her hand. As if awakened, she said, "My name is Irene Egle, and this is my husband, Pastor Egle, and this is our daughter Marta. We're all indebted to you and are very grateful."

Milda, mindful of Alma's warning, remained standing. She listened as Mrs. Egle, in a monotonous, tired voice told her how she picked up the blanket and wrapped it around her head when rocks and bricks threw her against a wall, pinning her inside some nook for many hours, while above, her husband dug through the ruins, his hands bleeding. He had returned after the bombardment and found *Martiņa* in a pile of ruins clinging to her friend, screaming.

"So these children, like I and my aunt, were saved."

"That's right. Your thirst saved you all. Or was there an angel we did not see?" Mrs. Egle said, her voice rising up, almost choking her.

"Only one drink of water. . . . Oh, it took an eternity before I was dug up from my live burial," she said as she folded the blanket, stroking it at each turn. "Yes, this saved my life. I didn't hit my head against the raw concrete with iron bars sticking out."

"Our shield and our salvation," her preacher husband confirmed, taking the blanket and handing it over to its rightful owner. While they all marveled at how small the world was and how the Lord's Hand was mighty and His love beyond human understanding, Milda backed out the door.

When she returned to her room, she saw that Alma was sound asleep, and put the blanket lightly next to her. Like a baby, Alma reached for it, propped a corner under her head and went on sleeping soundly. But Milda looked out at the sky and saw many stars shining in their little window. She couldn't wait until the morning, when Alma would wake up. *What a story I'll tell her! How surprised and moved she'll be! Perhaps she will turn, believe that God's hand does guide and protect His own; perhaps she will find peace and room for kindness toward our neighbors. It would please me and make the going up and down the stairs easier, almost pleasant.* She pondered these things long into the night, remembering many of their strange, unplanned, uncharted turns in the long road they had traveled thus far. Gazing at a part of the starry sky, she thanked God. She thanked Him with all her heart and asked that He would continue to lead and guide.

*

The next morning Alma was surprised but not shocked by the resurgence of her lost blanket. After hearing the story, she paused at the incredible and shrugged her shoulders. She said that so many odd things happen during wars that nothing surprises her. Sure, she'll speak to Mrs. Egle but in due time. She will not spread herself out sentimentally. "I feel like a snake who has recovered her lost skin. It's odd," she said, pushing the baffling find to the foot of the bed, "I'm not sure if I want this around me anymore. It still smells so much of Matilde and Latvia and endured pain. It hurts me." She stared at the blanket as though it were alive. "Throw it away," she shuddered, "I don't want it!" and then she said she had to go to explore the theater setup. But Milda stuck the blanket under her bed, inside Lutz's suitcase. *We might need it in the winter.* But she too was in a hurry. She had to sign up for school. Together, they went down the stairs and then continued on their separate ways.

The Gymnasium (high school)

Milda registered for the first class of gymnasium. The semester had already started, as had the school day. Embarrassed about her tardiness, she hurried to the assigned classroom. At the door, she stopped. All was quiet inside and out. With a nervously timid hand she opened the door. The hush deepened when she appeared as from nowhere, suddenly, interrupting some serious uniform writing. Many curious eyes turned toward her and, eventually, the teacher stepped forward and received the extended registration slip. She re-arranged the class alphabetically. Milda was again in her accustomed second seat in the first row, the one she liked—next to a row of large windows. The teacher, a tall reddish blonde, in a black satin uniform accented with a white color and cuffs, seemed shy. Confusedly, she said that she had been made aware of a newly arrived actress and her daughter.

"Niece," Milda corrected her in a clear, poised voice, at which the class recoiled and the teacher, blushing, escaped into the next paragraph of the ongoing dictation. As Milda wrote the uninteresting words, her mind sidetracked. Now she understood why Alma had pulled away from her at the station, when they got off the train: *Alma would not want people to assign to her a grown daughter and turn her into an aging mother.* "Class, pay attention!" commanded the teacher. Obeying, the class wrote on, at times glancing at Milda, who now sensed that ambivalent fame, for some reason, had run ahead of her and that she and Alma would be singled out and, at least for a while, censured and observed. The teacher, pausing during the dictation, kept eyeing her new student, until, at one pause, Milda turned her clear, blue eyes unflinchingly on her, letting them travel critically down the whole black torso. She saw the confused blush deepen. Then Miss Zāle closed the book and turned to the blackboard. For the rest of the day, she followed directions, eager to be accepted by her peers and excel in her studies.

At noon, on her way back to Lido, she felt free and happy, as though she had come back to her country, a home of sorts, but under a strange, humid sky in a strange and foreign land. She slackened her pace and looked at the people coming toward her, trying to pick out the Latvians. She identified some who walked arm-in-arm quietly and seriously, dressed out of local fashion. The natives walked and talked freely in their regional language. They scowled at her, and Milda's mood darkened. Again she was the foreigner, one of the intruders who cluttered their streets and parks and had taken over their school and other buildings, even the best houses. *What do they call us? Displaced persons—DPs. It's always the same, that frightened, strange feeling of being misplaced or displaced. You are without a home. You once had a home, but now it is far away or gone, while unwelcome strangers squat in your bedroom. . . . I am an orphan, without a mother and father, like a loose wheel rolling on and on, not knowing when and what will stop me.*

In the evening, she and Alma ate bread and cheese and drank tea, using up nearly half of the week's rations. They discussed things and shared impressions. Alma bubbled, full of information. She told Milda that apparently the top crust of Riga was congregating in this town. There were ministers, ambassadors, factory owners, even members of

President Ulmanis's cabinet. Milda didn't know any of them; still she was impressed.

"You see, dear girl, the war has made us all equal," Alma declared. "We will be standing with the lords and ladies in the same food lines and sitting on the same toilettes." Alma laughed, enjoying the prospect. "It's like in British plays of shipwrecks where the butlers rule the lords. Oh, what material is here for a true farce! But we cannot laugh yet, no, not yet. We are still beating the waves, trying to find a plank to lie on and paddle. Yes, it's too soon for laughter; we aren't done with crying."

She stubbed out the cigarette and put the butt in the gold box Charlie, her black friend, had given her. She sat quietly on the edge of her bed, blotting her face with jerky hands. "How did you grow up so fast?" she asked. "What am I to do? What shall we do? The schools are good, I am sure of that. What names! What teachers! Still—you, my darling, are especially fortunate because you already know German and English, and—you have learned life from me."

"Yes, and I'm still learning."

The Theater

"The theater is well on its way," Alma announced. She had found the theater's exclusive settlement in yet another school building on the south side of the bridge, close to the UNRRA headquarters. The actors, directors, set designers and dressmakers all shared the building. It was real Bohemia, a fantastic milieu, but no, she wouldn't want to live there; she wanted to stay separate; she wanted to be a star, ready to shine again on a stage in Latvia, once it was free. Lost in a daydream for a moment, Alma opened her gold case and stuck the cigarette butt back between her lips and lit up, inhaling slowly, a teasing smile tugging the corners of her mouth. "Guess what?"

"You got a part," Milda said, for what else would call up that mysterious smile? "Yes! And why not? — I'm Baiba in *Pūt Vējiņi*! (A much loved play by Rainis: *Blow, gentle wind. . . carry me back to Kurzeme. . .*) And the director welcomed me with a kiss on my hand and gave me the star role, after hearing only one short recitation—*per forma*. He knew me, remembered me from *The Sea Gull* and *Three Sisters*. Imagine that! What's more, he had come from Riga only to be there in Liepāja just to see me in *Faust*! So what do think of that?"

"I'm impressed. Perhaps he saw me too."

"Yes, maybe. But isn't it amazing how your works run ahead and around you without your realizing it? We live on so many different planes, in so many different people's minds."

"So—we must have been on the same ship," Milda interrupted

"Yes, for sure." Alma stopped to think. "There was no other ship for refugees, was there? I don't remember. . . . Hm. . . Yes, we are among a thousand invisible creations the waves tossed about and threw us out on these shores, who knows why and to what purpose." She went on, saying that she was virtually promised other star roles in the classics: Rainis, Aspazija, Blaumanis, Brigadere, Ziverts. "Oh yes, I'm thrilled. Happy. Almost as happy as I was in Latvia. I am a real actress again, only much better than before because I have lived and suffered, loved and lost." She wound down and, closing her eyes, collapsed, like a sea gull on the sand, shut in the wing and understanding many things. . . . She was asleep before Milda had found any words worth saying.

That night, a first chill came through the open window. Milda pulled their lost and found blanket out from under her bed and tucked it around herself. For a long time, she gazed at a star, stuck, like a clear amber pin in a tuft of dark, floating clouds, and then she too slept.

Establishing a *Latvian* Esslingen

Throughout that year, more Latvians were admitted to the settlement, and gradually the State of Exile started functioning smoothly. Energetic activities whirled about on both sides of the Neckar River. Subsidized by the UNRRA, the DPs were not burdened by the need to find paying jobs. Instead, they lived and worked for the community under a separate wage system, which paid poorly in actual currency but generously in psychological income. People, generally had time and opportunity to reclaim and perfect their professions and trades: the teachers taught, the writers wrote, actors acted, preachers preached. Only the dislocated government agents seemed idle, without proper status. However, in due time, important positions were created and honor and respect reclaimed, and it was not long before people knew, if only vaguely, who the outstanding persons were and who they had been, and soon the former authorities ruled again—rigidly, inflexibly, uniformly. Thus governed, the people felt secure, as if they were citizens of a real country.

Excellence flourished, and great was the pressure to work hard, behave well, and make Latvia proud. Education was greatly emphasized and for that books, journals, and newspapers were necessary. Former publishers took the initiative and reprinted the classics and more recent pre-war adult and illustrated children's literature. Encouraged, new writers took up their pens, and a body of exile literature emerged. School text books—plain and concise—were provided quickly so that no child would be left behind in the darkness of ignorance. Plays and poems, which some people had left behind and others grabbed along when they escaped, could be bought for a dear price at the small but always crowded kiosk. Pressed by the need and hunger for the printed word, the printing press had already become the crucial cog of enlightenment and the security against threatened loss of identity.

Avīze and other periodicals became not only vehicles for information, but they also set and enforced a particular nationalistic tone and vigilant mood the refugees accepted and adopted. The media, of course, was also entertaining and informative, but only within the prescribed perimeters. It drove public opinion to the right, forming a tight worldwide network that would last as long as the sense of exile went on.

It was a complex task, this governing of exile, for it was extremely difficult to be in a world with a voice, yet having none. To be a nation, yet have no seat in a legitimate national parliament. To be split in half by an iron curtain that left one side of the people—as the eminent exile playwright Martiņš Zīverts had put it—without land and the other without air. To have Latvia, Lithuania, and Estonia erased off the new world maps and painted red and marked USSR seemed like another genocide. It marked absolute homelessness and bred anger and outrage. It left no geographic spot to point to and left masses of people hanging in a limbo, as if beyond or even outside of exile. Exile at least implies home, lost though it may be. But nothing! Are the people who come out of nothing, therefore, also nothing? Or merely *others*? *And others...* So said the statistics and charts that the world accepted and taught in schools. It was truly a shocking thing for the DPs to see all the borders washed out and the people swept away.

Meanwhile, the displaced trembled and appealed to their leaders to correct the unjust error. "Don't let the world print and say the lie so long that it will sound like the truth!" so pleaded the lost as they fixed up their small refugee dwelling places, proving to anyone who looked their way that they had once been home owners and could very well mange their turf. "Prove, prove, to the world that you are worthy of life, liberty, property, and the pursuit of happiness!" the leading voices called out, and the subjects worked harder, some rising, some falling under the constant pressure and more constant grief.

But, people do not live on sorrow alone. The leaders understood that joy is an elixir of life and brought it to the public in many established and sure art forms. Concerts, art and craft exhibits happened in the best high-class tradition and according to the old Latvian calendars. Scout and guide troupes were organized in the tradition of the 1930s; that is, by absolute principles of order, work, and obedience to superiors. On formal occasions and weekly meetings, the scouts and guides were required to dress in uniforms. How and when they were stitched was a mystery. They were simply there, shining buttons, emblems and all. Everybody in uniform was expected to be an example of best behavior and walk straight, shoulders back, chest out, shoes polished, fingernails clean, for all was inspected. If a button was left unbuttoned, the leader pulled the button out, while the careless culprit blushed in silent shame. "Dis-ci-pline! Where would you be without it?" admonished the scout leader, inspecting the line-up of boys, as if they were soldiers.

Dressed in uniforms, the scouts and guides had to participate in all solemn assemblies, marching and standing at attention under the national banner, at times for hours. But there were also easier and enjoyable activities, such as, various sports events, dances, and excursions. No one could complain that life in the DP camp was boring and that time was wasted.

Milda joined the Girl Guides and soon became a troop leader.

The Lutheran church, too, was a mighty fortress, shepherded by black-robed ministers. The exile church and state leaned on each other for strong and continuous united, moral support. Together they appealed to God Almighty for vengeance and justice and redemption. Unwearied, they held up the return of lost homeland and freedom as a distant and golden award. "Therefore, hearken my people, be patient and steadfast, and the Lord God will reward you in due time, in the right season. Only through suffering you will learn the meaning of His love," so spoke the preachers.

The people accepted and trusted the unity of church and state and could not imagine things any other way. They especially liked the way the holy days and the national holidays reinforced each other: always a religious service and national assembly was followed by an elegant ball. This helped the people forget the past and prepare for each celebration with a mixture of reverence and excitement, enforcing national and moral unity and hope in a better future.

Alma especially liked the way the pagan rites and religious rituals fused. She loved to dance at the confirmation balls that followed the religious ceremonies. Milda was not sure about the correctness of all that; she remembered Aunt Matilde and Uncle Imants saying that God will not be mocked and that He was jealous. But she listened to Alma and obeyed her leaders. For her, certainly, the national broad way was easier than the narrow Christian *via dolorosa,* and she wanted to walk and dance as much as possible with easy, pleasant steps. And, really, she noticed that their Baptist neighbors, squeezed tightly against the Lutherans, did not dwell as much on the differences of rituals and traditions as on the necessity for common social and national purpose. So, it must be all right, she reasoned, and gladly took part in as many activities as she was able.

*

Alma, in principle, agreed with everything as long as it was properly impersonal. Above all, she wanted to be the best actress. In the same way, Milda wanted to be the best student. However, having lived alone for over a year, they had learned to be independent and choose their own open and secret paths and could not abide being lectured and watched. For both, the personal always broke through the national, the specific through the general. "Who do these men think they are?" Alma would spout all of a sudden as they crossed the bridge after lectures heavy with, what she would call impossible imperatives. She would drive the impractical propositions just heard to their absurd conclusions and throw them over the railing. "They don't need to tell me how to live!" She would say and spit down into the black river. "I have walked this far on my own, and I'll go on. I will not be bullied! Anyway, their power is only as secure as UNRRA." But Milda would warned her not to talk so loudly. "They listen and watch."

Indeed, hardly a month later, Milda was questioned about her aunt. "How would you like to live with a real family?" Milda answered, "Oh, but we are a real family!" and left the dreadful office as quickly as she could. After that, she became especially cautious, walking on edge, tiptoeing across the river. She shielded her private life like a fox and watched Alma with sharp eyes.

But Alma said, "Ha! I'll say what I want to and go where I please! I'm an actress and I take my schooling from Life. I shall shape my own destiny. Let those men watch me, let them come and question me! I am a woman, and I can disarm them—if I choose." In such a mood Alma was magnificent, Milda thought and learned from her.

She also observed life around her. Living more inside the German community, she noticed how, initially nervous, the Germans soon accepted the refugees and called them *unsere* (our) *Letten*. She saw how from their windows and side streets they watched the refugees carry out their rituals, celebrate their festivals, and march in their demonstrations without disturbing even a flower in the park. The local people noticed that the ladies of Riga brought a certain style and fashion to the old town, splashing it with unusual colors. Milda heard people comment in the small shops where she bought special delicacies, whenever Alma had extra money, that the *Letten* were a good influence in local slovenliness. "Now, have there ever been so many concerts and art exhibits here before they came? And our women, look, they are styling their hair, even painting their lips!" But the plain and moral women watched the changes through open windows and lace curtains and sighed, *"Ach Gott!"*

*

Milda was enchanted by the traditions of old Württemberg. She could not stay away from the market on Saturdays. She always found ingredients to make for them a good Sunday dinner. But most of all she enjoyed the simple entertainments all around. The monkeys and the organ grinders made her laugh and the circuses made her gasp in wonder. Once a year a traveling circus arrived and quickly erected whole make-believe towns on the shores of the Neckar, only to be just as quickly dismantled, like cities in the clouds. For almost a week, after school, Milda raced with her school mates to watch acrobats balance on tightropes as they walked from one church steeple to another and motorcyclists race in circles inside a barrel-like structure.

And she never would forget the town of *Lilliputs* that arrived after the circus on one fine summer day. Fascinated she watched the miniature people, children the size of dolls, go about their business around their miniature houses. She was a giant next to the tiny women in their high heel shoes. "How small their hearts must be," she remarked.

"They would never be too small for pain, though," Alma said. "Or for pleasure either."

"Yes. How right you are!" Milda agreed, as they saw children crying and laughing. They watched some little old men make passes at little young girls, while the big people laughed at their diminutive pleasures and pains. *Es ist doch der Zirkus* (it is the circus).

And then there were the boat races. On hot summer Sundays, people were out walking, following the boats along the canals watching and cheering. Alma was especially enchanted by the bright darting boats with their beautiful oarsmen as they wove through the city's waterways as easily as the fish that swam below. But moments later she pulled Milda abruptly off the quaint iron bridge saying, "I cannot stand it. It's so beautiful. See how they belong here, how they fit in as in a painting."

"While we don't."

"No, we don't," she murmured. "We belong to Exile Latvia, and we have to learn to make art of our sorrow. We, dear girl, have to learn to stylize our melancholy so that when the pain wears down we shall still have something to hold up. We must keep on acting."

"But shouldn't things be real? Isn't anything real for you?"

"This is. This dream. This exile. This whole drama, and when it's over, it will be over for me too."

"Oh."

Autumn 1946

Milda Bērziņa lived on both sides of the Neckar River; she also lived, as she always would, on both sides of the iron curtain. In this, she was like all other DPs, full of barbed wire tangles inside them scraping their hearts and minds. The crusting scratches always hurt. They were supposed to; the leaders saw to it that the scars would never become invisible, and so the people learned to live and make the most of them; some even enjoyed this divided, scarred exclusiveness and scorned those who had never been uprooted, never suffered like they. This sense of being special was gradually creeping into the exile consciousness. Milda, too, became aware that she stood above her peers, making them shy away from her as from some glamorous fashion model. Her golden hair, trimmed in a halo around her pretty face, made all the plain heads turn in envy, admiration, or suspicion. And the more they turned, the more Milda held hers high—even high above Alma. The teachers and leaders watched her, perhaps assessing her usefulness for the national cause.

Sensing their attention and scrutiny, after classes she would hurry home, across the bridge, up to her attic room, where she could be alone and spend her time as she pleased. The dusty volleyball court with its eager athletes and shy girls bored her and only made her feel more isolated, as if she were wrapped in veils of gauze. When some brave girls asked her how her life was before coming to Esslingen, she said little and, wrapping the invisible veils around her, remembered her and Gert inside their cave and Alma leaning on Charley's arm. . . . Smiling, she said, "Nothing" and left them guessing. Sadly she knew that the girls could give her nothing special, not the way Gisela had soothed her homesickness with her simple goodness and wisdom. She wondered how she was and felt guilty for their falling out at the end. *But that was the price for love. . . and I would pay again for the thrill of that love!*

Longing for something to happen, for some call to come or someone to find her, as soon as her classes were over, she hurried to her little room, she had made cozy with her creative, diligent hands. There she did her homework and let her mind wander in romantic visions and dreams. When Alma was away, she worried about her like a mother, like Alma had worried about her, and was relieved and happy when Alma would return at sunset, hungry and exhausted and they could be alone together. They invited no outsider into their room. Alma had strictly forbidden it, and Milda obeyed, because only in this little nest their insulating veils fell off and they, knowing themselves inside out, could be free and honest—if they so chose. When Alma was in a happy mood, they would coo and cuddle like doves hiding from crows, with the shade pulled and only a night-light burning; when the actress was despondent and melancholy, Milda left her alone until a casual smile or a touch of the hand signaled a changed disposition.

Saulcerīte (Hopeful for the Sun) and
Zelta Zirgs (The Golden Steed)

A month after their arrival in Esslingen, the call Milda had waited for came suddenly. The cast was chosen for the all-schools Christmas play. True to tradition, the play was *Zelta Zirgs*, by the eminent poet Rainis. To Milda fell the heroine's role of the princess *Saulcerīte*, who had slept for seven years locked in a glass casket, on top of a glass mountain. Inside the casket, the princess, true to promise, has waited for *Saulvedis* (who brings the sun), to save her by calling her name. Her name will open the lid, his kiss will infuse her dormant body with new life, and a happy wedding will follow. The chosen cast members had to read the whole five-act play and understand it before rehearsals could begin. Milda was nervous but excited.

"*Saulcerīte* is the symbol of locked passion and freedom," explained the director. "She is Latvia, which had been oppressed by foreign powers for seven hundred years. *Antiņš*, who is the good and innocent farm boy whom his brothers call a fool, but who symbolizes our people's highest ideals, namely, those who want freedom more than life. Because of his willingness to sacrifice himself, our *Dieviņš* (pagan god—always in the diminutive) blesses him and gives him supernatural powers as symbolized by the three horses: *bronze, silver,* and *gold*—also a reference to the ages of man. Because of *Antiņš's* idealism and commitment, he is able to ride the golden steed to the very top of the mountain and thus, symbolically, usher in the golden age. So, there, seeing locked freedom, our god, our help and protector, changes him into a prince—*Saulvedis*—who must act, and act quickly, because this is the moment, and it will pass if he does nothing. He *must now* call out the princess's name. The name (his knowledge and innate wisdom) will open the casket's lid. But that is not all: for her to really wake up, he must kiss her. Ah, don't you snicker! Grow up! – Hm. . . Well, may we go on? — Yes. So. Even you all should know that great acts and deeds to be credible must come from deep love, as symbolized in the kiss. So *Saulvedis* kisses her, and she feels the power of his sincerity and love and opens her eyes to a new age. She sees spring. Sunlight dazzles her. She hears a skylark singing high above her, and she believes that the mysterious caller's unselfish love, as symbolized in the kiss, will give her life. To seal that love, the happy princess gives him her ring, which no one—especially you," the director points to the youth who is the *Black Knight*, "can take off *Antiņš's* finger. That settled, the golden steed takes them down to the ground, to the waiting people. But as soon as that act is finished, the golden horse and the mysterious rider vanish. The *Black Knight* takes credit for saving the princess, but he does not have the right ring. When *Antiņš* hears that without her ring she will go back to sleep, he comes out with the truth. The imposter has him thrown into a dungeon where his finger is cut off. —This would symbolize a war, wouldn't it? Wars always call for sacrifice, don't they? But in the end—and remember that this is a folk tale and must have a happy ending—the truth and love triumph and break down the prison doors, and we have *the finale*—the happy wedding celebration, while the *Old King*—you over there!—confusedly looks on. Keep in mind that this is a symbolic drama about our nation's journey from oppression to freedom. Any questions?"

The *Black Knight* stood up and asked, "But why couldn't Rainis write about the revolution and all directly?"

"All right. Good.— Now, let's analyze. Why did he use the folk tale medium?"

No response.

"Well, because when he wrote it, Latvia was still ruled by foreign forces and scarred bitterly by the repressions of the 1905 Revolution. Rainis and Aspazija lived in Switzerland, in exile, like all of us here, and they knew that any mention of national ambitions would be dangerous;

hence, he had to clothe his ideas of freedom in symbols so that the play—and all the others he wrote—would pass the censors and be staged, because he did not want the people back home to give up the struggle for liberty and independence.. The time that is referred to—the awakening of the princess—is the 1905 Revolution, when the people rose up in revolt and tried to throw off the oppressors' yoke, but, as you may or may not know, the revolution failed and many were arrested, gunned down, deported, or—like Rainis and his wife Aspazija—escaped to other lands. That is what the imprisonment and cutting off the finger symbolize. Time, you must understand, in plays is squeezed together, but in our history, it was not until 1918, when our nation declared her independence, though still weak from the revolutions, the repressions, and World War I. And that is the reason why the princess is not quite strong to live and act. She is lethargic and uncertain and knows that only her *Saulvedis,* that is, the unified will of our people can make her strong. Freedom can never thrive under oppression, remember that. And imagine that, all of you! I remember those times and my whole body still trembles knowing the dangers. I feel the daring and the fear, the risks the participants took so we all would be free. So, please play up the fear and the courage. Remember that the princess is threatened with another internment. Like we are now, afraid to be turned back to the communists. But *Antiņš's* love and sacrifice—think of our soldiers!— must defeat the Germans, the *Black Knight,* as well as the Russians, the old *king.* Our soldiers were exhausted and short of ammunition, still they made our land free. And we were happy for twenty years. We really lived in a golden age. So much for the background. Any more questions?

Milda raised her hand. "Excuse me, Mr. Director, but how do I be a country and a woman? How must I act? I always thought this was just a folk tale. A good story."

The director hesitated, then, smiling down on her, said: "And you are right. It is a good story. It is interesting, and that is why we follow its plot to the happy ending. Yes, on another level, it is a universal story of love, longing, sacrifice, and fulfillment." He stopped, as if lost for words, then he stepped off the podium. He looked at Milda and spoke softly, like an ordinary man. "Forget all that I just said! Forget history and symbols! Think of love and suffering, of dying forgotten and alone. Miss Bērziņa, have you ever longed for someone to kiss you? Have you suffered for love?—Yes, of course, you have. We all have." Milda blushed. "So give yourself again to that longing, that dream you have been dreaming inside yourself, inside the casket. And you, Andrej, you *be* the prince, the one who wants her more than anything in the world! Your love and desire must scale the impossible, like a mountain of glass! Don't just recite the poetry, but feel it! The *words*, I emphasize, must drive you. Therefore, know what you are saying, and when the time comes, kiss Miss Bērziņa with your heart in it!"

So instructed, Milda immersed herself in the part and lived in a long-gone time, dreaming and wishing atop of her own glass mountain. No one and nothing mattered more than the play. There were rehearsals every day for hours.

Meanwhile, the most eminent set designer spread canvasses on the floor of a classroom and there created an enchanted ancient Latvia, where the Three Brothers, White Father, Black Mother, good and bad kings and princes, a whole cast of people, seven black crows, a butterfly, a skylark, and the transformed Third Brother—*Saulvedis*—would live out their destinies.

Simultaneously, the play was read and discussed in all the classes, from first to twelfth grade. "Great drama is for everybody," the director emphasized and urged the actors to be aware of this and act on all levels. "The human and the abstract, the personal and the universal. I know it's asking a lot, but I ask nothing more of you than of myself. So don't let me and yourselves down. And mostly, don't disappoint the audience. As Rainis would say, change and rise to the limit. Thank you."

After the Performance

The premier was in the afternoon on Christmas Eve 1946. Alma, naturally, was there, in the front row. She watched her *child's* every move, getting very agitated with each scene and act, and when the applause and curtain calls would not quit, she rose in breathless panic. She left the packed hall without a wave of her hand, without a word.

When, after the reception, Milda, her arms full of flowers wrapped in newspapers, went out the door, a man stepped out of the shadows and stood before her like an apparition. In the pale lamplight, he looked gray and gaunt, his face overgrown with stubble. A broken brim of a soldier's cap covered his eyes. He wore a long, battered trench coat, its left, empty sleeve tucked in the pocket. He moved up a step, blocking her way, and, saying nothing, eyed her fiercely, paralyzing her in cold fear. After some seconds, he pushed back his cap and grinned. Above the unshaved face, his eyes shone with electrifying intensity as they held her in place. Staring at him, she shivered from fear and cold and at last asked, "Who are you? Where do you come from?"

"I don't know," he said. "I lost my name, and I come from hell, but you may call me *Antiņš*. See," he pushed forth the empty sleeve with what was left of the arm. "I sacrificed plenty for my country, and I was in prison for the love of you."

"Please let me go."

"No, not yet."

"What do you want?"

"You. I'm waiting for the golden horse that will take me to the mountain where you sleep and wait. I want to kiss you."

"No! You're crazy!" she shouted and dashed past him. Never looking back, she ran down the slippery street toward the river. She stopped on the bridge and glanced back. He was not there. She hurried on toward Lido. She wanted to hear Alma's praises and feel her protective embrace. She wanted her to erase the apparition, but when she unlocked the door, the room was dark and empty. She switched on the light. There was no note. So Alma had vanished, leaving her in dark terror without a word. *Had she rushed away so she would not miss some black train?* Milda was dumbfounded.

As if sleepwalking, she filled the vases and glasses with her frost-bitten flowers, then went to the window and looked down. After some fearful moments, she saw a figure in a long coat shuffling down the street. Quickly she switched off the light and stood still, looking down. The man stopped, looked up, lit a cigarette, smoked it, and went on. Her eyes followed him until he turned the corner and was gone. Cautiously, she switched on the nightlight. She washed her face and, with a pounding heart and a bouquet in hand, went to knock on Door #1. She told the surprised Mrs. Egle that she was alone, that her Aunt had an important engagement and would be gone for an indefinite length of time. Seeing everyone dressed in coats and ready to go out the door, she asked if she might go to church with them. "Of course! Of course! But please come in and have some warm *piragi* and hot chocolate. We'll wait."

Little Daina ran up and touched Milda's dress, saying, "I know who you really are! I saw you, we all saw you, but you didn't see us because your eyes were full of ice. You are *our* princess, you belong to us!"

Christmas Eve Celebration

An hour later, Milda inside the circle of the three Baptist families, walked and glided through the narrow old town streets, along the canals and across the park. Every church bell rang as the town blurred in misty drizzle and the street lights diffused into dimmed nimbuses of silvery light. The children slid and pulled her along, away from the six adults. She laughed and blew the pin-prick snow from her muff and out of the children's hair. As long as she felt a part of the family and not just a cut-off branch, a frosted foster child, she was unafraid. By the time they reached the church gate, her show and the apparition mutated into dreamlike phantoms and slowly receded. The laughter and children's clinging touches had calmed her so that she dared to be glad that Alma had given her this gift, this rare feeling of warmth and safety in the middle of another strange winter.

Inside the decorated church, a young lady softly played the harpsichord. The tree sparkled with electric candles. The sanctuary filled quickly, as the children shed their overcoats and rushed to sit in their assigned front seats, while the mothers went their way to the choir room for a quick practice. The ministers sat down with the congregation. There would be no sermon. There would only be the words of the prophets, recited by the children, Christmas songs and the Christmas story. Afterwards there would be warm apple cider and pastries, as well as paper bags with cookies and apples.

Milda found a seat by a thin pillar. She was aware that some heads turned to look at her, but she ignored them. She watched her neighbors, the women and the children, each in their turn, singing and reciting. She heard the prophecies and the Christmas story, feeling the momentum of the greatest drama on earth. It was greater than all the staged plays she had seen. It was greater than *The Golden Steed* because it was true, without riddling symbols and garnished poetry. But suddenly she felt Alma's invisible and distant hand slapping her comparisons out of her mind, out of her thoughts and feelings. To dodge the slaps, Milda straightened up and turned herself into the Ice Princess on top of her glass mountain, knowing she had to stay there until she would be carried down—until the right time came. *When will it be? Who will carry me down?*

She leaned back and closed her eyes and listened to the preacher's description of the hills of Bethlehem and knew that he was really describing his own Kurzeme landscape of rolling, snow-covered meadows. She imagined him with his family riding in a sled pulled by dark brown horses over snow-covered roads. The fields and woods were white, glistening in the starlight. The air was crisp and biting and the stillness so deep that the crunching of snow seemed loud. She imagined the sled gliding to some little church, like the barn where Jesus was born, at the edge of a small, sparsely lit town that slumbered, its roofs tucked under deep tufts of snow.

And then she remembered Uncle Imants and his family and her sister—feisty, rebellious Zelda. *Where were they? Did they ride in an open sled to their cozy, little church or was there no church but a buried heap of coals and ashes?*

Her eyes traveled over the plain congregation and rested on the quiet, sad face of a woman. "And Mary kept all these things in her heart," the preacher said, ending the Christmas story, and closing the Book. And Milda understood that that was all anyone could do: keep things in the heart. At that instant, uninvited, he—the ragged stranger— suspended and invisible, came to her mind. He usurped her thoughts and her heart, turning them away from the angels and the manger. She visualized his every feature to the minutest detail and crossed her arms over her heart. She wondered who he was and where he would be going. Was he hungry? Had he walked from some prison camp or bombed-out shelter? He said he had lost his name and had come from hell. What hell? And where did he lose his arm? He seemed sick and weary, yet his eyes had glowed with a strange fire that singed her. . . . She pressed her hands on her heart, afraid everyone would see the heart naked and running after him, giving him bread, giving him her lips to kiss, giving him life.

She wrapped her coat around herself, eager to slip out and away, but just then the harpsichord started playing the postlude, and she realized she was hungry. Her room would be dark and lonely, and she was afraid to be alone. She might slip and fall on the sidewalks.

"Come on!" Daina called and was at Milda's side, pulling her hand, taking her to the side room where delicious vapors enticingly floated out the door and invited her in. She saw that her neighbors were saving a seat for her, beckoning, calling her name. Grateful, she stepped into the light and took her place beside them.

1947

When Alma showed up, on the second of January, herself strangely glowing, revealing and asking nothing, Milda did not confess that she had briefly followed the Star of Bethlehem. And she told no one about the man in the trench coat.

*

The recess over, Milda was glad to return to school. It was a cold, drizzly January, the kind that chills the bones. Behind her back, she heard some people referring to her as *the Ice Princess*. In her classes, the girls hesitated to approach and bother her in any way, while the boys seemed to look past and around her. Her "prince," sitting as usual on an ordinary school bench across the room, did not look at her but stared at the bleak hills in the distance. She, with sidelong glances, recalled that he had not dared to kiss her, as the director suggested, but, standing on a high ladder, awkwardly leaned over her, while she, lying in the transparent casket cried real tears.

"Really," she confessed to Alma, "I did not act at all. I simply lived the role."

"I know," Alma took her hand. "I live my roles also. The rest of my life is the acting."

"Oh!" was all that Milda had to offer.

In a flash she recalled the many tragic scenes she and Alma shared which no script could match. She saw her Aunt kissing her lover for the last time before they boarded the ship. In the blink of an eye it seemed that he and the one-armed man in the army coat fused into one colossal figure: the Latvian man caught in the cross fires of war. His sad gaze pierced her soul, forcing her hands to clasp in anguish. She wanted to tell Alma about him, about the way he disturbed her—not all the time but in waves, it seemed—and with a kind of supernatural force. But she did not like the way her Aunt was made up and how she smelled. "I don't know," she said exhausted and frightened. "I don't know anything," she said looking out. But the window was iced up, and she saw nothing.

Miss Exile Latvia

After her success as an upcoming actress, Milda found herself being chosen for all kinds of positions: she became the class assistant and the leader of a Guide troop. The organizers of freedom parades and anti-communist demonstrations chose her to be in the lead, where she and another young lady would be walking besides the young man who carried the Latvian banner. The leaders also chose her for a poster of ideal Latvia, naming her *Miss Exile Latvia*. One day, unexpectedly, she was summoned to an office where she received the brilliant orange-red *Nīca* national costume, complete from shoes to jeweled crown. She was told that it was a sacred garb to be worn only on special occasions and with special written permission. Any deviation from this rule and any improper private or public behavior would be cause enough to relieve her from her duties, whereupon the costume would have to be returned. "Is this clear?" the leader asked, and she answered that it was—perfectly, saying that she was honored and would do her best. She did not say that all her duties would turn to pleasure, when she would be at the right side of the tall, blond, handsome young man—the ideal Latvian male, the *exiled Mr. Latvian*—who held her suffering country's banner.

She imagined herself walking next to him in every parade and standing at attention during every assembly. Together they would listen to the speeches and recitations about national pride, lost country, and the mission to tell the world about the evils of communism. They would form an impressive picture as they would stand at attention under rented laurel trees and blessed by the enlarged golden stars of the national emblem. Milda was sure that if any man in any kind of a coat would cross her path and insult her in any way, he—the flag bearer—would rescue her. If she fainted, he would revive her. But she swore she would never faint, never flinch.

Yet often, after the formal, lengthy assemblies, she returned to her attic room utterly exhausted. After taking off the costume, she felt like Cinderella after the ball, sweeping the ashes and dreaming, remembering, wishing. . . But then, uninvited, the soldier in the trench coat would appear and sadly, seductively gaze at her. She would try to blot out his image with that of the flag-bearer, but the soldier would push him aside and take the flag, stretch forth what was left of his arm and say, "See what I must sacrifice, while you walk in sunshine."

Out in the streets, mixed with fear and curiosity, her eyes would search for him, even expecting him to stand at some corner waiting. But when days and weeks passed and he never crossed her path, her heartbeat slowed down and she would calmly walk on, at times involuntarily glancing back, whenever she heard a man's footsteps. At the veterans' assembly in March, she searched for him among the invalids, many without arms and legs, all looking beaten and lost, but she did not see him. By the time spring came into bloom and her heart wanted to sing, she pushed him out of her mind, telling herself that he had gone away to some other settlement and that he had only traveled through Esslingen that Christmas Eve and happened to be there for the play and she happened to be in his way. She tried to be casual, saying to herself that he too had been surprised and tried to save face by teasing and scaring her. *Perhaps now, somewhere, if he still remembers the night, he's laughing at me.* And then she thought about the shy young man and smiled. *Someday. . .*

She was very busy. As Exile became a normal way of life, her time was taken from her with such free hands that she began feeling like a mechanical doll, but that was all right. She was glad that her life was ordered and decisions made for her. As long as she served her country and could be next to handsome Kārlis Arājs, she felt safe. No stranger would dare lay his hand on her.

Besides, her busy schedule gave her good excuses to pay little attention to her aunt, whose moods followed the pattern of spring ebbs and flows. She did not see that Alma was hitting herself against the hard possibilities of what was left of her torn life. She failed to see that she deliberately confused the real with the unreal and danced to many dissonant tunes. But when Alma slept, Milda heard pained sighs and cries escape her parted lips.

"We live in such a bizarre dream," Alma said the next morning. She seemed happy on sunny days, when things went well, when all the rafters cooed and twittered, sending out their mating calls. On such days, she would preen, painting her lips and nails a bright violet-red and pin her yellow hair back on one side, letting it fall over the other, its wave partly covering her eye. She glanced at herself in the mirror, smiled at her niece, and went out. She traveled lightly, with one oversized handbag. Milda assumed she had rented another room in Stuttgart and there lived another life about which she refused to talk.

Nothing, however, stood in the way of Alma's acting. She never missed rehearsals and performed her challenging roles brilliantly. She knew and felt that people loved her and waited for her soliloquies and electricity-charged love scenes. No one knew that she cried in her sleep. No one saw how, moonstruck, she would rise from her bed and reach up and out over the roof and treetops, calling, calling him by name, "Viktor, my Vikki!" Nor did anyone see Milda gather her up and lie down next to her and hold her like a child, her sweaty head on her breasts, until both would fall asleep. In the morning, embarrassed but at peace, both would go their separate ways.

Among her colleagues Alma walked inside her bubble of pride and excellence—a lone star glowing inside a misty halo. She had no close friends, only colleagues and partners. "If you want our people to respect you," she forewarned her niece, "don't let them see you up close. Hide all that's personal from the public eye, otherwise they will hate you. Worse. They will despise you."

"Why?"

"Because, Miss Exile, you will disappoint them, wreck their visions of Latvian perfection. You see, we're no longer just people. We are the chosen remnant. Don't you hear how the speechmakers define us? We are the trusted ambassadors of *their* idea of Latvia. It's because they cannot see it anymore, so they need symbols. They look at us."

"You're crazy."

"Don't say that," Alma flared, her eyes glowing as if she were trapped, but when Milda laughed and taking her hand, calmed her down, telling her to keep talking, she finished saying. "You see, my darling, with our people it is all or nothing, good or bad, right or wrong. Nothing in between. Like with Faust."

"Then we must hold tight and be all and good and right."

"Yes."

"Like the acrobats walking on tightropes without safety nets."

"That's right." Alma looked at her deeply. "So, my precious, hold on! Keep your eyes on the distant steeple as you try to balance. Never look down at your feet or you'll crash. Play the role, keep it up as long as you must, and don't ask any questions. Don't fumble over your lines. You can be certain that someone, some old Riga dame, will hear your mistake and beat you with it. You must realize that her images and memories are more precious to her than any life of yours or mine." Suddenly Alma started to weep, the tears falling in dull drops.

"Is it that hard?" Milda asked soothingly.

"Yes, oh, yes, especially for symbols. And it's doubly hard in this perfect set-up we call Exile. It's so different from being in one's own country where people are people and there are many other things to worry about, like milking cows, running stores, the government, you name it. Here it's different. We're like in a Zeppelin. Floating in thick clouds of ideas and ideals that never touch the ground. So, don't you see, this is a training field in ideal nationalism, and we must all learn to jump through our assigned invisible hoops."

"Like our acrobats."

"Yes. Precisely. And you must learn well, my darling. You must learn to walk on air, and that is dangerous. One shot can blow the Zeppelin to smithereens, and then what's to become of us?"

"What *is* to become of us?" Milda stared in a pair of glassy eyes.

Entertaining the Veterans

On the Saturday before Easter it was Milda's turn to lead her Guide troop to the Mountain Colony to entertain and cheer up the veterans. The girls, all dressed in uniforms, pulled a wagon full of meats and cheeses, pastries they had baked, apples, a barrel of *Most*, and bouquets of flowers. As they labored up the steep incline, they practiced the songs they would sing for the old heroes. But Milda was uneasy, again wondering about the whereabouts of the one-armed stranger. What if he were there, waiting, confronting or teasing her? But in the unlit hall, with inadequate windows and clouded with cigarette smoke exhaled by uniformly drab men, she did not see him. Relieved, she lined up the girls for their songs and skits that lasted about an hour. When they finished, the men, having already drunk some of the *Most*, roared and clapped, some calling out provocative comments, while others started singing familiar lyrics about loss of country and love, filling the air with desperate signals of loneliness and desire.

The girls, obeying Milda's order, went into the side room, where they poured out the *Most* into pitchers and set the food on the tables. Milda nervously arranged the flowers in glasses and went to set them on the table, starting at the far end, where a group of men stood waiting and watching her quick movements. Suddenly, a warm hand fell upon her arm. She looked up. The glass dropped and shattered. Crying out, she bent down to pick up the flowers and the shards of glass, but the same hand pulled her up. For a second that seemed eternal, their eyes met and her face burned. She saw that he had changed. He stood tall. He was cleanly shaven, his hair combed to one side. He wore a dark brown suit that fit him well. She saw that he was unmistakably handsome—a blond Carry Grant. Feeling her whole body on fire, she sent a fierce glance at the empty sleeve tucked inside a pocket. As if stung by that glance, he turned abruptly and stepped back. She mumbled an *excuse me* and rushed to hide inside the busy girls, while other men cleaned up the broken glass, saying it meant good luck. Then they all fell to eating, drinking, and flirting, without paying any special attention to her—except the one with the empty sleeve in his pocket. He waited for her to fill his glass, but she did not go near him.

Nervous and tense, she urged the girls to hurry up with the food, telling them that they needed to be in their homes before dark. She scolded them for flirting and lingering, for forgetting the Guide rules. "It's all right to be friendly, but you don't have to sit on their laps. Don't you ever let them touch you again!" She wanted to say *don't excite them and don't let them excite you,* but the words would not come out, for she was extremely excited as she struggled against the magnetic pull of his eyes from across the room, sensing that something dreadful, even violent, masked his staged gallantry. She was curious, yet afraid to find out what that something might be. What had that now clean hand touched on the battlefield? she wondered. What triggers had it pulled and what blood spilled?

What happened to his left arm? Where was it now? And, anyway, where did he come from, and who was he? She glanced his way through the crack of the open door and new that his eyes had followed her and now met hers in the crack of the door and for a long moment hypnotized her until, with a shudder, she slammed the door. He did not eat, did not drink but sat, his gaze fixed on the door until another girl opened it. He saw that Milda had not moved, nor had tried to but stood as though waiting, catching the signals of his thoughts and desires. Her blush deepened as he measured her with his eyes, a grin playing on his lips, knowing that she watched him in helpless curiosity, knowing that the fly could not help herself and would, sooner or later, step into the spider's web.

At twilight, their duty done, the girls hurried down the mountain, the empty little wagon rolling of its own volition. Like children, they giggled and said silly things. They gave each other rides all the way down the narrow stone street and talked about the men, whom they liked and who appalled them. They tried to joke with Milda, but she wouldn't laugh, wouldn't play their games. At the fountain, she dismissed them, wagon and all, and cooled herself with the pure spring water. Wiping her face with her handkerchief, she looked up at the distant mountain where, she imagined him standing and looking down, and then turned toward Lido. Her body felt as if torn apart. "A Mephistopheles," she said. "Such a man could destroy any woman, and I must guard against him with all my might. . . . And I will! I'm no Gretchen!" On that day she learned the mighty power of real temptation and said The Lord's Prayer.

*

Nights of dreams, terror, and guilt followed, when suddenly Milda would wake up in cold sweat, unable to go back to sleep. The days were better—filled with work and sunshine or rain. Still, even when the sun stroked the earth, the torments of desire and resistance would suddenly arise and war against each other and, much to her relief would, just as suddenly leave off. She kept all this secret, telling no one, carrying the burden herself until, after days and weeks went by without her running into him by some pre-determined chance, he slipped out of her mind. She blamed herself and her imagination for her exaggerated emotions and forced her mind to dismiss him from all her night and day dreams. Still, there were times when she would want to hold on to some magic bunch of garlic or a crucifix, just to be sure. For lack of these, she would find an excuse to small talk with the Baptists, wherever they happened to be on the stairs or down by the pump in the courtyard. She would then exchange easy words and pleasant smiles, knowing that all of them—the children and adults—liked her and were always happy to see her and glad to help out. The fathers gave her extra coal and wood, saying that by pooling together they had enough, while she and the *honored actress* only had so much and nothing more, not enough for the soup to finish cooking. She thanked them and complained about the weather and that it was difficult to keep the stairway and hall clean. They promised to wipe their feet with more care. The wives and mothers were pleased that she spoke up so freely, because they too took turns cleaning the stairs and keeping the top floor presentable. Milda cheerfully said that she admired their not minding to stoop that low, adding that her aunt would never stoop or touch a wet rag or a broom. "What would I ever do without you?" Milda would exclaim whenever a helpful hand and a cheerful smile made the day better. *I'd be lost and afraid, my mind tangled in an empty sleeve.*

The First Song Festival of Free Latvians in Free Germany

It was spring 1947. The much discussed and carefully planned all-Latvian, all-Europe first Exile Song Festival to be held in August was would be here sooner than it seemed. About the middle of March auditions were announced, and Milda with other girls lined up to be tried and tested. Milda passed easily, as she expected. Choir rehearsals started right away; they were long, hard, exciting, and exhausting. Also, because of the festival, the school year would finish up a week sooner, so that those who had to study for their final exams would not suffer.

Caught up in all the excitement, Milda prepared for her Guides a short presentation about the last free song festival she had attended in free Latvia, because the younger girls knew nothing about what happened in 1940 and how Latvia lost her freedom.

Sitting in a circle, she recalled how she, with her parents, her sister, and nanny had taken the train to Daugavpils, where the festival would take place. She told about the excitement and how all the people were excited as the train carried the choirs along the Daugava River, going south up to the large border city Daugavpils. The singers were dressed in their national garb, many wearing flower wreaths they had made. "I can still see it all—the whole train decked with flowers and garlands. There was no sad face to be seen—until the choirs were onstage and President Ulmanis interrupted the song and announced that Russian troops had crossed the eastern border into Latvia. The President told us to be calm, but the choirs did not listen. They started singing *Dievs, svētī Latviju!* God, bless Latvia. They sang it over and over. My parents were also in the choir singing, but my sister and I sat in the audience, close to the front with our nanny, who cried and sang. We all cried and sang, I don't remember for how long."

She remembered the ride back to Riga and told the girls how quiet it was. She had fallen asleep against nanny's shoulder. When she awoke, the world had changed. "My happy childhood ended at that song festival. I understood little at the time; only much later, actually, only now I fully understand the meaning of *occupation* and *exile* and how it hurts and how it will hurt until we can sing our songs again in our own free land." The girls listened, watching Milda's eyes flooded with tears. They sat quietly and let their tears flow. They promised to be at the festival and never forget it.

On the beautiful August afternoon the whole Esslingen DP population walked to the festival site, filling the Neckar valley. About a thousand Latvians from other caps were there. The local people, many up on the mountain slope, listened to the concert from afar. They had never heard anything like it. They had never seen so many people turn their sorrow into joy. The keynote speaker, a former cabinet member, recalled that last festival and the tragic occupation. He spoke dramatically so the world would hear and understand why they had escaped the "clutches of Stalin." His speech was translated into English for the invited American guests who sat in the front row. Following that, in a short translated address, the American delegate delivered his country's sympathy and support and promises of help. The festival ended as the choir of a thousand voices sang the most rousing patriotic hymn: "Latvia, you must live forever, like the rising sun. . ." The choir sang the hymn twice, making the hills echo and tears flow, sending the song to their brothers and sisters behind the Iron Curtain. They could not sing the same song, nor pray for Latvia using the words of the National Anthem. They could only sing what was permitted and ordered, like a song about Latvia being a new red star in the Soviet sky. Alma was sure that their concert ended with the *Marseillaise*.

The audience called for an anchor, and the thousand voice choir sang the Star-spangled Banner. The Americans rose for a standing ovation.

When, in the gathering darkness, Milda with the whole soprano section filed down from the risers and passed the invited guests and delegates, she saw him. He stood between two Americans, talking, no doubt, explaining the plight of the Latvian soldiers. She hoped he did not see her and quickly turned and, passing others, rushing forward to where the Baptists would be. She caught Daina's hand that pulled her into the safe circle. Nervously Milda looked back to make sure he was not following, calming herself that surely he would be in a jeep, riding with the honored guests, who, no doubt, promised him America.

The First Wave of Emigration

"Guess what?" little Daina said about a week later, when she met Milda at the pump. "The Ābele family is going to America, and when they get there, Mr. Ābele will help everybody to sail to America too, and he will find a place for us and also for my friend Marta, and we all will be very rich and happy."

Milda listened in disbelief. "Oh, no!" she exclaimed. But it was true. Before the month ended, the Reverend Ābele and his wife and their two children were gone—escorted to the station with flowers and best wishes.

"We are going to prepare the way for you," promised Reverend Ābele. He would appeal to President Truman himself, if needed. He would come in the name of the Lord and say, "Let my people come in and forbid them not!"

As the train pulled out, he called, "Have patience, my brothers and sisters, have faith, if no larger than a mustard seed, and our Lord will deliver you as he delivered the children of Israel out of Egypt. Fare you well!"

Minutes later, train noises wiped the sound of his voice out of the humid air. Milda, with Alma's hand in the crook of her arm, watched as four white handkerchiefs fluttered and were gone. Even Alma believed the promise shouted from the train.

"If anyone can break the stagnation of exile," Alma said, "it would be these simple people with their simple faith. Who knows," she mused, "perhaps it will move some mountains after all. The war has shaken the whole world order out of joint. So, we'll see what happens next."

Thereafter Alma greeted the remaining neighbors with small smiles instead of her cold, masked face. "I must admit," she told Milda one fine day, "I rather enjoy the way these Baptists have come into their own. Even the theater people respect them. Some have gone to them for help and have received clothes and food. Yes, they do know how to help each other and how to share the nothing they have. And, now with President Truman, also a Baptist, they don't act so left out. They walk taller, as if they held the door handle to American. You never hear these people cry for what they lost."

"They are for saving," Milda mumbled.

"You mean—souls?"

"More than souls, I think. They always seem to salvage the good out of life," she spoke up, glad that Alma was conciliatory. "Let's not forget that they even saved our blanket from the bombs."

"So we can cover ourselves."

"Yes."

*

The unsuspecting Baptists did not know that they were being discussed and observed from a curiously utilitarian angle. They lived and let others live their daily lives, as best they could—as they had to. They went to church on Sunday afternoons, when the home congregation could spare the building. On certain Sundays, the Lutheran, Catholic, and Baptist congregations would join in some garden arbor of blooming roses and celebrate together certain holidays. This would never have happened in Latvia, but in exile it was different, since all suffered the same sorrows and cherished the same hopes. Out of necessity they learned to tolerate and understand one another, bypassing their doctrinal differences and leaving the old baggage of prejudices stranded.

Exile was biblical. It was easy for preachers to find appropriate passages with which to identify their plight and comfort the suffering. The Psalms were full of laments, praises, and assurances of God's purpose and blessing. The people listened and many were persuaded to admit that the Hand of the Lord is mighty. They had been delivered miraculously from many a perils and could hope for a better future. And so the small church that did not even have a steeple was packed on Sunday afternoons.

In food lines, sometimes Milda heard people talking about the long church hours the Baptists had to endure, but she also heard others defending them, saying that these *sectarians* were nicely integrated into the Latvian community and got along quite well— also with the Germans. "They are cosmopolitans," some patriots remarked and doubted their commitment to pure nationalism. Milda heard some of the men saying with a kind of lewd smirk that the Baptist women did not seem so saintly after all, especially when they went out by themselves to meet American soldiers. "I saw one all painted up with a netted veil over her face parading in the park with an American arm sliding down her back." Other men grinned and remarked about peroxide colored hair and red lips.

Milda listened, pretending not to hear, but she could not help comparing even the ladies of Lido as they had been when she first met them and as they evolved as time went on. Mrs. Egle, for example, had cut her hair and gotten a permanent. She colored her lips ever so slightly as she rushed down the stairs for her singing lessons in the Studio on the ground floor. Mrs. Strals, her hair also bobbed and lips brightened, took piano lessons and played waltzes and even tangos. Milda would hear her practice next door and open her door a crack so the melodies would float around, bringing back her romantic days and starry evenings with Gert. Listening, she would bask in her bitter-sweet memories until Beethoven's or some other angry man's chords would push innocent Gert aside and bring forth the man with one arm. With her eyes closed she imagined him standing in the doorway, watching her. When he would not leave, she would jump up and close the door, but he would only move over and watch her struggling through the lace curtain of her window, raise an eyebrow and smile.

When she cleaned the steps, she would also hear the excitement in the Baptist women's voices and see the blushes in their cheeks as they rushed by her to meet their instructors down in the studio. At the pump, Daina, the little gossip, bragged to Milda about her Mamma's playing the piano at church, while Mrs. Egle sang solos. The child would imitate the adult by pressing her clasped hands into her chest, stretching her neck and trilling in high vibrato. "Like that!" she would say, a little devilish grin on her face.

Meanwhile, the reverends, their husbands, did not only stand behind pulpits. They traveled to other refugee centers to preach and to distribute the goods that came from American churches. By mid '47, the food and clothing packages came regularly, and the ministers, as the disciples of Christ, carried their five loaves and two fishes with them, just in case— in case the hour was late and the multitudes hungry. Lacking food and clothing, the visitors humbled themselves and accepted help from the people they avoided in the good old days of freedom and prosperity. When their string bags were full, they returned to their cramped living quarters satisfied and full of hope for emigration.

In the beginning, Alma was surprised to see the Baptist clergy sitting in the front row in the theater, which would not happen in Latvia. Once, feeling a bit wicked and smiling like a temptress, she offered a pair of tickets to Reverend Egle for her first show. When he stretched out his hand, a cynical *I don't believe it* escaped her bright lips, leaving the tickets in mid air. "But, Reverend, I don't want to lead you into sin." The Reverent looked at her and smiled the wise smile of a father who did not want to embarrass a wayward child. "Lead *me* into sin? Why there is no sin in seeing a play unless, we make it sin because our nature is corrupt and we ourselves see sin in the things others do. My dear lady, more sinning is done by self-righteous people than by infidels."

"I'm not sure if I follow you," Alma said, going to her door. "So you and your wife will come, yes?"

"Be happy to! Thank you," he said, while she backed into flat #4. "I can get more tickets if anyone else would like to see me jump into the river and drown."

"Only to come out of the waters for a curtain call," he said in a kidding tone. "Rather like a baptism every night."

"Then I'm saved."

"That's something for our Lord to tell you, but I'll find out if the ladies would like to go and let you know. Until then, have a good day."

A few days later, Alma delivered four more tickets.

Milda smiled when she heard about the strange conversation. It seemed rather like Jesus talking to the woman at the well, but she said nothing to Alma, who had no more free tickets to hand out. Still, as the seasons changed, Lido became quite a closed, liberal community, a separate small world, where the air was free and the comings and goings exciting.

Often, from a park bench, where Milda studied on hot afternoons, she could hear the music coming from the studio and see ballerinas whirl and leap and, at the final chords, fold their swan feathers as they died on the liquid floor. One day, looking up, she saw Marta, the little *prima donna,* take her pose and tilt her head, listening to the music below. When the right note was struck, she started turning, whirling, her pleated short skirt going out. She seemed as small as a porcelain figurine on a high shelf, fragile and alone, spinning round and round in a dream of her own—now a sugarplum fairy, then a snowflake, melting on a chestnut leaf and, roll down a sheet of glass like a drop of rain. Unaware that anyone watched her, the child would dance, dance, dance, her long brown hair lose, her toes pointed, her arms curved, light as a pair of wings. But then, suddenly, she stopped and disappeared. Milda, hearing footsteps, turned and saw Reverend Egle. Minutes later, the ballerina came running out the main door of Lido and danced into her father's arms. He picked her up and set her on his shoulders. She rode him through the open door like a conquering princess.

New Arrivals Next Door

After the Ābele family left, the balance on the Lido top floor tipped unfairly: the Egle family of three now spread out over three rooms and a kitchen, while Alma and Milda remained cramped up in their little room. Alma was about to launch a vicious complaint, when all of a sudden strange feet ran up and down the stairs, carrying things, talking and laughing loudly.

The word spread that another Baptist minister's family of six by the name of Gramzda was moving into the emptied apartment. Mrs. Egle watched the change through a crack in Door #1. Her face, in the dark, as much as Milda could see, peered strangely ashen, her look nervous and closed. Little Marta stood by her mother, while Reverend Egle, full of welcoming sunshine, helped his brother up the narrow flights of stairs. Door #2 was propped open, and all afternoon people were going up and down stairs, carrying things and arguing about where to put them and how to pack everybody into the inadequate space. Milda stayed out of the way. She had to study. Besides, she missed those who had gone away—gone out of her life for good—and she was wary of any newcomers. She did not look forward to learning new names and seeing new faces, attaching herself to new smiles only to be cut off again. She had wept when the trains carried her neighbors away, and she especially missed chatty Daina, who loved to splash around the pump and spill any news her alert little ears had picked up. Now only the birds chirped around the puddles of dirty water. . . . And she missed the other children: shy lanky Gunars, Daina's brother, who like this father was a scholar, always reading, always so very serious.

She remembered Reverend Ābele and his wife and children, whom she hardly had time to get to know. She tried to recall little Zinta and Andris. They were good and quiet, the girl always mothering her little brother. They seemed like a pair of cherubs—innocent, and loving. Yes, Milda missed them all, as she realized that all those children who had scampered up and down the stairs, the boys sliding down banisters, the girls giggling and shy, were growing up far, far away in America—much too far from Latvia. How could there remain a connection, Milda wondered. How could any of those children possibly remember the tiny land where their mothers first cradled them? How could they remember the Latvian words in a strange, big land and keep their language from dropping out of usefulness? How? And why? Why was all this mixing and coming and going happening to her and her people? To what purpose?

She also missed their mothers. She missed the excitement when Mrs. Strals with Mrs. Egle dashed off to the theater, the concerts, the music lessons downstairs. She chuckled as she remembered how they turned their made-up faces away, as though she would mind the make-up and tell on them. . . . But whom would she tell? How would she betray? And why? Didn't they realize that all of them, including herself, were always running off to some secret unpredictable rendezvous to meet their own fascinating and frightening destinies? She remembered how they skipped down the stairs freely and dressed flashier when their husbands were away and when they had left the children alone, asking her to—please—look in on them once in a while, if she would not mind. Of course not, especially when Alma was away! But often she, too, would be out, attending the same concert, play, or poetry reading. Then she would see the mothers chatting in the lobby or thrilling to the words and music onstage, experiencing, no doubt, the agony and ecstasy of passion, like she did in her secret darkness and under covers.

After the Strals family left, Mrs Egle seemed lost. Too often Milda would see her gaze intensely, her face flushed by a dangerously secret fire just like Alma's. When noticed, she would turn away and, in her troubled mind, would flee—run or fly—where no one could follow.

On warm spring and hot summer days, these ladies had sunned themselves on the flat rooftop; occasionally she and Alma, too would go up and lie down, keeping a polite distance. They giggled, turned over, and cover themselves with their discarded robes, whenever some young factory men across the street pulled them close with binoculars and gave out loud, shrill whistles, like wolfish mating calls.

Now all that was gone. Vanished. Milda could understand quite well why Mrs. Egle stared into the dark hall forlorn and alone, her lips pale and tight. At times she wanted to pull the bomb-shelter blanket from under her bed and wrap it around the mysterious woman and tell her, "I am still here—at least for a while. And your husband is good and strong, like a rock. He does not see sin. He knows no such sin that burns in us." But she said nothing and passed her by with hardly a nod. She was afraid.

The Reverend Gramzda family

Before the week had turned, Milda and, unavoidably Alma also, met the Gramzdas—one by one. The first person she met one morning going down the stairs was Vizma. She, like Milda, was a gymnasium student and turned left as soon as they closed the Lido door. Awkwardly they walked some steps together, eyeing each other until, simultaneously, rather shyly, they extended their right hands and introduced themselves, saying they might as well walk together.

Vizma was eighteen, a senior. She seemed self-conscious next to her beautiful neighbor, but Milda only noticed the kindness of her eyes and her attractive smile. She saw her natural blond hair and well-proportioned figure. *A Latvian poster girl,* she thought.

"Let's be friends," Milda said but, as Vizma's smile brightened, her sister Zelda suddenly usurped her mind. *We could be sisters,* she thought. *. . But no! I must not always think that. . . I have a sister, only she is not here. . .* "I have a sister who did not get out," she said, as if affirming to Zelda her faithfulness.

"And I have an older brother who was drafted and is lost to us," Vizma said. Tangled in their own thoughts, uncertain what to say, what to ask, they walked on. When, a half hour later, they reached the schoolyard, they quickly separated and, with lighter steps, joined their own classmates. Thereafter, Milda left earlier and walked faster, reviewing her lessons and thinking her thoughts. Vizma did not seem offended, for whenever their paths merged or crossed—at the pump, wood pile and in food lines— no one pouted. Vizma did not seem offended. Milda liked that kind of vague friendship.

Shy with words, Vizma spoke through music. In late afternoons and evenings, she practiced in her room on the old upright piano. On Monday evenings she had her lessons in the Studio downstairs and every evening, between seven and eight, she struggled with a new piece until, by the next Monday, it would be mastered. Then Milda tried to be in her room with the door left ajar. The waltzes of Strauss and Brahms, the mazurkas of Chopin, the *Lieder* of Schubert would surge through the air and flood her being with a pleasantly, tormenting pain of longing and desire. Sometimes, when she heard the rapidly rippling variations of complex notes and chords, her emotional responses were so strong that she had to close the door. At other times, tearless and dreary, her heart often beat in jealous rage: *she has everything. . . a great talent, a pleasant disposition, enough beauty, a father, mother, two sisters and a brother—a whole family. What treasure, what blessing among so many ruins!* And blind envy would keep taunting: *while you have nothing, except your impossible Aunt, a battered, misappropriated suitcase, and an old blanket. . .* Whereupon, her conscience would strike back, scolding, *Shame on you! Be thankful! It could be worse, much worse. . .* To dispel Envy and Shame, she would step out to complement Vizma, calling her a rising pianist, wishing her good luck. But Vizma, lost in her music, would only smile and rush down the stairs with her book tucked under her arm. *If I had a piano maybe I would be as good as you. . . . No, no. . . . Maybe I have one or two talents, but you have the full five. . . God bless you and forgive me!*

Jānis, Vizma's younger brother, also came out of the same door, about the same time every morning, sometimes nearly colliding with Milda, but he turned in the opposite direction, up *Bahnhoffstrasse* and then crossed the *Pilsener* Bridge. He was in his last year at the elementary school. Milda had crossed paths with him before. They had been together many times in parades and demonstrations, staged for Americans to impress upon them that Latvia was unjustly occupied. At the head of the processions of the younger school children, he was the designated carrier of the American flag. He was also in Scouts. Her Guide and his Scout units were *sisters* and *brothers*; hence, they often had joint activities: hikes, camping, and special events, where they staged skits, sang, and danced. Jānis played the accordion, at times causing excitement among the leaders when he would play American cowboy and country songs. But other than that, he was quiet and shy and rather invisible. Seeing Milda suddenly appear next door, made his cheeks blush and his eyes look past her, searching for a getaway. When this went on for some time, Milda, at a right moment, caught his hand and called him her brother and friend, saying that whenever they had common activities, they should walk together. He nodded and blushed, for he knew her—as everyone did—and hoped no one would see them together and tease him. Mercifully, soon another family with three boys was moved directly below the Gramzdas. Then thumping boys' feet went up and down the stairs regularly, bypassing any girls that might be in the way. On fair-weather afternoons, their homework done, Jānis and Valdis, leaning out of their windows, would send their whistle signals, and minutes later, Milda would see the gangly youths dribbling a basketball up the street, as they rushed to the athletic field across the river.

Helga, the third child, Milda had also seen round and about: in food lines, at the end of the long parades at freedom demonstrations and on national holidays, when all school children would be mobilized. She had also seen her when *Little Flames* and *Big Guides* had joint activities. One episode, earlier in the summer, at an all-Scout and Guide camp flashed immediately to mind: Helga was in trouble. She and another girl had been punished for being unable to control their giggles at a line-up and were ordered to sit outside the camp all afternoon. As everyone was having fun, Milda saw the two girls standing defiantly for many long, hot hours without food or water. On a more recent, 10-km hike through the old kingdoms of *Württemberg*, Helga had dropped out of line to take off her shoes because her feet hurt. When the leader told her to put her shoes back on, she refused, crying and showing her blisters. She was then ordered to walk at the end of the line. Stubbornly, dragging herself, she had limped home, carrying her shoes.

At the next meeting, the leader called her up front for a talk and used her for a public warning, saying that if she complained again, she would not be allowed to go on other hikes. But Helga liked to go hiking and, in self defense, pointed out her scarred heels. The leader watched and threatened to dismiss her for good.

"I shall tell my father about this," Helga said and went home to report her to her father, Reverend Gramzda, who listened as he wrapped her ankles in layers of gauze. The next day he went to have a talk with the leader, whose turn now was to be nervous. In the end, she apologized, saying that Helga was too unruly and strong willed, whereupon the reverend agreed but stated that his daughter also had a strong sense of justice and knew right from wrong. "And in this case, you are wrong," he said, asking her if she would like him to take up the matter on a higher level. She didn't. "All right, we will leave this here between us. However, it is my understanding that one of the moral obligations of the scout and guide movement is for the leaders to set good examples and be fair."

The leader apologized again and, from then on, she left Helga alone.

Shortly after that incidence, as if sent from heaven, a shipment of shoes arrived from a Baptist church in Texas. Helga found a pair of saddle shoes that fit her perfectly. Happily, she announced to all her mates that there were shoes in the cellar of their house (The Gramzdas then lived in a private house.) and anyone who needed shoes was welcome to come and find what would fit. She had pleaded with her father to let her group, including the leader, have the first pick. He agreed and praised her for acting in a true Christian spirit, and so, on the next hike all the girls—and the leader—-wore comfortable shoes and walked up and down the hills singing.

But around Lido, Milda often saw Helga barefooted or in sandals she had made herself with a piece of plywood and strings. She wore these when it was the Gramzda's turn to clean the stairway so she would not slip. Unlike Vizma and Jānis, Helga was not shy. Whenever she met Milda, she would always be eager to converse and speak her mind. She treated Milda as an equal, especially when they cleaned the stairs and the hallway. Many times Helga complained: "Why should I be the scouring maid? Doesn't Jānis and Vizma have hands that can touch water? *Vizma has to save her hands for the piano,* Mamma says and *Jānis is a boy.* Well, so what! Don't they see that I too have a spirit? I like to read and write and be the best in my class just like you do, even if I'm not beautiful like you, but God loves me too, so they tell me in church all the time, even if He didn't give me a singing voice, He gave me a speaking voice, and I'm going to use it! And I write well. Even the grumpy leader says that, and so does my teacher." She spoke scrubbing hard, her small hands twisting the dirty cloth with fierce anger. But when the work was done, her scowls changed to smiles. "I like to make things beautiful," she said. Their chores finished, they usually would go out walking, picking flowers in the ditches, arranging them in a neat bouquets until their hands could hold no more.

It really did bother Helga that she was told that she had no singing voice and no talent for the piano. It made her feel deprived, somehow crippled, for all the Latvians she knew boasted about Latvia being a singing nation. "So I must like poetry," she told Milda and, to prove it, she quoted long poems she had memorized. She said she liked to recite poems in church and would like to be an actress, but that was sin, and she should not wish to do sinful things. "But sinful things are fun," she said, "and I must be good at something and not bring shame to my family and our church. Oh, life is not fair! When I say that to father, he tells not to hang my head, but lift my eyes to the Lord. That's what papa says. He cannot carry a tune either, but he can start any song on the right note without a tuning fork, so there!" She boasted about knowing the words of many songs, and then extracting a promise that Milda would tell no one that she wanted to be a writer when she grew up. "I see stories everywhere," she said, her eyes glowing. "I see *you* in a story."

"Oh, you do, do you?" She was afraid that this girl saw through her cover-ups, that she knew her secrets, for why else would she look at her with such sympathetic, curious, wise eyes as though she were reading and memorizing her? Looking down at Helga, she thought for a moment that she was seeing her sister Zelda.

"You make me see things in a new way, you little imp," Milda said and, spontaneously, hugged her. When Helga with questioning eyes turned to face her, Milda told her about her sister and their fated game of checkers.

"That *would* make a good story."

"Yes, but please don't write it yet. Don't tell anyone. It hurts so."

"I promise. I won't. I won't tell anyone anything about you, but you can tell me things, so I can save them all up and someday write a real book."

This made Milda laugh and hug her harder. And so a bond was tied for life.

Helga's little sister Aija was a most beautiful child. She was five, and wore large ribbons in her golden hair. Very shy, she looked up at big people with timid glances. She and Marta were best friends and went together to Sunday and day school and everywhere else—skipping along, hand in hand. Milda saw them in the park riding scooters and taking their dolls for walks, always looking pretty and happy. Yet, they, too, had their troubles and pain. Milda saw that, clearly, Marta ruled the relationship. She saw how the secretive ballerina would withdraw like her mother, and not speak to Aija, who, bewildered, would weep silently and for many days afterwards become invisible, waiting for Marta's mood to change. Unwillingly she would go with Helga for their daily walks and play games with her, which the bigger sister let her win. Being only a substitute hurt Helga's feelings, she confessed to Milda.

"Perhaps if I could sing or would be beautiful, then Aijiṇa would love me." But Milda, thinking about Zelda, sighed, "Sisters can hurt each other very much."

Reverend Gramzda was a fine looking, friendly man, with a nice, inviting smile. He joked and spoke to everybody on the floor and teased the children. He impressed Milda as being fearless and imaginative, excited about life—in spite of the countless tragedies of the war. She caught herself wishing that he would be her father, for then she would not be afraid, and, perhaps, Alma would be at peace, *but would I like his rules? Would I really want to give up my freedom?—No, not really.*

Milda was curious about family, and Helga was more than glad to tell as much as she wanted to know. When encouraged, Helga spun stories about their life in Kurzeme. She described how her father rode around on Sundays to different small country churches, preaching and, at least once-a-month took the whole family along, telling how those Sundays would turn into festivals, with tables full of food and games for the children. "The country people admired him and all of us," she boasted, "because father was also a good farmer." They had twelve brown cows, "the kind that give milk with lots of cream on the top, and a flock of sheep, "so our Oma would have enough wool because she was a knitter. We had pigs and hens, and a bunch of other critters—chickens, rabbits, cats, dogs, and mice. And I could tell you stories about them also. I hated the geese. Yes, and horses. Papa planned to build large barns and fence in the pastures so I wouldn't have to be a herd anymore.

"Oh, my Papa had big plans for us all, and whatever he did turned out well. We had the tallest and best rye, wheat, and oats because he used fertilizers," she rattled on as if she had memorized the speech or heard it from him so often that she knew every word by heart. "Yes, we would have been rich and happy in our land if the communists hadn't ruined everything and. . ."

Milda imagined Mr. Gramzda as her father, galloping, riding through storms over green meadows or driving in chariots, with her leaning against his side safe and happy. "But it was not meant to be," Helga was saying. "The communists came and there was the war. The day we escaped—October 8, 1944—the Germans took all the grain they could, shot the pigs and cows, and took our Sunday horse and, lucky for us, left the mare and the colt. They pulled us in our big wagon when we fled. She actually saved our lives, and here is how it happened. By the time we reached the Lithuanian border behind us was a long line of refugees, many we knew. Right behind us was the mayor of our town, sitting like a lord in his fancy wagon pulled by his stallion, who was in love with our mare and would let no other horses come between them. Papa liked to tell this love story. He said it was like riding in fiery chariot to heaven. They pulled us right through a battle where the bombs fell, and then through Memel that was packed with refugees. But there the love horses were separated, and we don't know how it happened. We had to stop at the harbor where a ferry was taking tanks across to *Kurishe Nehrung.* The mayor's chariot got on, but our wagon was pushed aside until Papa gave them honey and bacon. Then they let Mamma and us girls to cross over on a lifeboat, but Papa and Jānis stayed behind. It was night. I remember how bright the stars were and how cold it was when our feet broke through patches of thin ice.

On the other side, we crawled behind a wood pile. Mamma wrapped a blanket around us, and we slept. In the morning sirens blasted, and we jumped up and crawled out. Oh lord, were we scared. We looking for Papa, but he wasn't there. The shore was lined with stunned fish, their silver bellies shining like mirrors. A way up were soldiers looking out of their trenches, but on the other side a bomb fell. It whisled and exploded, and so it went all day, and the ferries carried the fleeing Germans but not our wagon.

Meanwhile, we were hungry. Mamma said she could fry the fish, but where and how. Then, higher up, we saw a line of summer cottages and went there. They were empty, but in the gardens were vegetables. We went inside. The kitchen was stacked with dishes and things. Vizma picked up a bucket and went down to the shore for fish. Aija and I pulled up potatoes, onions and whatever else was there, and Mamma started cooking soup. Vizma brought up the fish, cleaned them, and Mamma put a big one in the soup. The smell brought soldiers to our door. We gave each a bowl, but more were coming up. All day Mamma cooked fish soup, and I with Vizma carried buckets full to the trenches. Just so you know, Mamma can make the best soups with whatever is on hand. I don't know how she does it, but on our long trip, we always had soup, so we never starved like other people. Visma is also good with cooking, and I'm learning. Anyway, so it went until the sun started sliding down into the sea.

Yes, also just over the dunes, we saw a white beach like a ribbon winding along the shore. It was beautiful, with the blue sea lapping against the white sand. When Mamma came looking for us, she could not take her eyes off the waters, at the moment turning golden from the sunbeams. She said that she had always wanted to see this famous resort, but Papa never had time for rest. It took a world war to make a wish come true, she said. We made her sit down and rest. She breathed heavily. Another blast reminded us that we were in a war zone, and we hurried back to see if Papa and our wagon would be on our side, but it wasn't. An important looking officer or something was standing where the ferry came in. Vizma walked up to him smiling and flirting and promised to make pancakes if he would only help our wagon get across. I saw her put her arms around him and give him a kiss. The wagon with Jānis and Papa and our horses arrived on the next ferry. Vizma still feels guilty about not making the pancakes. But night was coming and the horses stampeded and neighed like mad. We climbed the wagon, and off we were! We were on the *Kurishe Nehrung*. It's about a hundred kilometer strip of dunes. The winds blow, shifting the sand, so there are no sure roads. It took two days to plough through before we reached Germany. During the whole flight we heard bombs whistling and exploding, driving the horses crazy, but they were far behind us. One night, at a turn, the horses jumped over another refugee cart and gallopped until Papa stopped them and went back to see what happened. No one was hurt, but a man came at him with a knife. Lucky for him, a truck was coming down the slope. The headights blinded the man with the knife, and Papa escaped. We rode on until morning dawned. We rode into Germany with the rising sun. At the end of the straight we were stopped and directed toward a muddy field. It was full of more refugees. Our Minna gave out a loud neigh and another answered. The lovers, so we called them, were again together, kissing and licking each other.

We traveled on, I don't know for how long and how many kilometers—stopping at farms and sleeping in hay barns, gleaning the fields for cabbages and potatoes and cooking them like Gypsies over fires. And so it went until we—with a carevan of refugees behind us, because we were up front leading the way—were again ordered on to a side road leading to muddy field. There the Germans took our horses and wagon with everything in it."

"Then what happened?"

"Papa saw a farm, and we went there. He offered to help with clearing the fields, and, leaving us behind, went back to speak to the camp leader. He found out that the adults would be put to work and the children in special camps, unless they had a place to go. So Papa wrote names and addresses on slips of paper and passed them around. The people showed them to the guards and walked out of the camp. Where they ended up, we don't know. Our family stayed with the farmer until his sugar beets were dug up. A pitchfork went through Vizma's middle finger and for a long time she could not use her hand, so our brother took over. I had to walk behind a ploughman and pick grub worms from the ground. Bucket after bucket. Brrr. . . It still gives me the creeps and nightmares. But by end of November, all was clear and we were out of there and went on until the war ended and Americans came in. And so—here we are!" Helga finished. „There is much more to tell but this is enough and I'm tired."

"Yes, so it was," Milda said softly. "So your father was the savior of many people, quite like Moses."

"Yes. But he says there is more to do."

*

Some time later on, when supping with the Gramzda family and listening to the preacher's version of the escape, Milda blurted out: "Why, oh why, did God allow evil people to destroy our lives and dreams?"

"Perhaps we loved our land and our dreams more than we loved Him," he said, coming to God's defense. "Our people sang and danced and forgot to praise God and thank Him for giving us freedom. Perhaps He is scattering us into the world to teach us or punish us—or show us the wonders of His world that He loved and for which He gave His Son."

"But why?"

"Don't ask. I don't know. The Lord gives and takes away. Let us bless His name."

"But it is hard."

"Yes, so it is. Still we must seek the Lord while He may be found, for the time will come. . ."

"Oh, please, don't say it! Are we also going to lose God?"

"No, He promised to be with us and give us strength and courage. So, my dear, take heart and live."

In time Milda learned the sound of his footsteps coming up the stairs, and then she relaxed as when she was little and her father came home. She noticed that she slept peacefully the whole night through, knowing that he was next door. But he was busy. In daytime, as he by chance passed her, he didn't slow down, barely smiled, said a short, kind word and was gone.

"He works for God," Helga explained.

*

Next time Milda talked to Helga, she told her about her first Christmas Eve in Esslingen, when Alma had abandoned her and how she had gone with the other families to their church and how good it was. "I recognized all of you, especially Vizma, who had played the harpsichord, and even you impressed me with your recitation of Poruks's *Christmas Eve,* but it was your father who told the Christmas story like I never heard it before, like it was the latest news. And when he described the field where the angels came down and sang to the shepherds, I guessed he was really remembering his own fields and home. I wondered where those fields were, thinking about my aunt and uncle and wondering what was happening to them and my cousins."

"But Papa doesn't look back often. Right now he is worried about what will happen to people when these DP camps close. He says he has no time to moan and mourn and must not slumber or sleep. He and his brothers must lead the people on. He hopes to America, but we won't go anywhere, he tells us, until at least all our church members of this and other camps are settled. So, I guess, we'll be the last to leave this town."

"Yes, I wonder where we shall go, my Aunt and I," Milda said. "There is no return home because of communists."

"And even if we would try to go back," Helga went on, "they would not let us go to our homes but put us on cattle trains and send us off to

Siberia. That's what all the grown-ups talk about now. They talk late into the night, drinking cups of tea. They think we are asleep and don't hear anything, but we hear it all. They are afraid that we might be forced to go back and that parents and children would be separated, put in work camps and orphanages. But I tell you, my brothers and sisters would hide and run away. We would take care of our parents too, and the Lord will guide as like He always has."

"Amen to that. You would not want to be made orphans like my aunt and I. All alone in the world."

"No, and that is why we want to escape to America and help you too. You could come with us."

"Well! Thank you."

*

As the Gramzdas settled in and assumed their daily patterns of life, Milda felt at ease with everybody but was especially drawn to Mrs. Gramzda, a quiet, sad woman, who panted as she climbed up the stairs. Often she would carry her bags up the stairs, but they spoke little, yet something deep and honest held them at close range, like some mysterious magnet. And when Mrs. Gramzda looked at her with her gray, piercing eyes, Milda felt her carefully contrived protective halo of aloofness break and disintegrate. She sensed right away that this woman had no time or use either for small talk or false airs. Too many children tugged at her, but she did not complain and lament. Instead, she insisted that life was beautiful and each day was a gift.

Milda knew that the woman sought out her soul, while she, in turn, simply wanted to touch her hand but was afraid. She was afraid that by touching Mrs. Gramzda she would touch her own vanished mother and lose the independence she had worked so hard to establish. In the face of this strange woman's powerful maternity, she would be nothing but a sad orphan. And so, as the souls' magnets operated by themselves, Milda held back. She was glad they moved in very different circles, their paths coming together only on the stairs and in the hallway. Milda hardly ever saw her or the preacher at the theater and at concerts. She did see them at the solemn assemblies. Then they listened calmly to whatever authoritative voice filled the auditorium, their faces sad and blank, like so many others. Milda, observing the audience, as she stood next to Kārlis Arājs, would rest her eyes on her neighbor's face and wonder how she felt and what she was thinking and remembering. When she learned that they had a common first name, she believed that destiny had brought them together. On May eleven was their name day, which they agreed to celebrate together. Mrs. Gramzda would bake something special, and Milda would come with a bouquet of lily-of-the valley she had picked, and they would share cups of tea and talk heart to heart. But Milda did not mention the man with one arm.

Impressing Americans

But meanwhile, toward the end of spring 1947, as Lido re-shuffled, the whole DP community was also being disturbed, shuffled, worked upon. Suddenly Americans seemed to be everywhere—inside the camp, at concerts, churches, schools, patriotic assemblies. The leaders honored all men in uniform and reserved front row seats for them. Frequently, without even a day's notice, Milda had to be ready, in her national costume, to present flowers and make short speeches of welcome. Once she was prompted to greet General Dwight Eisenhower, but he cancelled out. Instead, came some diplomat with a reporter and a photographer. Milda smiled charmingly and said her piece, while the photographer circled around, angling her with his camera.

Afterwards, one of the community leaders complemented her, saying that she was a fine representative and that on her behavior might depend Americans' attitude toward the Latvian refugees. She was told that in the United States, Congress is debating the DP question, trying to decide what to do with East European refugees and where to place them, since they would not return to their home countries. "You may well be the golden key, which, if turned, properly, might open the doors to America," one of the self-appointed diplomats laid it out. Milda smiled.

She did not know what Congress was and how it debated but, unwilling to show her ignorance, she asked no questions. She only knew that a great responsibility was put upon her and that she had to cram into her head new words and strange concepts. She wondered why Americans wrote so many words only in capital letters: CARE, MP, UN, NATO, and another MP that meant Marshal Plan. UNRRA (United Nations Refugee Relief Administration), to the dismay of all, gave way to IRO (International Relief Organization), yet people noticed no significant changes. Lastly came EQ = Emigrant Quotas, which inspired imagination and gave weight to the whole concept of THE FUTURE. When she questioned the meaning of EQ, an official explained that only a certain number of people would be qualified to emigrate to the United States of America, while others may be scattered all over the world, perhaps to dark continents and unimaginable climates. Milda saw herself lost in some deep jungle or alone and shipwrecked on an uninhibited island. Noticing her alarmed expression, the official assured her that there would be no reason for her to fear. She certainly would be allowed to immigrate into USA. The agent further stated that people who applied would be carefully screened, not only for their physical flaws but also for their moral and political attitudes, since the Latvians had technically stood against the Allies, especially Russia. They pointed out that a Latvian division had fought on the side of the Germans—as if everybody did not know that! Therefore, the man explained, veterans living in the American Zone could not be allowed into the USA, no matter how much some argued that they were not for the Germans as much as they had been—and still were—against Russians. "Your internal affairs and political attitudes are not clear to us, and we don't want any trouble in America," he told Milda.

"But, you Americans don't understand Communism," a frustrated translator broke in and turned to Milda: "So it is our duty to patiently educate them, and you, Miss Bērziņa, must tell them what it was like living under communists and what happened to our people, even your parents. Then ask them, *What would you do?* and see what they say." Afterwards the diplomat/translator prompted Milda to be direct and unafraid. She promised to do her best.

Thus, excited, frustrated, and bewildered, the DP leaders of various political shades and stripes admonished everybody, especially the most successful students who were learning English to clear the name of Latvia and whenever possible explain communism to the Americans. In that spirit, when the schools re-opened in September, the history teachers became politically aggressive and gave out imperatives: "Dear students, wherever you may be or wherever you may go, you must tell them that Latvia was a free and independent democratic republic until *communist Russia broke the Non-aggression Pact, of 1939*, and only a year later invaded our country and performed cruel acts of genocide against the population." Milda's history teacher wrote the statement on the blackboard and made the students copy it in their notebooks. Then he laid the chalk down and said, "Yes, the Russian Bear swallowed us, and I hope he will choke soon." The class listened, still copying the long sentence. "America," the teacher continued in his formal voice, standing straight and looking over the bowed heads, "must never recognize Latvia as part of Russia. . . . That is most crucial. . . And you must never recognize it either," he added, "no matter where you may emigrate and no matter how long the current situation of uncertainty persists. Always remember that some day Latvia *will* be free! You *must* teach that to your children—even though you are still far from being fathers and mothers."

New Parts to Play for Milda and Alma

Mercifully, at the beginning of November, auditions began for the annual school Christmas play *Maija un Paija* by Anna Brigadere. This is another dramatization of a folk tale, where the forces of good and evil war against each other. In the end, goodness wins and is rewarded, while evil is punished. Maija symbolizes diligence and goodness, while *Paija* is mean, overindulged, lazy, and selfish.

Maija is an orphan whom her mean stepmother overworks by making her do the hardest chores. Among them, she is forced to spin flax and draw water from a deep well. Blessed by good spirits and Laima, the goddess of fortune, all Maija does turns out well. This makes Paija jealous. To cause trouble, she tricks Maija into making mistakes, but no matter what, Maija does not falter and remains loving and pure. At last the evil spirits, which help Paija, snatch away Maija's spindle and throw it into the well. As Maija leans over to reclaim it, she is bewitched by voices luring her to follow the spindle. She falls into the well. Seeing that, Paija is glad and dances with her evil spirits. Meanwhile, Maija has reached the underworld. Singing she walks through the darkness, helping everyone along the way: she picks apples off a heavily-loaded tree; she pulls large loaves of bread out of the oven; she frees a tree and a brook from evil spells and, at the end of her journey, emerges covered with gold. Seeing her stepsister again victorious, Paija also dives into the well, but, as she goes through the underworld, she helps no one and comes out covered with pitch. Everyone shuns her, except Maija, who wants to save her. She calls upon Laima, who has transformed herself from an old woman into a splendid heavenly being visible only to Maija, as she prays for help, assuring the goddess that Paija wants to be saved and has promised to turn from a bad to a good girl. However, for Laima, promises are not enough. Paija must walk the path of thorns for nine days and learn the meaning of suffering, goodness, and love. The play ends as the people sing praises to Maija, while Paija departs on her path of repentance.

Milda won the part of *Maija* and, very excited, immersed herself into her character of high ideals. Before rehearsals would begin, all were expected to know their lines. Milda studied them as she walked back and forth to school, as she did her chores, and at night before she fell asleep. Not able to work with the real cast, she secretly assigned roles to the people who lived around her, thinking that she could then learn the lines faster and better. Thus, Mrs. Gramzda became *Laima* and Aunt Alma—the stepmother, for throughout the golden autumn months Alma hardly paid any attention to her. She was often away, never telling where she was going, and when she showed up, she was short-tempered and jealous of Milda for even looking at the doors across the hall. "You don't belong there, and don't hang around like a beggar. Have some pride!" she scolded, holding out a wad of printed pages of a new play. "I need your help," she said, waving the script around, but Milda, as if protecting herself, leaned back squinting: *I'm the abused orphan, who is unjustly attacked for being kind to all the helpless creatures in the woods and under the ground. My stepmother blocks my way and forbids me to go where the sun shines and the piano plays. . .* "What are you smirking about?" Alma shouted. "I need you to help me learn the lines and fast!"

"I have my own lines to memorize," Milda said firmly.

"I don't care. You do as I say or else. . ."

"What?"

"What?—I can get you thrown off the stage, where you love to twirl and shine and pretend you're a real actress."

"You wouldn't dare!"

"Try me!" she said, staring down, as she replaced Milda's script with her own.

Alma is also a Maija—the heroine of Rainis's tragedy *Mīla stiprāka par nāvi* (Love is stronger than death). The tragedy is based on the true story about a real and beautiful Latvian virgin named Maija of Turaida. The setting is in Vidzeme, the former Livonia, in the castle of Turaida, a 14th century brick structure, built by the Teutonic knights. It sits high on a mountain above the valley of the River Gauja. The castle is fortified by high walls. Paths lead down into to the gardens and the fields and the valley, made fertile by a spring that flows through a cave and on, down into the treacherous Gauja. Beyond that, on the next hill, sits the town Sigulda with its inns and markets. Milda knows the tragic story:

Maija, known as the Turaidas Roze, *frequents the town and is admired as the loveliest of maidens, though envied by some women. Jakubovskis, a temperamental and superstitious soldier of the allied Polish regiment, desires her special favors, but Maija ignores him. She loves the castle's gardener Viktors Heils, whom she meets secretly down inside the cave. There they make their wedding plans and dream of future happiness. At one time, Viktors gives Maija a red shawl as a token of their fiery love. The gift frightens her, because instead of love she sees blood in the delicate threads. Frightened, she pleads with Viktors, begging him to marry her right away, even though he is not rich enough to support her as wife. She assures him that they will be happy, that their love makes them rich. Reluctantly he agrees and soon leaves the castle in order to make their wedding arrangements. But, unbeknown to both, in the shadows lurks Jakubovskis, burning with jealousy and lust. He overhears the plans and hastens to cross them.*

In the next act, Jakubovskis bribes his foot soldier who, in turn, employs Maija's attendant, a sly girl who is also in love with Viktors, to lure Maija into the cave. The girl gives Maija Jakubovskis's forged note, in which he asks her to meet him in the cave. Believing the note to be from Viktors, Maija, wearing the red shawl, goes to the cave. She enters cautiously, but, instead of finding Viktors, she is confronted by Jakubovskis and his accomplices. Driven by uncontrollable passion, he tries to seduce Maija. She resists him with all her might. When he does not leave her alone, she offers him her shawl, telling him that it is endowed with magic which will stop the strike of any sword because it has soaked up so much blood that it cannot take any more. He is skeptical but tempted and, being a soldier who would like to own such a magic weapon, takes the shawl. Urged by his superstitious underling, he agrees to test the shawl's power. Maija wraps it around her neck, then tells him to prepare to strike. However, she tells him, that for the magic to work, she first must be left alone so that she can invoke the right spirits. Reluctantly he steps out of the cave. Left alone, she says her farewell to life.

Milda reads the instructions: "*With uplifted arms, turning to the cave's opening, then to the brook.* Take it from here!" she says, and Alma begins working through the lines:

"*You, beautiful light of day! You, the high, white, all-seeing sun! At this moment I still see your divine brightness, but soon I shall go into eternity and behold another, paler light! I recall the immeasurable happiness I have enjoyed, while you allowed me to feel the brilliance of eternal love and the rapture that pulled me into that bright world!*" Alma pauses and wipes away an onslaught of tears. Milda is impatient and helps out: "*Good Spirits. . .*"

Alma interrupts, "Yes, I know!. . . *Good Spirits, you sent me forth into this world, so that in one moonlit night I would glide over a thousand empty fields and make them bloom with beautiful flowers that never wilt. Now I am going back to you so that I may inspire more people to experience the excitement of victorious and glorious love! . . . I go so that the eternal fountain of goodness may never run dry. . . . Oh, lovely, sparkling brook, don't ever cease to flow! Whisper forever about love that is as unceasing as your flow! Tell future generations about my suffering and my victory! Say the last farewell to my lover. Tell him not to mourn for me. Tell him so he would know that love is stronger than death, so that every one would know that love is stronger*

*than death, and that there is no other power greater than love that can
save the world.*

"All right," Milda says, "but you need to be more convincing."
She ignores Alma's resurgence of tears and summarizes: *"Impatient
Jakobovskis re-enters the cave and tells Maija to stop mumbling. He
draws his sword and strikes, killing her."*

Alma says nothing and stares intensely at her niece. "This is very
difficult for me," she stammers, "not only because the story is true, but
because the gardener's name is Viktors. . . Oh, where is he now?" she
cries, dramatically probing the sky. "I don't hear a word, not a sound."
She speaks leaning out of the window, looking up to some fleeting
cloud, "You see, I am not like Maija, the lovely Rose of Turaida. I have
not kept my love pure. I don't choose death rather than a life without
love." Abruptly, accusingly she turns and faces Milda, "It was and still
is because of you," she blurts out. "What would have become of you if
I had killed myself?"

Milda does not respond. "Let's go on with the play! I don't have
time for soul searching now." Again she takes on all the other parts
and tells Alma to concentrate on Maija's lines. She rises and paces the
narrow confines of their room. She listens and drills, nervous about her
own play. In her mind she becomes the mean stepmother of *Maija and
Paija*. She turns Alma into the selfish Paija, who pushes innocent Maija
into the well. She imagines her pushing hard, sadistically, enjoying the
torment and the tears. Milda reads: *"Jakubovskis (very angry): What is
it? Are you playing tricks with me? It sounds like you're reciting some
gibberish. Put your head down so I can strike and see if you've told me
the truth or not! Maija (proud and determined): . Please. . . go on!"*

Alma: *"Strike! Love is stronger than death!"*

"Good," Milda says. "You sound sincere."

"Of course I sound sincere! I only wish I could believe it."

"Aunty, please stay with the text! Let's go back to the beginning," Milda commands, and reluctantly Alma complies. Hours later they put the script away. "You still have a lot of work ahead of you, but don't count on me to help you," Milda tells her, reaching for her overcoat. Leaving Alma behind, she rushes out the door to her own rehearsal.

Every day Alma, angry at her niece, stubbornly practiced her lines in front of the small wall mirror, which reflected only the head and neck, as if they were already severed. At last, near the opening night, exhausted, staring into the glass, she shouted that she did not like the play. "I think Maija's last speech to the brook is much too long and unreal. Her submission to the irrational sword is extremely stupid. Of all the characters I've impersonated, I hate this one the most. Innocence! Ha! Who is ever innocent? Not even a baby, not even you! Don't your preachers tell you that we're all born in sin and will die in sin? Go to hell, right?"

"Yes, I guess so. So it is written in the Bible," Milda says calmly.

"Well! You see? So what's Rainis doing with us? He's worse than all the preachers put together with his absolute morality and unreal innocence. Besides, Maija was never that innocent. Maybe her gardener was, but he's also dense, clumsy, not understanding either men or women. The whole drama is a bluff."

"Still, it sounds to me like you enjoy this play even more than *Faust*. You do know it all by heart and it will touch many hearts. You will be splendid."

"Yes," Alma took the compliment and smiled. "I know all the lines, but I cannot be splendid because I don't believe them. There is a song I heard the Americans sing:

What is this thing called love? I don't believe love is stronger than death. Death is the strongest. It rules the world. At one time or other, we all submit, and when we do, it's the end."

"Not so, the preachers. . ."

"The preachers preach lies. Nothing is after death. When I die my love dies also, and death wins over any kind of love or hate. We love only as long as we live and not a second more. Love in the past tense is not love. When Maija's head is cut off, so is any possibility of love. She'll never go to those other realms she's imagining. She'll never prepare the way for anyone. She'll prove nothing. What do you think?" Alma faced Milda with eyes of fire that slowly flooded. She let the tears fall, then fell on her bed and sobbed. "If I killed myself, would my Viktors even know it? Would it matter? Ah, but my love is not innocent, it never was.—Oh, the more I think about it the more I hate this play!" She sat up and wiped her eyes with angry gestures, like Lady Macbeth, rubbing her hands.

"Oh, stop thinking and just act! Or do you like to torture me? Are you really talking to me between the lines? If so, what are you saying?" Milda rose challenging.

"If you don't understand, I'm not going to spell it all out for you. You're a big girl. You've certainly been acting big, reversing the roles, huh?"

"Please. . . Let me go. I have things to do. I also have a role to play, but no one is helping me."

"There you go judging and accusing me again!"

"No, I'm only telling you that I have to go and not be late for *my* rehearsal."

"Yes, sure. . . Oh, go! Get out!" Alma said and fell back and buried her head in her pillow.

Milda left the room.

*

Love is Stronger than Death premiered on the first Saturday in December and was staged throughout the month on every Saturday.

Alma was magnificent onstage but moody offstage. When her mood was good, she helped Milda with her lines and gave her tips for acting the part. This drew them together, and by the time *Maija un Paija* appeared on stage, on the Christmas Eve matinee, the two stage Maijas were almost inseparable. Milda was surprised that Alma did not seem jealous, as she had been a year ago, when Milda was in *The Golden Steed.* Now she promised to stay with her throughout the premier performance and the ball that followed. They also agreed to go to church together for the midnight service.

"Anything you want, my dear," Alma said. "I want you to be happy."

But when the play was finished, Milda was in no mood for dancing. She took off her make-up and wig and, slipping into her overcoat, caught Alma at the door. With arms full of flowers, they went out into the cold, crisp night. Heads tucked inside their collars, they walked against the wind, when, looking up they saw a man standing at the gate. Milda cried out and held onto Alma's arm. The man wore a long army coat and a beat-up hat above an unshaven, pale face. With one bare hand he smoked the butt of a cigarette. The other arm was not there. The empty sleeve was tucked inside his coat pocket.

"What. . . what are you doing here?" Milda stammered, feeling the blood run down to her shoes. She stared at him, but his face seemed strange, yet all the familiar features were there. She wanted to reach out, invite him to come along where there was warmth, where he could get a bowl of soup, but no words crossed her lips. She stood as if glued to the pavement. She wondered what had happened since she saw him last at the Mountain Colony. Had he been away? She had not seen him, had heard nothing about him. She wanted to know why he was wearing his old clothes, when the last time she saw him he was well dressed, clean-shaven, and very handsome. What was the matter? Was he a bum drunk? Had he been kicked out of the camp or what?

"Go away, beat it!" she heard Alma say. "We have nothing to give you. Why don't you go there—up to the mountain, just follow the narrow streets, they'll take you there. That's where the used-up soldiers live." She softened a bit and said, "They will take you in. Where do you come from?"

"Hell," he said and turned and began his shuffle toward the mountain, which loomed like a black wall behind the old town's spires.

"What's the matter?" Alma asked, taking her hand. "You look like you've seen a ghost."

"I have, and I don't want to go anywhere."

*

And so, on that Christmas Eve, they stayed in their room. They ate the food Milda had prepared and drank a bottle of hot red wine that quickly went to their heads. Hours later, they heard the Baptists leave for church. All became very quiet, and in that quiet Milda told Alma about the armless soldier that had come from hell exactly a year ago, as if he had decided to keep an annual rendezvous with her.

"But I know that he was living in the Mountain Colony. We took food up there and. . ." She stopped before telling Alma that he had touched her as if putting a stamp on her, as if marking his territory.

"And then what?" Alma asked.

"N-nothing," Milda stammered, not telling that he seemed to have vanished only to appear again, like a ghost to frighten her—just when happily she had erased his image from her mind. "What does he want? Who is he? What hell do you suppose he has come from?" Milda asked, rising and pacing between the door and the window.

"The prison camps, of course. Could be from Belgium. I've heard terrible things about the camp where German prisoners are sent to starve. You do know that to the Allies generally treat Latvians as if they were Germans—Nazis, Fascists—and try to prove otherwise! I heard how the prisoners are so starved that they eat grass and drink rain or snow."

"Oh, God! Still, that man gives me the creeps down to the marrow of my last bone. First this apparition on Christmas Eve, then a strange transformation, and now back down the ladder like in a board game. And somehow I'm an object, a target, something he's watching and stalking."

"Symbols," Alma said. "You are the symbol of pure Latvia, and he is the warrior, the Bearslayer, whose ear has been cut off. You are expected to mend it, don't you see?"

"Ah, stop that nonsense! You are too full of Rainis and the theater. No one thinks that deeply. He is just a man who's been through hell and has come to find a place for himself but cannot fit in, cannot accept the fact that we lost the war and his arm was cut off for nothing."

"That's what wars do to you. There are losers and there are winners, but in the end everybody loses and no one wins."

Milda was shaking and Alma gave her more hot wine, which she drank quickly, thirstily. In the twilight zone of her mind, she felt Alma undressing her and lying down beside her. In the morning they woke up in each other's arms and stretched slowly, lazily, their heads hurting. It was Christmas. It turned out to be a gray, drab day with nowhere to go, nothing to do. Across the dark hallway, the Baptists were celebrating. Vizma played *Joy to the world. . .*

1948

A Letter from Zelda

Shortly after New Year, like an unexpected bolt of lightning, a black-edged letter arrived from Zelda. It hit Milda like an arrow, right through the heart. The envelope was dirty, the ink smudged. It had traveled over a month and been opened and sealed by strange hands several times. The layers of glue told a fearsome tale, as did that black rim.

With trembling hands she ripped at the black edge. She pulled out a thin graph paper torn from an arithmetic notebook and read the inky words written as if by a ghost:

I must tell you the sad news. (Zelda's handwriting was so grown up!) *Papa died there, and Mamma is in the red brick asylum. Her window has iron bars, and I cannot go there. I live with Aunt M. We are all healthy and very happy in our free land. I hope you are also happy, but how could you be when you are away from our homeland? Don't forget me. I cannot write more because our old uncle gets very angry when I use his ink. I must obey him always. I weep for our Papa and Mamma and kiss you. Your Z.*

The news hurt unbearably. Milda could feel the giant points of the Iron curtain bars pressing down, deep into her heart and conscience. "I locked Zelda up," she sobbed in her pillow. She understood all that Zelda had *not* written because Stalin ruled mightily. "I will have to burn in hell for cheating my sister."

She saw again the pile of discs rolling next to the checkerboard on Zelda's side and remembered every move of her cruel game.

Her cramped attic room was cold, and she was famished, but the idea of lighting the old pot-belly and cooking a gray portion of oatmeal, the only staple that never seemed to run out, nauseated her. She made herself get up and do something. She washed her face, put on her wool skirt and sweater and went across the hall. She knocked on #1, the Gramzdas' kitchen door. All was quiet behind it. It was Saturday. She knew the children would be gone to their various morning activities. Reverend Gramzda was not home either; he had gone to some other DP camp to hold Sunday morning service and would not be back until Monday. That was good, for she only wanted to talk to Mrs. Gramzda; she desperately needed to borrow a mother, if only for one stealthy hour.

The door opened. She stepped quickly over the threshold and without a word held out the letter. In one glance Mrs. Gramzda read its full content. She said that she, too, had received a note from home lately. "Something must be happening there now," she said, her eyes wide open. She invited Milda inside and closed the door. She urged her to sit down in the dining nook off the kitchen and put a kettle on the stove. She cut bread and set out sausage, jam, and butter. Milda sat silently and watched. She took in the privileges of a large family: there was plenty of food, a stove with gas burners, running water, full shelves, an array of dishes, and—space. Oh, she, too, would have a large family! She, too, would have such a neat little nook!

Mrs. Gramzda poured the tea and then sat down across from her guest, insisting that she help herself and eat all she wanted. She also poured herself a cup of tea, which she sipped slowly. Used to giving other preference, she nibbled at the food, all the while watching her beautiful neighbor eat, drink, and slowly relax. She saw her eyes flood and blink as they repeatedly turned to the letter, which lay between them, filled with summaries of unbearable tragedies, mutely accusing and crying out. After a while, Milda folded it up and put it in her pocket, and then she began to talk. She told the story about her family, her father's deportation, her mother's nervous breakdown, and finally confessed her dishonesty in losing the game of checkers. She said that she was constantly being tormented by her guilt. "I am free, but I locked up my sister," she cried with tears flowing down her face, her hands covering her eyes and wiping her nose.

"All our people carry this burden of guilt," the elder said, rather awkwardly, groping for the rights words so she would not minimize the girl's unique, personal grief with general phrases. She was fully aware that this was the girl's hour of need and that out of this great need, the proud girl had come to her. To her and no one else. She was also aware that she was not the kind of a woman who pulled people to her bosom;

neither was she one to cry and lament, certainly not in front of others. So quietly she began to speak her mind, letting the words come as they might and hoped that they would address the girl's oppressive, festering guilt, which like an imbedded sliver infected her whole being. She had to somehow pull that sliver out. She knew that only then this beauty, whom she had observed for a long time, could be free and truly beautiful. She, therefore, had to allow her tweezer words their sharp points.

"We all have suffered more or less the same fate," the woman spoke, "but maybe we are too conceited in thinking that we are uniquely responsible for everything and that by much talk we could change things. No. . . . We are not that mighty. A much greater hand, I believe, is ruling over us and has set us here to live this way and no other. Perhaps we had very little to do with what happened to us. At any rate, nothing can be done about it; at the same time we cannot allow ourselves to turn into pillars of salt like Lot's wife. We cannot help ourselves, nor those on the other side by walking with our heads turned backwards."

"But why were we saved and not the others?"

"I don't know, and it is not for me to ask questions that have no answers. Do you know the story about Joseph and his brothers?

"Yes, of course."

"Well, he did not end in the pit. He was also in exile. He lived through it in order to save his brothers and his people. Perhaps it will be like that with us. Perhaps one day we will be able to help those we left behind. We don't know any of this. Or—perhaps they will save us. It could be that those who are now struggling on the other side will be greater than we. We don't know these things."

"But what must I do? What must we do?"

"First of all, you must go on living and be strong. Next, you must forgive yourself and honor your parents and sister in living a good life, not in sorrowing. Remember, you are not alone and perhaps not as unique as you may imagine, though you are exceptionally beautiful.

Beauty is also a gift. It was laid in your cradle and with it you must honor the Giver of all good things," she said smiling gently, sadly.

Still, Milda turned her face down as if she were scolded, but Mrs. Gramzda touched her hand and gave it a squeeze that conveyed deep sympathy but not pity. "The strong and the beautiful actually have a very hard lot in life. From them so much is expected, and certainly I see our DP world expects great things from you. My advice is don't let it abuse you. And don't abuse yourself. Our Lord says in His Holy Word that God does not put on us greater burdens than we can bear, so let's not surpass God and pile burdens upon ourselves."

The preacher's wife paused, aware that she now had the pulpit. She saw Milda sit uncomfortably at the mention of the Bible and God, and so she stopped. She poured out more tea and then began to tell her story to show that when it came to the ravages of war and losing relatives, she had suffered her share. Her brother, so she had learned lately, had died at sea. He was a captain on a passenger ship, sailing from the Baltic to the North Sea. It had been torpedoed at the end of the war. While still in Latvia, she had lost her two sons, the oldest and the youngest. The first was drafted into the Latvian army. Since their escape, they had lost contact, and she did not know whether he was dead or alive. Her baby had died of diphtheria right after Christmas—their last at home—when the whole family was celebrating together, not knowing it would be the last time. "How were we to guess that death would be invading our house just when we were so happy, so enjoying the baby's words and all the funny things he did?"

She brushed her tears away and, adjusting her voice, went on. Her only sister, who with her family lived in Riga, had lost her five-year-old firstborn son only three years earlier also from diphtheria. It so devastated the mother, pregnant at the time, that she—malnourished during the war as all city folks—died two years later of leukemia. She left her year-old baby and her four year-old daughter.

"But I know it was grief that killed her. And, yes, hunger. It was during the German occupation. They had nothing to eat in the cities and no medicine and coal wherewith to heat their apartments. Roads were blocked, so we could not take food to them. You must remember how bitterly cold those winters of occupations were—one more terrible than the next. We could not even cry like normal people because the whole country was crying."

"Yes, I know. I remember that. I remember Mother crying all the time."

"So after my sister died, her husband brought the children to us. It was not long before he found a good wife, a good Christian and member of the Baptist church in the next county. She was pretty and kind and loved children, and so our sweet orphans left us. They went to live on the farm with the new wife's family. Her parents had been deported in '41, so they needed a man around the house. For the next three years we were close and helped each other—until October '44. They escaped about the same time we did. How we found each other, only God knows, but they lived here for a while and were among the first families to leave for America. Do you remember the Ābeles?"

"Yes, yes, of course! Little Zenta and Andris? Oh, what a small world this is!" Milda lightened up, and they talked more about the family. "Reverend Ābele is in America and works for the Baptist World Alliance; he is on the receiving end of the forms my husband sends off to America."

"Oh."

But Mrs. Gramzda did not catch the surprising tone of *oh*. She went on with her story: They, her family, had escaped quickly, in two hours time, with their horses and an oversized wagon full of themselves and whatever they could carry out of the house teaming with soldiers. "We escaped literally through fire and water, and not a day too soon nor too late. At the Lithuanian border we watched how Liepāja was being bombed, scared to death for my parents and all our people. The whole sky seemed to be burning, while we sat in our open wagon, in a line of refugees watching. I remember how bright the stars were on that clear crisp night, and I said to my children, 'Now we have only what we are.' We sat very still, not daring even to cry, and then my husband, standing up on the wagon, prayed to God so all could hear. Miraculously, the bombing stopped. The night seemed to turn darker, the silence more eerie, and only then the whole truth came over me: we were homeless and without a country. We had left our house and barns, our cattle and our fields and the many dreams needed to build a life. All the familiar places of our childhood and youth, as well as our flourishing country churches that my husband served we had left behind. My husband had tried to calm us, saying that we'll come back as soon as the dangers of the war are over, but then, on that night, I knew we would never go back. We would never see our country again, not the way we left it. We knew that it would be all torn up. So. Yes, all we had was what was inside us. We were pulled up, but the roots were still stuck in the ground, and that hurt, hurt terribly." She stopped talking, stopped looking out the window. "Please excuse me," she said. "My heart is heavy as I wait for news from my parents every day."

"But how can you hold out? How can you be so calm?"

"Oh, my dear girl, what choice do I have but to hold out and to uphold? Who would pick me up if I fell? Besides, I do have a bad heart and must be careful."

"How can you help being bitter?" Milda asked, comparing her to Alma's many battles with life's furies.

"Because, I admit, I am afraid of it—the sin of bitterness. It is poison to the spirit. I have seen it turn on itself like a many-headed dragon."

"But aren't you angry? Angry with God for allowing such things to happen? Isn't He supposed to be Love? So why has this happened to us, our people? Why?"

"Oh, dear child, don't ask that huge *WHY?* again! We'll both cry until we'll burst and still not know the answer. Of course I am angry, but not at the Lord God. I am not angry with Him. He created a wonderful world for us, and we make a mess of it. He is the Perfect and Great Light. He wants to save us with His love, but we crucify it. No," she shook her head. "I would not be angry at my God. I find it difficult to even talk about it like this, when I really want to tell you that my faith in God helps me get on with the hard parts of life, but maybe that would sound too simple. I don't wear God like an apron. I need to worship and trust Him. I think that is what believing in God really means. So, I want to press upon you, if I may, trust and live your life the best you can. Finding that balance between fate and free will and ridding oneself of anxiety and guilt may be what it means to be saved. It may be the answer to many other questions. A very hard answer, I confess, but an answer all the same. Yet, I really don't know. I'm never that sure, still. . ."

"Do you hate them, the communists, I mean. All those who destroyed our lives?"

The kind woman laughed a short, bitter laugh. "Yes, I hate them! I hate all who bring evil upon others, but I cannot build my life and my children's future on hate. I must nurture and love them as much as I can; that is all I can ask of myself. . . . Making a fetish of hate scares me, and I think some of our people are doing that right here, in this valley. Instilling this hatred of communism, like Hitler did of the Jewish nation, will lead to no good. Whenever we hate movements, we can be sure that innocent people suffer. But I don't know how we can separate one from the other, how we can blame and not blame people for embracing ideologies and all those great movements that shape history. Oh, it is all so very complicated! And I don't have the kind of mind that can sort things out logically and hope that others will do likewise and all will be well. So, I really don't have any answers, only hope and faith that He rules the world. . . . It seems to me that is all we can do, especially we women. All we can do is take care of our front doors; the big things happen without our hands.—More tea?"

"No, thank you."

"Do you feel better?" Mrs. Gramzda asked, looking at her name sister solicitously, sensitively.

"Yes, I think so. And I will think about what you said about guilt and hate and trust." She sat silently looking out the window. She saw the dormant vineyards basking in the afternoon sun, pregnant with grapes, waiting for the sunrays of spring to draw them out and give them life that would nourish and intoxicate other lives. How different the day felt on this side of the building! How open and splendid the view! "I shall be glad when spring comes," she murmured.

"Yes, it's so very lovely here in springtime."

"Should I write to Zelda?" Milda asked, clutching the letter in her pocket.

"Yes. But only a word or two, so she knows you live and care. Take the hint from her, and choose your words cautiously. The risk is very great, especially now when the borders are so ruthlessly sealed."

"When America looks the other way and when even we might forget."

"Yes.—But we won't ever forget. We all—those whom we left and those of us who escaped and those deported—are all parts of each other and nothing can change that. Our blood and our pain bind us forever, don't forget that, my dear, no matter where you may go."

"I won't. I cannot," Milda said and, clutching the letter inside her pocket, slid out of the sunny nook. She squeezed the aged hand and with another warm, smiling *paldies* departed.

At an Art Exhibit

To show Latvian culture as completely as possible, a special exhibit of arts and crafts was set in Stuttgart, at the end of April. Refugees from the whole American Zone competed, but only the works with highest honors were selected for display. The people who would monitor the stands had to pass a test in the English language. They had to be good looking, poised, and dressed in the national costumes. Milda, naturally, was among the chosen.

In high spirits, talking and singing, the chosen rode through the Württemberg countryside until they arrived in the bomb-damaged city. Among piles of bricks and rubble, in a clearing, they found the exhibit hall. At the door the organizers introduced the selected representatives as guides to the Americans, who stood in a group smiling, talking, smoking. One guide was responsible for two or three Americans, who seemed impatient, for the shuffling took too long. But in good time, the parties pared up, the Americans thanked the leaders, evaluated their guides, some trying to pronounce their names. They let it be understood that they were busy and would have no more than an hour to spare. And so that no one would be crowded, each guide led his and her guests to the assigned starting point and proceeded.

When Milda, with her two officers entered the hall, she stopped short, "Oh, how beautiful!" she exclaimed spontaneously and turned her face toward the men, who also stopped and put out their cigarettes, as if they had entered a cathedral.

"I had no idea that there'd be so much to see!" said one man, while Milda wondered how to begin saying the phrases she had been taught. The wavering sunrays touched the amber and silver jewelry, making it sparkle and shine, making the room seem like a mirage that would disappear at any moment. But the other man lightly touched her elbow, and, suddenly awakened, she led both men onward along the display cases, pausing at each. She ignored or forgot her instructions but answered questions only when asked. She hoped the works would speak for themselves, but felt the men's eyes on her more than on the displays. Blushing, she ignored the phrases and gestures and led on, realizing that these conquerors were not as curious or interested as every one expected, and so there was no use talking, while she was most dazzled and marveled at the rows of hand-woven wool and linen costumes and decorative items of every kind. She had never seen so much Latvian talent and beauty displayed in one room. She had not seen anything like it in Latvia, when she was a child and Latvia's beauty had been wrapped all around her. Here it seemed the soul and heartbeat of her country was transported as if by magic; every piece told its story about how it had come to life and what price its creator had paid. "It's nice," said one man and the other agreed. "Yea, sure is!"

On the wall of children's handwork, she spotted Helga's pair of mittens. They did not quite match, but the design was flawless, painstakingly knitted, her fingers hurting from the thin steel needles and itchy wool. Helga with her mother and sisters had dyed the yarn in onion skins, beet juice, moss, and whatever else, until her teacher had accepted the colors as ethnically correct. Another table showed the work of a silversmith: he had turned lids of cans and old coins into brooches. He, she knew, was the master and Scout leader who had made all their Scout and Guide emblems. He stood by his display case proudly, in his uniform, ready to elaborate, but the strangers had no time to stop and listen.

Nearing the exit door, one of the men asked, "How did you all do it?"

"It is a mystery," Milda said, smiling mysteriously.

"And so are you," said the other. "So how did you all do it?" Still smiling, she tried to gather her words as directed, but they seemed lost, and she had to find her own way through the maze of the English language, which she had never been required to speak in long impromptu sentences and paragraphs. She took a deep breath, and tried to explain that the things were created in workshops held in the school buildings in the evenings. Professional refugee masters taught the classes, drawing the geometric designs from memory, even drawing their own graph paper. With a slight smile, she confessed that she did not attend those classes, but said she knew the mothers of her classmates who learned to dye yarns, unravel discarded scraps for threads, even use old American army uniforms for the skirts of certain national costumes. "Yes," she said, "all this is the handwork of our people. In each piece of art are woven not only our people's pain and sorrow but also their joy and longing for beauty and harmony." The sentence exhausted her. Unwanted tears rose to her eyes. The Americans noticed. One said, "That's nice."

"This exhibit was prepared for you," she said cautiously, feeling living words stirring within her, and lining up for a speech she had written out and memorized in case she would need it. Seizing the moment she spoke: "All this what you see, gentlemen, is our people's letter to the world. In the woven and engraved hieroglyphics and subtle designs you may read our long history. The ongoing lines along the borders of shawls and skirts repeat over and over that Latvia has a right to live. The golden threads that spread throughout are like ancient amber routes that stretched from the Baltic Sea to the Mediterranean. Through the routes traveled rich cultures and the ideas of great civilizations. Our language is one of the oldest Indo-European languages that is still spoken. We have a treasure of folk songs and sayings such as no other people have."

"Really?"

"Don't you just love to hear her accent? Where'd you learn English that good?"

"Well," she said. "In school, but mostly by myself."

She led the men on in silence, and silently they followed. "In the designs," Milda continued, "you may also read the influence of the occupiers who tried to extinguish our people. But in the end they failed, as will fail the current occupation."

"Why do you have swastikas all over? Do they have anything to do with the Nazis?"

"Oh, no! It is the cross of the thunder god. It is a very old symbol and has nothing to do with German uniforms. Hitler, so we've been told, took it and turned it backwards and painted it black, but I am not quite sure about that.—Please note that our garments and things are also full of stars, the sun, the earth, and sky, not only thunder and lightning. Our signs are good. They connect us with the cosmos, and we honor the earth and sky that God gave us but which the powers of earth are systematically destroying." She heard the hurt and anger rising in her voice. She wanted to shout about the horrors of war, accusing the Americans, the British, the Russians, and Germans for not even feeling guilty for having bombed so much, for killing so many innocent people. She was hot. The room felt like a greenhouse, and she wanted out. But she remembered that the leaders watched her, that she was only a representative and had no authority of her own, and so she turned toward her guests, smiled and said, "Gentlemen, we have come to the end. Thank you for your attention."

"Such people would be good for America," one remarked to the other. "Would you like to go to America?"

"Yes, perhaps, but when Latvia is free again, I shall want to go home."

They laughed rather too loudly. Milda was offended.

"You, young lady, are also a work of art." The higher-ranking officer tried to make amends. "It really is a shame what has happened to your small country."

"We won't let you down," said the other, adding, "You'll like America."

"Perhaps," she said and guided them into the side room, where a stage was set up.

And there she saw him—the one-armed veteran, as handsome as ever—wearing a light gray suit with a white shirt and blue tie. She stared in shock, blinking, wondering if she was seeing doubles or visions. How could he have changed so much since she last saw him, on Christmas Eve? Or had she not seen him, but only imagined, expected for him to be there and, therefore, assumed things in her nervousness?

She was sweating and felt faint. It was that time of the month. She clasped her hands and brought them to her heart that hammered, she was afraid, for all to see and hear. She tried to turn back, but one of the leaders told her to go on and not abandon her guests. She had no choice, and so she moved forward where a stage was set up. The room was too small for the large crowd, so people squeezed together. The veteran stood at one side of a stage, his hand holding the edge of a podium, waiting for the guests to find their seats and settle down. His eyes scanned the room and, in matched surprise, lingered over Milda. The blush on his face deepened, as he gazed down. When, unable to resist she looked up, he smiled and then began addressing his audience.

He spoke in quite fluent English, taking too much time to explain the evils of communism. The Americans rose, ready to walk out, but the program director stepped up to the podium and cut the speech short, saying, "Please, honored guests, I see that you wish to leave, but I would like to invite you to come forward." They obeyed and took the reserved seats in the front row. A children ensemble, looking like dolls in their costumes and sparkling crowns, walked up on the stage. Perfectly disciplined, they lined up and sang a medley of folk songs, followed by a round of dances. The Americans seemed to forget their time limits and applauded enthusiastically when the show was over. The girls curtsied and the boys bowed, as other girls rushed forward with bunches of flowers for all the Americans, who patted the blond heads, as other soldiers came forward with crates of oranges, candy, and toys. They handed them out to all the children, who were as surprised and happy as if angels covered them with gold.

Out in the sunshine, amidst piles of ruins the liberating bombers had left behind, there were American and Latvian reporters, who interviewed the people and wrote their comments in their notepads, while photographers worked their cameras. When a lens turned on Milda, she tried to smile, but then stood as if she had turned to stone. An arm had wrapped itself around her waist. She felt the pressure of all his fingers that held her tightly against his side. The photographer said, "That's beautiful. Now smile again," and she tried. "Look up at each other and turn a bit toward the camera. . . . that's beautiful! I'll send this into *Life* magazine. Thank you!"

"So we meet again at last," he said casually, being polite and correct in his every move. "If you don't mind," he said, releasing her, "I would be honored if you would ride back with us. Two of the American guests want to drive to Esslingen and see our situation, and I would like you to sit with them and answer any questions they may have. I heard that your English is excellent." Before Milda could agree or disagree, his hand took a hold of her arm at the elbow and was maneuvering her toward an open jeep, where three men in uniform waited. Milda was welcomed with big smiles and low whistles. She was tucked in the back seat between two of the men, while the third took the steering wheel. The one-armed man sat in the front passenger seat, but he kept turning around, looking at Milda more than at the road and the blooming hills.

"I don't believe we have been formally introduced," he said extending his right hand so she had no choice but to offer her sweating hand to him. She watched his hand swallow hers like a hungry pickerel would swallow a thirsty butterfly. "I am Pēteris Vanags, and, at the moment am the supervisor of the veterans at the Mountain Colony, and you, I know are Miss Milda Bērziņa, our pride and joy." He spoke in his accented English. His smiling eyes met hers, and then the introductions went all around, while the chauffeur sought the quickest way to Esslingen.

As Mr. Vanags had promised, Milda had to answer many questions. Reluctantly she told parts of her story. Subdued, the Americans listened. She hoped that Mr. Vanags also was listening and that she was doing justice to her people, that she was setting the right tone and making the Americans change their minds about Latvians being fascists and their alleged former enemies. She was not astute politically, but she knew enough to make the case for the Latvian soldiers, like Vanags and many others, who were caught in the whirlwinds of a world at war. At times during the ride through the beautiful landscape, veiled in early spring greenery, her and Mr. Vanags's eyes met in the mirrors. He smiled and nodded approval, as he listened to all she was saying. But just as she relaxed, feeling her fears fall off and thinking that her heart had only played tricks with her imagination, a sudden turn of his head, a seemingly casual touch of her hand, caused her whole being to vibrate in hot and cold flashes. His amazingly blue eyes held her, if only for brief moments, as in a sharp ray of swirling light. As she half-heard the Americans say words, her body trembled inside her heated folk costume. She wriggled, opened a top button, rolled up her sleeves, couldn't stand the heat of her feet. She was afraid of him, the way he looked at her. She had never felt such male desire and never felt her body leaning forward, almost resting her head on the back of his seat. But she jerked back, tightly between the Americans.

Mercifully, the ride lasted barely an hour. When the jeep stopped at the Lido door, one of the Americans stepped out and held out his hand. "We'll never forget this day," he said, very politely thanking, saying, "Keep your courage up and remember that all's well that ends well. There will be a place for you in America, I can guarantee."

Vanags also embarked and formally extended his hand to Milda, which she clasped, shyly lifting her eyes to his. He took it all in and smiled. The seconds turned into eons, and then he said casually, as if she were any woman, that he was sure they will soon meet again, and slowly withdrawing his hand, wished her well. Without a backward glance, he got back into the jeep and was gone. As if thrown out on the curb, she watched the empty street and then turned as if in pain and opened the door. She went up the stairs slowly, holding on to the banister. Inside she pulled off her clothes and sponge bathed herself with the sun warmed water. "What a never to be forgotten day this is!"

Migration of Displaced Persons

And then—by the time the trees had fully leafed out—it happened! The word was out that America would not recognize *forever* the incorporation of Latvia into the Soviet Union and that the Latvian refugees living in the American zone, carefully screened, would be allowed to immigrate to the United States. What to do with the refugees of East Europe was a big issue for the United States government. Already in 1947, in his State of the Union address, President Truman raised the issue about opening the doors to the refugees, appealing on moral grounds and the fact that those who escaped had refused to go back to their communist-governed homelands. But Congress did not respond immediately, and it would be June of 1948 before the immigration law was passed. It was legislated that the Latvian refugees could use the quotas on two-hundred year credit, since Latvia, as such and, for all practical purposes, was closed and would be for the next two hundred years. Certainly no one would emigrate from behind the Iron curtain to the United States or anywhere else—not for a hundred years! (*Oh, Dornröschen, sleep a hundred years, a hundred years, a hundred years. . . .* sang the German children as they played games in the castle park.)

But during the spring months, the DP leaders, having received messages from refugees and earlier immigrants living in America, encouraged their waiting compatriots to be positive and wait. The Reverend Ābele, who by this time was in Washington working for the Baptist World Alliance Refugee Relief Program, lobbied with others for extending immigration quotas. He also wrote long uplifting letters to brother Gramzda, explaining how the wheels of democracy turned and assured him that he was doing all he could to pave the way. He was traveling all over the vast U.S.A., speaking in countless churches, telling about "his Joseph, who was still in prison, waiting." He said he lived more on trains than at his temporary home with his family. His good wife worked in a textile factory and his children attended a one-room school house. Life was not easy, he wrote, and told his brother to urge people to study English, not be proud, and learn some useful skill so they can honestly fill in the forthcoming application blanks. Old degrees and diplomas would be of no use, not at first, not for getting sponsors who needed working hands on cotton plantations and orange groves, etc.

And so, inevitably, hesitatingly, almost, imperceptibly the refugees turned about face. They turned from looking back at the East toward the West, not only the United States of America but to the other communist free countries and continents. In Esslingen, almost every night in the various school buildings films were shown about far-away lands: Alaska, New Zealand, Australia, Canada, Argentina, Venezuela, Brazil. . . Those lands would be open for people who could not, for some reason, enter the U.S.A. "So, please, take your pick! The applications are on the table," urged the envoys. "Fill out the forms and wait. You will hear from us. The world can use hard-working hands and honest minds. Sign up, sign up! A home is waiting for you somewhere!"

One evening Milda, with her friends, had gone to see a film about South America. On their way out, the girls talked about how they would not like to go there. It would be too far, like another planet where they could not find each other. If they would not be admitted to the United States, they agreed, they would rather stay in Germany. As they pushed their way out, they passed a long table with brochures and people who handed out application forms. At the end of the table, by *Venezuela*, Milda saw Mr. Vanags, listening to some explanation as he was trying to shuffle through papers with his one hand. Surprised and feeling the lumps gather around her heart, she stared at him, her hands reaching out of their own to help him, to pick up the booklets that he dropped. At last he turned his head but showed no sign of recognition. He did not nod, did not smile, and did not drop more papers so his hand would be free to take hers. He simply turned his attention back to Venezuela. She felt snubbed, offended. *How dare he not even bow his head in greeting after all that line he gave me in the jeep? What's going on, and why is he going about all of a sudden dressed like a tramp? Who is this man, anyway? And why does he upset me so? Well, let him go to Venezuela or wherever he wants, I'm going to America!*

She wriggled through the congestion and came out in the open. She linked arms with her friends and went to get some ice cream that was finally available at sidewalk cafes. "I'm going to America," she said as they licked the chocolate cones, thinking *I'm glad—relieved, thankful that he won't be where I will be.*

Milda and everybody soon learned that America took only the healthiest and the best, those with clean bodies and hands, those who could prove they had not been executioners of Nazi orders. *That certainly will exclude him and all our veterans!* She took a deep breath and began walking with a sure, purposeful step, in her mind heading westward.

But everyone wanted to go to America, and there began a great search for identification papers. Many did not have any; they had forgotten them when they heard the shots or they lost them on the way. Hence, new papers—new birth certificates—had to be issued. Some people, while at it, revised their birth dates and re-named themselves; they made themselves a bit younger and better educated, and then they signed up for lessons in English and workshops that taught needed and useful skills. Some took crash, condensed courses that would help anywhere with any job, and put a plus sign in the square next to *fluency in English.* They wrote on the applications that they would be willing to do anything—anything at all, as long as they could sail to America!

There was much work to be done among the excited DPs. They mended old suitcases, studied, and stretching their necks, looked westward, where the sun set and the sky touched the earth—far beyond the German hills—as far as their imaginations could reach. And they dreamed, almost forgetting the snapped-off roots which still festered in the Latvian soil.

But Alma did not forget. She still looked back. Desperately she again waited for news from behind a very hard iron curtain.

Milda did not argue, but continued slicing apples for applesauce. She knew very well that Alma's reasons for living were not like everyone else's, not even like hers. Just when others at the theater became lax, Alma worked harder, taking on the heavy roles of Rainis's dramas with greater passion and knowledge. "I want to be able to play opposite him when the time comes," she said deadly serious. When others discussed leaving, she talked more and more about returning, about going back to her actor lover Viktors Vētra, believing that he waited for her. "I know he does," she uttered simply, quietly.

"But the communists?" Milda asked. "Could you suddenly go back to a Communist country? Stalin still lives, doesn't he?"

"*Ak vai*! Why do you pester me? Even the mighty Stalin is not forever. Latvia will be free, you'll see. There will come a war or revolution or salvation. The Americans are turning around. They are beginning to understand, as you yourself say, and then, well—you'll see. We will go home! I have also studied history. Everything that happens now has happened before, and it will happen again. One day our people will return home, and Latvia will bloom again!" She was magnificent as she spoke, and Milda could not guess whether she spoke to her or whether she was rehearsing a new role for the stage.

"But you," Alma said, taking Milda's knife from her hand and cutting up the apple herself, awkwardly, her long, polished fingernails getting in the way, "You must go to America and wait there. You must marry and have many sons and daughters and raise them to be Latvians so that one day, rich and free, you can come home to me. I will only go a little ahead of you—to prepare the way, as it were." She pushed the cut-up apple aside and wiped her hands.

"Yes," Milda said, picking up the knife. Alma's words or acting frightened her. She thought Alma was delirious. Her eyes had that glow again; however, she caught her words and immediately thought about tall, handsome Kārlis Arājs, who carried the flag and by whose side she had walked in many parades. She was not sure he had even noticed her, although his face always turned red, whenever his glances strayed her way. But he never spoke to her or anyone else during the parades. His eyes looked ahead. His hands held the flagpole firmly as though the whole country were in his grasp. Milda admired such disciplined steadfastness. Besides, he was a real patriot. There was no doubt about that. There was no blemish on him that might offend or embarrass. He was always so sure, so firm. She knew that he would go a long way to defend his country's rights, and she would walk with him and help him.

"Yes, he would be the right man for me," she whispered.

"What? What did you say?"

"Nothing, nothing at all."

But she had spoken and decided to begin paving her wonderful and purposeful Road of Life. "We already know how to walk in step."

"But we cannot go on together!" misunderstanding, Alma cut in. "You must find your own way."

"Must I?"

"Yes!"

Milda emptied the bowl of sliced apples into the kettle that simmered on the potbelly stove and slowly stirring, her thoughts floated like sweet vapor toward the man she had just chosen to be her husband.

Stairway to America

By the end of the summer of 1948, by which time the Immigration Law was passed by the Congress of the United States of America and the clear and green light of open skies and sees sent its beams across the Atlantic Ocean, the DP communities all over western Germany were on the move. One day, while Milda scrubbed the hall and stairway, she heard the slow but determined clicking of a typewriter. The inexperienced sound, escaping through the closed door #2, labored and paused, paused and clicked on and on all afternoon. Squinting at the door, she read: **Baptist Relief & Emigration Office** hand-printed in black ink on a sheet of paper. That same day the first strange people—a woman and two teenage girls—came up the stairs and asked where one could sign up to go to America. Milda pointed to the door. The woman knocked, and Reverend Gramzda let her in.

Now what's all this about? Milda wondered as, sitting up on her heels, she wiped up the fresh footprints around the door. She leaned her head listening. Within seconds she heard strange words and puzzling concepts: *sponsor, affidavit, visa, Baptist World Alliance, screening, inoculations. . . wait. . . . Wait!* The last word came through to her, it seemed, with an up-beat intensity, charged with *hope* and *future* and *America.* Satisfied for the time being, she moved away and mopped all along the edges, going into the corners, the toilet, then working her way around the hall to the middle and on down the stairs, all the time going up and down to change water, all the time thinking, imagining life in unimaginable America. When finished, she went out to sit under the chestnut tree until the floor dried. She saw the woman and girls come out smiling as others approached the Lido entry confused and lost. "Alma won't like it," she said to the sparrows. "She won't like it at all. It'll be like living on a sidewalk." But it did not matter what the Star liked or disliked. From that day on, people came in greater numbers so that they disturbed her quiet afternoons. She did not like it.

The Reverend Egle also employed himself in the relief work. Milda caught in glimpses the two pastors sitting across from each other at desks tightly pushed together in the middle of their crowded room. She saw the stacks of papers grow and spread all over the room, even onto the piano, which Vizma did not play as much as she used to. "I don't like it," Helga said at the pump. "Papa never has any time, and he shouts at Mamma and makes her feed strange people. Papa and Brother Egle drink tea late at night, so I can't sleep. But he tells us to be patient if we want to go to America."

And so it went. America shone like a bright star in the distance and people reached for it, in spite of the many daily discomforts.

Reverend Egle practically lived in #2, while an eerie calm prevailed behind the locked #3. Sometimes a pale Mrs. Egle looked vacantly through a crack but closed the door as soon as she heard any footsteps. Little Marta spent most of her free time with the Gramzdas. Aija treated her like another sister and seemed happy, especially after they discovered a litter of kittens at the bottom of their packed wardrobe. How the mother cat had sneaked in, was a much-discussed mystery.

"What can we do? Mamma says, 'What's one more mouth to feed?'" Helga said. When the kittens' eyes were open, the girls took the box down to the courtyard, where strange children suddenly showed up ready to play, making the mother cat nervous. Aija and Marta picked out their favorite kittens they would take to America and pouted when Mrs. Gramzda explained that it could not be done. "Then we don't want America!" Marta said loud enough for her mother to call her to their room.

Milda did not like the way things were falling out of place, the children and cats running up and down the stairs out of control. She did not like to wipe up the footprints people left behind on their way to America. The people who climbed the stairs seemed to her a pathetic lot. The men appeared timid, past middle age, walking low, while the women in front of them pushed full force. They pulled their children who seemed to be permanently embarrassed as reasons, evidence, proof for their necessity to emigrate. But usually the women came alone, without men, without children and knocked uncertainly. With each day the typewriter clicked faster and longer, and Reverend Gramzda spoke louder and faster. At times his voice rang with humor, at other times with impatience. As the summer went on, it became tired and irritable. His steps also changed. They became firmer and faster, going up and down the many flights of stairs at odd hours, even in the night to catch the last pick-up of the mail.

The Reverend Egle did not rush about. He was a big man, born in Russia. He moved slowly and spoke gently. Being a good shepherd of his assembled flock, he oozed peace and goodness and caring; naturally, the timid, uncertain people turned to him first. He held the door open and his dimpled smile pulled everyone in. No one was turned away. But Milda hardly ever saw Mrs. Egle, in or outside of Lido. When they did meet, the lady passed by with downcast eyes, without seeing anything. She had become colorless. No secret lipstick, no stray curl and bright scarves, only shades of gray, brown, and off white. Her hair was parted in the middle and pinned down behind the ears. Sometimes she would sit under the chestnut tree and weep, her face hidden in her hands. Whenever Milda saw her, she imagining the once-exotic woman as a symbol of devastation, of broken down femininity—like Faust's Margareta—harboring depression and fear in a seemingly sunny, indifferent world.

Meanwhile, Alma, being far outside the fold, did not like the goings on one bit and stayed away as much as possible. When she crept up the stairs late at night, she always saw a flat ray of light at the threshold and heard the typewriter click and stop: click. . . stop. . . click. . . stop. . . click. She complained about the noise and her awful headaches, but no one heard her except Milda, who hurried down the flights of stairs for cold well water with which to cool her aunt's troubled face. Then Milda's head would also ache, not only because of Alma or the annoying Relief Organization, but from its own silent, unspeakable tension. Besides, the water in the pail—whenever she scrubbed the toilet, hallway, and stairs—turned dirtier and dirtier.

*

Then, one day, when hot and angry, Milda carried a full bucket of water up the stairs, she slipped and almost fell, for at the top flight she saw her handsome flag bearer—Kārlis Arājs himself, following a large, commanding woman who made the stairs creak. Milda felt like Cinderella caught in her ashes and quickly slipped out of sight until the #2 door closed. Her heart was hammering, and she slid into her room and lay down on her bed. The room was hot. She muttered unkind phrases at the heat and her fate. She pulled off her clothes which stuck to her skin like stale bandages. She soused herself with the lukewarm water from the pitcher. She felt like a dirty floor and kept scrubbing her hands, neck, face until she was cold. Then she lay down and hid inside her sheets, shivering. "A huge hand is pushing me around," she whispered. "I am a checker piece, the black one," she said, thinking about the little red pieces that rolled under the table when she and Zelda played their last game. "I have nothing to do with my fate," she said to the ceiling. She closed her eyes and waited. She waited for a blank time. She could not sleep; she could not read or sew or think. "So, that's his mother, a huge roadblock. . . . Some day I'll be forced to call her *Māte, even Māmiṇa.*" She shivered and remembers her own vanished mother. "Oh, where are you now, when I need you so much?" Tears welled up and slid down the sides of her face. She reached up to take the handkerchief from Mother's hand, but all she caught were light rays full of dust. The tears stopped, as they started, on their own, and then all was quiet. Her body lay between the sheets, waiting.

At last she heard the door open and the words of assurance and then the footsteps going down. She rose, dressed, and returned to scrubbing the floor. She must get everything clean quickly, before more people would be invading her space, but she won't mind them. Their steps wouldn't matter. The ones she scrubbed matter a whole lot. They left such huge imprints!

She scrubs and scrubs, but still she can see them, both pairs, side by side, one behind the other, going across the floor and down, down, down the stairs. . . . The water inside the bucket turns dark brown as her hands turn red. Her heart also turns. It is white. It is a white dove beating her soaked wings inside a tin bucket. She scrubs harder and does not notice Reverend Egle standing in the doorway. She looks up only when she hears him saying, "My child, why do you work so hard? The floor is clean. Rise and go out into the sunshine!"

She hears and obeys.

Above the Vineyard

"Why don't you go and talk to the Baptists?" Alma asks when they sit on a stone wall in the vineyard watching the grapes ripen.

"Why?" Alarmed and squinting Milda faces her. "Why me?"

"Because it is time for you to think about your future."

"*My* future?"

"Yes, *yours.*"

Then she looks at Alma as she had not in a long, long time. With the bright sun shining, she sees tired lines around the large eyes, and beneath the platinum hair are gray roots. Around her mouth, Time's mean lines have begun their cruel furrowing through the silk-smooth skin. Her hands clutch themselves nervously, uncertainly, picking at some tall weeds around them, pulling off the insignificant heads and dropping them carelessly on the limestone walk. But her figure is fine, especially in profile. Onstage it is still eighteen.

"You're almost eighteen," Alma says. "You'll soon be done with gymnasium. . . . Your confirmation is coming up, though it's impossible to believe it." Her voice sounds like Katerina's—Milda's mother's, Alma's sister's.

"Yes," Milda hears her mother and wonders why she had not heard her in Alma before. Perhaps she had not listened, not listened enough. "But now I am seventeen," "Don't argue," Alma snaps. "Time flies. You'll be grown up before you know it and then what?"

Milda sees that they sit literally at crossroads. One path goes up, the other down; one goes east, the other west. "I don't know which path to choose," she says.

"Let's go on up," Alma says and jumps off the wall. They walk silently northward, up to the orchards. "The way things are going from what I can gather," Alma talks, her breath heavy, "the DP camps will soon be liquidated. UNRRA is hands off, and who knows how long IRO will bother with us. In America people always vote about things, and, who knows but they might vote against helping the messed up world, and that will be the end for us. They hate dependents and high taxes."

"What are taxes?"

"Money. Money the government makes people pay for things they need and use, but also pay for wars and peace. And for refugees like us.—The American people are sick of having their money taken away and will vote against helping us, and I don't blame them. I wouldn't like it either. No one does. . . . We cost America a lot of money."

"I didn't know that."

"That and lots of other things you don't know," Alma goes on. "Yes, things could change for us very quickly, and, therefore, we must act quickly. Our Latvian Esslingen is slowly fading out," she says, nodding and shaking her head. "It's almost over. The theater is breaking up also."

As they climb higher, Alma names the actors who are waiting to leave and making their plans about setting up stages in New York, Boston, Chicago, Philadelphia. Those who do not qualify for the United States weigh their chances for Canada, Australia, Venezuela, Brazil. "And so," Alma says as they rest on the wall that separates the terraces of grapes from the orchards of apple and cherry trees, "This dream we have been living out here in this lovely oasis," she sweeps the horizon with her actress' hand, "will soon be over. The time when we shall have to leave this paradise, this happy illusion, is rubbing at our heels. I feel the blisters."

"Nice, the way you put things," Milda smiles, then turns her alarmed eyes on her Aunt: "But won't we leave together?"

"No."

"But why?" She slides off the wall and stares at Alma's feet dangling against the weathered stones. The feet are large and bare in clumsy sandals and do not fit the rest of her body. Red blistering lines mark the heels, where straps rub. Milda turns her stare away and looks at her own feet, which are small, almost dainty, as though she had left all walking to Alma, as though she had not done her share of trudging; and now, therefore, she will have to walk on alone—even walk for Alma and her Mother and Zelda—to a strange land and live among strange people.

"You must go and live your own life," Alma says, guessing her thoughts, seeing her guilt. "You must not be afraid, my little one, my only child, my precious darling."

Warm and sticky, the words buzz around the darling child, and she simply looks at her Aunt in whom, for the first time, she recognizes also Aunt Matilde and bits and pieces of her forlorn mother, whose voice she keeps hearing in the wind. She sees a little cloud like her mother's shawl floating in the blue and remembers the night when she and Mamma and Zelda sat with the window open waiting for Papa.—

"I cannot help you anymore," Alma says. "You must go to America, as I have tried to tell you all along. Europe is finished." Silently they look down on Esslingen and see the Neckar, low in its bed, yet sparkling like a bead of aquamarine, winding on eternally in its secure and ancient bed until it will flow into the mighty Rhine and then be no more. "Maybe some day it will be strong again," Alma talks on. "But not now, not while you need to marry and build yourself a home and family. So, you listen to me! You must go and talk to the Baptists."

"But you? What about you? Where will you go?"

"I?" Alma gazes into the distance. "I?" She takes on a dramatic pose and quotes Aspazija: *I shall go where tempests dwell. I shall go to find fulfillment.*"

"I'm serious."

"Oh, so am I. Very. But—I see—you want to know in more practical terms, in terms of time and place and all our other limitations."

"Yes."

Alma smiles and strokes her niece's hair, again bringing on Milda's head the ever-missing touch of a mother. "I cannot go to America. I believe I've made that clear. I will not cross the ocean. I am bound to Europe, and I must stay close to Latvia just in case."

"But, for all our singing and talking about it, isn't Latvia really dead? Haven't the communists killed it?"

"My precious darling," Alma pulls Milda's hands inside her own. "If there is one thing I have learned in all our wandering and suffering—and from the dreadfully long plays of Rainis—is that nothing ever gets lost or dies completely, not even we. Not even when we die. Often dead people and things are more real than the living. All right, let's take Latvia, for instance. By constantly holding it in front of us, we keep it more alive than ever. Neither you nor I were ever as aware of our country when we lived in it as we are now. . . . Oh, it's not dead, not dead at all! Quite to the contrary. It is so very large and perfect and alive that we can hardly stand it. It lives in all of us all the time. And there are so many of us—how many? One, two million, it doesn't matter—who, like seeds, are being scattered all over the world, some even re-planted back home. Don't you see how on every national holiday a newer, more polished Latvia is created? Don't you see how millions of Latvians will yet be born, like new stars, and each star its own world? To be sure, there will be wars among the stars; they will want to outshine and out burn each other, but the nation will never die. And we will never die. Not a one of us." She puts her arm around Milda's waist and pulls herself tightly against the warm young side. Milda rests her head on the angular shoulder and closes her eyes, swaying as gently as the grass at their feet.

"Yes," Alma speaks on, her words soft and resigned. "We, too, will go on changing into invisible elements, confused, miserably shuffled, but we'll go on. We will carry each other inside ourselves, our poetry and songs, our work. We shall live in each other in a myriad ways. Crazy, unpredictable world events and accidents will help pull us along without our being aware of it, without really having any say about it. Perhaps, too late, as always, some historians will wake up and explain communism as another historical mistake, and we'll be vindicated. Who knows? We can't ever know what the world does or does not do with us. Whatever will, will simply happen and, as people, as a nation we shall go on living. Oh, Latvia IS, my dear." Now both arms wrap around Milda, and she snaps out of the trance and pulls out of the vice and jumps off the wall.

"Please, dear Aunt, you sound like a book, a very good book, I'll grant you that, but all I'm really asking is—when I sail to America, where will you go?"

"Yes, yes, that's what you ask me. . . . Well, I don't know. Sweden is a possibility, but it's hard to get into. I don't know what their attitude toward the Baltic States is. When our people risked their lives and escaped to Sweden by fishing boats, the boarder guards succeeded in turning some back into sure jaws of death. And not too long ago, as the spoils of war were settled, they sent our soldiers, who sought refuge there, back to the welcoming Soviet Union, into the arms of daddy Stalin. So you see what I mean. The Swedes don't want foreigners, but who does? They try to be neutral, but nobody is. Not now, not at any time. We all side and have to take sides, or others put us on one side or another. Latvia also wanted to be neutral, but how could we, with everyone pulling us to their bloody sides. So here we are. Still, Sweden would be nice, close to home. It's on the Baltic Sea. I could lie next to the sea, on the beach, close my eyes and feel the same waves that touch my dear Kurzeme stroke my body also. It would be like touching home or keeping a hand on the handle until the gates open. . . . Yes, I'd like that, to be connected at least by water and air, if not by land. It would give me life. It would nurture me."

"It's that important, that necessary?" Milda asks in disbelief, thinking *she will sacrifice me*, as she realizes that she has no wish to go north only to stare at the sea and wait for boats that never sail. Too much of the southern sun has already warmed her blood for her not to shiver as she imagines the unending expanses of ice and snow over a land heavy with granite.

"Yes," says Alma. "It is that important." They leave the wall and, hand in hand, walk higher to the very top of the ridge. They swing in rhythm, their shoulders and hips touching, their hair blowing in the warm wind that turns stronger with each step. "You know," Alma continues, now hooking her hand in the crook of Milda's bare arm. "I still feel, deep inside me, that he lives and waits for me."

"I know. I hear you in the nights."

"Yes. Only you know me. I cannot hide anything from you," Alma says, stopping to catch her breath. She wraps her arms around the slim young waist, "and you will understand me better when we are not together anymore. It's not only for his sake we must part. It is also for the sake of them. I mean, our sisters. At least one of us must not forget them. One of us must stay close by, like watching at a cradle."

"Or like not missing the train again."

"Yes. Yes, my darling."

To stop the onrush of emotional torrents, they disengage and walk faster, breathing harder. They sweat. Alma is soon out of breath, while Milda only feels the more rapid beating of her heart. In spite of Alma's gentle tones, Milda walks accused and guilty: she had missed the train, and she has decided against going north.

They have reached the highest ridge. The path ends at the last turn. They have taken off their sandals and continue walking barefooted in the grass, so silky and warm, unlike the rough blades that edge the path. Above them lies the silent and blue sky. But with each gust of wind, clouds fluff over the hills across the river and gather along the horizon, promising a splendid sunset. Expectantly, again hand in hand, they stand looking down on the ancient steeples and gables. The old town's steep houses appear like children's blocks, medieval and pretty and all in neat curved rows laid carefully by small hands. . . . The Neckar—a blue ribbon—flows on, breaking only at the falls, until it meanders out of town and flows freely through fields ripe for harvest.

"So, my pretty," Alma says looking at the vista as she holds Milda's warm hand tightly. "I wish we could be up here forever, but we cannot.

You, therefore, must go quickly to the Baptists. You must go and do it right away. Go to the church, sing in the choir, let them baptize you! Anything, but get yourself to America." Alma's voice suddenly shifts. Again it has that mean, frightening edge. "Go," she repeats, dropping the stiffening hand, pulling her own hands together, pressing them so the knuckles turn white. "Go! Get down from this enchanting, bewitching mountain and do what you must."

"I cannot be like that," Milda says firmly.

"You must learn to be practical," Alma commands. "Do as I tell you."

"But you? What about you?" Milda remembers that long-gone Walpurgis Night and Alma wearing a thin red thread around her throat. "What will you do?"

"Nothing." The voice resumes a maternal tone. "I only want to stay here alone for a while longer. I want to rest and dream awhile, go over my lines." Alma sounds tired, very exhausted. "Go, please go. . . . Don't worry. I'll come soon. I need to see the sunset once from this height. I always wanted to but had no time, so now that I've climbed this high, I must stay and see the silver veils of the day turn red before black night gathers up everything."

"Very poetic," Milda says, looking up, and then she turns and picks up her sandals. She feels a great big lump of pain pressing her heart, but she does not want to cry, does not want to ruin the beautiful day with her salt, and so she blinks and rushes down the mountain, down through the orchard and vineyard, down to the city. She comes out into marketplace, still full of people. The organ grinder grinds out the same old tunes, and the monkey dances up and down his back. The children skip around laughing. She loses herself in the crowd and meanders aimlessly, finding no place to rest.

At last she comes upon the fountain around which eternal children and pigeons splash, and she, too, dips her hands in the cold spring water and brings handfuls up to her face, splashing it until she feels cool and clean. Above her, in the Rathaus tower the faithful clock strikes a very late afternoon hour. The gonging jars her. She feels strangely awake and free, as though unshackled and untangled. *The Glockenspiel may sound its ominous, warning notes! They do not concern me. I am seventeen!* But the clock strikes at her in Alma's commanding voice: "Go, go, go!" She starts to walk—fast, faster. . .

She wonders how to approach that door with the sign. Of course, she would not simply knock and ask. She would not risk losing the respect of her neighbors. Had not they saved Christmas for her? Don't they share their coal and bread and make her feel safe the many nights Alma sleeps in some strange bed? Oh, she would never knock suddenly, shamefully, desperately like so many others. She would not beg like the ragged Slovak girl who knocks every evening on the doors of Lido, begging for a piece of bread. *"Ein Stickle Brot, bitte."* The children call her *Ein Stickle Brot* (a piece of bread), as though she had no other name except, perhaps Hunger or Despair. Oh, she could never beg for crumbs! She will wait for her own counsel. She will wait for her hour.—

She looks up at the vineyards that glow in the setting sun. She tries to find Alma, but all she sees are people as small as grapes, as small as dots. Those dots cannot help her. Yet, she draws comfort from the grapes that trust the sun and wait for their season of ripeness. *To everything there is a season,* wise Solomon said thousands of years ago. And Jesus still asks: *If God so clothed the grass of the field, which today is and tomorrow is cast into the oven, shall he not much more clothe you, o ye of little faith?* She looks at the sparrows hopping in and out of the bushes along the street and inside the garden fences, and she hears Aunt Matilde singing *His eye is on the sparrow, and I know He watches me. . .*

Milda hums the old hymn as she turns on to *Bahnhofstrasse.* She would have supper ready for Alma. She would whip up apple snow for desert, and they would talk about her confirmation and about a white dress and shoes and flowers and how she should style her hair. . . .

But Kārlis? Who is he really and what is his Baptist connection, she wonders. When would he be leaving? Where would he go? Could she ever find him in as large a land as America? Would he hold the flag high enough so she could see it when she steps off the boat?. . . Her white confirmation dress takes on a massive veil. She sees herself leaning on Kārlis's arm, white lilies in her hand, a myrtle wreath on her head. The organ plays the march from *Lohengrin*. . . . They become one, man and wife—one body, one soul—and they must live their lives happily. All marriages promise happiness and harmony; that is why people marry, is it not? And they, too, will marry and be happy!—She imagines a brilliant ball, and they waltz into a life of riches and joy.

She hastens on, her fantasies driving her, lifting her up, and before she reaches Lido, she has decided that at the next parade she will distract Kārlis. She will make him turn his face toward her, and then she will smile a shy, conquering smile, and he will fall off the platform. But she, the Ice Princess, will pull his head to her bosom and awaken him with kisses, and all the people will rejoice. . . . Veiled in such visions, she rushes up the stairs and hides inside her room. As she prepares the supper and waits for Alma, she is convinced that all the angels in heaven are planning her wedding. Still, she will not knock on #2. She will wait for the right time.

Kārlis Arājs

Once Milda had fixed her mind on Kārlis, she forced her heart to obey her will. *I must love him because he is so right for me, not like the other one, who rips me apart with his looks and his secretive hide-and-go-seek games and would clamp me with his one arm, when I would want two arms around me and not be embarrassed when he takes his jacket off. Anyway, he will soon be gone and that will be the end of this mad feeling, this unreasonable burning inside me, this*

*forbidden, no-good desire. Mrs. Kārlis Arājs. I like the name, the sound.
It's so down to earth, where I would be safe. Yes, I will love him—him
alone! But while lazy Cupid sharpens his arrow, I must find out more
about him.*

Trembling and tossing inside, she became a detective, picking up
bits and pieces about Kārlis wherever she went. At the end of her days,
she fit each puzzling piece into a portrait, and before the leaves finished
turning, she had a fairly accurate image of her future husband. Although
there were still many missing pieces, she could see the full portrait
emerging and, like a good detective, she scrambled to find whatever
pieces she needed with increased excitement. She was aware that her
heart had started to beat quicker whenever she thought of him, and
it pounded, sending blood to her face, whenever they marched side
by side. She took this as a sure sign of love made in heaven, and, as
the brilliant leaves whirled and fell at her feet, she walked with sure,
deliberate steps into her eighteenth autumn.

There were biographical details of Kārlis Arājs, which she had
picked up even before she had chosen him. For example, she knew that
he had finished gymnasium in Latvia, in the spring of 1944, which
would make him about five years older than her. She knew that he
attended the adult evening classes offered on the other side of the river,
but she didn't know what he studied. She assumed it would be the
English language and something that had to do with electricity. Most
young men seemed to be dealing with electrical currents and atoms,
connecting wires, building radios, exploding things. To Milda the
particulars didn't matter; she knew that whatever he would choose to
do, he would do thoroughly. She also knew that with him she would not
be lost and would stay a faithful and pure Latvian no matter what she
did or where they lived.

As she began paying more careful attention to any mention of him,
she heard his name often, suspicious that in many curious minds they

were already paired. She had heard *Aren't they beautiful together. . . What a pair!. . . With such, Latvia has a future.* So said the people. And they also talked about his mother. Milda learned that Mother and son had fled from Latvia on the Vidzeme highway, like so many others, in the autumn of 1944. Mr. Arājs had been a general in the Latvian army and was the victim of mass executions at Litene, perhaps in June 1941, but she wasn't sure. This fact would make any member of the family vulnerable. Their names would be listed automatically for the next deportations as soon as Latvia would fall again under communists. Therefore they had fled. But in the good days of independence, the family was privileged and definitely considered aristocratic, socializing with top government officials, noteworthy artists, and clergy. They would shun the bleeding half-communist social democrats, who messed around with Bolsheviks, and support President Ulmanis, who worked with his America-educated mind toward a free and prosperous Latvia. Strong nationalism flowed in the Arājs' veins; it was their life force. And Milda liked that.

When she found out about Kārlis's father's tragic fate, she sighed, *Oh, God, he had vanished like my Papa, like so many, so very many.* Instantly, she felt the ties of fate bind her with the victimized orphan, her counterpart. She also learned somehow that, with the help of German officers, the noble widow and her son had contacted some distant relatives in Berlin and had lived there until after the war, when the borders were set and Berlin was locked inside the Russian Zone. Then they, banded with other refugees and fled west or south until, in the usual mysterious way, ended up in Esslingen. She learned that, while living in Berlin, Kārlis would naturally be in *Hitler Jugend* and marched in the Sunday morning parades. *So that is where he learned how to lift his feet and keep his head high and his back straight,* Milda noted, as she put another piece in the imaginary puzzle of his life. Inevitably, she also heard mean and jealous words, saying how the Mother always pushed her son to the front, how she forced him to look up and stand apart. Milda, however, sensed that those who talked about the powerful woman still feared and respected her for she had circled in the midst of powerful people during the shifting dictatorships that pressed down on Latvia. Mrs. Arāja had seen the power struggle; she had seen the way important coats turned. During those brief but crucial years between Ulmanis's authoritarian rule and the brutal dictatorships of Hitler and Stalin, she had learned how to survive, how to keep her eyes open and her mouth shut and how to keep secrets and use them as weapons in self- defense or blackmail.

Aware of that, Milda saw how some of the Exile leaders stepped aside when she passed by, her head high and chest out. They greeted her humbly and treated her son with respect. In one food line, which Mrs. Arāja ignored by walking straight to the counter and receiving her rations, Milda heard some women shout out mean words, while a well-known newspaper man kindly stepped aside and let her pass. Only when she was out of sight and sound, people began talking, saying how her husband had been a four-star general and how his son looked so much like him. They said Kārlis was legendary, very special, and that some day he would be their leader. "Our tragic President has blessed him. Yes, he will lead us one day," a white-haired man said, sounding like a prophet.

Milda, once this pronouncement had fixed itself in her mind, could not quite imagine the circumstances of his leadership, nor the territory, nor the looks of the masses that he would lead from one place to another. Yet, she could see him; she could see them both, side by side, leading their people—perhaps, if Alma was correct—leading them back to Latvia once it was free of communists. The more she looked forward, the clearer she could see a glorious day, when they—and the masses of the dispossessed and displaced—would walk in a victorious parade through the streets of Riga, down the repossessed Freedom Boulevard, with throngs of all the suffering people whom they had left behind when they escaped. The unfortunate ones would welcome them with flowers and songs, like, at the end of World War I, the people had welcomed Rainis and Aspazija from their fifteen-year exile in Switzerland.

"Why wouldn't it be possible?" Alma also asked, imagining herself coming home, wearing a fur coat and motioning for people to put the flowers in the back of the open convertible, while she would reach out her arms to embrace Viktors Vētra. "Everything is possible. No borders are locked forever. . . . History repeats itself, going in cycles, from one generation to another. The hardest thing is to hold out, not buckle under the pressure of assimilation."

Milda pondered these things and knew that with Kārlis she could hold out. She would have no choice, for he would be firm and unbending. They just might make a glorious entry into a liberated Riga at some far-off golden point in time!

Meanwhile, the proud, broad-shouldered wife of martyred General Arājs kept the leader image of her son alive, spreading the idea whenever and wherever she could. She carried it about with the sound of proverbial trumpets and was always close by, admonishing him to walk straight, be like his father. Her words and commands put fear in him; Milda could sense that by the way his hands gripped the flag pole, by the way his lips tightened when he knew Mother was watching. She noticed that, when he did not carry the flag, he was very shy, downward looking awkward and embarrassed.

Then, unexpectedly, the mysterious legend about President Kārlis Ulmanis's blessing was revealed to her. It happened at the public bath. Kārlis's former elementary school teacher was there, and so was the eminent Mother, as well as the usual end-of-the-week group of women, all steaming hot. Milda heard the teacher and Mrs. Arāja talk about the event, now some ten years ago, in free Latvia, all the while wiping and massaging their naked, abundant bodies. Milda, offended by the open nakedness, hid under her towel, drying her hair carefully strand by strand. After Mrs. Arāja left, a woman asked the teacher what had happened between the President Kārlis Ulmanis and the young Kārlis Arājs. "Where was the connection?" the strange woman asked the half-clad teacher who glanced at Milda, whom she, of course, recognized. But Milda, all wrapped up in her pink terry cloth bath towel, which Alma had given her for a birthday present, went on drying her hair.

"It was the summer of 1938," the teacher began. "The President was going around the country and came to our town of Madona, which we who loved him had decorated with banners and garlands. Oh, how grand it all was! Our hearts beat with such joy, when we saw him enter through the arches of oak-leaf garlanded gates of honor. Our prettiest girls, clad in our district's dress and carrying meadow flowers waited at the arches. When the President and his entourage approached, they spread their flowers on the road so his feet would not touch the mud. On the distant stage, sang the town's choirs. There was a band and soldiers and land guards. The scouts marched in a parade. As you know, the President put great faith in our youth. He had learned the value of the young while studying in America. He believed that farmers—and our country would prosper only through farming—had to be forced to love the land while they were young. Therefore he supported the Scouts and *Laifs* (4-H clubs). Anyway, you asked about the young Mr. Arājs. This is what happened: our school had made a sentence out of the children: *SVEIKS TAUTAS VADONI!* (hail, nation's leader). We centered it in the sport field so it would face the platform where the President would stand. Oh, it was something to see! We knew he would be pleased, for, as I said, he loved the nation's youth. And, we the teachers, had carefully selected every child. I chose Kārlis Arājs for the exclamation mark. He was so handsome and tall for his age, and his father was so dashing and famous that there was no contest, really. Who else would be like him?"

The teacher paused and then started rolling up her cotton stockings that were damp and would not slide easily. "He also had a good head, the best, in fact. He knew the President's Handbook by heart and could recite all the paragraphs without stammering and with great conviction. Yes, he was the best, that is why I chose him for the exclamation mark." She began hunting for her garters.

"Is that all?" Milda asked softly. Then, jokingly, "Who was the dot?"

"A girl, of course," the teacher snapped at her garters and pulled her skirt firmly over her knees. "She was very small and sickly," she said, packing her towel away. "It was not my fault she got sick and died."

"Oh. . . ah. . . really," the women sighed and waited for more.

"That happened a whole week later," the teacher, suddenly agitated, spoke louder. "And it was not my fault that it had rained all night and the meadow was wet, and it was not my fault the President's train was late, and she had to crouch in the cold, wet grass longer than we had planned. Everybody got wet feet, even me, even Mr. Kārlis Arājs, but he did not give in. He stood as straight as any exclamation mark I've seen in print. I know. I stood next to him." She patted herself.

"How did she die?" Milda asked.

"I don't know," the teacher snapped irritably. "You, young lady, keep cutting in when I wanted to tell you all who're waiting to hear what I know."

"I apologize," Milda said.

"So, at last our President arrives. He and his cabinet and guards walk through the oak-garlanded gates and down the flower-carpeted road on to the platform. His arms stretch over us, his smile shines down on us. . . . Oh, what ovations, what love oozes from the people! Even the sun breaks through the clouds to welcome him! He speaks, and we applaud. And then he steps down and walks among the people. He shakes hands, wishes us good fortune, a bright, prosperous year and so on, and then he steps down onto the field where we stand and comes straight to me and shakes my hand and tells me that I am a good teacher. I curtsy, suspecting that Mrs. Arāja must have praised me to him, but I cannot say a word, I am so in awe of the big man. I only know that I stand before our great leader and his shadow passes over me and stops on Kārlis, my pride, and he puts his hand on the blond head and blesses him, saying, 'may you grow up to be a leader of our people.' Yes, I heard him say that. I heard it with my own ears."

"What about the dot?" Milda asked. She was fully dressed and looked down on the teacher, who was still sitting in a row of half-naked women, struggling with a button.

"I told you what happened! It was not my fault."

"Didn't anyone lift up that dot?" Milda persisted. "Didn't Kārlis Arājs give the poor girl a hand?"

"No. He had to hold his head up. He was facing the President, I told you already! He would have no time to look down."

"I see," Milda said and left the steaming room, letting the door slam behind her. She was outraged, but, simultaneously, pity mixed with sadness filled her heart. She wondered if he carried a load of guilt as she did because of the checker game. As she crossed the bridge, she vowed that she would save him. "It is my duty to rescue him from this cold insensitivity so that when another chance comes again, he would bend down to raise the insignificant and the poor. Not even a dot should perish at his feet, if I can help it."

*

After this episode, Milda wooed Kārlis with greater energy. Seemingly quite by chance she showed up, often in the company of some classmate, at the volley ball games, where he stood out as the slammer, or at political workshops for the young that did include women, and here and there, hoping that, just in case, he might notice her and run over with a friendly *labdien*. Occasionally she saw him, smiled, waved, and cheered along with others, but still he would not run over or lift his hand and wave back from a safe distance. Once, at some parade, her foot slipped, but he would not even offer his free hand but held on to the flag pole as though it was slipping off the platform and stood firmer, straighter, his gaze fixed on some far-off lofty goal.

Milda waited. The days dragged on, and then came one of those *to be* or *not to be* days. It happened in the Lido courtyard at the pump on a warm Saturday when, skimpily clad, she came out of the doorway to fill her pail for her stair scrubbing. Through the large opened windows of the ballroom flowed the notes of a Strauss waltz. In step, she waltzed up to the pump and started pumping to the *Blue Danube*. Before the pail was half full, the piano stopped and, after a while, the elegant dancing instructor appeared her. Startled, she stopped pumping, eying his black paten-leather shoes, covered with spats and some drops of water. She said *Oh*! and apologized, as he put his hand over hers and said never-mind.

"I have been watching for you. Have time for a word?"

"Yes, of course."

"Of course you know *Arāja kundze* and her son."

"Yes." Milda blushed. "So?"

"She signed her son up for ballroom dancing lessons."

"So?" She feigned indifference.

"Well, she gave me your name as a possibility for being his partner." Milda took a deep breath and lifted her wide open surprised eyes to him, squinting as the sun blanked him out for a moment.

"I would encourage you to accept and join us. There are, of course, more young ladies than men, so I can easily find a partner for him, but—the *dāma* is right—you would be the best choice, and I could teach you also some exciting new moves," he said, touching her thinly clad shoulder, applying his expert pressure, then sliding his hand casually down, over her spine. *That means he will be coming here twice a week,* Milda told herself and almost agreed, when the man's hand suddenly arrested hers that grabbed the iron pump handle. Together the hands went down, down, down, splattering more water on his shoes.

So she has watched me. Chosen me. Spoken to this man and made a bargain with him! They bargained over us without even introducing herself to me. She laughed, thinking, now trembling from the instructor's seductive pressure, like the pressure of Vanags's hand, like the pressure of other men's hands, and when she looked up, withdrawing her wet hand, his eyes caused the pail to tip over and the water spill.

"I know how to dance already," she said, as he tap danced to avoid the puddle. She picked up the pail and started pumping again.

"No, thank you," she said, pumping hard, filling the bucket to the rim.

"It would give me great pleasure to teach you."

"Thank you! But I'm not willing."

"Good," he said and moved a step closer, reaching for her as if they were already on some dance floor.

"Sir, you misunderstood me. I said I'm *not* willing."

"Oho! Proud are we?" And suddenly she was in his arms, his lips hunting for her mouth. Outraged, she pushed him away, slipping and grabbing for the bucket, she left him standing in a puddle of water.

*

In her mind, Milda brushed off the unwanted advance as she would brush off an irritating wasp, but held on to the information the gentleman had given her. She found out the time of Kārlis's dancing lessons and timed her coming and going so they would meet, but he seemed awkward, pretending not to notice her until one day she blocked his way. Their eyes met for a second and then, his face turning red, saying excuse me, he brushed passed her and was gone. Humiliated, she too disappeared before the dance instructor would notice. They ran into each other like that accidentally on purpose several times. Sometimes he looked at her like he wanted to say something but then, suddenly, he turned away in a hurry. She tried to break his searching, wondering gazes with an encouraging smiles like clear, bright lights that would give him direction, but he remained mute and blind. This was terrible, tormenting, causing her such anguish that she couldn't sleep, lost her appetite, and was short-tempered, especially when Alma asked her what the matter was.

"That's LOVE!" Alma said and snickered. "You should've accepted the dance lessons. Again, you let great chances go by. . . . What are we to do with you?"

"We?!" Milda cried out. "*Et tu!*" She fell on her bed and turned her face to the wall, calming down only after her aunt closed the door behind her. She turned on her back and gazed at the blue square of sky beyond her window frame. As she gazed at a white cloud that slowly floated in and out of her vision, a delicious anticipation of Kārlis's embraces and kisses came over her. *Perhaps he too is lying on his bed thinking about me. Maybe he too wants to take me by the hand on his own, not talked into by his mother, not pushed and questioned and pushed again as if he couldn't do anything right on his own. She and everybody push us together but then stand in our way. It's as if they all wanted a piece of us, wanted to watch us kiss like in the movies or the theater*

"Oh, this crowded closeness! This everybody being everybody's business!" she shouted at the ceiling with its one, fly-spattered dull lamp hanging blindly in the middle. Frustrated, she got up and, with spiteful hands, took up her books. She had to study for final exams. *I'll show them*!

"She's the one!" Milda said in her sleep one night and sat up, suddenly wide awake. She had seen his mother, the indomitable Mrs.

Arāja, in a dream. She was like a mountain with jagged edges, which she had to get over before she could as much as lay a finger on her beloved target. "But you must do it! . . . you must save Prince Kārlis by working through his mother, the queen," she whispered and tried to go back to sleep.

She took herself at her word. The very next time they marched for another assembly, she bowed to Mrs. Arāja, who sat in the front row, next to an important guiding light of the Kingdom of Exile. The grand dame slightly acknowledged her in the manner a queen would an unimportant foreign princess.

"She sees me!" Milda told the stars that night.

Neighbors Can Help

She was glad that the Gramzdas lived within reach. Since Alma had pushed her future into the Baptist hands, the doors between them were often left open. Many times, when Alma was away, they shared their meals and their thoughts. She also spent much of her free time with Helga, going on hikes, reading and sewing together. Helga adored her and was happy for any endowed minute of friendship. She trusted Milda to look over her themes and correct any mistakes. When the mood was especially congenial, Helga would open her diary and read aloud her first poems, blushing, yet hoping for some bright words of approval. When Milda said them, Helga had touched heaven and for days basked in its glory.

"I must find a way to America," Milda told Mrs. Gramzda, one afternoon when they had conversed while drinking tea. "Could you help me?"

"No, not really, but my husband can. So you must talk to him. He'll find a way."

"But, you understand, I don't want to become a Baptist," she made it clear. "I'm a Lutheran and will be confirmed after my graduation. I respect your faith, but I want to keep mine." Her hands twisted a napkin into a rope.

"Why are you so nervous all at once? . . . Who has asked you to become anything? Faith is not something you can keep or give away. One simply has it or does not."

"Please forgive me," she stammered in a voice ready to break. "It's, it's just that people think there is a reason for your doing what you do, like making your church bigger, more acceptable," she stumbled on awkwardly, while Mrs. Gramzda warmed up their tea.

"Tell me," the elder asked, "do people really think we run some kind of a trading post here? Do they think we give out visas for blasphemous lies of salvation? Ah, there's the sin: this lying, making fools of us, of my husband and all the others in our congregation who try to help, who try to make sense, in a way, of why our fate is what it is. My husband is a simple man, an orphan who had to raise himself on his sandy acreage by the sea. He struggled against poverty all his young life and knows what poor people need. Food and lodging and love. Then other things must follow. He really likes to help. It's his calling, his reason for living—to lift others up, to tell them that they are princes because Christ is the King. Yes, he believes strongly that God has guided him to do this work and that he must bring as many Latvians as possible out of bondage into freedom. Oh, but why do I go on? Of course, he will help you. In fact, he has wondered about what you and your aunt will do."

"Thank you," Milda said. "You have lifted a huge burden off my back." She smiled and untwisted the napkin. She ironed it out with her hand. "Please forgive me for being so blunt."

"It's all right, my dear. At least you have talked straight, not like so many others."

"What do they say?"

"They talk in circles. It really gets to be quite funny, but I better not say more."

"I must go," Milda said rising, then stood still, gazing out the window. "I have one more question. Mrs. Arāja, you remember her?" Mrs. Gramzda nodded. "What did she say? What was her connection with the Baptists?"

The woman chuckled. "At the end of the last century, her servant's grandmother had been baptized in a frozen river. I heard her go on about how a hole was chopped in the ice and how warm the old woman had felt when she came up out of the river and was wrapped in a horse blanket. Her son was embarrassed, so different from the way he appears at the parades. By the way, you both look very handsome together."

"So I've heard others say. When we get to America we will marry."

"I see. . . . Congratulations! I'm happy for you, and I will talk to my husband, but you must talk to him also. He will find a way, I know that. He always does.

Milda Prepares for America

Milda let the days pass. She reveled in her newly-found security, thinking and allowing her fantasies a free reign. At last, when Alma seemed somewhat relaxed, she told her that her passage to America was being worked out. Alma, disappointingly, did not cry out in the expected glee; she did not refer to the turn of events for days but continued to probe deeper into her *Maija un Paija* dreadful cave scene. When the drama was finished, Alma, without a word or a note, vanished. When many days later she returned, she offered no explanation, only put a box of chocolates on the table. Milda asked no questions but tried again to broach the emigration issue: "You too must come with me to America." Alma pretended she did not hear.

*

Days later, Reverend Gramzda called Milda into his office. He was friendly and set her at ease right away. For a while they chatted. She found out that he knew her Uncle Imants and had preached in his church. He liked Aunt Matilde's cooking. He knew all the children from their cradles and had blessed them all as infants. He was glad that at least part of the family was well and living on their farm and not in Siberia behind the North Pole. When Milda told him that their son Juris had fallen in battle, he asked about Atis. She didn't know what had happened to him. No one knew.

"Such is our nation's plight," he sighed and then talked on, saying that the bloody part of terror might be over. "Even communists must eat, and it would be insane to hurt the farmers, yet. . . one never knows, but we must go on, so let's get this done.."

Sitting across from each other, they filled out the emigration forms. All the questions were easy except the one, which the Preacher asked looking over his glasses: "Your parents. Both dead, is that right?"

"No, oh, no—not Mamma!" Milda exclaimed.

"But I have classified you as an orphan. Or did I misunderstand?"

"Mamma is alive," Milda whispered and repeated Zelda's last words from the letter.

Silently they looked at each other, and then the man began explaining about sponsors and other technicalities. Orphans belonged in a separate category, he said. The procedures were simpler. "Besides," he asked, "will you—could you—go back now or in the next year or the years after that?" He, speaking softly, tried to show her that for all practical purposes she was an orphan. She had no mother. None who could travel with her, care for her, advise her. And she was still under eighteen. He did not use the word *dead*. He only said that her mother was not and would not be of any help to her, not now, and perhaps never. "It may be that in twenty-five or fifty years things might change, but by then you will be older than your mother is now."

"Then she will be gone," Milda said, unable to hold back her tears. The Preacher waited. After she wiped her eyes, they finished filling out the form. They agreed that she would leave Germany after her graduation and confirmation. "I want to have as much of my life done right as is possible. . . . I would like to finish one stage before starting another."

"Of course. We all want to restore some sense of order. I also have set aside my application until my job here is finished." He told her that it might take at least a year, perhaps longer, before all the people would be re-located. "Pastor Ābele recently wrote to me, saying that the debates in the U.S. Congress are still going on and no final word has been said. So we all have to hold on and wait. But that doesn't keep us from getting the paper work done so we can be ready to go when the trumpet shall sound."

"Could I travel with your family to America? . . . We could all go together."

"Why, yes, of course! Why didn't I think of it?" He paused. "Would you like to visit our church again?" he asked as he shook her hand.

"Leave the young lady alone!" his wife poked her head out of the adjoining door. "She is not like the others."

"Very well!" He shrugged indifferently. "She is and she isn't. How would she know that she is welcome unless I invite her?" He smiled. "You are always welcome." He put his hand on her shoulder. Her fate was in that hand that felt like a blessing.

"Thank you," she curtsied and left the office.

Out in the hall, Mrs. Gramzda met her. "So it is done. I heard it all. I am very sorry that you had to answer that one cruel question like that. We had to adjust our forms also. We put down four children, not five," she said. "For all we can guess from the coded notes from my mother, he is a prisoner of war and is somewhere in Siberia, but to the Americans it means that our armies were allies of Germans and fought against them. Our veterans cannot immigrate to the United States."

"I know."

"Well, then, what could we do? Our staying here would not help him. Here we would have no way of rebuilding our lives, but once we are in America and we find out that he is alive, we could very well help him. . . . Oh, it is hard, so very hard, and none of it is our fault. We have fallen between the cracks of the great powers that rule the world."

"Yes."

"I am very happy that you want to travel with us, when the time comes. . . . Let's have some tea and a bite to eat. We should celebrate."

They talked the remaining afternoon hours away in an easier mood. They made plans and indulging their fantasies of far-away America. When the time was up and each had to return to her duties, Mrs. Gramzda said apologetically, "You must excuse my husband. He tends to be insensitive. It comes from growing up alone. He was an orphan and had to look after himself. Lived in the crude backwoods of Kurzeme that had no use for gentle manners. And then the war came—the First World War, that is. God saved his life and his soul, and that is why he became a preacher. He is a free man. He fought for our freedom. Oh, he will tell you all about that himself, I'm sure. Over and over. We'll be ten days in the crossing. . . . But why the tears again?"

"Because. . . because he talked to me like—what I have always imagined—a father would, not like the teachers and leaders, but like a father, and I can see the road in front of me clearly. Oh, I'm happy! So glad and relieved. I must tell my *Kārlītis,* somehow, but how?"

"With patience comes wisdom, as the saying goes. You will know the right time. And you will have the right words."

Milda and Kārlis

The right words came to her, when at last Kārlis Arājs succumbed. It happened at the Christmas ball. Milda had starred again in the lead role as *Saulcerīte* in the school play *The Golden Steed.* After the performance, she had rushed across the river, back to Lido to change clothes and meet Alma, who would return from wherever she was and had promised to be her chaperone. Like Cinderella, very excited, Milda arrived late for the ball, knowing that Kārlis would be there. She was dressed in an exquisite gown of midnight blue velvet she had designed and sewed herself. "A Christmas present," Alma had said at the end of November, as she spread the royal material on one bed and equal yardage of wine red velvet on the other, adding, "For your gift to me. Please make me a dress out of this."

Milda was relieved, for she had tried to come up with the right present, because everything seemed trivial for her aunt, who hated clutter and kitsch. Milda set to work immediately, as sewing relaxed her, and created two beautiful dresses. When she and Alma entered the ballroom, all eyes turned on them. They heard the *ahs* and *ohs* and, mercifully, the starting notes of the orchestra. Alma quickly disengaged herself from her niece and went to the table of her theater acquaintances, leaving Milda standing dazed and alone, squinting at the dim lamps spaced out like streetlights.

She sees the students and teachers, by classes, at one side of the ballroom; the actors and actresses have congregated on the other side. The men rise as Alma approaches. One man doesn't allow her to sit down, but puts his arm around her and off they waltz. She stares at the dancers whirling past her, and then she sees Kārlis in the candlelight of the huge fir tree. She sees his mother also. She is dressed in a dark blue lace dress, through which the white skin of her arms exposes itself in dappled flecks. Then the woman moves and becomes a large, twisted shadow. Milda feels as if the candles were singeing her face, making it glow. Her heart drums. The music stops and starts. And then Kārlis comes toward her, walking as if on air, coming out of the lighted tree as out of her dreams. He bows, and she extends her arms. They waltz away on the strings of *Wine Women and Song.* She closes her eyes and lets him guide her, carry her from dream to dream, from cloud to cloud. She likes the way he holds her. The grip is strong and possessive. He holds her the way he holds the flagpole, and she is glad. She is sure that only he could carry her through life without dropping her. She would be safe with him, protected from the likes of Mr. Vanags. At the many turns, her eyes search the dark corners and the tables where men sit in circles, fearful that he might be there and at any moment might intercept their dance. But she doesn't see him, and closing her eyes leans back, testing the strength of his left arm. She feels the pressure of his fingers guiding her as he had been taught. She recalls the long-gone scene at the pump and the instructor's advances and regrets that he had forgotten his manners, which made it impossible for her to take dancing lessons also. But—Kārlis danced well; and he would lead her. He knows the rules and had learned the steps well. She smiles approvingly and follows his lead. They pass Alma and the Mother but don't pause. The Mother is a shadow, and Alma seems far away, lying by the Baltic Sea in the cold North, while under her own feet burns a strange desert sand.—

The dance ends, and Milda stands again on the same spot where Kārlis found her. In harnessed torment she yearns to dance the night away, but Kārlis merely bows and backs off. She tries to stop him by raising her hand slightly, but he does not see it and is gone. She sees Mother quickly going through the door, wrapping her seal coat around her. She is a passing storm. . . .

Alma takes Control of Milda

Milda pulls herself back into the present. She sees a classmate bow before her, but she brushes him off, her eyes searching through the enchanting darkness. Suddenly, as if fallen from the ceiling Pēteris Vanags stands before her, bowing, extending his whole arm, toward which she leans, almost yielding, but then catches herself and looks at the half-empty sleeve pulling itself out of the pocket and hanging loose on the stump, reaching as far as it can. She tries to speak, tries to say that she thought he had gone to Venezuela or somewhere in the Southern Hemisphere, but the words don't cross her lips; instead they circle around inside her head, chanting *See how handsome he is tonight! Dark blue looks so good on him, making his eyes blue even in darkness. How can he change so often, so completely? And where has he been all summer?* As if reading her thoughts, he says, "I have been away. In Paris and. . ."

"We must go," Alma says urgently, throwing an overcoat around Milda's shoulders. She pulls her away. As she does, she scans Vanags from head to foot and gives him a hard look that makes him back away. "I think I've seen you somewhere before," she says. "You were a nuisance then as you are now, but I don't remember when and where it was. . . . Now, get out of our way!" Vanags opens his mouth to speak, remind and explain, but she has already turned her back and, pushing Milda forward, leaves him alone in the cold.

Outside drizzles and freezes. The streets turn slippery. The women hold on to each other. The bridge is all a glaze, with lamps glowing inside misty nimbuses. Angry tears freeze in Milda's lashes. The black water down below gurgles and ripples in unruly waves. Milda stops and holds Alma's arm. They look down silently; then Alma embraces her niece and pulls her head against her cheek. "Don't cry," she says and kisses her face. "You have slain him. And you were magnificent, true to our lineage!" They manage to get across without falling and meander on. Alma tries to remember, "That invalid, I know I've seen him before.... Yes, I know! He used to hang around the theater, staring at us, waiting for any small part he might fill, but I may be wrong. There were many boys lurking around, and then the war came.... They ran to enlist, and now they're invalids and still lurking around, but you must not pay any attention. You cannot save the world. Everyone is on his own, sink or swim."

"Still, I feel sorry for him and others like him."

"Feel all you want, but stay away, and remember your heart's promise to the whole, undamaged boy you must turn into a man."

"Yes."

They walk on in silence. The night, shrouded in mist, lies silent— except for the chiming of church bells. The old town in Christmas attire is enchanting. The two displaced women, wrapped in their separate thoughts, wander the narrow streets that slowly turn white from mounting granules of sparkling snow.

"*Meine Ruhe ist hin, mein Herz ist schwer*," Milda chants, and Alma picks up and echoes the same heart-breaking lines. "So it is," she sighs. "*My peace is gone, my heart is heavy*." They lean on each other, their arms tightly around their waists, their faces battling the sharp snowflakes. They stop at pretty window displays and catch their reflections looking back at them as from glassy pools. They go on, murmuring softly to each other until their feet grow numb from the cold, and turn onto *Bahnhoffstrasse* toward Lido and go up to their room. Milda has spruced it up with evergreen garlands and a tiny tree she had bought at the *Weinachtsmarkt*. She lights the white candles fastened on its tiny branches and kindles the wood in the potbelly stove. Alma turns out the electric light. They take off their coats. They pour out a bottle of red wine and heat it and then pour it into a glass bowl. They set out slices of bread and sausage, an orange, and some cookies. They eat, drink and giggle. The velvet dresses brush against each other, the skirts tangle and twist, hands lock, lipstick smears.

"My darling," Alma talks dramatically, "Isn't life fine, just fine? Better than the stage, more dramatic than any made-up thing. "Happy Christmas! to us—the broken off branches of our family tree all intertwined, acting out our parts on the dusty stage of life."

Milda offers no comment. She sips the last of the wine and watches the candles burn out. They make weird shadows on the ceiling. She sets down the empty glass, and Alma pulls her down beside her on the bed. In a tranquil daze, they watch the shadows, reading in them blurred faces and forms. They name them, talk to them until, one by one, the candles burn out.

1949

Throughout January, Milda caught only rare glances of Kārlis. But she seemed to be running into his mother frequently and quite by chance. Each time the matriarch indicated good will and encouragement with uncertain smiles and evaluating glances. As if by mutual resolve, when the new year was already on its way, they were taking their late Friday afternoon baths at about the same hour. Milda felt the woman shamelessly examine her body as if it were a piece of meat at a shop. Her bold stares made her shiver, yet she knew that unless she was fully approved, she would have no chance with Kārlis. The unexpressed, seemingly casual appraisal was clear and provocative, and so, Milda spitefully submitted to the challenge.

After the next bath, sitting at a slight angle, opposite the naked and wet Mrs. Arāja, she did not wrap her pink bath towel around her but dried herself slowly with the towel's edge, starting from her head and going down to her toes. With proper shyness, she finished the drying process by lifting her arms to pull up her hair. She twisted herself ever so slightly, allowing the examiner a full front view, then turned her back and blotted the lower parts of her torso. She rose and stood for a moment like Aphrodite on a seashell, and then reached for her clothes and dressed fastidiously, piece by piece, displaying the neat border stitching of her underwear, the more elaborate tatting on her blouse, and the straight hem of her skirt. She rolled her Alma-supplied nylon stockings with artistic grace, extending her well-formed, strong legs, and snapped the garters. She slipped her feet into black, fur-trimmed high-heel boots, put on her coat and, with a slight nod, left the half-naked, red-faced lady sitting on a bench in a row of steaming and curious women. As Milda left the bath room and before she reached the outside door, muffled sounds of high-pitched voices seeped through the door. With a feeling of having won a race, she rushed out with a light bounce into the frozen air. As she crossed the river, she saw a blue-gray pigeon flying into the sunset, tilting its wings against the wind. "Perhaps this is my bluebird of happiness," she said, following its flight.

Kārlis Departs for America

Sometime during the freeze and thaw of early February, the transient Latvian remnant of Esslingen spread the news that Mrs. Arāja and her son had received their clearance to emigrate. On March, stiff and formal, Milda and Kārlis marched side by side in General Kalpaks memorial parade. They stood at attention during the solemn assembly. As Milda heard again the long speeches, recounting the bravery of the first General of the Latvian army—she calculated that it was exactly thirty years ago when he fell in battle, but she did not mourn, buy turned her head and looked at Kārlis, her eyes imploring *why are we standing here, wasting our time?* But Kārlis reacted with a disapproving grimace, putting her to shame. She turned from him and stared straight ahead wondering why there was such a fuss every year over a man whom his own foot soldier had killed by mistake. She wished she too were going to America. She was tired and bored with all the holidays and always having to stand at attention.

*

Three days later, early in the morning, Milda hurries to the train station to see Kārlis off. She is extremely distraught because nothing is settled. No words of love and engagement and marriage have been spoken. *Maybe he's waiting for me and saving those life-changing words for the very last.* With every step time and chance slip under her feet, splattering her with slush. She sees the train and, pushing ahead of the line, buys a platform ticket and races through the under path and up the stairs. Before she steps on to the platform, she sees Kārlis tightly packed in a crowd of milling people. Mother stands by like a bodyguard. To Milda's immense joy, Kārlis gives her a smile of relief and welcome. She presses on toward him. With her cold fingers she sticks a blue crocus in his lapel, saying, "It's from my window garden." Then, rising on her tiptoes, she whispers close to his ear, "Blue is the color of longing" and kisses him on the cheek.

At that, she sees Mother nudge him hard and, blushing he takes her hand and holds it so that she feels his quick pulse. Thrilled by his nervousness and pressed by the crowd, she moves up against him. She pulls gently at the buttons and belt of his trench coat and opens it. Another maternal nudge causes his arms to open and take her in. Her arms reach up, and her hands clasp his padded shoulders. She brings his face down. Their lips meet in their first kiss. Their bodies touch, and she feels his imprisoned manliness arising, making her legs go weak. She locks her eyes and kisses him passionately, burrowing inside his open coat, but quickly pulls back, disengaging himself and wrapping his coat tightly around him. She opens her eyes and sees him looking at her bewildered, helpless, his face turning a deep pink. As though caught stealing, he looks around for someone to handcuff him, but the crowd pays no attention. Everyone is holding, kissing, separating, saying words. Mother watches, eyeing Milda doubtfully, then straightens out her son's twisted belt. Kārlis looks frightened, as if in pain, ready to cry. He clutches Milda's hand, saying, "I don't want to leave you now!"

She kisses him lightly, sadly smiling, whispering, "Soon I shall be with you—forever—if you wish." He pulls her close to him and holds her fiercely. Mother watches, and catching Milda's eye, nods in a kind of conspiratorial approval.

The train's sharp whistle tears them apart, as the crowd tramples through and around them. "Think of me always," he shouts, looking over his shoulder. "Yes!" she shouts back. Some minutes later, she sees him inside the train. He opens the window and leans out to touch her outstretched hands. "All the best to you, my dear," Mrs. Arāja phrases the cliché with deep meaning, as though summoning the crowd to bear witness to the virtual engagement, then stands tall, filling the window, watching from above. When the train jerks, Milda tucks her finger inside the corner of a white, embroidered handkerchief in an effort to soak up the tears that ought to be gushing from her wide open eyes, but they stay dry and cold. The train starts moving, slowly chugging out of the station as white handkerchiefs flutter in the wind and slowly fold away.

Minutes later Milda walks down the station stairway on to *Bahnhofstrasse*. In her peripheral vision she sees Pēteris Vanags leaning against a lamp post. She doesn't know that he had gone before her and shaken hands with Kārlis Arājs and made him swear that he would not forget him and do all he can to bring him to America. Having extracted that promise and felt the younger man's tight hug and seen his blushing cheeks, he had stepped aside as Milda rushed up the stairway. He had observed the whole last scene from a safe distance, jealous of the trench coat, the kisses, and the hands, the fingers reaching, pressing, and interlocking. She had not seen his one fist clench nor heard his heart swear *one day you will be mine, even if it takes half a lifetime! I can wait. I will outwait the boy. I've survived trenches, and I'll survive this one. He will never know how to love this Princess whose heart belongs to me!* She does not see—would not comprehend if she had seen—the tears he was hiding behind an open newspaper. She increases the speed of her steps as she passes by, now looking straight ahead, carefully crossing the street, hurrying on, pretending she doesn't see him, who makes her heart pound in fear or excitement. She cannot tell which it is. She must not be late for school, and school is on the other side of town.

All the world blurs as she probes into her future. With each hurried step she reviews the brief contact with Kārlis. She goes over it second by second, excited, yet confused, forcing the other out of her tangled nerves. She hangs her thoughts only on Kārlis, reviewing every gesture, every glance. She knows their kiss was his first. It was awkward and ignorant, and she knows that she cannot open herself to him too quickly, too irrepressibly, as she liked to imagine—even after they will be married. She knows she will have to nurture him, lead him slowly to the bubbling fountain of her love and desire. She must act like the innocent orphan, idealized in folklore and poetry. Foreshadowing that, she trembles in a new-born fear, worried that she had given herself away too much, that she had stepped over the line, that Mother surely had seen it all and would discuss her with her son in some unimaginable moment of privacy. She is sure that Mother saw her as she often had—undressed—and would make her hang out the sheets on their wedding night. All right, she will do it and prove that she really was innocent and chaste in her body, if not in her imagination, but imaginations are invisible. Still, she cannot deny, cannot forget herself and Gert in the cave and Alma in the attic room, nor the ride in the jeep with Mr. Vanags. . . .

Separation and Anxiety

Within a month, when Esslingen bloomed in all its splendid colors and filled the air with dizzying fragrances, Kārlis's first letter arrived. Milda's spirit soared, winging her to rush up to the vineyard, where closer to heaven she could feast on his words, where she would find deep meaning in every phrase and behind each sentence. She thought it a most wonderful letter, describing the trip, the ocean, and life in American. The letter ended classically, simply, *Kārlis*. She answered immediately, sitting under a blooming apple tree.

Thereafter, more letters arrived, each longer than the one before, setting down details about New York, the people of America and the Latvians who disembarked upon the shores. Kārlis wrote about the formation of a Latvian community and about the possibilities for a rich life. No letter referred to their platform farewell, no letter indicated that he suffered from her absence. The sentences were flawless, balanced, coherent. Relieved, Milda wrote back equally flawless and balanced letters.

*

Still, there came no word from Door #2, although more and more people dirtied the stairs. The DP settlements all over Germany were thinning out quickly. By mysterious agreements and policies, things were being rearranged, people were being moved and shuffled about, and everyone seemed as ready to fly like migrating storks or take to ships over troubled waters like the pilgrims of old. Into the vacated housing in Esslingen, across the Neckar, displaced Polish refugees were placed. The Latvians did not like it, and the Germans hated it. "Damned foreigners, they complained. "Will there ever be an end to all this?"

"Yes, there will be. I see it coming," Milda answered the butcher, the baker, and the florist at the end of her street. "The day will come when all Germany, including our Esslingen will be swept clean of us *Ausländer*. The four winds will scatter us over the globe."

"*Ach*," sighed the butcher. "I didn't mean to offend you. *Aber* people are always happiest in their own countries."

"I know that, but *your Führer* did not, so here we are," she said and left the shop. It never failed to amaze her how untouched by all the troubling changes the people of this town, this province, were. To them what happened had already happened and seemed only a disturbance of their *Ordnug*. They could not wait for things to return to normal, the way they had been before the war, before the waves of strangers flooded over them. At times, Milda felt sorry for these people, who still did not see beyond their pretty hills, not even beyond the end of their streets. The butcher did not know who occupied the Lido and that it was a rare cultural center, indeed, a world within a world that would become a historical landmark in the Kingdom of Exile about which musicals and stories would be written in future years. What did the butcher care that the School of Dance closed when the patent-shoe maestro left for New York? What did the florist care that the Egle family left and Aijiṇa cried and that those who went to say their farewells at the railroad station had bought flowers at his shop? And no one cared that the sign was moved from Door #2 to #3 and that Reverend Gramzda had a real office now, and again Vizma could practice her piano in peace and, oh, so beautifully. No one cared, except the displaced. For them, every change, every train, carried away yet another part of their uprooted, uncertain selves.

*

One evening Alma announced that the best comedy actor was gone and her steady partner waited for his final papers. She told Milda that she was making arrangements to immigrate to Sweden. "And I still don't know what you will do," she said angrily.

"I'll go to America," she answered. "I'll marry Kārlis Arājs—all at the right time. Reverend Gramzda has promised, so I must wait."

"Oh, you goose!" Alma yelled. "I can't stand it anymore. You drive me mad."

"Forgive me, please."

"Forgive me, please," Alma mimicked. "My forgiveness will get you nowhere! What the devil are you waiting for? Angels from heaven?"

"Yes." Milda said and lay down on her bed and pulled the covers over her. She prayed for help, like she and cousin Anna had prayed for the sun to shine on that rainy Sunday morning long, long ago. Alma went out.

*

Of course, in spite of Alma's outburst, Milda trusted the Preacher's promise and waited. Her mind was at rest, and her life followed its set routine. School, study, housekeeping, handcrafts, costumed public appearances, and stolen hours of tea and discussions with Mrs. Gramzda. During those hours, when they talked, the hands never lay idle. Mrs. Gramzda mended constantly, while Milda knitted a sweater for Kārlis. She had gathered every possible length and color of yarns and was working them all into a most astonishing design, herself surprised and delighted. "It is love you are knitting into that work of art," Mrs. Gramzda said in admiration, very much like Mrs. Niert did so long ago, when she taught little *Mildchen* how to cast stitches. It was a large sweater she was knitting now. Kārlis was a large man—larger than life.

As the autumn days grew shorter and drabber, the knitting became more exciting, like a dramatic poem, like a tapestry, like an infection. Then Vizma caught the knitting germ and also started knitting

Christmas presents. Helga looked on and soon she, too, picked up five very thin steel needles—the same ones she vowed she would throw into the Neckar—and cast on the necessary eyes for a pair of gloves. She was positive. When the eyes dropped and her fingers cramped, she closed her eyes and saw her ethnically correct but not exactly perfect mittens hanging on the display wall of the gallery in Stuttgart and, setting for herself an imagined goal, struggled on. She took many deep breaths and knitted and purled, drawing inspiration and competing with her sister and her friend, who made knitting look easy. She tried hard not to be *just a girl* in transition. She also reminded herself that at the end of the last school year, her theme was read in front of the class and received second place in an all-school writing competition, so next to that knitting a pair of gloves with ten fingers should be easy. She smiled when she remembered the small celebration on the top floor of Lido in honor of her winning the prize. There had been a full plate of wonderful cookies and hot chocolate. All the neighbors came and stayed on, the older ones talking, the young singing around the piano that Vizma played so lightly and effortlessly that Helga recognized in her soul the sin of envy. It seemed to her that every time she did something right, there were expressions of surprise and half-hearted joy, telling her that no one really believed that she could be outstanding in anything and certainly not permanently. But that one time, even her father had paused from typing to join in. Jānis, to show that he was not to be ignored, played unheard cowboy songs on his accordion.

Milda also recalled that occasion and, seeing all the hands in a circle knitting, the fingers dancing, laboring, playing, felt that she had naturally and easily knitted herself into the family of her guardians. Alma was left out. She couldn't separate the yarns, could not unravel the intricate geometric designs, so Milda said and let it be known that gossip about her aunt was strictly off limits.

After Milda finished the sweater, she asked Helga to go with her to the post office to mail it. "I cannot do it alone," she said nervously. "What if he doesn't like it? What if he doesn't understand my designs?"

"Creative people have that problem," Helga said, having heard it somewhere.

"Yes. I understand, still. . ."

The following day, Alma gave her niece a lecture on privacy, reminding her where her home, though temporary, was and where her loyalties lay. "Not with them. . . Well, maybe until you have the emigration papers in hand. But after that you don't have anything to do with that family but only with your own, broken or not!" Milda listened and felt again that deep, mean shadow fall across the floor. She tried to obey, tried to shrink back into her little room, crowded with her Aunt, whether or not she was actually present. The tension made her despondent, sick with colds and headaches. That autumn she did not march in the November 18 parade. She had chicken pox. It was a severe case, and she was mortified that her face would be pockmarked forever. Alma feared it also, or did she gloat as she glanced in the small looking glass and smiled at her smooth image? Vizma, the would-be nurse, tiptoed into the room, when all was quiet and applied potions of chalk and vitamin mixtures to each bump and encouraged her friend to drink the herb tea she had brewed. Afraid that someone else might take her part of Maija in *Maija un Paija,* which was scheduled again for the school Christmas play, Milda swallowed the vitamins and teas as much as her stomach could hold, wrote long letters to Kārlis, and perfected her lines. As, feeling miserable, she immersed herself more and more into her character, she forced her body and soul toward absolute goodness and perfection. In her sleepless hours, she remembered and confessed to Jesus her past sins and the desires of her unruly flesh and asked His forgiveness. She was so afraid that God would punish her with ugly facial excavations so that Kārlis would surely reject her and that she, like

Cain, would enter the New World forever marked. Repeatedly, every night, she prayed for forgiveness and promised to be eternally faithful to her betrothed, if only He would not rob her of her beauty or punish her in some other way and not let her cross the Ocean so that she would never glide into the safe harbor of matrimony.

She firmly believed that it was in answer to her prayer that her last blemishes dropped off and soon after that her face cleared, except for one stubborn blemish at her hairline. Still weak, but happy, she dressed and went to the rehearsal, leaving Alma alone with her Maija in *Love is Stronger than Death*, which was also being staged throughout the fall season. And, as a year before, on the main stage, a more distraught Alma, wrapped in a red shawl, wearing a blond wig with long braids, shone brighter than ever. She had stopped arguing with Rainis and accepted the character as a part of herself. The public, what was left of it, adored her, and she basked in that glory and triumph that all knew would be brief.

Roses on Ice

It is mid-December. A very cold day. Milda walks up the stairs. The Lido smells of sauerkraut and fried pork chops. Vizma plays Christmas carols. Children jabber in warm voices behind Door #1. She longs to knock on the door. She is hungry and sick with loneliness. But she dare not. Instead, she finds the key in her pocket and goes toward her own room that seems suddenly like a prison cell. She trips over something and looks down. It is a bucket full of roses. She opens the door and pulls the bucket inside, to the middle of the floor. She kindles the stove and then counts the roses. There are a hundred. One hundred dark red roses! In the middle is a gold-edged card, unashamedly open. Milda reads: *"To my betrothed. Vilis."* She stares, blinking at the intruding flowers that take over the whole room like an army. United, bunched together, blooming—when only ice flowers bloom on her window glass—and intoxicating, they have come to ravish weary Alma.

"What is all this about?" she screeches as soon as Alma throws the door open and almost falls upon the roses. "Who, in heaven's name, is Vilis?"

Alma kneels down by the roses and spreads her arms around them. Her fingers cannot touch. She buries her face in the red mass and comes up smiling like a deceitful child. "He is what it says there: my betrothed. Can't you read?" She speaks in a bland voice that does not match the dramatic display. She rises and goes to the window, where Milda stands bewildered and angry. She puts her arms around her niece and calmly, wearily reminds her that she had said that she would make plans to go to Sweden but, that in order to do so, she would have to find someone willing to marry her. "So.— Through a friend of a friend we found a willing man. Vilis. Willy, as the Americans would say. He *will* do." (She puns in English.) "And if he wants to shower me with roses, why that's all right. Just fine. Romantic in this bomb blasted age." Alma takes off her coat and hat and glances in the mirror.

"There should be some reward for his pains," Alma goes on speculating. "Perhaps he is not as dull as I feared. Electricians and engineers usually are, as we know. Perfectionists can be difficult, but Vilis, as he has explained in his beautifully perfect handwriting, has a good situation, so we shall live well. Just think, I might have my own house and garden. Can you imagine that? Can you imagine me anywhere but in an attic room? Well, I will surprise you, you'll see—maybe—if we ever see each other again. So if he has a romantic side that sends a bucket full of roses, I'll be all right. And—most importantly—he is a Latvian. One of those who escaped to Sweden in a fishing boat. So I'm curious about him, and I think I could put up with him and go through the motions of marriage and then, after a polite time span, simply divorce. I would have served my term. By then Latvia, too, might be free, you'll be settled, and I can go home. Oh, it'll be a hard role to play, but I can do it, don't you think?"

"I guess so."

"All right. I'll return to Latvia like Puccini's Manon or a prodigal daughter, and then I'll fall in the arms of my true and only love and beg his forgiveness. And he will forgive me, and the lights will go on in the theater, and there will be great joy because the diva was lost but is found; she was dead but is alive! Then he will put a ring on my finger and call me his bride. And all the other actresses will be jealous. Oh, what a day and night it will be! Yes, so it will be. . . . wonderful! *Wunderbar, wunderbar. . .*" sang Marlena Dietrich.

Alma sings and rambles on madly, in circles, confusing many lines and many roles, she dreams of playing on stages upon stages. Milda fixes her gaze on the roses and remembers the bouquet in the crystal vase, which Alma, in her wild struggle with Mr. Viktors Vētra, had knocked off the windowsill so long ago, in that other world from which they had escaped. As in a dream, she hears again the glass shatter and muffled, strange screams and burning whispers she did not understand than but would now. She only stooped to pick up the broken vase and two roses. They watched and wept.

"Dear Aunt, don't go there. Come with me to America," she pleads, taking Alma's hand that feels cold and thin. "Please, please come with me!"

"That is out of the question," Alma says and frees herself. "And don't you bother me about that anymore!" she shouts. "Don't confuse me! You must go your way and I must go mine. You know very well that a big hand rules our fate."

"Stop it!"

"All right, I'll stop. Stop what? Talking to you, putting some sense into your head? So, listen! You know I cannot go with you. I have seen enough of black and white America right here, and I can't say I like it.

As a matter of fact, I know I would hate it. I would get lost in the bigness because I am made for small stages, small countries, cozy little corners, like this room." She turns sweet.

"So you can shine."

"Of course! What's a star if she cannot shine? Yes, I would hate not to shine at all or be outshined. I would die, kill myself."

"Don't say that! Don't hold that specter always before me!" Milda shouts in a matching tone. Madly she starts breaking up the roses, separating them, putting them in whatever containers she can find.

"What are you doing?" Alma screams so the whole Lido might hear. "Are you crazy?"

"I don't know who's crazy and who's not, but I can't stand them. They look like a pool of blood, and I see you in it. . . . I'm scared, Aunty," Milda sobs, kneeling over the roses, shaking and gasping for air. And then Alma slaps her and they cry together. In the stove, the burning wood shoots up a high flame and crackles. The women laugh and start up again to arrange the roses, strewing them all through the room, singing crazy songs about roses and lovers, until, drunk and dizzy they plop on their beds, silent and hot.

"Let's get out of here," Alma says sitting up and reaching for Milda. "Don't worry. I'm not leaving you yet." She pulls her up. "Come on, let's go to the cinema, there's something I want to see. It's quite appropriate for the occasion. It's called *The White Dream.*" She giggles. "Let's dress up. I know where there is a secluded little *Gasthaus* with good food and where no Latvian watchdog will find us. We'll hide inside the garlands and candles."

They dig in the wardrobe for velvet skirts and satin blouses and dress quickly.

"When will you leave for Sweden?" Milda asks.

"When you leave for America."

"Is that a promise?"

"Yes. I swear. We'll take the last train together as far as it goes, all right?"

They finish dressing. "You're lovely when you are angry," Alma says and pins a rose on Milda's pink blouse. "You are becoming more beautiful with each day. I'm quite jealous, you know."

"I know."

"I couldn't stand to be in your shadow."

"Oh, my darling Aunt, you could never be in my shadow! It would never be large enough to cover you. I'm in these plays only for fun or because they ask me. I'm not going to be an actress. I will be a wife and a mother. It will take a lifetime and all my energy."

"What a pity, poor darling," Alma says and takes her in her arms. "You are so beautiful, so very talented," she whispers and kisses her on the lips. "My poor, poor orphaned darling, you want to correct all the horrible mistakes of the world." She kisses her again and pulls her closer. Their satin-clad breasts press together, exciting all the sleeping, anesthetized nerves. Milda gently leans back, staring wide-eyed at Alma, who only smiles and opens their blouses. "Let's not get them wrinkled," she whispers and they kiss. Alma's hand slides inside her niece's blouse, inside the brazier. Her fingers circle around the hidden rose until she feels the thorn, until she feels her niece's head slump unto her shoulder, her lips kissing the bare neck hungrily, dizzily, while her arms clamp her around the waist. They sink down onto the bed and kick their shoes off. Their nylon stocking legs twist and lock. Time stops in their embrace. And then Alma screams out and clutches her niece as if she would pull her inside herself. The girl's breath also becomes rapid and shallow, and then she, too, trembles and exhales a deep sigh of joy or pain as she digs her fingers into her aunt's moist back. All their pulses throb together like synchronized drums until they fade out and the hands relax. When Milda opens her eyes, the sky is a dark blue, pricked with stars. Alma strokes the young, messed up head, fingering back the perspiring ringlets, gently kissing the damp forehead, "You see, my most precious," she whispers close to her ear, sending new tremors through the subdued body, "it's no good for us to go on living together. We would destroy each other."

"But why?" Milda holds her tightly, kissing the hand that is pulling away, leaving her shivering as in fever or from cold. "Oh, I love you, love you so much, and I worry about you all the time."

"I know, my darling," Alma kisses her again and they rise up, out of the bed that had taken them, like some magic boat, to yet undiscovered islands of dangerous pleasure. "Let's go on out, away from here while we still can." She buttons Milda's blouse, slowly hanging her fingers with her bright red nails in each buttonhole, "and let this be a one and only time, never to be forgotten and forever kept secret." Milda clasps the hands and kisses them, tears flowing, sobs shaking her shoulders.

"Let's go," Alma says and disengages the hands. "Wipe your eyes," she commands and steps to the wardrobe and pulls out their overcoats. They put them on. Alma wraps the old fox around her neck and secures her hat with a sharp hatpin.

"Why don't you get rid of that dead beast?" Milda asks. "I don't like it."

"But I love it. It fits me, and he gave it to me. It's my pet." Alma strokes the dead fox and laughs a shrill stage laugh that clears the air. They paint their lips with the same lipstick and pin roses on their lapels, and then they go out into the night.

*

Days and nights of gnawing guilt and incestuous longing followed. Milda tried to escape by throwing herself into the final examinations of the winter semester and in the Christmas play, while Alma crawled deeper into her assigned tragic role. She stayed out of Milda's way, returning to their common space only very late and then going straight to bed. When they talked, the words came out jingling of superficiality, irritability, and with unbearable formality. Over the coming days, from either side of the cramped room, they watched the ninety-eight roses wilt, one by one, until they dried up and hung like curdled blood on little shriveled thorny poles. When the last rose wilted, Alma crumbled the rest also to dust—one by one. "They are mine," she said as she rubbed the petals between her hands with sharp, red nails, smiling sadistically. Milda swept them up and tossed the red-brown dust into the fire that crackling shut up a purple flame.

Alma takes on another Role

Suddenly, out of character, Alma started dusting and polishing the room. Her senses seduced by a delicious aroma which was seeping into their room, she ordered Milda to go and find out what Mrs. Gramzda was baking. There were only three days until Christmas. "Time is running out. . . . I must be left alone so I can scrub the floor really clean," she said, her hands deep inside the bucket. Puzzled, Milda put on her coat and went to the market instead and bought the smallest fir tree. She also bought red candles and stars made of straw. It was nothing much, as always; yet, the beauty was exactly in the Nothingness from which she had learned to draw out Something. From nothing she had made token presents for all her neighbors, and from patches she had secretly made a vest for Alma, having seen a patchwork quilt in one of the American magazines. She bought colorful wrapping paper and then wandered around, with the tree resting on her shoulder, until she was sure that Alma would be gone.

The next two nights Milda was onstage; she was Maija—the good and virtuous—who, at the end, shimmers in a shower of gold. As always, the applause was loud, full of adoration, the flowers many and dazzling.

Alma was there as well, in the front row, clapping. When, hand in hand, they left the hall, people made way for them reverently, as though they were phantoms that should not walk on common ground. They chose not to stay for the ball, for neither would put her hand in the hand of any man. They went back to the Lido carrying their freezing flowers.

Christmas 1949

The following morning—it was Christmas Eve—Milda spent in Mrs. Gramzda's kitchen, as agreed earlier in the week. They talked about *Maija un Paija*. Everyone had been at the play. Little Aija could not stop telling Milda about the wonderful Maija and the bad Paija, who had long black fingernails. She believed in the play as she believed in Father Christmas. She had not simply looked at the play, but for two hours she had lived in a world of enchantment. Next to her, Helga, so grown up during the last year, only smiled down on her little sister, her mind swirling, creating her own world of make-believe she would place in orbit when she grew up.

Later on, while they made *piragi* and *piparkūkas*, Milda noticed that Mrs. Gramzda observed her with a troubled look and Vizma seemed to be especially kind, too sweet and caring, like the cookie faces they made. Feeling the heat of her sin, Milda worked with downcast eyes, rolling the dough, snatching the pans out of the oven quickly and taking the fragile cookies off ever so carefully. Unmindful, she gazed up at the bare vineyards as if she were looking for someone to come down and save her—some wise angel, not a baby in a trough. She seemed to hear some Sunday school teacher or her conscience whispering, telling her, "But my child, don't you know that it is written in God's Word *not by works are ye saved?*"

Coming out of her trance, she looked straight into the gray eyes of Mrs. Gramzda, who seemed to know and see everything. "Why don't you celebrate Christmas with us?" the woman asked. "Please."

But confused and taken by surprise, *Mildiņa* thanked her and said she would come over only for a while, only to see the lighting of candles in the large tree, which stood all spread out in Room #2, next to the piano. "Yes, I can say a poem, the one about the angel who comes to visit the earth on Christmas Eve."

*

Hours later, dressed in white, she did go to her guardians, in spite of Alma's scowls. She came mostly for the sake of little Aija, who also believed in angels. She brought presents for everyone and stood at the closed door taking in the scene. The tree shimmered in candlelight. Vizma played the piano, and everyone was singing without books, knowing the words by heart. Some of the songs were German originals but had mutated into the Latvian culture and were quickly appropriated. They also sang a medley of Latvian originals, words and melodies Baptist poets and composers had created. Hearing these caused the preacher to take off his glasses and rub his eyes. "Perhaps, *Fräulein* Bērziņa," he said, clearing his throat, "you do not know that the creators of this music were also among the deported. We knew them well. I baptized the poetess, a sincere Christian girl, so full of promise, and the composer! What talent, what a personality!"

"Wonder where they are tonight, if still alive," Mrs. Gramzda sighed. But Vizma struck the chords of *Joy to the World*, which they sang in English. Milda let her voice join in and opened the door a crack, hoping that Alma would hear them, hoping the light rays would reach her dark spirit. Reverend Gramzda then raised his hand and took Aija upon his knee, "Enough singing! Now let's listen to the Christmas story." He reached for Helga, but she scowled and stepped back, close to Milda. "Doesn't he see that I'm too grown up to sit on his lap?" she whispered. Milda had to move over, pressing herself against Jānis, who was almost a man, ready to carry the Latvian flag in the next parade, when Milda would be at his side. Perhaps he thought about being too close to famous Milda. The thought made him fidget and turn his attention to the Christmas story. When Vizma played the soft chords of *Silent Night*, the Preacher left the room, nodding to Milda to say her poem. Finished, she wished everyone a happy Christmas and left. In the hall she ran into Father Christmas, who carried a sack full of presents over his shoulder and a switch in his hand.

"I deserve the switch," she said and went to her room to be with Alma, who had set a table for two. They ate in the candlelight, talking casually, awkwardly, not touching hands, not scrutinizing their flushed faces. After the small supper, they put on their overcoats and went out into a slippery, slushy night. They went to the Lutheran church service across the Neckar, up on the opposite hill. Both knew that this would be their last Christmas together and, therefore, it had to be a night neither would forget. After this silent night they went back to their room absolved, while all the church bells were ringing.

On the lamp-lit bridge they stopped and looked at their shadows stretching over the water, but Milda didn't want to look down; she looked up at the stars, so bright and pure. For a moment, she imagined herself as a falling star, yet circling through the universe with incredible speed, pulling away from the center, pulling away from her Aunt as she felt deep, dark waves rise between them.

New Year's Eve

The clocks strike twelve midnight. It is the half-way point of the 20th century. It is a century divided in half in a divided world. In the

Kingdom of Exile the celebrations were nervous, too triumphant, too loud and guilt-ridden. And also too quiet. In the Lido bar a band played *A String of Pearls*. Couples danced. A bare-shouldered, overweight blonde, with a peacock feather growing out of her head, sang *In der Nacht ist der Mensch nicht gern alleine.* . . (in the night a man does not want to be alone).

Alma sat next to her niece at a cabaret table with some other actors and measured out their fortunes. They poured led into ice water and watched it solidify into shapes that teased the imagination. One of the actors peered at his fortune and shivered. "What do you suppose is going on behind the iron curtain?" he asked. "Not a letter or card has come to anyone." Milda said she had not received any news from her sister. Neither had Mrs. Gramzda received a word from her mother, who wrote in code.

"I have no news from my fiancée," Alma said, adding, "the real one." But no one responded to what anyone said. Silently they poked around with their baffling fortunes and silently wondered what might be happening to their other halves, their sisters, brothers, mothers and fathers. The men tried to read the future of Latvia in a piece of lead, which had the shape of Latvia like on a distorted map. Some saw trains and ships, but Alma said *Terors*. She stood up, but another lady, an actress who was always cast in the roles of queens and wise grandmothers said, "I see a time, far in the distance when Latvia will be free again."

"When?"

"Perhaps in the odd year, as the old Oracle Fink predicted, when the numbers will read the same from both ends."

"Ha!" Alma snapped, "that would be 1991 or 2002. That's fifty years away. I'll be dead by then. Good night!" She motioned Milda to rise. They and went up the stairs to their room. In their window bloomed ice flowers. The night was clear and cold. Bells and fireworks brought in the new year of our Lord—**1950!**

The Marriage Proposal

Throughout the new winter nothing extraordinary happened in the life of Milda Bērziņa, nor at Lido and, generally, throughout the Kingdom of Exile. Both Milda and her aunt sloshed again on their separate ways, crossing the Neckar countless times, going up the mountain slopes and down again. They caught colds and stayed on separate sides of their room. Both wrote letters: one sent them to Sweden, the other to the United States of America. Both received replies regularly, in excellent handwriting. Only Alma was irritated and depressed after each letter, while Milda rejoiced, looking into the distance with shining eyes and, when alone, she wrote letters to Kārlis and kept a diary. At times, when alone, she looked out of her small window at the sky and tried to send messages on waves of air. She now visited Mrs. Gramzda whenever she liked, regardless of Alma's lethal stares. They did not seem to affect her as they used to, for Alma was losing her grip on all things present. Milda heard her crying in the night.

At the end of January Kārlis Arājs proposed: *"My dear Milda, I offer you my hand in marriage. Will you accept it? Your Kārlis."* That was all. The letter looked like a telegram. Milda stared at it from all angles, and then she folded it up and hid it so Alma would not see and offer her condolences. Some days later, she uncorked her small bottle of black ink, dipped her sharp pen in it and, taking up a piece of simple lined paper, wrote: *"My dear Kārlis, yes, I accept your hand in marriage. Yours always, Milda."* With a cold hand she dropped the note into the yellow mailbox. *So it's done.*

HOW LONG IS EXILE?

*

It is settled. My mind is at rest. . . . She knew that somewhere the emigration papers were being shuffled and filed, and in Brooklyn, N. Y., Kārlis's mother planned her wedding. Milda's routine remained unchanged; only she looked with more panic at the thinning refugee settlement, the unraveling of her temporary tent. The trains that departed seemed closer, their whistles sharper, leaving empty spaces all over her accustomed domain, as if exposing her to the elements. She felt the draft in the half-empty buildings and along the shores of the mindless Neckar. She was anxious about her teachers' leaving before the school year ended—before her graduation—and afraid that she would be hanging again in some kind of open space unfinished, uncertified. Or—that there would be no minister to confirm her in her mother's faith and she would stand excommunicated and only at the mercy of the Baptists. At times she would wake up in the night, crying for Alma, telling her that she dreamed that she left her standing alone on a platform. Then Alma would comfort her like a mother and tell her that she would never leave her like that.

Thereafter, for a while, peace would prevail—at least until another bouquet of roses would suddenly arrive, followed by impatient pleas to come quickly. But Alma would only laugh, her eyes cold and glassy as she stared at the flowers, seldom bothering to put them in water. She wrote short letters, sometimes standing up. She spit at the envelopes to make the glue stick and then let them lie on the table for days. At the same time she struggled hard to keep her interest in the theater. "What's the use?" she would lament. "The best actors are gone and we are only marking time with stupid plays, filling our heads with trash. Only the uncouth and the invalids are left in the audience, and they depress me. I can't act freely around so much settled misery and I cannot escape from this life anymore."

"It will be better once the winter is over," Milda tried to comfort.

"Why? Because the waiting will be prettier?"

"Yes. Maybe. And I should know soon, when my boat leaves, says the preacher."

"Oh."

"Why do you sigh?" Milda asked drawing closer, opening her arms for an embrace, then stepping back, afraid, "Don't I hold you here as in a prison?"

"Or keep me from one." Alma snapped back.

"Oh, oh!" Milda cried out as in pain. They fell into each other's arms. Alma kissed her on the lips and, with the tips of her fingers, dried her cheeks. They lay down together.

The Engagement

Once Kārlis Arājs acknowledged Milda's consent to marry him, his letters took on a certain practical, instructional, informative tone, and Milda reacted in kind. Somehow it was easier, safely impersonal. Her romantic, storm-and-stress soul, unsure of any firm ground, hid under cover, embarrassed next to her future husband's logic and certainty. Seen from her small and high window on long distance airwaves, he seemed much taller than he was. He seemed straighter, more upright, ready to point out errors—not only in her thoughts and feelings, but also in others—even the President of the United States. He offered his opinions with confidence, obviously based on traditional attitudes carried over from free Latvia—at least so it came across in the letters, which often seemed nothing but long essays on *her* flaws that must be corrected. She read his words carefully and believed that he was right. Even people she loved and respected at times dared to point out that she was too emotional, too impulsive, acting as her moods—not reason—dictated. Without being told, she knew that in a married, well-settled life she must be steady and rational. She must not act like Aunt Alma. And she must be grateful to mature Kārlis, who certainly loved her and wanted them to be successful, happy, and respected. She told herself that she must listen to and accept his systematic, principled guidance because she did not know how to become all those things, and so she must try hard at least to learn and submit, and—thank goodness—there was still plenty of time for her to *grow up,* as he put it. But her defensive and proud side was hard to bend because, it seemed that his and others' criticisms were directed at her left side, where her heart beat and where she was most sensitively romantic and artistic. *Must that go? Torn out of me? No, no! I should just learn to tame it, to put it in balance, to think things through before I act. Don't wise people also tell you to be yourself?*

She pondered these things continuously and never received any clear signals, any clear illumination. But she did not write to him about her doubts and fears of eventually living in some cold *age of reason.* In her letters she revealed less and less of her inner self. She crossed out any of what she considered on re-reading to be romantic and poetic passages. She took out the adjectives and adverbs, the exclamation points and dashes. She pruned and clipped out all ornaments and left the sentences simple, the messages short and crisp. He liked that and praised her for the improvements and wrote back with new flourish, saying that she would be a great help, when he had to write newspaper articles. She read that and was angry. She hated newspapers and hardly glanced at their redundant bad news. She liked books, essays, and poems, where she could drown herself, where she could freely converse with any character she chose and through them learn about herself and the people around her. She had hoped that she and Kārlis would read good books together and discus great themes and ideas but his letter told her that again her *romantic notions* were too far out and had to be reined in. She did ask him if he liked to read good literature and who his favorite authors were. *Do you like going to the theater and concerts,* she asked, and he answered that he had no time for useless pleasures. That closed the subject, and she understood that again she must hide her desires so he would not accuse her of frivolity and base, selfish motives. She also knew that he could not ever understand her craving for sexual joy she had barely touched. *How could that man understand that only out of the most painful longing Alma and I had embraced and kissed each other? How could he understand it, when even I cannot?*

With increased frustration, unable to confess the truth, she crumpled many sheets of paper, crying and thinking that she should break off the engagement but did not know how to do it. After she read another cold, unfeeling letter, she went straight to Mrs. Gramzda and poured her heart out. The elder listened with a pained look and, after some fidgeting, asked, "But where would you go? What would become of you all alone in the world?"

Milda stared at her with angry, questioning eyes and squinted as though the woman's face was out of focus. She watched the lips form cold words of reason, like those in the dull letters. Again the words struck her heart that hurt.

"There are times," Milda said, taking a deep breath, "when I feel that the best part of me is being crossed out by each stroke of his sharp pen. . . I don't know what's left of me. . . . How can I be sure I love him?"

"Love blossoms inside of marriage."

"But what if it doesn't?"

The question made Mrs. Gramzda uncomfortable, embarrassed, searching for words. Waiting, Milda's thoughts drifted away, back to Kārlis and her parting at the train station and their quick kisses. She was about ready to confess all and tell the sad woman how she wanted more kisses, how she wanted the whole thing, but just then Mrs. G. spoke up:

"When a man does not ask for IT but looks into the depth of a woman's character, then. . ." Milda watched the pale, thin lips move, say more things about purity of love and children and joy, but heard nothing. The message that did come across told her that, as always, *she* would have to adjust herself to someone else. It would never be the other way around. She would have to take all the clues from him as she had from her aunt and even now, from this woman—a preacher's wife, who might be more frustrated than she—who also could not figure life out and assumed that certain obligations were simply a woman's lot. It was the way life was made, Milda concluded. So it was her lot too, no matter who her mate would be.

"Child, don't you see how much he needs you?" Mrs. Gramzda now seemed to stand on a more familiar ground, though her voice was breaking, her gaze going beyond them into the next room, where the typewriter clicked. "He needs a strong and beautiful woman to hold him up. They all do, and if the woman breaks, like poor Mrs. Egle, for example, who has to be put through shock treatments. . ."

"Oh, dear God! Really?"

"Yes. Poor woman," Mrs. Gramzda sighed. "Yes, so it is, when the woman breaks. Disaster follows. The whole family falls apart."

She filled their teacups and went on: "Man alone is often awful and pitiful. He cannot hold out. . . . Still, it is men who make big plans and rule the world—large or small. Mr. Arājs is already involved in building an ideal Latvian society on nothing but a handful of displaced, sad people. He cannot give up, even if he wanted to, and he clearly does not want to. He sees that as his mission, and he is a proud man, strong in his principles. Besides, the people need him. If someone like he does not lead, who will? I'm thinking about what you told me—how our President, so to speak, anointed him. So, there you are, and he has chosen you to be his helper. So you must be with him, to guard and protect him, for he—blinded by his vision—may be forging crippled and exaggerated attitudes on a foreign, unfamiliar turf."

She took a deep breath and looked out the window, as if pausing for a prompter. "It must be very difficult, especially with his mother always there pushing him, forcing him to think and look a certain way—a kind of Latvian way and no other. I doubt if he reads *American* newspapers, especially those clever editorials, even as much as we do here. No, he wouldn't have time and the ideas would be much too liberal for him as they are for most of us who are afraid of communists and see red where there might be only a tinge of pink. I am afraid of the so-called Cold War I read about because no matter by what name, wars cause pain and suffering to innocent people. It will hurt our loved ones back home. . . . Yet, I can see that he and others who propose to lead us, will be involved. Therefore they must be strong, even inflexible but also sympathetic and wise. Their strength must be balanced out by a woman's more romantic, gentle, understanding spirit. . . . Oh, it is difficult to set oneself up as a leader."

"Kārlis has written as much," Milda injected and told her how he had laid out his plans for organizing Latvians abroad. "*Living within the vastness of America, our people must still conduct themselves with unity of purpose,*" she quoted him. The leaders, he wrote, had to establish *a firm core and then a large network that would reach all over the Free World. We have to tie all the people together by our common language, pain, and hatred of communism. And, yes, hope of course! The goal has to be the re-emergence of a free and independent Latvia within our lifetime. We have to set the example, keep the flame of freedom burning,*" she quoted with a staged flare. "*How we establish ourselves in the very beginning will set a precedent for years to come.*"

"Please don't be cynical and try to see his side of things."

"Yes." She rose, impatient to leave and then blurted out: "But what if I am not strong enough to hold the weight of such a man as he? What if I want and need IT and that IT is a most important reason why I want to be married as soon as possible?"

She did not wait for an answer. She was tired of words and more upset than before she came for help. She excused herself and left the kitchen.

Inside her quiet room she stood looking out her window, trying to calm down, but released her thoughts raced all over the Mountain Colony where, she imagined, the man with one arm wandered about trying to find his other arm so he could embrace her and carry her off. . . . She wondered why she had not seen him for a long, long time. . . *Oh, but I must not think about him. . . and IT. . .*

Mrs. Gramzda Gives Advice

The next afternoon, Mrs. Gramzda knocked timidly on the door across the hall, which happened rarely. She apologized and said that she had thought things through carefully and wanted to say a few words.

"Yes. Please, go ahead."

"I don't know how to start, don't want you to misunderstand and perhaps I have no right, no authority, to speak to you. It's only that I care deeply and have grown to love you as if—as if. . ."

". . . I were your daughter?"

"Yes. Perhaps. But you aren't, still. . ."

"I know, but please say what's on your mind—and heart." It was Milda's turn to put the kettle on and make tea. "Please, sit down. I'm glad you're here—as a friend."

"Thank you. Well. The words don't come easy. I want to admonish you, tell you, not to push yourself under the load of guilt. . . . Thank you." She stirred a half a teaspoon of sugar into the hot cup. "That helps nothing and nobody. Remember only that your chosen man has already measured your strength or he would not have asked you to marry him. Don't try to work out your future before its time. Everything will fall into place, and, days or years later, when you look back, it will seem that there had been a plan, that things could go that way and no other. We all live day by day, and often nothing turns quite the way we imagine, so don't rush to the end before you have lived through the beginning and middle—which is hard enough."

"I know and that's what I'm trying to do, but something isn't as it should be."

"I see. I know."

Mrs. Gramzda paused and studied the settled tea leaves. "Letters can be misleading. . . . Don't kill your soul—how should I say?—only cover it up. Put a veil over it and tend it when he is not looking. Above all, you must keep developing your spirit—also for his sake and for the sake of your children." She clasped her hands, concentrating, it seemed, at her ingrown wedding band she could not even twist and continued with her speech: "I don't especially like the pearl metaphor of the Gospel. It's very harsh, yet it is a commandment our Savior laid down. *Don't cast your pearls before swine!* Why did He say that? I've had to explain it to the children of my Sunday school class, and so I told them that swine cannot tell the difference between pearls and slop and let it go at that."

"I think that most people cannot tell the difference either," Milda injected.

"I've thought that too but wouldn't dare say it. It's very offensive to men, don't you think?"

"Could be. Women might be better at finding pearls and digging them out of slop buckets."

"Well. You know what I'm driving at. Yes, women might have more patience, a bit more understanding, less ready to condemn, knowing that it takes time for those slimy discharges the oysters produce to turn into precious jewels. You understand that, and Mr. Arājs sees the potential, the non-perishing beauty in you." She stopped trying to twist her wedding band and, as if finding the lost thread of her thoughts, made the eye contact. "He sees that potential now only *as through a glass darkly*, and that is why he needs you. To help him see things clearly so he can guide others. He cannot do it alone and he knows it. He may even be afraid. So, meanwhile, you must develop your inner self, no matter what he writes.—Be assured that there will come a time when you can hold that precious pearl up high for all the world to see. It will surprise and shock him, perhaps put his love through a test, but it will happen. If he would be great, he will call you blessed, if not. . ."

"What then?"

"I don't know.—But until then, you simply must go on day by day and forgive him his limitations even as you support his work." She paused to see how her words had fallen on the troubled face. "Life is hard," she sighed and rose from the chair. She took Milda's extended hand, as if they would be parting for a long time, and left the room. "Yes, life is hard."

And lonely. . . At least in Esslingen, the crumbing capital city of the Kingdom of Exile. People keep on leaving, train after trainload. But one's loss is another's grain.

Kārlis writes:

With each landing of a ship, the old Latvian communities that were formed here, in the U. S. after the 1905 and 1917 revolutions and World War I receive new injections. In the cities I have visited--New York, Boston, Philadelphia—that in the beginning of this century had culturally active Latvian colonies which were dying. I met only old people who have managed to survive as Latvians; that is, they still can speak the language (though poorly and with American accents) and feel some loyalty to the "old country." They like to talk about the revolutions, World War I, and remember the beeches and pine forest of Latvia. Some are old revolutionaries and cannot understand why we hate communism. John Reed is their hero. They collaborated with the U.S. Communist Party. Can you believe it? That infuriates me, but I try to be kind and patient, for, after all, they are still with us, unlike their children and children's children, who are assimilated and lost to our suffering country. This old, mellowed, and sobered up remnant gives us a bit of a foundation; it provides a foothold, so to speak. They find jobs and housing for us, which is no easy task, and help us acclimate culturally, being happy that new blood is coming in, giving them unexpected joy and a boost of identity. They convince me that we, above all, must not allow our children to become Americanized and lost in the so-called melting pot. Once something is melted and dissolves, my dear, it cannot be unmelted, nor undissolved. Therefore, we—and I mean also you—must lay down firm policies on language, marriage, and general attitudes. There is no other way. We must, as a community, stay connected if we are to stay "solid" and not melt, as you will understand. Therefore, when people leave, as much as you can, find out where they are going. Ask them what their final destination is so that we may contact them as soon as they arrive and persuade them to join a Latvian center as soon as their obligations with their sponsors expire. That would take about one year, and then they would be free of any further restraints.

Kārlis discussed in such and like essays all points in turn, in serial letters. With each installment Milda's spite withered in shame. She became excited, like a princess whose evil spell is about to break. She could see more and more clearly how a new Latvia was being conceived and delivered across the Atlantic Ocean, the way Alma had predicted when she revealed her vision on top of the vineyards. With each letter, like with an adjustable camera lens, a new life and her part in its creation came into clearer focus:

Our women will also have much to do, especially you, as my wife," Kārlis wrote. *The managing of social events, following lectures, performances, and so on, will be of greatest importance. We want to see and taste our traditions in our superior culinary arts. We want our tables covered with ironed tablecloths, graced with live flowers and tasty dishes. We would not want to take any tasteless shortcuts, such as would come from canned goods and packaged foods, which are invading this culture through advertisements and catering to the frivolity of women, luring them out of the kitchen and away from teaching their children good manners and the art of gracious living. . . . So, please, concentrate and observe how ladies behave and what their duties are, not only on the family stage but also in a social setting."*

Milda did not know where to *observe*. She could not look at Alma for help, nor at Mrs. Gramzda, who was a Baptist and belonged to their *Sisters* group. The German women would not do at all. And so she started observing the wives of the leaders and the widows of the war-fallen men. She tried to break into the DP's high society's inner circle, the same she had avoided and Alma shunned. She did this gradually, carefully. Whenever it seemed appropriate, Milda offered to help and then performed well. She accepted praise humbly, feigning surprise—like Maija in her play. She also increased her activities with the Guides by participating more in entertaining the veterans at the Mountain Colony, in spite of Vanags, whom she saw at a distance and who, surprisingly, seemed to ignore her. This puzzled and angered her. *Has he lost interest in me? Am I no longer attractive? What has happened to his seductive overtures that used to throw my spine out of alignment?* At night, alone in her room, she decided she hated him and would not ever extend her hand even in a formal greeting. She would not allow him as much as her little finger. *The rat!*

So resolved, she threw herself into whatever task was assigned to her. She helped to plan another art exhibit; she drew designs for the high school Olympics at the end of May; she suggested the dramatization of *Daugava* for the June 14 memorial for the deported, and agreed to create a short play for the Midsummer night program. She visited her Guides in their living quarters, where she assigned each girl a part, discussed the costumes they would need and texts they would have to memorize. Keenly aware that this would be their last chance to perform together, she impressed upon each that nothing but perfection would please her. She did not mention to anyone that she needed something concrete she could describe to Kārlis and give him cause for high praise.

All these activities spread throughout the summer, at reasonable intervals, so that there was still time left for herself, her chores, her dreams and pleasures. She practiced being rational and reasonable. She was very careful, knowing that she was being evaluated at a much closer range than ever before. As each event drew near and tensions mounted, she was fully conscious about many eyes staring at her from unexpected angles, lips whispering, fingers pointing and felt as if the earth shook under her feet as she made the usual rounds throughout the town. But she held herself firmly in control, trying to learn, as Kārlis wished, so when the time came she could be among the leaders of a new Latvia. Taking mental notes, she marked how the best of the ladies mixed elegance with maternity and housework. She saw how those ladies upheld their men and smiled when they spoke. She noticed also that they dressed in suits and shoulder-padded dresses, high-heeled pumps and silk stockings, keeping the seams straight down the middle of their legs. They wore lipstick and rouge and styled their hair in a variety of ways, but never plainly pulled back in a bun like Mrs. Gramzda. She saw that those ladies of Riga were not just housewives. Having no houses and being crowded, they lived beyond their limited quarters; they lived on the outside, where they displayed their beauty and virtue and were appropriately appreciated.

They wore their children like finely made garments, judging themselves and others by their offspring. Milda saw how they turned each public function into a grand event. They took care that every buffet after each function was unique, memorable, and pleasing to the men, around whom they circled like ordained satellites. The ladies knew that, really, the buffets and balls that followed the solemn assembly hours formed the ties that kept the nation together with all its truths, lies, and myths. Naturally, the ladies knew that they were indispensable, and, therefore—but also out of an ingrained sense of pleasure, beauty, and harmony—each sub-committee strove to surpass the other with its fine embroidered tablecloths, arrangements of flowers, and creations of food. The women outnumbered the men. This consequence of war granted the men certain privileges, made it imperative and polite not only to entertain one's own wife but also the women who were not sure weather or not they were widows or wives. Milda observed that when the ladies stood behind the buffets or served around the cabaret tables, they themselves appeared as tempting and delicious as cream puffs. Yet, they stayed beyond reach and feigned shyness whenever men winked or spoke to them. The husbanded ladies refused invitations to dance with other men unless their husbands nodded, giving permission, and then they danced at arm's length and never more than twice with the same gentleman. Milda also noted that the ladies allowed their husbands to stray slightly but when they overstepped the invisible line of propriety, they would be suddenly at their sides, filling their glasses or cutting in on imposter partners. At the end of all festive evenings, uncomplaining, the women picked up their men and patiently guided them to the cramped places they called home. Oh, Milda was observing and learning so much! She knew that the initiation test into this displaced high society would be much harder to pass than her final exams. She understood that very well.

Kārlis wrote: *"America is not like Germany or Latvia. Here are many choices. Only a few could serve our people and our national goals. Therefore, one must be strong and resolute. You must be the best. . . . My wife must be a queen. She must have the correct attitude."*

"What does he do for a living?" Alma suddenly asked. "How will he feed you?" Strangely, Milda had not thought about that. She had somehow assumed that food and all the other necessities would simply be there for the taking. "That is what a lot of people here, under American care, assume," Alma said with a smirk. "But I know better. In America all is work, and you pay for what you get or you don't get it. Nothing is handed to you. So you better be prepared for that. There everything is measured with money."

"How do you know?"

"I just do. So you better make sure that your husband *makes* good money, as they say. He can't support you on a flag pole," Alma laughed again. "Haven't you asked him any practical questions?"

"No, guess not."

"Well, well, well!" She turned to face her niece head on. "It's time you did that." She made Milda sit down and write what she dictated. She ordered Milda to demand that Kārlis answers with numbers, measurements of housing, the description of his street in Brooklyn, etc. Did he have a car? When Milda frowned and hesitated to seal the letter, she snatched it from the reluctant hand and, on her way to the train station, dropped it into the yellow *POST* box.

To their surprise, Mrs. Arāja answered. Kārlis had been too shocked, and if she had not intervened—so wrote the matriarch—he would have broken off the engagement. He could not imagine that underneath all the sweetness, his betrothed was crassly materialistic. "I calmed him down, because I do understand your concerns. We women must put the bread on the table, after all." She stated that Kārlis worked in the engineering department for an electric company. His salary was $300.00 per month, with advancement in the future. She described what the money could build and buy and that it was a good start for a young man. "Do not worry, my dear, my son is very smart and, as his boss has assured him, *he has what it takes.* He is also working hard to master the English language, which in America is not the same as we studied in our Latvia Institute of Foreign Languages. People talk very fast and often incorrectly, but he will learn, be assured of that! By the time you arrive, he will speak as American as the best of them."

Alma was comforted and satisfied and left Milda alone. In the next letter, Kārlis ignored the whole money issue but stated that he had filed for U. S. citizenship, *not for any selfish reasons, not to betray Latvia, but so that in the future I could have influence with the United States Congress and the President, where Latvian rights would be concerned.* He wrote saying that he would not be afraid to climb any steps *that would lead my nation to freedom. . . . We will lead our people, you and I, and we will educate the American leaders so that they understand what communism really is all about. We shall work together to help destroy the evil system that plagues the world like growing cancer. I see changes in attitudes already. There are responsible and influential people in U. S. government who are serious about curtailing the expansion of the Soviet Union, but hopefully it will not come to war, at least not where we live. Perhaps in Asia, but that would not concern us. President Truman does not want war and is ready to compromise even with the devil.*

The newspapers and radios, however, tell us that the Democratic Party is infiltrated by leftist elements and that there are communists in the State Department. Even as I write, there are investigations in Congress. Mr. Truman is charged with being soft on communism, and people in the South hate him for his upsetting their way of life by trying to do away with racial segregation. Therefore, we must be vigilant against the naive ideas of liberals who do not understand the subtle ways of communism and oppose even the investigations of suspected persons. They see nothing wrong with Russia having a seat in the United Nations. But I ask: does a fox cooperate with a hen?

Still, we must be grateful to Pres. Truman for the Marshal Plan, which helps to rebuild Europe and has opened the doors for our people to immigrate into this great country. Because much is written in the liberal press about the Holocaust, Americans, on the whole, hate Hitler worse than Stalin. In fact, they don't hate Stalin because they don't know what Stalin has done to half the world. Because he helped to win the war, they trust him. Can you believe that? Therefore, we must work hard to destroy that trust. Fortunately and thanks to our retained diplomat, the United States government has not yet acknowledged the incorporation of the Baltic States into the Soviet Union. There is hope that the Displaced Persons Act of 1948 will be enlarged so that our veterans and German-rooted spouses will be allowed to immigrate. So, my dear, you see, we must work very hard to help save our people. We must hold out until the Soviet Union will collapse and fall like a rotten apple from a warped tree. For that goal, I emphasize, we all must be united—our whole society—wherever it happens to be further displaced in this changing, diminishing world. And that, my dear, includes you too."

His words lifted Milda above her fears and the concerns that Alma had stressed lately. She could see Kārlis again carrying the banner, with her at his handsome side. She loved his idealism and understanding and how they complemented her own romantic dreams—naturally and without any arguments. This firm faith of his, this vision, in time let her overlook any problems that had troubled her before. She realized that she had, in fact, *grown up* and was glad to confess this to Mrs. Gramzda, who was pleased. Milda told her that she was ready to rise with her beloved to whatever height he would take her. She would even hide her soul so it would not disturb him, do whatever he wished because it was right and proper, and, anyway, she assured her neighbor, that he would always wish the right thing because he was good. So what if her soul would have to learn to sit out for a while as he weighed and measured everything carefully, even her!

So convinced, Milda was sure that, in time, she would find a way to his heart and desires. She would do what the other ladies did so well. She would cook and set tables, and, satisfied, he would put his head in her lap and lay his handsome body next to hers and she would teach him the many ways of love. Then all would be complete. She would see to it that they would be forever happy.

A Package from America

Mrs. Arāja, having received Milda's polite letter, now started corresponding with her regularly, giving her version of her son's virtues and America's vices. She showed some sensitivity to Milda, coming across almost like a caring mother. This feeling was confirmed in a package that came to Door #4 on one fine spring day. Mrs. Arāja endowed her future daughter-in-law with yards of white nylon and lace for her confirmation dress. A bit later, fancy undergarments, stockings, and shoes followed. Still later, arrived a package of staple foods and rare spices and delicacies in time for an Easter feast.

Nearly breathless, Milda started working on a most exquisite dress. She said nothing about it to Alma, afraid she would soil it, if not with her hands then with her words. *Let her be surprised! Let her, too, kneel before me! I—her little niece—am about to enter the adult world as the queen of the invisible New Kingdom of Exile!* Alma would never enter that kingdom, since she chose to stay in Europe among the ruins of old kingdoms and principalities, hunger, and derision. Milda stitched carefully, by hand. The long seams, like secret passages, led her to the visions of a heavenly married life.

Then, right in the middle of Holy Week, she heard Alma's steps rushing up the stairs. Milda shoved the dress fragments into a pillowcase and pushed it under her bed. At that moment Alma entered and thrust a very little package in her hands. It was from Kārlis. "Open it!" Alma urged. Milda excitedly tugged at the strings and tore off the outer wrapping. Inside the larger box was a dark blue velvet case. She stroked it, closed her eyes, then opened the soft little case. A solitaire diamond shone out, dazzling her. Tucked inside was a note: *Put this ring on your finger and wear it always. It will bind you to me forever. Kārlis.*

"Well, do as he says," Alma said as if she were looking in the eye of a dragon. "Put it on!" But Milda closed the box and sat still.

"Must I put it on myself?"

"And why not? What more do you want? Do you expect sudden violins and roses?"

"Yes. You get roses."

"Oh, me! Poor me. They cover up an awful lot, don't they, those sad roses."

"Sorry," Milda said, clutching the little case in her right hand. "Will it always be like this?" she asked in a cold, distant tone. "Will he never touch me, I mean, really hold me so that I can feel and hear his heart beat?"

"Of course he will, poor darling," Alma soothed. She sat down beside her and held her close, kissing her face, murmuring, "He won't be able to keep his hands off you. You are so beautiful!" For a second Milda almost sunk into Alma's perfumed sweetness, but, suddenly appalled, she elbowed herself free and pushed the temptress away. She put the ring on her finger like a shield.

"It is the rock, you understand, upon which you are supposed to build his statue while still on this side of the Ocean," Alma said bitterly. "I'll do my part in spreading the news of your clever wit, you little witch, you burning *Spīdola,* with the diamond *The most beautiful here on earth and down in hell!*" Milda looked down on her Aunt and held out her hand so the diamond shone above the distorted face. "It is beautiful, like a fallen star," she said.

Alma sat up slowly. "No, no, not fallen but rising, shining high and alone, which is the best way to shine." Then she lay down and spoke softly, looking at the ceiling. "You almost fell with that Nazi Gert, almost buried yourself in his cave, sweet boy though he was, until I pulled you out. With Kārlis Arājs you will shine out in the open, only I won't see you." She spoke sadly, and Milda sat down on the edge of the bed, prepared to say some words of pity, but Alma put her hand over the young parted lips so they would not breathe on the subject of falling and rising stars or planets with the usual symbolic undertones. "Shh. . . . It's best to be the star in one's own sky, such as it turns out to be, than be crowded in a mass like the Milky Way, where nothing stands out, where one needs telescopes to find the best. His Mamma will find the right end of the necessary telescope, you can be sure; she knows what she is doing. She picked you and the diamond well." Alma closed her eyes. Milda couldn't think of a rebuttal and studied the lines around Alma's eyes and the tight mouth. She thought she saw her mother.

"Oh, how will I ever live with his mother?" Milda questioned sadly, bitterly. "She clouds me already."

"Now, you let her be! She won't live long, not longer than she needs to, so use her for all she offers. Turn her around. You know how." Alma sounded like a cunning witch.

"Like you would, you mean."

"Well. All right. Like me or however you need to, but don't crawl! Don't you ever crawl! I didn't save you for that. Walk, climb! Walk over him if you have to, but don't stoop and bend!"

"Oh," Milda moaned, "I'll have to lift my feet very high."

"You can do it. Exercise!" Alma commanded. "Submit until you are married and then rule him, but never let him know it." Alma reached for her hand and invited her to go to a real night club, to Stuttgart, at the American base, but Milda refused. "I don't want to soil this diamond.

From now on I must stay pure for Kārlis, like this gem." She smiled sweetly, acting the part.

"The gem is not pure," Alma came back. "Do you know how many dirty hands have made it what it is, you silly dreamer? It is precisely because of all the handling that it shines so innocently and beautifully."

"Well, you look at it your way and I—mine."

And before her temptress spoke again, she took a sweater and rushed out the door and down a flight of stairs. Then she tiptoed back up and softly knocked on Door #1. She showed her hand to Mrs. Gramzda, whose hands were white with flour. "How lovely! Congratulations!"

They looked at each other in awkward silence. They had not had tea for some time. But, again the gray eyes peered deeply, past all glitter into a heart that beat in caged darkness. "Do not be afraid," the elder Milda said and then added, "I was just thinking about how to catch you. On Easter Monday we—our family—are planning to take the train to the Magnolia Garden—weather permitting. Would you like to join us?"

"Yes, oh yes! It's exactly what I would like to do. It's exactly how I would like to celebrate my engagement. You saved the day!"

"Bless you. May God bless your life."

Milda thanked her and then rushed down the stairs and out. She was so happy that this Easter would be a true day of resurrection. She looked forward to a bright day, full of joy, magnolia blossoms around sparkling fountains, all caught in the prisms of her diamond ring.

Under Watchful Eyes

After Easter, Milda divided her time between studies for her final examinations and the social obligations she had assumed in order to please her betrothed. Each event, however, loomed like a mountain with jagged peaks. And she was no mountain climber. The attention directed at her at close range disturbed her, making her very nervous.

Consequently, she came across to those ladies who easily floated at the top of society as uncooperative, capricious, even lazy. Milda heard low whispers about Alma and her questionable influence: *How can they dress so well and be so proud?* asked the ladies who wore the dresses and coats they had brought out of the fires of Latvia. *Who are they anyway? We don't know, do we?*

Milda heard the hush that fell in the room whenever she entered, always a bit late and out of breath. The critical looks cut her up, the unsaid words chilled her, but she would not allow herself to be injured. She pulled her insulating veil of pride and fortitude around her and endured. She saw each meeting as a test of her virtue and love for Kārlis, who, on the other shore, waited and watched. She assumed that Mrs. Arāja corresponded diligently with certain ladies of the committee and knew that any one of them would be happy to write and describe events and people in great detail. There were times when she felt Mrs. Arāja's distant eyes on her; then she would turn herself into *Maija,* who was lost in the underworld. Steadfastly she kept her eyes on him—the shower of gold. She told herself that she had to go through the slime of gossip, malice, jealousy with a light step and helpful hands in order to prove her goodness and grace. And so, she kept her head high even though her heart was sinking. Whatever task was assigned to her, she performed flawlessly so that no one could find fault with her. And there was still so much to do before she would be united with her man.

She circled the big events on her calendar: *Walpurgis Night* (only because of Alma); *May 1st* (not to be celebrated, a communist holiday, but *remember!*) *Mothers' Day.* (A Scout & Guide event in the school assembly hall. *I do the program.*) *Olympics* (Gymnastics with hoops. I'm in the lead.) *Graduation* (my day! responsible for decorating the hall, the day before.) *Whitsunday* (my confirmation! No responsibilities.) *June 14th* (responsible for the whole Memorial of the 1941 deported. Must take Guides to Mountain Colony.) *June 23-24. (Jāņi=*Midsummer

celebrations. Responsible to direct my Guides in a show of the ancient
Līgo fest, to be held at the marketplace. Must write script from folk
songs. *Must study folklore!)*

Milda looked at all the dates in May and June she had circled. They
stood like posts at the side of a long and risky road she would have to
travel all the way. Still that would not be the end: in July there would be
a local song festival, but she didn't bother circling that. It was an entirely
separate event where many people worked together. She would not be
noticed. After that she would rip the summer off the calendar.

In between those special events she focused on her studies and did
her chores. She hardly talked to Alma and only greeted the Gramzdas
as she hurried past them. She allowed no disturbances, no pleasures
or discussions. She wrote very short letters to Kārlis and read his only
once without dwelling on them, telling him that she did not need his
dissertations on the preservation of nationalism. There were enough
lectures on that all around her, all belaboring the same points, all
reminding those who still waited in the DP camp that no one lived for
him/herself but for the nation—for the higher, greater good. Milda grew
tired of the tone and resented it as an unfair indictment. "As if I had no
right to study for myself, for the sheer joy of learning," she complained
to Mrs. Gramzda. "Why does it always have to be for something else:
father, mother, nation?"

"And God," added the woman, nodding.

"Yes. And God, whom I don't see and hear."

"Only He is merciful, so be kind to yourself."

Milda closed herself behind her door and went on studying. She felt
herself ice over even though everything around her bloomed, and the
sun walked in the valley of the Neckar. But she had no time to smell
the flowers and to sunbathe. She feared Kārlis would not approve her
exposing herself in any secret or common dale. Lately he wrote how
he expected her to be submissive to the elders and graduate with top

honors. He wanted to be proud of her. . . . She tore the letter into tiny bits and raged, her fists pounding the bed.

Of course, she finished at the top of her class. The graduation was solemn, the decorations appropriate: white bouquets of carnations held together with maroon and white ribbons were fastened all along the center aisle. On either side of the stage were large baskets of white carnations surrounded with greenery; a black curtain hung at the back of the stage; down the middle hung a huge Latvian banner with the coat of arms centered in the middle. The stage provided the perfect background for the choir; the women wore national costumes, the men dark blue suits. *"Though possessing little of material goods, you are rich in spirit and strong of will that shall carry you toward yet unknown horizons,"* so spoke the principal. The graduating class, seated in the front rows, listened to the speeches, poems, and songs. At the end, as in a dream, the graduates walked up the steps to receive their artistically inscribed diplomas.

Milda, up on the platform, stared into the crowd for one long, searching moment. She saw Alma, Mrs. Gramzda, and her children sitting in a row. They all seemed proud, proud, proud, as though they had done the work, as though they had all pushed her up the jagged mountain slope. Helga waved at her quickly, spontaneously, she thought—as Zelda might wave. *Ah, Zelda. . . Would anyone give her a diploma? What's happening to her schooling anyway? And Mamma, where is she?*

She clutched her diploma, knowing that she would treasure the scroll for the rest of her life. She curtsied and gracefully stepped off the stage. Sitting in her chair, she raised her eyes to the coat of arms, admiring the three golden stars and the red and white winged lions, so strong and brave, like her people, her torn nation. She remembered her father and mother and everyone behind the dreadful Iron Curtain. Her eyes misted, and again she felt the Curtain's sharp iron points piercing deeply into her heart, turning the day of joy into mourning. She sighed, knowing that so it would always be as long as exile would last. She knew that inside every silver lining there would always lay a dark cloud. Sometimes it would be huge, at other times it might not be bigger than a man's hand, but it would always be there—over and inside her. . . . *Such is my fate*. . . . She brushed her eyelids and, glancing around, saw similar melancholy hidden in bitter-sweet smiles on all the faces. Seeing the people sitting quietly in rows of benches with no back rests, she was filled with love and sorrow for everyone. *Yes, dear Kārlis, I will help you lead! I will uphold you in your great work. That is my mission, so help me God!*

The applause and ovations startled her. The ceremony was over. She rose with her class and, in a procession, walked out of the hall into sunshine, flowers, congratulations, well-wishes. She smiled at Alma, who seemed relieved.

Confirmation

Whitsunday was the next major event on Milda's calendar. In her white nylon and lace gown—every stitch made painstakingly by hand—she knelt at the altar in *Frauenkirche* to receive her first Holy Communion and absolution of her sins, and then, with eleven other young people she listened to the sermon that seemed to go on forever. Much to her distress, the ceremony was not executed by the bishop, as she had hoped, but by a little clergyman who would not be able to emigrate because he had not passed the physical examination. The bishop was already in America and served as a vital pillar in the construction of the New Kingdom of Exile.

Kārlis had explained this in detail, but she did not quite understand how the construction was done. She still could not understand how everyone would fit in his proper place; she did not understand how she would be placed. In the confusion, her mind wandered off to retrace the path of her life that had taken her this far, and then it paused, drawing a curtain to an uncertain future, where Kārlis stood waiting. She smiled and returned to the present. The little man inside his black robe was still talking. He preached on about the duties and temptations and how life in exile was very difficult for a young Latvian Christian. "There would be even greater temptations in America because every one will have to be responsible for himself." *But I shall have a husband who will watch over me,* Milda argued back. And then it was over—the sermon, the liturgy, the Lord's Prayer, the hymn, and benediction. The confirmed processed down the long aisle toward the open door.

As she walked that long last span into adulthood, Milda, in the half darkness, saw Alma wipe her eyes. Sitting in the dim church, she seemed so very small—like a pale star inside dark clouds. Like a pebble tossed on some shore. Milda saw Mrs. Gramzda put a handkerchief to her eyes, *but not for my sake*, she thought, recalling their conversations, feeling herself falling away from such intimacies in the future. *Now I am an adult. I must take care of myself, but still. . . . Does the need of love ever go away?* She saw Vizma and Helga, very serious and observant, perhaps envious because their religious practices did not allow such ceremonies. Little Aija stood on the pew between the two sisters, stretching to find the one face she knew among all others and waved. Milda was grateful to all of them, even those she did not like. *There is nothing in life that cannot be useful*, Mrs. Gramzda had said, and Milda understood. The good and bad, dull and exciting, just and unjust—all twist together into some grand design—a work beyond the best art—that she called *her* life. *Vita mia.* And yet, she seemed to be far from everyone, gliding alone in her white dress, a big black Bible in hand, gliding on past and over the crowd, leaving everyone behind. Her gaze traveled far, far into the blue at the end of the aisle, and then across to that distant shore, where he waited. She wished she could keep on walking, flying, dressed as she was in billows of white, and become his wife—all in one step—skipping everything that now seemed an interference, a pointless delay. But, of course, only the mind is limitless and unbound. The body has to walk the earth. Milda had to walk in step, watching those in front and behind, putting her feet carefully so she would not soil other ladies' white trains and veils. And then, all the confirmed were out in the sunshine, pressed on all sides, being congratulated and showered with flowers.

Milda's arms filled quickly; they overflowed with roses, carnations, lilies and meadow daisies. Photographers focused their extended lenses, snapping. Black and white photographs would immortalize this hour, this moment. The young adults smiled, shed tears, and glowed in the sunshine and the shadow of the old *Frauenkirche,* as its bells rang out softly and clearly.

*

Suddenly a man with a huge bouquet of red roses pushes through the crowd. People make way for him. He goes straight to Milda. The sun makes her squint, but she recognizes him. Who else would it be than Mr. Pēteris Vanags? He carries the dark red roses in his right hand. The left sleeve is folded up, empty. She notices the upper bulging half arm. Her eyes become large; they blink and furtively glance around. She searches for an escape, but people block the way. The only clear path is the one the crowd makes for him. If she would take that, they would collide. She stands still. He is only a step away. He offers her the brilliant roses, bending over her, smiling, lips open, saying words, then coming down on her hand moist and lingering. Milda grows pale and withdraws the hand. He bows and takes a step back. She sees the people around her watching, smiling, hoping. *Hoping for what? Don't they know that I wear the ring of another, and does not that ring protect me? Why does he bring me roses? What right does he have? How dare he?* But no one hears her internal screams. No one chases him away. *Of course they could not.* He is handsome, tall, a true Latvian hero. A poster man of the self-sacrificing soldier. She stands still. He holds the roses impatiently, passionately, and then she hears herself saying, "No, thank you. I have enough flowers. Give them to her who has none."

His face turns into a pained grimace. Beads of sweat gather on his forehead as he pushes the roses on her. But she does not touch them. They fall at her feet, on the stone pavement, where people are already stepping on them, accidentally, apologetically. "You can't toss me away so easily," Vanags whispers close to her ear and then backs away, leaving her trembling in a flood of sunlight. Alma steps forward and leads her away from the church. They walk fast as in a nightmare, holding on to the mounds of flowers, their feet hardly feeling the pavement, the white dress sweeping the streets. They turn toward Lido. Far behind them Mrs. Gramzda and her daughters follow in disturbed silence, untouched by the tempest of Milda's heart. Out of a side street, the Slovak girl, *Ein Stickle Brot*, comes toward them, her hand open, begging, but they pass by, knowing that others will put a piece of bread and some worthless coins in that rough little hand. Once they have entered the shadows of the chestnut trees, heavy with white blossoms like huge candles, they slow down. Milda quickly looks back and sees the Gramzdas, her guardian angels, following her at a distance, following the lovely white dress like a vision.

Dinner with the Gramzdas

Mrs. Gramzda does not go to her church that afternoon. She stays in her kitchen and prepares a meal for Milda to which Alma is also invited. In her haste, Milda had almost forgotten the kindness, but now she looks forward to it. She is very hungry and is glad that the family had saved her again. Alma had been angry at her because she had wanted to throw a real party downstairs in the dance studio, but Milda did not even consider that. Neither would she want to do the rounds of other confirmation parties. She would have no man touch her and no alcohol taint her lips. She did not want to fall into temptation. She would not sin, not on this day, not anymore.

In late afternoon, while the sun gilds the vineyards, Milda, in the same white dress, now cut and hemmed slightly below the knees, goes to the dinner. She goes alone, with a large arrangement of mixed flowers. Aunt Alma, she explains, had to leave suddenly. The theater troupe would be touring other DP camps with *Love is Stronger than Death*. She would be gone for a week. Mrs. Gramzda and Vizma exchange suspicious glances but say nothing. The momentary silence hurts, but it is a small pain that can be quickly brushed away. The family give Milda a copy of *Pilgrim's Progress,* a precious volume that somehow had escaped with them and survived the flames of war. "We all have read it," Vizma says. It is a sacrifice. Milda sees that in her face and knows that love and sacrifice render any gift invaluable and accepts it graciously. She thanks everyone and sits down in the place of honor—in a garlanded chair. The preacher says grace, and then the women carry in the dishes. There is roast beef, mashed potatoes, creamed carrots, sautéed sauerkraut, wild mushroom gravy, garnished with fresh dill and chives, and fresh leaf lettuce salad in sour cream. Milda praises the food but eats very little. Every one else eats heartily. Jokingly, the preacher thanks Milda for the confirmation, else, he says, there would have been only bread and sausage! Time passes pleasantly, even while they remember all those who cannot be at this table because they are suffering behind the Iron Curtain. In a silent prayer, Milda remembers her parents and sister, aunts and uncles, and cousins. The food is hard to swallow, for sudden tears threaten to choke her. Mrs. Gramzda watches and sees all as a pained silence descends over the bowed heads.

When the meal is finished, the girls start jabbering about the day that is passing—the momentous day, only one such in a lifetime. As if urged, Reverend Gramzda commences a debate about the meaning of conversion and the Biblical base for adult baptism instead of confirmation.

"Leave her alone," his wife orders. "It was a beautiful ceremony and our guest was serious in her commitment."

Obediently the preacher fills up his plate and turns to praise his wife as the best cook. "She knows how to salt everything just right." He eats with pleasure. When the meal is finished, Milda rises to leave, but the preacher stops her. "Wait please! I have a gift for you also," he says and goes into the next room. Seconds later, he comes back with a folder and gives it to her. "All the emigration papers are in order," he says pleased. "A woman in Bethlehem, in Pennsylvania—close to Philadelphia—is your sponsor," he explains.

Milda takes the folder and holds it, saying thank you, but she doesn't want to go anywhere. Not yet. She does not wish to part from Alma for all the women in America. She wants to run away and hide. She wants out but must stay and listen. The hand of fate on her white, lace-clad shoulder presses down on her. But the preacher, smiling with great satisfaction, is saying that their family's papers are also ready and that they are destined for North Carolina. "To a land unknown and hot, but we must accept the Lord's will." Helga says she wishes they would be going to New York, where her best friend is; her father cuts her short, saying we cannot always have what we want. "I hate hot weather," Helga mumbles, stubbornly. Excited, frightened glances dart from one to the other. A strange quietness settles around the table, while somewhere, far away on the other side of the world, strangers are paving their way and molding their lives into new forms.

"If all goes well, we shall leave in the middle of August, while the sea is still calm," says the preacher. "My work here is almost finished.

Fortunately those who have passed have their departures fixed. The quotas are just about filled. So. We must get ready!"

Vizma and Helga clear the table, while Jānis brings out a map of America. They lean over it, their fingers traveling from one coast to the other, along the shores and over the wildernesses and the mountains. "Such a big country," Mrs. Gramzda says and sighs. They try to estimate the distances between cities and states. "Philadelphia appears to be quite close to New York but far from Charlotte," Jānis says and calculates the distances. He turns the miles into kilometers. He points out the mountain ranges and the rivers that would be hard to cross.

"We may not see you again," Mrs. Gramzda says, looking sadly at Milda.

"Oh, yes, we will!" Helga exclaims. "We'll find each other again!"

"I hope so." Milda smiles. "America could not be so big that we might lose our friends and brothers and sisters. Besides, America has no iron curtains."

"True. And thank God for that!"

"My Aunt says that people there don't have to carry passports."

"Impossible!" the preacher cuts in. "But soon we'll find out for ourselves. Jānis folds up the map and puts it away. Mrs. Gramzda asks Helga to set out the

coffee service. It is a beautiful set of the finest *Bavarian* porcelain, white with silver edges, bought—Reverend Gramzda jokes—for a carton of American cigarettes.

"Father, can't you keep some things to yourself?" Vizma pleads, while Jānis burns in shame, but Papa jibes at them for being judgmental. "We live in abnormal times," he says seriously. "And we have to manage the best we can, my dear children, because this is a dirty world, where the devil has brushed everything with his tail. Nevertheless, meanwhile, we have to eat and try to maintain some elegance and a sense of our Latvian humor that has helped our people to survive through far worse times than these. So be thankful and make the most of it and remember that we are cultured people." He pauses and takes a sip from the delicate cup, too fine for his thumb and forefinger. "Yes, you accuse me, wondering how a minister who preaches that smoking is sin, can be trading with cigarettes. Shame on me, you say, but now let's see if these thimble cups will hold the coffee that cost me a whole pack!" He laughs, leaning back.

Vizma brings in a mocha cream cake. "Where did that come from?" the preacher asks. "What have you traded in?" He scowls at his wife, who shakes her head helplessly. "Mama saved the ingredients for a long time, cutting here and there out of our rations. She traded nothing," Vizma comes to the defense and sets the cake in front of the guest of honor, who cuts into it, letting the knife in slowly and lifting up the first fragile, many-layered piece. She sets it on one of the transparent little plates, passes it forward and continues cutting.

"Never has such a cake been set even on a king's table!" the preacher praises, but his eyes fog over. His family knows that he is remembering, wondering if his son has a piece of bread to eat. "Thank you, Mamma, bless you," he says, looking at her across the table.

At last they rise, but Milda still cannot get away. Everyone gathers around the piano. They sing as Vizma plays. The religious songs are about sailing upon life's seas, heaven, and ties that bind. The folk songs are about the sun setting, winds blowing, the maiden waiting for her lover to come home from war. . . . They sing until the sun slides down beyond the vineyards, leaving the room in twilight. Milda again thanks the preacher for her papers and his wife for the food and returns to her room as from a long, strange journey, as from a passage through the mysterious underworld. She is very tired.

The poem *Daugava*

Throughout the following week, Milda rested. She worked on the June 14 program and made notes for her Midsummer Night script. She took her Guides into the nearby foothills, where they picnicked and practiced for the program. She liked and loved the girls, those few who were still left; she guarded them and praised their efforts and, in turn, they adored and obeyed her. But the teachers and leaders watched her; they did not quite approve of the improvisations Milda allowed on Rainis's greatest, most sacred epic poem *Daugava*. They did not like the cuts, nor the fluid moves depicting the waves of the river. "But waves are irregular, turbulent, disturbing," she argued.

"However," said the advisor, "you certainly should understand that such movements may provoke the men to unclean thoughts and be offensive to the women and children." Milda promised to make amends and to correct other errors. She assumed that the misunderstanding was cleared up. Yet, the clouds of doubt seemed to hover in the air. She felt spying eyes scrutinizing her seemingly overly confidential acts. "Perhaps someone is waiting for me to blunder," she told Helga.

"It couldn't be. Your imagination is playing tricks. Everyone loves you," she answered seriously. But Milda was not convinced. As she counted down the days on the calendar and re-lived the desperate, accelerated push of Mr. Vanags's strong arm after her confirmation, his hand full of burning roses, her body trembled. "What does this mean?" she asked the mirror on the wall. Out in the public, she leaned on her girls, drawing courage from their innocence, laughter, and quiet admiration. Days before the event, her nervousness increased; the least imperfection upset her and she snapped, her face tense with disapproval, then going soft and apologetic, saying that this will be their last big event "before we all are scattered by the four winds." In the night before the 14th, she had a dream: the imposing man pushed a diminutive

Kārlis under the flag and made love to her. As she yielded, she woke up with a cry, her body on fire and all her pulses throbbing in savage pain. Her sleep escaped, and she lay wide awake, watching the dawn brighten, glad that Alma was gone. *Oh, where is she? What dreams does she have?* When the sunrays broke through her window, she rose, telling herself that all is nonsense, that dreams are nothing but invisible vapors and that she will go up the steep incline to the Mountain Colony unafraid and confident. "This evening will be the examination that will test my love for Kārlis. I must pass this test."

The day of June 14, 1950, in the valley of Neckar, was hot and humid and full of blossoms of every kind. Toward evening the Latvians from all over town headed up to the Colony. They walked slowly, reverently, carrying gifts and flowers. Milda guided her girls up through the castle and then on beyond it. They took a shortcut through a meadow next to the outer wall. There the sun shone warmly, while a gentle breeze cooled them, blowing the humid air away, disturbing the tall grass that sparkled full of daisies. There, close to a budding rosebush, they rested, protected and invisible. They went over the lines of *Daugava* one more time and then, spontaneously, as if they were lost in some meadow of Latvia, started picking the daisies. Bunches of them. They would decorate the hall with these innocent flowers. It would be so sweet, so very folkloric! They chatted, saying how the bright blossoms would make a striking contrast against the dark blue "water" — streamers of Milda's leftover nylon material they had dyed and stitched together. "The daisies are the perfect symbols of hope and joy, which we all need," said one of the girls. They were sure that the veterans would understand the symbolism and appreciate every detail. "Oh, it will be a good show!"

"Unforgettable!"

Singing, the girls bent and twisted in and out of the flower-sprinkled grass in happy abandon, picking the flowers, not minding the flight of time.

*

Milda blows the whistle, ever so softly, like a meadowlark. The girls spring to her side. They brush off and straighten out their uniforms and follow their leader on to the wide-rose-garlanded *Alee* that takes them to their goal. The large buildings cast huge shadows as they near the gate. The low sun shines in their eyes.

They reach the crowded courtyard in plenty of time, but other Guide and Scout troupes are already there, lining up. Milda sees Jānis, who waves and teases her for being late. Helga runs up to her, but does not know what to do, how to help. Milda gives her a large bunch of daisies and tells her to go and tack them on the *waves*.

"There are still so many men here," she says to no one in particular as she scans the veterans. "No country wants to take our invalids," a young scout comments. "The Germans branded them and the Americans believe that our soldiers fought against them because they killed Jewish people," adds the scout leader.

"Did they?" Milda asks.

"Of course not."

"It's very sad," says one of the quiet guides. "Leaving them here is like burying them alive. . . unfair. . . perhaps they would be better off. . ."

"Quiet!" commands Milda. "Please observe the code!" she says, her voice too harsh, her face too flushed. "Order!"

One by one, as through sunrays, smiling or grinning, the invalids come toward them, reaching for them—that is, if they have legs and arms; those who have no legs remain seated on the sun-warmed benches along a wall, waiting to be moved into the hall to perch along the inside wall. The girls give the sad heroes bunches of flowers and walk slowly through them as through upturned battle fields, stepping lightly, raising their feet high. They carry the white daisies and dark blue streamers and then disappear through the open door of the barrack that serves as the assembly hall.

In the doorway Mr. Vanags waits like some chief. He welcomes the girls, looking over Milda's head, ignoring her presence so deliberately that she is afraid everyone sees the deception. He puts his hand on each girl as she passes through the door, but he does not touch Milda, who comes in last. He then closes the door and promises help if he's needed. The scouts are already at work, draping the dingy hall with black streamers that look like black rain. The girls set the daisies all around, in memory of the souls whose bodies perished on June 14, 1941. They work silently, sadly. Each is lost in her own grief. Each mourns for her father, brother, uncle, friend. . . . Not a single person on the whole mountaintop is unscathed by the sickle that cut through Latvia, not only on that dreadful night but on many nights and days that followed until the war ended, but, as soon as the sickle could be sharpened, it swung again, cutting the innocent and the guilty.

Milda remembers. Vanags also remembers as he watches her now with hawk eyes. She does not look at him. She sees other ghostly eyes peering through the open windows. Do they accuse the healthy and the living? Do her father and Juris see her? Are all the fathers looking at their daughters and the innocent young men, charging them never to forget that day and the many other days, when Latvian blood poured out in streams, making the land they all lost forever holy?

"Don't you ever forget!" come words from outside the window. The boys salute, and the girls nod. How could they possibly forget? Who would ever let them? They know without being told that no matter where they would end up, they would always decorate halls for the deported and slain. They would decorate and remember the victim faces long after those faces and bodies will have disintegrated. The girls know they would pick flowers and make garlands even when they themselves will be too stiff to bend down. The boys would grow into men and give their lives to keep the flame of freedom burning and the memory alive. They would be as vigilant as young hawks. "Yes, we will remember forever," one of the scouts says. Those sitting outside hear him. They turn, some grin, others remain stone-faced. One invalid says: "You, the young and the living, must go on and tell the world until the last victim is avenged and until justice returns to our nation." The words hit like stones. Everyone stops and stares at the heads in the window.

"What now?" Vanags asks, rather kindly. "Let's finish our work. It's almost time."

"Yes!" Milda says, her fingers tangled in daisies, and goes to the farthest side of the room. He does not follow.

*

The sun is near setting. The decorating is finished. The Scouts take their stand along the center aisle. They stand at attention like soldiers, and then the hot hall starts to fill with people—the whole and the lame, the uniformed and the private. The ladies who live in the valley below help the invalids. They are mothers, sisters, and brides. Some turn their eyes away from the deformed bodies; some cry, others smile. They let the men hold their hands for a while as they speak gentle women words, and the invalids take what they can and are reluctant to let go.

The hall fills slowly, laboriously, until it overflows. There are not enough benches. Those who can, stand along the walls. They all wait, wait for another WORD. They wait for the reminders of historical moments. The veterans seem pleased with the brief hour of attention that comes up to them so seldom, but when it does, it flutters around them in girls' skirts and virgin smiles; it comes in brief moments but long enough to articulate their eternal loss.

A great hush settles over the hall; it is so still that the wind blowing through the open windows seems loud and howling, the draft dangerous.

Vanags closes the windows. The Junior Guides, Helga among them, proceed and light the candles. The elementary school choir sings. The clergyman gives the invocation, and then Mr. Vanags steps forward and addresses the assembly. His voice is low and strong; his account of 1941 dramatic and accurate. He moves the audience to tears, and then he pauses and remains standing. All eyes are on him who gave his arm for his country. People applaud. A teacher presents him with an oak garland from the Ladies Guild. Schoolgirls representing the various grades give him flowers. Milda, in the name of the Guides, gives him the latest volume of a history book of Latvia. He presses her hand formally, correctly. An adult chamber choir sings, and then it is time to perform the *Daugava*.

The words of the poem rise in a crescendo as they pledge eternal allegiance to the red-white-red banner. Milda, having changed into a white, masterfully embroidered Latgalian costume, leads the girls who carry the banner up the stairs to the stage. The banner lies flat and tilted, gently waving like a river. Other girls spread the daisy-pricked dark blue nylon over it. On both sides stand the remaining guides and scouts. Reverently, they stretch their arms over "the river" and chant the powerful lines of the poem. Milda stands on a platform beyond and above them like a priestess, her arms raised to heaven. And then they all sing:

Both sides of the Daugava—eternally indivisible—

One land, one nation, one language—ours. . .

It is a long poem that allows for the mind to wander, to look down on the river that flows through Riga, dark and deep. The poem tells that the river carries the souls of soldiers who gave their lives to unite both sides of the river. The people who listen know the history; they know about the fierce battles that started way back in the 12th century when the Crusaders' boats floated up and down the river attacking the tribes on both sides. They know that foreign conquerors ruled, each on his side, each coveting the land across on the other side. And they know how only some thirty years ago the Latvian men and boys brought the two sides together and forged them into one nation. Yes, they know. They knew the men who fought and died, who laid down their heads on the banks for the enemies to smite rather than split up and vandalize the country—their precious God-given land—where the enemy sits now, basking in the northern sun.

Tears flow, hands clasp, eyes look forward and backward and all around as if for help. Perhaps someone—some world leader, some American, God Himself, will hear and affirm their sacred right to live in their country. — Another spotlight illuminates the banner. Vanags gives the tune, and all the people rise and sing the National Anthem, the holy prayer: *God, bless Latvia.* Girls in white blow out the candles. A blue twilight curtains the windows.

A banquet follows. In another barrack, tables have been set. They are loaded with food the ladies had prepared as an atonement. But even the veterans must not live on food alone: they must listen to more garnished speeches, spiced stories, and tantalizing songs. The girls must entertain them with services and smiles. And those who don't serve must sit next to the soldiers—their big brothers for the evening. They have to sit tightly, since there is little room.

Milda is assigned to sit at the left side of Mr. Vanags. She is very hot. She cannot eat. She cannot breathe. She feels the sleeved stump rubbing the top of her arm. His leg flanks hers. She is a fly stuck on flypaper, and she cannot pull away, cannot fly even into the dim candlelight that burns right in front of her. Her leg won't move, while her heart pounds so loudly she is afraid everyone can hear it. She is sure Vanags can. He keeps leering, looking down on her chest, where an amber brooch holds together the slit of her damp blouse. She is conscious of the slightly exposed rim of her heaving breasts. He touches the side of her hand as he fills her cup. Her little finger extends, willing to help steady the large hand, but she quickly pulls it back. The room becomes hotter. They all sweat. Vanags sweats. His breathing sounds as though he were running a close race. She tries to rise but he holds her down. Desperately, as in a nightmare, she turns for help, but all around she sees happy, glowing faces and hears joking, story-telling voices that pay no attention to her. She sees that bottles are springing up all over the tables. *Where did they come from*? she wonders. *We did not bring any. . .* Vanags reaches inside his suit coat pocket and out comes a nice, flat little flask. He grins and pours amber liqueur in his empty water glass and offers same to Milda. She shakes her head violently. He laughs, says *bottoms up*! and drinks. He refills his glass and fills a lady's glass across the table. Milda recognizes the woman. She was on the program committee that censured her. Now she stares at Milda with hard eyes that soften and linger on Mr. Vanags' face. Milda's face burns. She tries to bypass the flushed face across from her and sees that everybody is having a wonderful time—*all on account of our deported loved ones. The Baptists were right in not staying on.*

She rises and tries to escape, to get away, but Vanags holds her back, whispering with alarming intensity, "Wait! I need to talk to you, Miss Bērziņa." His voice is thick, unbearably close, nicotine noxious. He smokes a strong American cigarette that stings her eyes. His hand shakes hot ashes on the tablecloth. The woman on the other side scowls at Milda, no doubt because she does not rise with her. Holding on to the edge of the table, the woman leaves in a slow sideways manner. Time freezes while Vanags' side flanks Milda's, gluing them together. She tries to pull away, but cannot. She hears the drone of meaningless words but does not listen. Her head hurts and she drinks from her bottle of lukewarm *Seltzer*. His side is still stuck to hers. They sit like that—she doesn't know for how long—until loud applause jars her. She sees people rising, shaking hands, bending, moving about, and heading out the door that is wide open. Like a gymnast, she quickly swings her legs over the bench and breaks away. She rushes toward the door, aware that he is close behind her. They are outside. In the darkness, he pulls her to his side, smiling affectionately, paternalistically, in case people are watching. "Please, let me escort you and your girls down from our mountain," he says loudly, ignoring the Planning Committee woman, who stands close by, willingly accepting his offer. He moves inside the circle of the young, still resting his arm around Milda's shoulder. "It is dark and dangerous for such lovely girls to be out alone. Come on, fellows, those who have legs, let's go!" The girls flirt and giggle, some move quickly to where the scouts are milling about, not knowing when to start down the mountain, while others linger, saying that the moon is bright enough to guide their steps, *but if you wish.* . . Milda cuts loose and runs.

She runs out of the crowded courtyard, out the iron gate, and down the *Rosen Alee*. She cuts through the castle, and only when she reaches the steep steps she slackens her pace. Down, in the marketplace, she drinks from the fountain and washes her face and hands. She scrubs furiously, but she cannot take out the stains where his hand touched her, where his leg rubbed hers. She cannot rid herself of the voice in her ears, hissing, seducing, calling her, calling the demons out of the dark crevices of her being. She walks on slowly, the night clouds enfolding her in darkness. *I'll catch up with you yet,* rings in her ears, making a joke of her flight. Again she takes to running and keeps on running until she is safely inside Lido. She walks up the stairs slowly, counting the steps, one by one, until she stands at her door. The other doors are dark and quiet. Even the typewriter sleeps. She goes to the toilet. It stinks. She hadn't had time to clean it. But she stays there, relieving herself, emptying her bowels, then pulls the rusted chain that will flush everything down the long drainpipe. Quietly, so no one would wake up, she tiptoes across the hall, unlocks her door, and enters her room. It is empty.

A Letter in the Night

She turns on the nightlight and writes Kārlis a letter, describing the solemn event and her part in it. She writes about the success of *Daugava, my première performance,* and about the fine banquet (*Our art of table setting and food preparation always amazes me, and I am learning.*), and the cloudy, moonlit night. She writes about the daisies and roses and black and dark blue streamers, but she does not mention Pēteris Vanags. She knows that, if the truth were told, he would not understand. He might point out: *after all, the old soldier only wanted to talk to you. Wasn't he kind, most solicitous?* Besides, she knows that Kārlis admires him in a special way, almost like a girl in love. He blushed whenever the older man talked to him or put his hand on his shoulder. She knows that Kārlis would do anything to please him, to receive words of approval, especially when it came to *great* causes for the sake of the nation. So, if she would as much as suggest anything negative about his hero, Kārlis would certainly take Vanags's side and scold her: *you behaved hysterically, you are like your Aunt... You must guard against imagining things. It is a very childish way to be.*

And he would be right, for she was indeed imagining things, terrible things. She imagined Vanags's hands, when he still had two, bloody and his face cruel. She imagined him pressing her down to the ground with his stump. She imagined how Kārlis could never protect her from the predator claw. She would have to somehow, somewhere defeat him all by herself or be defeated, and she was afraid. She looked at her solitaire diamond ring, helplessly reflecting the lamplight, then turned the light off and went to the window. High in the clearing sky grinned the moon; it was a vampire night.

"Oh, Alma, my dearest, where are you?" she speaks, leaning out and looking down, searching up and down the empty street. "What rocks and caves are you exploring tonight, and who is there to catch you if you might slip and fall?"

Numb from fear, she notices a man walking quickly up the street. He stops and leans against a tree opposite Lido and lights a cigarette. From her lace-curtained dark window she watches him smoke slowly, in prolonged in-and-out breathing, his face turned up, briefly illuminated by the tip of the cigarette. She stares down, clutching her hands so her body would not tremble. She is a moth that would, at any moment, fly into the fire and light if the window were not so high, the downward plunge so violent. Hypnotized, she watches him take the last draw, then pitch the butt into the gutter, where, for an instant, it flickers and dies. But the man still stands; his and the tree's blended shadows stretch across the street. Milda pulls herself back, yet leans forward, dazed and closes the window. He turns and with quick steps walks back toward the dark mountain. She double locks her door, undresses and goes to bed. For a long time she lies wide-eyed, until she sinks into a nightmare.

St. John's Eve

The next major event on Milda's calendar was the day and night of June 23-24. *Jāņi* (St. John's Eve/Day), which marks the midsummer solstice. However, the shortest night is always from June 20-21, the real turning point. "So why the 23-24? And why Jāņi?" Milda asked her teacher, but she did not know. Then she asked the preacher, who explained that the 24th was the birthday of John the Baptist and was instituted as a holy day by the Catholic Church when Latvia was Christianized. "All pagan holidays were outlawed," he said, but the natives still held on to the old feast days and simply implanted them upon the Christian holidays and went on—often in secret—with their doings—dancing and drinking and indulging in licentious activities, singing immoral songs and so on. They turned away from God and ridiculed John the Baptist and Jesus Christ. They washed the baptism off in the Daugava, so goes the story. Yes, such was our Christian beginning. Our ancestors were pagans well into the 13th century and many still are. Most don't hold on to the old beliefs, but the pagan practice has become a tradition, and immorality seems to be all right on this night. Maybe it's not as bad as it used to be, but it is no night when nice young ladies and men ought to be out alone. In short, it is a night made for sin, and I object to celebrating it. Hasn't God punished our people enough for turning from Him and following their old, ungodly ways?"

Fortunately for Milda, Mrs. Gramzda had come to the rescue and stopped the sermonizing. She knew that there would be a celebration in the camp, as there had been every year, and it was best to let the young people of their church and family go along rather than forbid them and make them sneak off and lie and complain that they can't have any fun. And she did not want to offend Miss Milda, who was working hard on creating a play for the evening's performance.

"I remember some very boisterous, *Jāņi*," Mrs. G. joined the conversation. "But such could only happen at the old farms, with their courtyards full of relatives, farm workers, and neighbors and not here in this town, where people go to sleep at a decent hour." The preacher excused himself and went back to his typewriter. Mrs. Gramzda wished Milda good luck. "But do be careful."

In her room, Milda felt uneasy. She jabbed at the dates with her sharp dip pen, contemplating the paradox of this holiday which deliberately—through songs and dances—invited temptation of every sort and spoofed at those who stayed on the sidelines watching. *On John's night you cannot tell/ Who is woman, who a maid. . .* Tradition made it all right for any couple to search the woods for the magic fern blossom that blooms only on that night. . . . In anticipating the holiday, even the ladies of the Festival Committee told each other about their fern blossom hunts with girlish excitement, certainly embellishing their promiscuity and their successes, Milda thought, unable to imagine the women as girls running about the woods. She heard one lady say that the word *līgo*, which is the loud refrain after each quatrain of the *Jāņi/ Līgo* songs, had a definite sexual meaning in the Sanskrit. *Līga,* she said, eying Milda boldly, is the name of some ancient sex goddess, and that it is no coincidence that the name in Latvian calendars is listed on June 23, the Eve of *Jāņi.* "So make of it what you all will," said the scholar. But Milda remembered the preacher's warning, "Why put yourself in the path of the tempter? Why take any risks?" But she had dismissed the warning and thought of Kārlis's letters stacked on a shelf like a rampart.

The festival was only a week away. She concentrated on her play. It was a one-act simple dramatization she called *Pusnakts sapnis* (A midnight dream), set "in times past." It was nothing special, just a medley of love songs, where all her guides had a chance to sing and dance.

On the Eve of St. John, Milda met her guides. Together they went up into the hills to pick flowers and cut oak branches and made wreaths for themselves and the American and German guests. Meanwhile, down in the city, the streets filled with the aroma of baking bread, as the Latvian women rushed back and forth between their dwelling places and all the bakeries. Further up, the hills echoed with songs which the older women sang as they made oak leaf wreaths for their men and the disabled. The Germans looked on the strange doings, as though they were expecting a circus. Toward the evening they, too, gathered around the marketplace and along the streets, waiting for the theatrics.

At sunset, on the south side of the Neckar, all the Latvian children and youths were formed into lines that snaked across the bridge and on to the marketplace. Milda, dressed in her special costume and wearing a wreath of daisies, led her girls across the bridge. Though her dress felt heavy and she was hot, she felt safe and excited inside the billows of the many costumes and banners, like boundaries and walls. Afraid of running into Mr. Vanags, she hid behind armfuls of flowers, the meadow grasses, and the *Līgo* songs.

By the time the procession reached the marketplace, the magic transformation had already happened. The DPs had, for the evening, inherited another land, usurped another kingdom that had no borders, no written signs and rules. They wandered in the vast regions of emotions and memories. They sang their songs, spoke in their own language, and held their hands in a chain of hope, knowing well that in Latvia and in other foreign lands more people like themselves were celebrating this holiday in spite of occupations and other restrictions. They knew that they were a link in a chain which, though weakened here and there, would never be broken.

The stage was set up against the old *Rathaus.* On one side was a farmhouse with garland-decorated posts. A painted tar barrel torch burned on a painted hill. The other half of the stage was a deep cardboard pine forest with ferns in the underbrush. Behind the stage, on a tall post, burned a real tar barrel. Its flames leaped up dangerously, throwing out sparks. The town's firemen stood below, looking up and watching out.

The program started with the usual speeches, the honors and respect given to the invited Americans, gratitude to the town's mayor and admonition to the young people to be careful and not destroy anything, especially Latvia's reputation. "Remember that we are guests in this land." And then Milda and her guides were onstage, performing her very own dream play. It went so well that the whistles and roaring applause startled her. The girls curtsied and bowed, as they gathered meadow flowers from many hands. Milda was proud of her little drama, thinking that Kārlis would also be pleased. At least she would have an achievement she could write about in her next letter.

When the applause stopped and the spotlights turned off, Milda, with her cast, stepped off the stage. "Disperse! Go! Have fun!" she told her girls, and off they ran. Left alone, she paced around the stage, going in and out of the shadows, getting too close to the bonfire, her hands full of flowers. She paused and looked at the people, who suddenly seemed foolish, jumping around, like lost children, playing childish games, singing their songs, pretending that nothing had happened and that they were actually back in the hills and valleys of their lost homeland. She looked up and saw the black barrel flicking up single little flames and lone sparks. It was ugly, she thought, like refuse, polluting the air.

The *Rathaus* clock struck—she counted—ten. It struck away her precious time, her youth, that would never return. Neither would this pagan night return, when sin was pushed aside. Alarmed and nervous, she craved for that sinful pagan love the preacher had railed against. She sighed and paced on like a nocturnal animal, her whole body becoming tense as in a hunt, throbbing with forbidden desire. Exhausted, she leaned against a dark post and watched the bonfire. *It will soon be over, this loneliness. . . this waiting. . .* But her thoughts did not soar across the ocean but pegged on Vanags, seeing him as he stood under her window a while back. *No, no! I hate him!* and forced herself to concentrate upon Kārlis. *What is he doing on such a night when ferns bloom and stars glide the earth?*

She wove through the crowd and paused to listen to group of older women who were singing bantering *Līgo* songs, which rowdy men answered in kind. A few yards away, other men lit the bonfire. Quickly the flames caught on and ate up the dry wood, but more wood was piled on so that the flames leaped high and sparks flew and danced. A circle formed around the fire, holding hands and dancing; she saw her guides having fun and felt old. When the flames died down, she watched young men leap through the flames, showing off to the girls, each outdoing the other. She too wanted to leap and dance, but felt the pressure of her diamond ring.

Distraught, she went to the fountain and splashed water on her face, dropping a bunch of the flowers into the water. She watched them float in circles, making her head spin. Tired out, she edged her way around the loud crowd and glided on, behind the dark stage, where the cardboard pines cast their shadows.

Suddenly, his strong hand grabs her. The flowers fall from her arms, and her feet step on them. She loses her balance and falls forward, but his hand pulls her back. She is tight against his chest, his leg is pushing against her long skirt; his lips press her lips as his tongue drives inside her mouth. She hits him. She strikes again and again, beating on his chest. His nostrils exhale nicotine and alcohol in thick, heavy puffs like bug spray that makes her weak in the knees, but her arms stiffen and push against him. He doesn't let go but holds her head, stroking her hair gently, soothingly until her arms rise and meet his hand and her mouth responds to his kiss. Satisfied, he withdraws his lips, only to whisper, "I caught up with you at last, my beauty! Why do you struggle, why pretend?"

"No, no! Let me go or I'll scream!" With her sharp knee she kicks him where it hurts and bites his hand. The stump hits her on the head, but he laughs, "Oh, you little witch," he says, still holding her, "We have found the fern, as you've been wishing."

"No, I don't want you, ever!"

She wriggles out of his arm and runs toward the fire. Like a satyr she leaps over the flames, clearing it better than the young men. The crowd cheers, but she races on, pushing through the wall of people. She runs toward the alley she cannot see but knows is there. She turns sharply and runs to the park, not up *Bahnhoffstrasse*. She means to throw him off her track if he tries to follow. At a corner she stops and listens. She hears footsteps, and is sure he is close behind her, but she dare not look back. She runs on and makes another sharp turn. Still, the footsteps follow. She slackens her pace, for she is confused. Do the footsteps belong to a whole mob or to one mighty man? She stops and hears only the distant singing, like a desperate mating cry: *"Lee-goo-o, lee-goo-oo!"*

Again she hears footsteps behind her. She zigzags down a path and runs along the canal and stops at the bridge. *Oh, if only I didn't have this dress on me!* She fears that it glows in the dark, while its little bells jingle. She stands until the jingling stops. She hears nothing. *What happened and what was I doing? Why? Oh, how I hate that man!*

She walks on. The singing has stopped. She glances back and sees small groups of people walking, gliding with their shadows. She hides from them. She leans against the trunk of a blooming linden tree, drawing in its fragrance, taking deep breaths like droughts until she feels lightheaded, too weary to go on. She hears new footsteps and clutches the tree trunk. — It's only an old drunk who shuffles down a path, cursing and hitting the darkness with his cane. She sits down on a bench exhausted, but her body throbs with fear and longing. It wants more of his awful, poisonous kisses. She sits on the bench a long, long time. Is she waiting? Hoping he would come and find her? They would be safely alone, hidden behind the heavy, blooming branches of jasmine bushes, and he would be gentle. But no one comes, and she knows she should not be out alone, sitting on the bench. She clutches herself and doubles over, crying, whispering harshly, *"No, no, no! This is madness! It's the night, and I am alone in a strange country.*

Casting cautious glances all around, she rises and hurries out of the park. When she sees the gable of Lido, she feels safe, but as she nears the building, she imagines him standing behind the chestnut tree. She tells herself that her mind is playing tricks. She thinks she hears him whistling ever so softly, sadly and tenderly. At the door, she stops to listen. *It's only the wind blowing through the trees.* Quickly she unlocks the door and drags herself up to her room. The room is cool and empty. She double-locks the door. Panting, she dips her hands into the look warm water and pats her face and then dips her fingers in a jar of Vaseline and runs them over her lips. They are large and swollen. They hurt. Slowly she undresses, carefully folding one garment after another and laying each down. She goes to the window and looks down, but sees no one. She stands still in the darkness, flooded by moonlight, and prays to the moon, not God, the Invisible. She closes her eyes and shivering re-lives the long day and night. *The grand finale of my sin. But where were the angels when I fell?* She stretches her arms up and looks at her hands and sees her diamond glowing like a furious eye. *"He sees me too, he saw me, and I am doomed!"* Like an awakened lunatic, embarrassed, she draws back inside and closes the window. She puts on her robe and tiptoes to the toilet, past the silent doors, behind which all is dark and quiet. *The innocent sleep. . .* Back inside her room, she slides under the covers, trembling from lust and guilt. She is unrepentant, like her pagan ancestors who came out of the woods with fern leaves in their hair.

The next morning, she finds a part of her midsummer flowers and grasses lying at the foot of the chestnut tree.

Sin, Guilt, and Expectations

Milda fell ill and confined herself to her room for many days. Mrs. Gramzda brought soups and tried to engage her in conversations, but she would not talk; she would barely turn her face from the wall when the good woman knocked. She did not want her to see her lips. Alma, as usual, was very busy at the eroding theater. Besides, she had neither time nor patience for sickness. Irritated, she shouted at Milda to speak, to explain. She said she heard people talking about her, saying, "See,

see. . . who would have thought she would do such a thing." But Milda said nothing. She wanted to die.

About a week later, however, she cautiously left her room and went up on the rooftop to lie in the sun. Vizma and another lady were already there, receiving the usual whistles from the factory men across the street. When Milda stepped out on the roof, all sirens seemed to go off, but she feigned deafness. She lay down as on a frying pan and looked at the sky through her dark glasses, thinking that it was pleasant to be alive, after all, to soak up the sun and hear trivial chatter. She went up again the next day and the next until she was well. One lovely morning she realized that her fears had ceased, her trembling stopped. That same day she began to work on a white shirt. A present for Kārlis. White over white, white woven through with white.

The work healed her. It forced her to forget Vanags like some plague, and soon she braved again the streets of Esslingen, even the paths leading up to the vineyards. She wrote bright letters to Kārlis, excusing herself for not writing because she had been sick. Only a summer cold, she wrote, nothing more. But Kārlis wrote in a different tone: *This is a very important work we are now doing. We cannot make mistakes. We are laying the foundation of a Free Latvia in a Free World. We must be strong like granite. We must resist all winds from the outside and all doubts from within.*

Milda pondered those imperatives. She did not see how she could stop the winds from blowing where they would, especially in a strange country. Since her collapse, she was again afraid and full of doubts about laying foundations and selecting building materials. She did not see things as straight as Kārlis, especially when the shadow of Vanags blocked her view. Besides that shadow loomed darker, whenever Kārlis gave orders. It seemed to watch her, enjoying her struggle, making her recall the kisses the likes of which she had never tasted before and, therefore, racked her being with shame and outrageous yearning for more.

Assimilation is our greatest threat, he wrote. *We must not allow our people to fall into the common American melting pot. Our people must break away from their sponsors as quickly as possible. They are not white slaves, and they must not subject themselves to any kind of slavery. Remember that America sold us out. Remember that America was an ally of Russia. Did anyone ask us what our rights were? Did anyone care? So why should we? We have our own work to do, and we need all our people together. This time is crucial.*

He wrote on, telling gruesome tales about Latvians picking cotton in Mississippi and fruit in California. They were overrun by rattle snakes in Oklahoma and sweated on barges on the Mississippi River. Some sweltered in the mineral mines of Missouri and coal mines of Kentucky; others were blown about the vast winds over the farmlands of Kansas and the prairies of Wyoming. *Our people are like seeds, scattered in all directions, so we must bring them together—to the East Coast, here to New England, and the northern mid-west, which looks like Latvia, and you must, you will help me!*

Yes, of course, I shall help. That is why I will marry you! To bring Latvians together, to keep the dream of a free Latvia alive. . . to give birth to children and raise them for Latvia. "I will," she whispers and wonders how she should do it, how it will be. And then, she blinks hard, not believing the words that came at her: *Please consult with Mr. Pēteris Vanags of the Mountain Colony. Tell him that, although he is an invalid and a veteran of the Latvian army and, consequently, not welcome in this country, I shall do everything in my power to bring him over. We need such men as he, and I know that he and I will work well together. I have talked things over with other men in leadership positions, and they believe that there might be a place for him in Washington in our embassy or even in some U.S. federal agency. So, please, encourage him and tell him that I shall soon contact him directly. He may not know you, but I am sure that he has seen you about and at my side as I carried our banner. Greet him from me.*

"No!" Milda shouted, then tried to reason: "Are you out of your mind? Are you truly blind or do you want us to be a permanent triangle—until death—mine first?"

Soon after this, she received a thick letter in a strange, careful handwriting. It was from her sponsor: Miss Mary Fern. She wrote saying that she wished to introduce herself. She had come to America in 1929, as *Marija Paparde*, to work as a domestic servant. She described her daily life and her surroundings. In the last page she clarified that she was unmarried but that she had a grown daughter who was married. She confessed to being lonesome and that was why she decided to risk becoming a sponsor. But, of course, there was more to it: she was happy to help someone now that she was well off because others had helped her. That is what America was all about, she wrote, layers and layers of people helping each other start new lives.

She further confessed that she had been in a bad state when she arrived: she was pregnant with a married man's child. The man was her master—a nobleman of German dissent in whose mansion she had been a servant. She had lived in an attic room, where the man had come to her. What could she, poor girl, do? She was all alone—an orphan—and he was so handsome, so gentle and cultured! "And I loved him very much and felt sorry for him because he had a mean wife who nagged him constantly. The woman treated me like dirt, always watching me, always finding work for me to do, while her own three daughters lounged about, spoiled to the core. My master saw everything and pitied me, at first from a distance, form across the tables and chairs and hallways. But our eyes met over the heads of others. As a flower in spring, my being opened to him, and I lived only for those short, caressing glances. Then, on one fine day, he came to me when his wife was away and the whole house was empty. And so the inevitable happened.—He came again and again, and when I told him I carried his child, he was desperate. He said he wanted to divorce his wife—a rich baroness he never loved but who was forced upon him by his unreasonable, money-hungry father—and marry me, but, of course, that was impossible, and so quickly and sadly he bought a ticket for me for America. He had connections."

In America, she was presented as a widow and worked again as a servant. But only until the baby was on her feet. Then she moved to Philadelphia, where there were other Latvian immigrants. A caring woman invited her to go with her to the Baptist church. She went gladly and soon gave her life to Christ and joined the small congregation. "After that I told people the truth, as I am telling it now. I also admitted, before I was baptized, that I never stopped loving the man who was the father of my daughter and who promised to acknowledge and support his child, even though he might never see her. When one of the deacons asked me how I could be a born again Christian and admit to such sin, I answered him saying that the Bible was full of *other* women and concubines and that God blessed them, so why not me? I reminded him that Jesus did not throw stones at the woman caught in adultery. I told the stern deacon that he should not judge me either but take care that he and other men sin not and lead innocent girls into temptation. Some of the women nodded in agreement. The vote was taken, and I became a member of the church to which I still belong and where I serve my Lord. It makes me happy to walk in the truth. It has made me free, and I praise the Lord for his goodness, love, and mercy."

She further explained how she had learned secretarial skills and that she had a good, secure job. "I have my own house. Nothing much, but it is mine, and now it will also be yours—for as long as you need it. I know that you, like I, will want to be independent as soon as you throw the shoes of the old world away."

The letter went on. The more the image of Miss Fern turned into a real woman, the more Milda liked her, but she would not confess to her any recent or old sins of her own. She would not take the time to write long character descriptions of herself. She wrote back a short letter of thanks and told her that she is engaged to be married and would not stay with her for very long. She ended by saying that America was not just an unknown wilderness anymore or a strange Brooklyn, where her betrothed lived, but a new and fantastic land to be discovered. . . . *Yes, she thought, as she folded the transparent air-mail page, there are green lawns and roads that curve around hills and meadows and towns. And for me there is a house with a garden, and in that house lives a nice, understanding woman who is preparing a room for me. There I shall be safe at last.*

When, in a following letter, Kārlis instructed her how she should do the decent thing and work for her sponsor for a year before he married her, she raged. *Will he always tell me what to do? Will he always be the master of my morality and immorality?* She studied the photograph of Miss Fern, standing in her flower garden. *Behold the lilies of the field. . .* she had written in the margin. *Yes,* Milda thought. *They neither toil nor spin, but they are flowers. I am a woman, and I must toil, even spin, though I don't know how. And so I must stitch and wait and sit very still and never open any windows and look down. . . . What is the matter with him? How can he hold off our wedding for a whole year? Doesn't he long for me or is he afraid? Doesn't he need me the way I need him—close by—sleeping with me at night and working next to me in the daytime? I simply cannot understand. Are we that different? Are men and women so very different? But no. I would only have to beckon with my little finger and Vanags (befitting his name) would fly up to my nest and then where would we be?*

But she did not beckon to Vanags (the hawk). She could not imagine herself married to a man so overpowering that his passion would wear her out, and she could not think of him beyond that intense, demoniac, sexual passion that would only destroy her, where she could do nothing as noble as Kārlis demanded but only serve their carnal desires. His insatiable love would wear down her spirit, as it did now, when his words burned inside her and the memory of his kisses consumed her thoughts, making her sick for more. Her time was wasted, she knew, warring against herself. In this struggle she was alone, but swore she would confess nothing to no one and then have to deal with their judgments, advice, condolences. *I'll have to talk to him—in the daytime, in the morning, hopefully in some crowded place,* she resolved and wrote a kind letter to Kārlis, the sort one writes to a son.

You are right. Patience is a virtue I lack, I admit. I understand that you do not want to be rushed and that preparations for a proper wedding take time. Besides, I am certain that I shall need a whole year to learn that as well as the confusing ways of American life. I shall need a job and learn the skills, my Aunt also tells me what I'll need. So, my darling, I shall follow your instructions and do as you say. I want to be your obedient wife in all things. And—here are also things I need to settle and overcome, but I won't burden you with myself. She read what she had written and was satisfied. Kārlis would be pleased. She hurried down to the yellow *POST* box on the corner and dropped the letter in the wide slot like a hungry mouth that swallowed it whole.

Screening and Inoculations for America

The next morning Helga woke her up. "You have to get ready to go with us to Ludwigsburg. "We have to get more shots. I knocked on your door last night but you didn't open. Are you sick again?"

"No. I must have been sound asleep. I didn't hear you," she lied. How could she tell her excited friend that she was battling her demons and had been sitting by the open window staring down, waiting for him, late into the night and then gone to bed because not even his shadow was there, behind the chestnut tree? "I'll be ready soon," she said wearily, for she had not slept much. "Oh, when will all this end?" she mumbled. "Bodily examinations, questions, long lines, hot and smelly rooms packed with people. Hours on the train."

"We all dread the ordeal, but Papa says that we must suffer before we reach the Promised Land."

"Ah, yes, yes, I know, so please go so I can get dressed."

An hour later, she and the Gramzdas were squeezed together in the tight compartment of a local train that stopped at every station. As people came aboard at every stop, they had to squeeze even closer and be the targets of hostile stares. They whispered in their own language and talked about America, each looking at that distant land for the fulfillment of some dream, some vision of him and herself. Jānis would wear only plaid shirts. Vizma would have her own piano. Helga would have shoes that fit, and little Aija wouldn't wear large ribbons in her hair.

Mrs. Gramzda said she could hardly imagine large Baptist churches, complete with stained glass windows and raised pulpits. She could not wait to hear the kind of intelligent sermons she was reading in church magazines that now came regularly from those who had gone before. Nor could she imagine hearing smart men discussing politics on the radio for all the world to hear and not in secret, the way it was all through the horrible war years. In America, she could see, intelligence, reverence, beauty were almost one; in such a land she would be happy; her spirit would be free; she would be learning. Her face glowed as the train rattled on. She was positively beautiful, Milda thought.

"You should cut your hair," Milda suggested. "Get a permanent, put on lipstick."

"Oh, that would be too much of a change," Mrs. Gramzda blushed, musing, "I wonder what it would feel like to express one's insights and thoughts freely. . . to read anything one wished! How can it be, how will it be—after all we have suffered just for that, just for words." She told unbelievable stories about old times when she was a schoolgirl: children had to kneel in a corner on dry peas for speaking even one word in the Latvian language. And then her husband began telling his stories about his escapes, his battles for freedom of thought and belief and how he and his family barely escaped from the massive deportation to Siberia by hiding in a neighbor's root celler. His crimes were that he had the knack for making a good, honest living, owned a piece of land, and served his country folk with the word of God. Added up, that made him a bourgeoisie and a criminal in the eyes of the communists.

"Milda, my dear" he said to his wife, "we will build a new home, you'll see. And our children will go the university. They will live in peace and plenty, the way we could not in our country. Don't frown and think we're too old to start all over! Still, we must never forget where we come from," he spoke now to his children. "We have come this far not of our own strength but only through God's mercy. Even if we cannot understand His ways, I and you and our house, we shall always serve the Lord, our God."

"We always agree on the big things," Mrs. Gramzda said.

"And one day," he continued, "our son will come to us, you will see. The Lord is watching over him and guiding his ways." Mrs. Gramzda seemed embarrassed. Everyone was watching them, listening without understanding. The children paid no attention and looked around, talking to each other. Reverend Gramzda put his hand over his wife's. "I'll buy a washing machine for you. You won't have to scorch your hands and lift heavy cauldrons with boiling sheets. It will be easier, trust me. And we'll have our own auto so we can drive around like noblemen wherever we want to. . . . Don't look at me like that! You must believe. I will learn how to drive, no doubt about that! Oh, it will be good in America, you all will see and you, too, Miss."

"Yes, I hope so," Milda said.

On the way back, they were quiet. The shots hurt and dulled their minds. They were hungry and tired, and they could not see America.

*

The very next day, Mrs. Gramzda started sorting things out. Her husband brought up a large trunk and two brand new leather suitcases he had mysteriously purchased for cigarettes and popcorn. Everything had to fit in those. "We are like pilgrims burdened by sin," the wife said. "How quickly things accumulate! How little we really need and how much we have!" She seemed happy as she threw things away, giving the surplus to the poor, including the shrewd Slovak girl, who stood in the stairway waiting.

Milda noticed how much more relaxed Mrs. Gramzda had become; she breathed easier as she walked up the stairs. She smiled more at her husband. To everyone's surprise, one day she went out and came back with her hair short, styled loosely around her face. She looked years younger, Milda told her, remembering similar transformation of Frau Niert, when they went into the woods to welcome spring and when the twins pulled out her hairpins. "But I am afraid of the Ocean," the elder said, when they took time out for tea. "I'm afraid that I will be seasick. . . . Oh, well . . . What's to be done? My life always has a dark edge somewhere," she said resigned.

"So has mine," Milda sighed. "Oh, so has mine, but we won't die. It's not that easy, even my aunt tells me that. And now we must be ready for a new life in America. Didn't your husband say that we, too, are God's chosen people?"

"Yes, that he did, but being chosen means more trials and tribulations."

"Yes," Milda agreed, almost ready to blurt out her confession.

A Scolding Letter

In the middle of such discussions and visions, arrived yet another, most disturbing letter from Kārlis. It was very short and full of anger. He had heard. *How could you insult the most prominent of the veterans? Where was your gratitude for his sacrifice? Where was your respect for those who suffered and laid down their lives for our country? And what were you doing out in the night by yourself? Aren't you ashamed? How could you put your selfish whims ahead of your duty? How could you leave the girls entrusted to you all alone in the dark? Have you apologized to Mr. Vanags? Have you delivered my message to him? If not, do so quickly before he signs up for Australia or heaven knows where. Tell him that we need him here, in New York or Washington. We are hoping for a promising situation for him. As soon as I know more, I shall contact him immediately by telegram. I hope you will obey me and go to him."*

Milda crumpled the letter into a ball. She had almost forgotten the June 14th episode and felt relieved that Kārlis referred to it and not her midsummer night's madness. Also, time and the expectation of her forthcoming departure had crusted over the rawness of those nights so that she was able to sleep through the nights without disturbing thoughts and dreams. Mercifully, it was already July. The weather was hot and muggy, deprived from cool breezes. Especially sticky was the attic room that irritated her mind and body. To push Vanags aside, she had marked each day, when her thoughts had not dwelled on him, with a tiny dot on the calendar squares. The dots had thickened lately, as she thought about Kārlis, her wedding, and America. She calculated that if she were careful, she could avoid any more contact with Mr. Vanags and, as it were, wade across the Ocean with dry feet. Fortunately, she had not seen him, nor his shadow, since that night and assumed that he had made a decision to leave her alone or—perhaps—he had left town.

Whenever her body became unruly, she calmed it down, knowing that soon she would leave Esslingen and be gone, where he could not follow because he was an invalid. If he emigrated at all, he might be going to Canada, Australia, Argentina, or some other place far, far away. But suddenly, on the other side of the world, Kārlis was muddling her carefully constructed possibilities and digging up what she was so carefully burying. *How dare he, when he knows nothing*! *He orders me, personally, to go to Vanags. . . Ha*! She emitted a twisted, sarcastic laugh like a gurgle. *How absurd, how ironic! . . . How very tempting!* She played with the crumpled paper. She tossed his words about like a ball, making them tighter, smaller, and at last crushing them inside the palm of her hand. *All right. . . I will, if I must. . . tomorrow. . . .* She put the ball on her footstool and, aiming, gave it a kick. It hit the wall. *No, now!*

Milda Obeys Kārlis's Order

She rose and dashed down the stairs for a pail of cold water. She sponge-bathed quickly and changed into a dress Helga had found for her in her church basement full of Americans' emptied closets. It was a golden orange jersey with white sprays of flowers that hugged her body, enhancing her perfect figure. The V neckline plunged just enough. She hung her small golden cross around her neck and combed her hair to one side, burying one ear, while leaving the other exposed, and secured it with a jeweled comb. She applied a touch of lipstick but no other makeup. Her cheeks blushed naturally, feeling sweaty. Nervous, she stripped and washed herself again, rubbed her armpits with Alma's deodorant, and dressed a second time. She put on her comfortable, white wedged sandals, took her purse with Kārlis's rolled up letter inside and began her dissent down the stairs.

Under the Pink Rose Bush

It was high noon, when she arrived at the Mountain Colony. The sun beat down on the huge trampled courtyard. The place seemed deserted, as she stood in the middle, wondering where to go, how to find him. As her eyes adjusted to the glare, she saw men sitting on benches in the shadows of the large buildings. She walked forward, scanning the line, but he was not among them. Some men rose and bowed, and the leg-less ones nodded stone-faced. She looked at the pathetic lot, then turned abruptly, ready to flee. With rapid, nightmare steps she hurried across the empty graveled space toward the way out. She slowed down once she reached the paved road that sloped downhill. It was empty, except for a woman who walked up, a string bag full of vegetables in her over-burdened hand. Milda paused. The woman was so obviously Latvian. *Does she recognize me? Why the smiling nod?* Milda barely nodded and stepped aside as they by-passed each other. She hurried on, now hearing rapid footsteps coming down and getting closer. She recognized them, but continued walking, increasing her speed. Abruptly she turned and took a path that skirted the castle, then turned off and made her way toward a huge blooming wild rose bush that hung upon the stones of the castle wall. The footsteps followed and stealthily slid over the down-trodden grass. She came up against the wall and turned to face him as he approached, usurping her whole range of vision. She stood still in the tall daisy-sprinkled grass that reached up to her waist; she trembled, while the bees buzzed all around and the shadows danced like fairy ballerinas, swirling in the breeze, cooling her burning body. The fragrance of the roses dazed her senses.

She pressed her back against the hot wall and wide-eyed watched him close in and loom over her. Without pausing, without a word, he took her in his embrace, his whole arm wrapping around her waist, then traveling up her spine, his fingers spreading out to hold her head. His half arm stopped on her shoulder, wriggling and fierce, jealous of the whole hand that raised her head like a ripe fruit and tilted her lips to his. They kissed. They kissed greedily, insatiably, and slowly slid down into the grass, inside the shelter of the rosebush and tall grasses. Cautiously, gently he prepared her tight, trembling body for his entry. She trembled in fear of the unknown, but she braced herself, suddenly feeling a strange surge or a wave coming to meet him from deep within her being, breaking through her virgin frame, like through a locked door, suddenly opened, eager for his entry. She hurt but only for a moment, only until she pulled him inside her and felt his palpitations rushing to meet her next, more powerful surge. She clung to him as if she were falling or drowning, her lips seeking his, her fingers digging into his back. And then it was over—her surprise, the wonder such as she never imagined in all her nights of longing fantasies. Slowly she opened her eyes and saw the roses swaying in the wind and smiled up at them as if they were alive, as if they knew her. He moaned in his separate struggle of joy and pleasure, taking deep breaths, until he collapsed in her arms. All their movements were strange, making her wonder. In a kind of daze, her disturbed mind pondered why she knew so little, for she had read many romances and seen movies and plays. She had even looked at nasty magazines and heard countless love poems and arias, but nothing had prepared her for this, this pain and pleasure like a sealed explosive.

Was there more? —She dug deeper for as long as he held her tightly, his head above hers, and his lips tangled in her hair. She wanted to rest, but her body went its own way, writhing on its own accord as her hands held on, clutching his heaving and subsiding shoulders, until there came one striking chord, like of an orchestrated finale. The baton fell, and all was quiet. Fulfilled, their bodies rose and fell in one breath and then rested. *Peace like a river flooded her soul.* She smiled as if she had discovered a new land full of hidden treasures. *Ah, life! So vast and rich!* She sighed. *So much to learn and explore!* She wanted to rise and shout, but he lay still, covering her, his cheek next to hers. When, measureless time later, they disengaged and lay on their backs, gazing through the pink canopy at a blue sky, their hands lightly touching, she confessed in short, measured words: "I had to come to you because my betrothed so commanded."

"Oh? Not because your heart drove you?"

"No."

"You're a bad liar," he said, not moving, only stroking her body, running his hand the whole width and breadth of her, making her stir with new desire. She caught his hand and held it still on her heart, but the hand would not be still and sought its own pleasure, gathering as much as it could hold, only to give it back to her a thousand fold.

"We mustn't ever meet again." She could barely force the words over her lips, while her hand held his in place and felt his fingers struggle under her palm, making small circles on her bare skin. She closed her eyes and took in the fragrant air in full droughts, her lips now brushing his hair, inhaling his desire, telling herself that she had never, ever tasted such pleasure and that she may never taste it again. Guessing her thoughts, he kissed her lips and let her rest on his arm.

She awoke, when a late afternoon sunbeam burst through the rose bush and stuck her in the eyes. He lay beside her, his chest heaving in sleep, his arm under her. Slowly, unwillingly she braced herself on one elbow and watched him until he stirred and opened his eyes. Still sleepy, he pulled her down and lazily stroked her head, running his hand under her hair and down the back of her neck, making her twist in oncoming desire. "Wait!" she murmured and held his fingers tightly. "Please stop. . . . We mustn't." His hand stiffened as in pain, as if it would freeze once it left her sweating palm. "We must talk," she said, gently disengaging herself and sitting up. She located her purse in the grass and, having extracted the crumpled letter, handed it to him. He cast a questioning eye up to her anxious face and untangled the paper ball. He read its message. She watched him. When he appeared baffled, even irritated at the intrusion, she explained to what Kārlis alluded: the episode after the memorial performance on June fourteen, in the Mountain Colony, when she left her guides and ran away. He, recalling smiled and kissed her. "Kārlis wants you in America, and he says there that he will do everything in his power to help you get there, even go to Washington where he knows the people who handled immigration matters." She told him that in previous letters he described a great need for men like him, always re-stating that we all must do *everything* (emphasis his) to bring him over. "So, I obeyed his instructions and came to you with the message." She turned away and looked up at the shivering roses high overhead. Pink petals over a stone wall.

She heard him press the letter back into a ball. He dropped it on her and watched it roll off. Amused, he pulled a timothy stalk and chewed on it, letting its feathery head tickle her flushed cheeks. "And was the command so difficult to carry out?"

"Oh, if only it were!" she said, and tilted her face to meet his lips. He kissed her gently like a child and rested her head on his chest and again ran his hand under her hair, the tips of his fingers gently massaging the roots, the nerve endings. Closing her eyes, she inhaled his body odor, memorizing it, storing the sensations for some unforeseen famine and empty longing. Guessing her struggle and pain, he took her left hand and examined her ring's diamond eye, brilliantly shining. "I'm engaged," she whispered.

"I see. But what shall we do?"

"Nothing," she said sitting straight, shaking him off. "I had to come to you," she repeated, with tears falling on his hand, holding hers. "I'll tell him that I obeyed his orders, but never again because we must never meet like this again. In America," she spoke in heaving, broken words, still crying, still holding him tightly, "we must be strangers or act like casual acquaintances. Kārlis and I will marry—next year—and we will have children. It must be. It is so fated."

"Fate may have other plans."

"I don't know them, only this that I do love him—not like this—but with a supportive, quiet, and pure love, and that I must be forever faithful. I will be the best wife and mother. Together we'll build a home and a new life and, when Latvia is free, we will go back to it. We'll all go home—even you."

"A grand scheme," he said and released her hand. He lit a cigarette and smoked slowly, watching the smoke curl and evaporate. "So we, the guilty and tormented must guard the boy, must work together to preserve his innocence—or ignorance. We must conspire. Very well. . ." He smoked the cigarette down to his fingertips.

"And you must promise that you will not destroy me and my life—and his—if you love me. We both must sacrifice. He trusts you. I think he loves you more than me. He wants and needs your help. We must never, ever betray the people who trust us, who believe in us, and I would never have come to you if he had not ordered me, but now I can tell him. . ."

"What?" He stamped out the small butt. His eyes probed her eyes deeply until she couldn't take his scrutiny and closed them. He kissed the eyelids, tasting the salt in her lashes, brushing them with his lips, then slid his lips over her closed mouth. His fingers dove inside her cleavage, caressing. The stump of his lost arm rose and fell, suddenly angry, furious, his body contracting, crying, "Yes, I see, I understand, I cannot even hold you because I don't have two arms and I am damned. I am a cripple through and through, and you would be ashamed of me if you really knew me, but it wasn't my fault that I was caught in the machine of war which was fueled with blood and which I was forced to drive. Now they hunt for war criminals, and, yes, I am one—forever punished. I am banished from your love and from such joy and pleasure that would rightly be ours."

"Hush," she said, stroking his hair. "Hush. . . my soul. . . . I am so very happy that I came to you, that we have this. Oh, how I have longed for you, how I haven't slept for nights, waiting and watching for you! But you stopped coming after that night, why?"

"Why torment myself? Why hurt you, when I love you more than my own life?"

She silenced him with her kisses and lay down tightly against him. They slid deeper inside the bower, hoping the tall grasses would hide them and indulged again. Vaguely they heard light, distant footsteps on the path. "Let this be my farewell to you," she wept, smiling, kissing his face, holding it close to her, rocking him. "It will never happen again, it must not, but it will always be there, between us—for us alone to remember and treasure—even in America, when we will belong to others."

"For me there will be no other."

"Find another! Don't torment yourself and me!" she said, holding him, sliding under the rose bush until they were tight against the wall. She let her tears flow and wrapped her arms around him. "Promise me," she whispered, forcing the words out, then holding back. "Promise me that when we meet in America we must be as strangers or mere acquaintances, and you must live far away—he said Washington, yes?— and never disturb my peace in any way." She clutched on, denying her own words, hoping he would laugh at them and, gathering her up, would carry her away. But he lay still, then propped himself up on his one elbow and gently stroking her face and, wrapping his fingers inside the ringlets of her damp hair, said, "I promise. But I also swear that I will hold out until you will be forever mine."

"Oh, stop! It cannot be! This didn't happen! I'm not me, and I'm so afraid."

"I'll watch from a distance. I'll be there when you call."

"No! Never! You must leave me alone."

With false anger, she rose to her feet and brushed off the grass and flower petals. They stood looking at each other, letting the uttered words penetrate and take meaning. Leaning against the warm wall, he looked down on her, smiling a wise, paternal smile, and then he drew her to himself again and spoke above her head, "Yes, we must part, but I will wait for you if it takes a lifetime. Don't ever be so afraid of me as you have been all these years here in this enchanting place." She bit her lip and shook her head. "You are not the beast I feared," she said.

"No, but I am a man."

"Yes, I know, and I am a woman."

She plucked a rosebud and stuck it in the buttonhole of his shirt, then slipped from his arm and quickly ran down the path. She knew that he watched her run away. When she looked back, she saw him far away, walking up the hill into a blue sky.

The Aftermath

When she burst into her attic room, Alma was there, leaning against the window, furious and poised to strike: "So here you are—finally! Where've you been all afternoon?" She glared, and Milda was sure that with one hard look, she saw it all. Her eyes narrowed, her red lips twisted into a cynical, ugly grimace. She took in a deep breath and charged: "Look at you! Grass in your hair, and what's that on your dress?"

"Water," Milda answered, looking down, her hand fumbling through her hair, finding the bits of grass and lifting them out, combing her hair with her fingers. "I must have splashed myself at the fountain."

"Yes, sure, an overflowing male fountain! Don't take me for a fool! Anyone can tell you've been laid upon. Water dries but sperms congeal and you cannot ever wash them out. *Out, out damned spot!* But it won't go anywhere! So, who is he?"

Milda said nothing. Alma moved forward and slapped her face. "Answer me!"

"Pēteris Vanags," Milda said, facing her, "and don't you dare hit me again!"

"So." Alma slumped into the easy chair. "Why?" she asked, gritting her teeth, her hands turned into fists. "Did you go to him? To the Colony? By yourself? Why?"

"Because my beloved fiancée ordered me, and I had to obey," she spoke in a cool voice, looking over her aunt's head, out the window, where the sky was still blue. "I went to him because my heart drove me because otherwise it would have no peace. You have no idea how I have suffered, how I have longed for exactly that—what we had today, in the soft grass, under a blooming rosebush. Nights, days, and more nights and days, here alone, while you are who knows where, doing who knows what and. . ."

"Don't you dare judge me!"

Milda laughed. "No, dear Aunt, I'm not judging you, nor myself— nor him. And there is nothing more to say. Only this: he will not frighten me anymore. It's over. He promised. He is only a man now, not a phantom of my imagination. I pity him. An invalid without a home, a hawk without a nest. . . . Kārlis wants to help him get to America, but America is large, and we'll be far apart, and so it will be all right because I'll be married, and, in time, today will have been only a dream—a wonderful dream on a sunny day in July."

"You're crazy! Take off that dress! It stinks, and throw it away!"

"No, not yet. . . I'm very tired." She lay down on her bed and turned to the wall.

"I wanted to tell you that all my emigration papers are in order," Alma said, her tone changed. "I thought we might go somewhere to celebrate, but now I'm in no mood, so, go on and sleep! I'm going out."

Milda did not respond. She thought about writing to Kārlis, telling him that she had learned to know Mr. Vanags and was glad he would be going to America, helping him, being his friend—their friend—but she didn't rise. She didn't even hear Alma leave the room. When she woke up, it was dark. She got out of bed, went to the toilet and then back to her room. She ate nothing. She took off her dress, rolled it up and, hugging it close to her naked body, lay down. In her mind, she recalled Kārlis's letter in a new light. How did he know that she had left her girls in the dark and insulted the honorable veteran? So—she sat up frightened—somebody must have written to him about her; somebody had been watching, spying, and wanted to hurt her. But why? Why, why? Who was he—or she? Ah, yes, of course, the mousy woman who sat across from them, watching all the time. . . . *But why wouldn't Kārlis take my side? Are not people in America innocent until proven guilty? Hasn't he learned that?* She had. She had read the *Bill of Rights* and the *Preamble to the Constitution* with Mrs. Gramzda, as part of their preparation for life in the U.S.A. Hadn't he read it? Would she have to teach him all that also?

She lay down again and stared into the darkness, being glad that he referred to June 14, not 23. But what if someone had seen her today? She closed her eyes, comforting herself, recalling the silence and dazzling loveliness under the canopy of roses and tall linden trees, all protecting them and shielding their secret union. She recalled the sound of footsteps along the path; they merely slid by without a pause. "This day was a gift," she whispered and re-lived it moment by moment, until sad, yet happy, she lulled herself to sleep.

When she awoke the next morning, Alma lay in her bed, open-eyed, watching her. "What am I going to do with you?" she asked, rising. "I cannot police you anymore, I cannot be responsible."

"You're right," Milda said, rising and going to the washbowl to rinse the congealed sleep from her eyes. "Yes," she said, brushing her hair and pinning it back, for he had whispered that he liked it that way, that it was most becoming. "I must take care of myself, and I will. So, don't worry. Come what may. . . Soon this finale of our so-called exile will be over, and, as you said once before, refugees and Gypsies can revise their past and tell their stories and keep their secrets as they go along. I'll be all right. But now I want to go for a walk and be alone before the day heats up." She drank a cup of instant coffee and ate a hard *Brötchen* with some jam. She brushed her teeth and kissed Alma on the cheek. "I love you. . . you, too, please be careful!"

Then Alma sunk down on her knees and, as if praying, pressed her head against her bed and cried, sobbing, "Have I cared for you and carried you this far only so you can ruin yourself? Are you that cheep? And what about your saintly friends? What will the old woman say when she finds out? And the preacher? He can throw those emigration papers away, and then where will you be?" Her shoulders heaved. Milda had never seen her so broken-hearted, so sincerely pouring herself out at her feet. She ran her hand over the vibrating shoulders. "I don't know," she whispered. "I didn't mean for you to know about this. I didn't know you'd care so much. You didn't before. . ."

"That was then, but this is now," Alma rose, turning her tear-streaked face up to the young, glowing face above her. She looked for the little girl, whom she had rescued and the teen-ager she had tried to protect, but that person was gone. Swallowed up by a proud, spiteful woman. "Go, where you wanted to go," she said, brushing off Milda's hand, "I cannot follow you, but I'm sure you won't get by as easily as you think. Night or day, someone always sees you. All acts have their consequences, and whatever you do follows you like a tail or a shadow. That is all I can say to you now."

"Yes. You've said quite a bit. I'll see you later."

On her way down, she almost bumped into Mrs. Gramzda, who was walking up, a string bag of vegetables in one hand. She paused, but Milda merely nodded and went on. But, in that one sharp glance, she was convinced that the woman saw and smelled everything. That she knew and saw through her. Like a fugitive, Milda ran down the flights of stairs, out the door, and down the street, then turned and took the path up to the vineyards. She climbed all the way to the orchards, where she and Alma had been, it seemed, an eternity ago. She sat on the same wall and looked down on the city. She gazed at the Neckar, sparkling in the morning sun, flowing on, a transparent blue ribbon. *It will flow like that forever, even when I am gone. The river will not miss me. It does not love and it does not hurt. How many sad lovers have such rivers gathered, how many stories could they tell, but they only flow on, rippling, sparkling over rocks and bones, while along its banks grow grasses and big trees. So I must go on, flowing until the end of my life, until the eternal sea takes me home.*

She sat on the wall until the sun forced her off. She found a shady spot under an apple tree whose fruits were still hard and green, and there she wrote a long letter of confession she would never send to her betrothed because he would not understand. She knew that if it were a matter of protecting his pride, he would use her confession as evidence of her immorality and would drop her. Still, her hand rushed on, spilling out her heart, making it light again, turning her into a star-crossed romantic heroine locked up in a tower, where pink roses climbed, where she plucked their blossoms and threw them down for her lover, in spite of her stepmother's jealous, threatening commandments. She wrote on, until she ran out of paper.

She filled up all the margins until her fountain pen was empty and the ink was dry. She would save her writing; take it with her to the new world. Perhaps some day she might tell her story to her children or the whole world, and then, she too, like the river would not die but flow on, and her desperate, impossible love in the course of its telling would live and echo in other hearts and would cause them to weep, to wish that there might yet be a happy ending somewhere, sometime. Later on, in her room, she took a clean sheet of paper and wrote:

"My dear Kārlis, I am very sorry that I caused you grief. As for my actions, I had my reasons, and I offer you no explanation, only deep regret that I have displeased you. But yesterday I corrected my negligence and went to the Mountain Colony to deliver your message to Mr. Vanags, who received it in a most excited demeanor. So, my dearest, I hope that this news will please you and set your mind at rest. I shall try to do what is right until we meet again. Your Milda."

Milda's Trial

A few days later, she received another letter. It was from the leader of the Committee of Culture. The terse message summoned her to his office. Alma's prediction, she knew, was fulfilled. Her heart began hammering, her knees going weak. She told no one, relieved that Alma had been gone since their confrontation and hoped she would stay away until the aftershock of her intercourse with Vanags abated. But it did not. It flared and subsided. Food choked her. She only drank bottles of fizzing Seltzer and avoided seeing anyone and going anywhere. But she could not cancel her order to appear before the ruling committee. And so, at the appointed time, she crossed the river afraid and alone. In the office, around a polished brown table, sat the leaders and a teacher she had not had. A whole committee of officials of the State of Exile!

As soon as the door closed, she knew she was in for an inquisition. She stood already condemned and found guilty. Not even one face appeared kind, not even one set of eyes offered sympathy. She had nothing to lean on. No one asked her to sit down, though she appeared faint and overheated. And then it began. Accusing, mean words hit her and faded out into silent ellipses: *You failed us. . . You were negligent. . . disrespectful. . . insulting. . . You left young girls alone in the night. . . You provoked and then insulted an honorable man.* Milda's face burned, and she looked down, then out the window at the leaves fluttering in the breeze. *You are ungrateful. . . selfish. . . seductive. . . Of course, we pity you because you have had no proper upbringing, but this is too much. . . How could a lady jump like an unruly boy through fire? And in the costume we entrusted you! How could you, could you, could you???*

"I was afraid," Milda said softly, relieved that it was only about that and turned to face the thin female voice that struggled to be heard: "You left your girls and separated from all decent people."

"What exactly am I accused of?" Milda asked in a calm voice, scanning her antagonists with her large eyes.

"Miss Bērziņa," spoke the chairman. "You know what you are accused of. You broke the code of conduct. You betrayed our trust."

Milda closed her eyes and remembered the famous trials of the innocent she had read about and, like those heroes, she kept silent, while her accusers spoke. She heard as in a bad dream: "I saw her standing in the middle of the courtyard, provoking, and tempting. Mr. Vanags went out to inquire, but she ran away. I saw it. He came back hours later."

"That, of course, is no concern of ours," said the chairman. "People may come and go as they please."

"Yes, but," resumed the female voice: "He came back with his shirt open and a rose in his buttonhole."

"That will be enough. Miss Bērziņa, please return, as soon as possible, cleaned and pressed, the national costume and your guide uniform. You shall no longer represent our people, and with that this case is dismissed."

So they are stripping me of all honors, chiseling at me, making me smaller and smaller. I am being stamped out and erased. . . Someone will write to Kārlis, and then. . . "*These people who judge you have no power over you,*" her soul's voice whispered. "*Their act is almost over, and you are free—like a bird on the wing. You are graduated, confirmed, grown-up. You are on your way to America, to Miss Fern and her white house and lily garden. These people can neither judge nor condemn. They are also migrants, nestless birds. And the chairman. . . remember, you saw him kissing the Latin teacher behind your chestnut tree, the night you suddenly came out the* Lido *door. He saw you too. See how he fumbles, how he wants you gone!*"

Yes! Milda stared at the man; she fixed her eyes on his mouth, watching the thick lips move as they formed strings of additional words that had no meaning. Then she raised her eyes to his and gave him a secretive smile and watched his face turned down. She looked at other talking mouths, feeling a sarcastic smile pulling at the corners of her mouth. She imagined being on stage, acting a part. She imagined all the people as cardboard cut-outs. She remembered Reverend Gramzda and his wife having tea one afternoon after he had had a hard time with some dispossessed official whose application he rejected. "I do have my standards," he had said, sitting in his usual nook. Full of righteous indignation, he had expounded on the elements of authoritarianism in the Latvian culture and traditions, and how, he thought, that had contributed to "the tragedy of our nation." Milda had not understood his political theories anymore than the religious, but she felt there was truth in all he said. Now she saw the faces of authority turned toward her with mean frowns that made her knees shake. She also remembered Alma's forewarning at the beginning: *Don't get too close to people. You are an image to them, and people cannot stand to have their images shattered.*

That is something they will never forgive you. And jealousy. It's lethal, so don't ever make them be jealous of you. I know that you are too pretty and smart for your own good, and that worries me.

Jealousy

Milda longed for a drink of water. Images blurred and floated in her head, while the talking went on unheeded, unperceived. *No doubt the jealous had accused me! These women and, maybe even Vanags himself—before, that is. Before I rejected him and made him furious. Who knows what he had said, what he had sworn in his blind rage? And this woman, the one who had seen me standing in the courtyard, and who, no doubt, that same evening, had taken the same path down and seen the circle of bended grass under the rose bush. She surely had come to the right conclusion, had put together the rosebush with the blossom in his buttonhole. Yes, I remember her now: she fluttered around him on the 14th and had spied on me on St. John's Eve. She had watched from her own shadows and seen the near rape and been jealous of that. Yes, it could be so!*

Milda looked hard at the small woman, alone and single. She saw her cheeks flame pitifully as her eyes turn down. She almost pitied the poor thing who wanted the very man she had repelled on that night but seduced on a bright day in full sunshine. Milda rested her eyes on the misplaced creature, who had gone to such great length as to assemble this mock trial, hoping that she would win Vanags's admiration and avenge his injured honor, but it was too late. Milda had won the war and the peace. "Ladies and gentlemen," she said, "I shall do as you wish. This trial is such a waste of our time!"

She saw the confusion. She saw the paper faces crumble. She saw the people's reflections waver in the varnish of the polished table.

For once Milda was glad to be on the western side of the Iron Curtain and living in a Kingdom of Air. She imagined herself in a similar situation on the eastern side, in Riga, perhaps, in those dark buildings of judgment—the one way gates, the doors that never opened out but in, the doors through which her father had been dragged and pushed. Perhaps it was like this: go after anyone whom you dislike and of whom you may be jealous. Get them all out of the way; the wagons are waiting.

Milda blinked and stared at the gleaming table, now reflecting the sun. In the sunbeams she saw streamers of dust. They settled on the table and on the people around it. The whole room seemed to be settled in dusty silence. Or was she still talking? Did they expect her to say more? And why did those dusty faces look at her like that, almost as though she were a heroine?

"I never have, nor ever would only represent you. I, at some wonderful moments in this our oasis, became my own vision of a beautiful Latvia. My leap over the fire was only a symbolic last escape out of tyranny. The flames did not catch the holy skirt. The costume will be returned to you—clean and pressed. And now I must go. We have wasted a lovely day in this stuffy room." With that, she turned and was gone.

Freedom of Choices

After Milda returned her costume, she confessed to Mrs. Gramzda almost everything, except her willing surrender to Vanags. She justified her deception by convincing herself that the saintly woman would not understand and that it would only snarl their relationship—maybe to the point where they would be forced to part company, and she would be left alone in an empty town. In her mind, the afternoon under the roses took on a translucent, dreamlike quality that she would never be able to describe without gross self-incrimination, when, in fact, it stood behind her like a garlanded gateway through which she had transcended from maidenhood into adulthood. It had been much more graphic than her graduation and confirmation—those accepted, traditional days of passage, which had left her standing in place, still holding her aunt's hand,

"It is good that we shall be leaving soon," Mrs. Gramzda said, rather alarmed. "Do not write any confessions to Mr. Arājs. He will not hear your voice, nor understand. And—he is not yet your husband. He does not own you, nor should he ever." Milda listened and knew that the woman saw through her, that she had also seen her dashing past her on that afternoon but sensitively did not probe, did not ask for any details but was ready to protect her and guard her secret. She spoke on, looking past her, averting eye contact: "In your marriage, my dear, don't forget to allow for breathing and walking spaces. We women, as you know so well, also have some accounts to settle with our Maker and our conscience, not only with men. God endowed us also with certain talents that might be death to hide, as Milton said it so beautifully. God gave you beauty, sensitivity, and intelligence. Don't trade those in for forced shame and submission. Make your husband rise up to you. Remember that only you know what really has or has not happened, and people will swear to having seen what they wanted to see. However, do be careful. We live in an age, where men rule and they can ruin lives." She again offered Milda the protection of her family and warned her not to stray alone.

"As for those who accused you, you have nothing to fear. You won the battle, and they would not admit to losing." They agreed to say nothing to Alma for the time being because it would only upset her and cause more problems.

Still Milda felt uneasy and guilty. She hurt. Everything was hurting—the triumph and the humiliation and the sacrifice. Esslingen burned under her feet. July sweltered; the sidewalks singed. Neckar trickled low in its bed as though hiding the polluted water, which appeared pure and blue only from on high. Close by, it stunk and buzzed with mosquitoes and dragonflies. The grassy shoreline where people usually sunbathed and swam was empty, except for some poor, half-naked children. The Americans had closed off the beach. Milda had no reason to cross the river anymore. It was as if *Pilsener, Vogelsang* and all other bridges were blown up and the other side of the city fallen off. It had no connection with her life anymore. She was relieved of all civic duties. Feeling doubly exiled, she confined her living to her designated area in the valley; she didn't dare look up to the Mountain Colony, which, mercifully, was camouflaged by large trees. Only when Vizma or Helga would go with her, did she venture out as far as the courtyard of the castle. Then they would wander about the sleeping *Dornröschen* and sit on the wall, overlooking the old kingdoms.

On one such outing she guided their walk along the wall where IT had happened. She feigned excitement and ran through the grass to the still-blooming pink rosebush. She tried to sever a small branch without pricking her fingers, when, in a tight fork, she saw a brown paper triangle. She pulled it out, unfolded it and read: *I know you will come here because your heart will drive you.* She looked up, her heart pounding. The sisters were picking flowers and paid no attention to her. *I heard what happened. Forgive me. So that I could keep my promise, I have left this town. You are always in my thoughts and my heart.* She tucked the note inside her blouse and told her friends she had a headache and wanted to go back to her room.

"But it's so nice here," Helga said leaning against the wall. "Someone has been sleeping here. Look how they pressed down the grass and flowers."

Milda put her arm around the girl's shoulders. She wanted to warn her about love's roses and thorns, but when Helga's innocent gaze met hers, she only smiled. *Let Life do the teaching, cruel though it might be.*

She would have to find her own strength and balance and the ideals that would carry her on when equal temptations will come her way.

Once Milda became used to not seeing the national costume and her uniform hanging in the wardrobe and filled the emptiness with her everyday garments, she experienced an euphoric sense of freedom every time she opened the double door. She felt like Christian in *Pilgrim's Progress*, the book she was reading, when the bundle of sin rolled off his back. With Vanags gone, there would be no temptation, and Kārlis's letters betrayed nothing. And so, with each new day she felt lighter and freer. Her demanding society had released her, and she had forgiven herself, as Mrs. Gramzda insisted she must. She learned to look at herself as from the outside and observe her feelings. As the days waned, she noticed that she had become less tense, especially when she was out of doors, for he would not suddenly appear before her as she rounded a street corner. Alone on her morning walks, she loved the way the cool wind blew her hair and her skirt, and, when in her room, she learned to apply just the right amount and shades of makeup. Her reflection in the mirror appeared glamorous, like the faces in American fashion magazines. At last, she dared to put on the slightly transparent blue sun dress Vizma had found in a shipment of American clothes. "It is so beautiful on you!" Vizma said, and Milda was glad that now no one had the right to point out that she should not wear such dresses. She was free! *I have no image to protect, so at last I am what I am—Milda Bērziņa, a Latvian girl. The orphaned daughter of a small orphaned country, entering a great, big open world.*

Alma had hardly spoken to her since their big confrontation; when they were together, she seemed afraid. She saw the transformation and never again treated her niece as a child. She even helped with the chores and cleaned up after herself. Milda noticed that, from behind, her movements were like her sister Matilde's, except she was thinner. She also knew that things were slowly turning around in their relationship:

it was Milda who now was gone much of the time, leaving only clipped notes or no word at all. Alma, on the other hand, stayed more in the room, writing letters to Sweden and preparing for her own lone journey. The theater was finished, the last props put away and the dusty burlap curtain drawn shut. Without her stage, Alma was lost; the sound and fury of her soul had lost its dramatic substance. Her body was becoming too thick; her hair grew too long, exposing the graying roots. She sat for many hours in the corner chair smoking and reading German plays and romances, things that did not interest Milda anymore.

A Trip to the Alps

Unexpectedly, Vizma invited Milda to go with what was left of her church choir on a week's excursion to the Alps. Helga, too, would go, even though she could not sing, but their mother had insisted. Reverend and Mrs. Gramzda had recently been in the Alps and spent a week with friends. They returned awed and excited, especially Mrs. Gramzda, who told Milda: "You need to see the glory of God's marvelous works, then you will understand Beethoven and Mozart and Goethe, and it will stay with you forever." It was a wish come true. Milda had always wanted to see the Alps, but there had been no way. Suddenly the gates opened, and she was free!

A covered army truck carried the choir straight into the heart of the German Alps. They went to Garmisch and Berchtesgaden. They saw the Eagle's Nest from a distance, and took the tram up to the Zugspitze. She, Vizma, and Helga climbed the rugged path up to the golden cross and looked down at the splendor of Europe from that height—the snow-capped ranges and the blue lakes amid dark green forests. Indescribable beauty lay at their feet, still and suspended like eternity.

The next day they were down in the salt mines of Berchtesgaden, down at the substance of the earth, in the netherworld of salty forms that, like bewitched wanderers, lured them in deeper and deeper. But they didn't stay long in the darkness. Soon they surfaced again into the world of bright sunshine. On another day, they rode on dangerously winding highways, edging deep abysses, rolling through Alpine meadows and across narrow bridges until they came to a lake. They boarded an excursion boat and rode the length of Koenig See, while old Watzman—the mountain by whose tip the local people predicted the weather—rose above them, its head buried in clouds. The guide blew a folk melody on his horn, and the mountains echoed it seven times, over and over, as the boat slid on, past splendid water falls and exhausted avalanches.

Once again on land, for several enchanting days, they took in cathedrals and crypts, castles and palaces—everything! Singing with the choristers, Milda, with adoring Helga always at her side, walked down mountain paths, through gorges and caves, across bridges over tumbling rivers and streams full of trout.

"What a grand finale to my life's drama in dramatic Germany!" Milda exclaimed, when Alma met her when the truck stopped at the train station in Esslingen. She told no one that throughout the whole trip Vizma had walked hand in hand with the choir's charming tenor. She and Helga had stumbled upon them in a gorge. They stood close together, and Vizma was crying. His arms were around her as she rested her head on his chest. When they saw them kiss, Milda took Helga's hand and silently pulled her away. "They need to be alone," she said.

Out of hearing, Helga told her how much her sister was in love, but that her father forbid her to even think about marrying him because he was shiftless, smoked on the sly and chased other girls. "But she loves him and cries at night," Helga said. "I certainly would not listen to anyone if I loved someone. I would elope. I would follow my heart to the end of the world."

Milda was surprised to hear that. She looked at her young friend and smiled sadly. "Love cuts its own paths," she said.

"Yes, but if someone loves someone they should marry and be happy. I would not let anyone stand in my way."

"What does your mother say?"

"She takes Papa's side. She says Vizma should wait until we are in America. She tells her she needs to go on to college and that, in the end, she will be glad to be free of him because he is below her in every way. But my sister keeps on crying. Don't tell Mamma about them. I'm glad that they will have at least this nice trip to remember forever."

"Yes, I understand," Milda said, sadly looking at the innocent girl.

"I know you'd understand—even better than I do. I know."

Summary Glimpses of Germany

This trip over, she traveled more—alone, with the Gramzda family and alone with Alma, who was despondent and had to be coaxed. Like short-changed, out-of-breath tourists, they raced through the land— now nearly rebuilt—where they had lived for years but had not really been a part of. They had lulled in another, transient world, in a state of welfare, memories, and wishes. They had lived in borrowed houses and rooms they never repaired; they had plucked fruit from trees they never planted. Their allegiances were confusing, as confusing as the human mind and experience—as confusing as history and the country where they sojourned. From the top of Zugspitze they had tried to see the Iron Curtain—the awful line that divided their worlds and their lives, but they saw only a calm ethereal blueness. They looked for other lines: the zones—French, English, American. . . The country was a house, a crowded, torn up house with many rooms, some clean, some still littered with debris but all full of ghosts, ghosts that will haunt and howl forever.

Still, they saw very little of Germany, around which the war had left many closed borders. They wished they had gone up to the Eagle's Nest, seen the Passion Plays, been to Wagner's and Beethoven's houses and more, much more. They had not floated down the Rhine because it was in the French Zone. In the evenings they looked at the map and regretted what they had missed, but nothing could be done. There were so many kingdoms they never would visit. Anyway, their days were running out. The clock in the *Rathaus* kept striking the hours away. And then, one day, Alma and Milda stopped and looked at each other: only one week left!

Last Week at Lido

That week they did not separate. Milda shut herself off from the Gramzdas, from everything, as though Alma were sick, as though she were at her deathbed trying to be cheerful. She then told Alma about her fall off the pedestal. She dramatized every detail of her trial. When she finished, she saw in Alma's eyes intense love, pride, and relief: "Now I know you can go anywhere in the world. . . . I can rest in peace." She confessed that she, too, had been summoned to the trial but refused to go. "Who do they think they are, these self-appointed moralists? Besides, I wanted you to face the ordeal alone—like a test, you know. I wanted to see you take them on by yourself and in your own way, like you did Vanags, who would still be happy to ruin your life if you would let him, but you won't, will you?" Alma scanned her with narrow, distrustful eyes.

A sarcastic, unconvincing laugh escaped Milda's lips. "Don't worry," she said. "I'm thinking things through, and I see my way clearly. I see two roads. The one is like an Alpine path that winds through rocks and over gorges. Roses with sharp thorns grow in those gorges. They are slippery from waterfalls and moss. One could easily slip and fall. Be killed. On that path I see Mr. Vanags, but his one arm cannot protect me. The slippery darkness scares me. The other road is flat and smooth. It winds through cities surrounded by prairies. One can see far into the distance and see a house with a garden and children. I see myself in that house, opening the door and waiting for him. There is love, peace, and harmony. And there is safety. There is my Kārlis, who loves me in a quiet way. It is there I want to be, and that is the path I have chosen. So don't worry. I am glad that I can choose well. My heart is at peace."

"Yes, your husband can play the knight in shining armor and defeat all dragons."

"Don't joke."

"I'm not. Good luck, my dreamer. Your sins have made you wise."

*

On the last day they packed their suitcases and cleared the room. They put away the photographs of their men, pulled the calendar off the wall and threw away the dried flowers. At last, on her hands and knees, Milda scrubbed the old wooden floor and laid newspapers on it so that not even one footprint would be left to tell the tale of the DPs who had lived in this attic room of a splendid old house they named Lido.

At night, late, late, at night, they leaned out of the window, looking at the stars and the rooftops of the sleeping town. Below them, the secret-holding chestnut tree spread its silent branches over an empty street. When they felt the early chill of a north wind, Alma closed the window and pulled down the shade. "We must now draw the curtain, my dear, and prepare for the next act," she said, her voice breaking. Milda took her hand and held it. They looked at each other in the darkness, their hands locked. "All this will soon seem like a dream," Milda whispered.

"Yes. . . All our life is like a dream that's rounded out with sleep."

"Oh, what shall we ever do without each other?"

"Live, my darling. . . We will live on—as long as we must."

Departure

As all anticipated days, the day of departure from Esslingen dawned with the usual sunlight gilding the sky and housetops, the usual birds chirping in the trees around the attic windows, the usual people rising and going about their activities and leisure. However, for the people of the top floor of Lido this was a never-to-be forgotten day—August 16, 1950. They rose early to meet the train that would take them out of their *oasis* forever.

As in a parade, once again in the lead, walked Milda Bērziņa, wearing a tan traveling suit she had made out of discarded U.S. army uniforms. An oversized shoulder bag weighed down her left arm, which also carried the old lost and found blanket. Her feet in wedge sandals, she went forth with heavy and sad steps, looking forward and backward. Packed inside the blanket, she carried so much life, so much personal history; yet, much had to be left behind, discarded, but never forgotten.

Alma, dressed in a bright blue suit with deep white lapels, her hair freshly colored, walked close behind her grown-up niece. A large travel bag hung from the crook of one elbow and the old overcoat with the fox collar from the other. Her feet were cramped in high-heel pumps, which at times stuck in the cracks of the sidewalk, throwing her off balance. But she would quickly catch herself and continue on her journey, as in a race, keeping her eyes on the finishing line—the train station at the end of the wide street. A short distance behind her, minding their father, walked the Gramzda family. Closing the line, an enterprising German boy who pulled the *Wagele* full of all the earthly goods of the displaced. There were two suitcases branded **Lutz**, a gray trunk packed full of clothes, and—to be handled with special care—a box containing the service of their fine Bavarian china and a Rosenthal vase. And a box of books: those precious volumes of Latvian literary treasures, printed by exiled professionals on various presses throughout

West Germany. The emigrants walked quietly; only their footsteps broke the morning silence. It took only minutes to reach the station. They unloaded the diminutive wagon and dragged the luggage up the stairway and checked it in. Then, pausing, looking back, they saw their friends, curious by-standers, and some rejected refugees—war veterans and elderly widows, who begged the preacher to remember them. He stepped out of line and in his usual cheerful voice said, "I shall not forget you, for we all are pilgrims, going to the land of milk and honey. Many trials and tribulations are now behind us. God has led us this far, and He will lead us on. Have faith and study English!" He shook hands with his brothers and sisters in Christ. He knew them all by name; he knew who would be left behind, having failed the screening, and who would wait their turn to leave the Neckar valley as soon as the papers were in order.

Inside the station others waited; Milda's guides and teachers and some of those elegant, critical ladies who should have stayed in bed. All carried flowers as to a burial, Milda thought. I don't need their roses and carnations," she mumbled to herself as she reached for the small bouquet of wild flowers from those guides, whose families had chosen to remain in Esslingen and wait for better times, when the road back to Latvia would be open and they would all go home. She put her face in the tender blossoms and inhaled the girls' love, mixed with many good and sad memories. "We always loved and honored you," said Rita, Milda's assistant, now the leader of the troupe, which would soon be fazed out.

"Thank you," Milda said, taking the sad, autumn-tinged bouquet, like the last breath of summer, like a farewell to her fading youth. The other girls looked on, holding back their tears. No words were spoken, for all had been said and was being left behind in the halls, the streets, the woodlands, and gardens of troubled, scarred, divided Germany.

A small remnant of the theater crowd had come to see Alma off, burdening her with more flowers and photographing her alone and with her partners—arms around shoulders, faces cheek-to-cheek—all in black and white. Everybody was photographing, clicking the scenes away, pinning them down for posterity, perhaps for some future archive. Everybody smiled and cried, looked backward and forward. Uneasily, Milda glanced all around, her face flushed, eyes searching like headlights. She saw along the outside fence, those who would not be allowed to enter America because some scar or shadow in the lung, a missing limb or a German spouse would block the way. "Perhaps later," the preacher said, as he hurried on. Through the mesh of the fence the children gave him apples and grapes and then waved with empty hands. "You, little rascals, don't you forget us either!" he said joking. "Obey your parents and study hard!"

The clocks struck. Milda did not see Vanags and turned to go through the gate, following the flow which rushed down and through the under-path to the congesting platform, where the train waited. All too soon the whistle blew, and the people climbed into the wagons and rushed to find the best seats.

The Gramzdas fit into one compartment, while Alma and Milda found places with strangers inside another. "Wonderful," Alma said. Milda, too, was glad and spread out the old blanket over the hard wooden seat. She took the place by the window, and Alma grabbed the next space, while a German woman nestled in the corner on Alma's right. A man slept across from them with a newspaper covering his head. "Tight," said Alma, "but this will do; at least we'll be alone. No one here will understand what we say, so we can talk our hearts out."

"Yes," Milda agreed, and together they put their handbags in the rack above and Alma's overcoat and the flowers wherever they fit and then leaned out the open window. Several windows over, the Gramzdas also leaned out, all framed in flowers, smiling, blotting tears, saying their last words to those who had bought platform tickets so they would be with the departed until the very end. The cameras snapped sporadically.

Suddenly Milda saw a distraught Vanags rushing through, coming straight toward her, a bouquet of forget-me-nots in his outstretched hand. The stump inside his sport jacket, also reached out to her, who stood framed like a portrait frozen in time. She looked down but did not reach out. She watched him speaking, saying quickly that he will follow soon, that he had heard from Mr. Kārlis Arājs. "Then we will be together again. Please greet him from me. Tell him that all expect great things from him—and from you. . . . Don't forget me!"

The whistle blew. He pushed his bunch of the forget-me-nots up to the window. The blue, moist mass touched her hand that opened and reached down, but a stronger hand cut in. "Go to hell!" Alma shouted and, grabbing the flowers, smashed them down on his dark blond head. Some bystanders laughed, others said, "Shame, shame" and tried to pick up the innocent flowers. Mrs. Gramzda saw Milda's face that betrayed her secret longing mixed with willful denial. She saw the girl's heart and mind again at war and wished she could help. For a moment it looked like Milda would jump off the train and run into the one outstretched arm, but the Ice Princess remained framed as in a trance. All saw the drama and the man's bold advance. "Leave her alone!" Helga shouted.

The whistle blew loudly, impatiently. Vanags made a joke of the whole scene, jesting, "I like proud women." He stepped back, next to the timetable display case from where he fastened his eyes on the young woman he loved. The whistle blew again, and the train started to move. Alma appeared again in the open window, next to her niece. Both waved their handkerchiefs like queens from a balcony, their hands touching no one in particular and everybody at once with cool, distant sweeps. Alma did not see that Milda's eyes held his face for as long as they could. *How did Anna Karenina do it?* she wondered as the platform slid by with increasing speed.

In seconds they were out of the station, watching the familiar houses, factories, and streets slide away. They looked up to the vineyards, hot in the slanting August sun. They saw the native people gathering grapes high up in the terraces. It was a good year. The kegs and barrels would be full, the people predicted as they looked to the hills. The grape gatherers loved hot and dry summers because they promised happy winters with long nights in the pubs and money in their treasure chests.

"Like in a well-made play," Alma said. "We came and left with the ripening of grapes. Old Bacchus must love us," she joked, but Milda, wrapped in her blanket, trembled. Through her sooty window she stared at the vineyards and the endless fields of cabbage. People cut the heads and threw them on to wagons harnessed with oxen.

"A Swabia pastoral," Alma mused. "At last we're out of it. Please don't sigh! Don't be afraid. He is nothing but a flapping braggart, a pompous pitiful fool, a castrated executioner who tries to play the role of a grand seducer. I tell you, he is a pervert and you better watch out!"

"How do you know all that? How can you say such things?" Milda asked softly, with the vision of that afternoon by the castle wall blinding her. She sought words to defend him, to justify herself again, but her teeth bit her lips, and she remained silent, while her eyes stared straight ahead, seeing nothing.

"Don't look like a mouse that's escaped from a hawk!" Alma tried to make light, pleased about twisting the man's name to suit her figure of speech. "I know and don't know the particulars. All I see is that he has a high opinion of himself that will get him nowhere with Americans. Latvians—perhaps." She leaned closer to her niece and spoke in her ear: "I suspect he has blood on his hands. I can see it in his shifting glances, his looking around as though he were afraid somebody is after him. And the Americans will go after his like. There are enough detectives who will dig and dig, until they dig up times and places and names. Who knows what he's done. In what trench did he lose his arm? How many women has he raped, and why does he stalk you, when he knows you belong to another? Don't you think that I don't know that he's been following you all these years, watching, seeing, knowing things about you that you may not know yourself?"

Milda hid deep inside her corner and closed her eyes. "I think you're exaggerating because you too are afraid—or even jealous. Maybe you want to punish me for making you leave your lover. I don't know, but something is happening that I don't understand. Why do you hate Mr. Vanags so much? Perhaps if it had not been for you, I would have stayed with him and my love could have save him no matter what he has done."

Alma laughed. "Sure! But you're off to America. He's nothing, I tell you. A man with one arm cannot support you in America, and I could not let you run into the arms of poverty. Anyway, he must be dead for you. He won't get a visa because he is no asset to the American work force. What can he do?"

"He is smart, clever. And my fiancé has already sponsored him and promised to find a place for him."

"Well, that's interesting!"

Alma took her cold hand in hers. "Let's forget all the men," she said softly. In silence, they watched the scenery slide by, the hills opening up, the woods displaying their colors. "Here we are again, on a train, as so long, long ago," Alma soothed her with soft Latvian words. Again they were in a world of their own. Again they felt the iron wheels of a train carry them on, rock them, even sing to them. They fell into the rhythm of the movement and felt the past falling away as if in bunches of forget-me-nots. "I guess, after all, I'm glad we're alone," Milda gave in.

Alma put her hand over Milda's, plugging into her being, connecting things, finishing up what they had started six years ago. Now they were two brides traveling to their future husbands—their weddings or funerals—each wrapped in her veil, each a world or a star, each going to her own cold and distant world or star. . . . They knew how to travel side by side, how to lean on each other and how to shake free. They knew so much.

Milda closed her eyes. It was hot, but the draft too strong to keep the window open. The trip to Bremen would be long—two days and one night. They would travel together that far, and then they would separate. Alma would travel on to Sweden and Milda would get off with the Gramzdas and all the other emigrating refugees and take a bus to Bremerhaven. There they would have to spend a week in a clearing camp, and then they would board the ship for America. The voyage would last ten days.

The Last Train Ride

Marred by Vanags's surprise appearance, the journey—this last trip for aunt and niece together—stretched before them endless and nerve-wrenching. Usually eager to see new sites, Milda's thoughts could not shake off his image, his words and gestures no matter how much she tried to replace all that with visions of her betrothed. She looked out but was bored with the dull fields and the hazy sky which, after an eternity, turned into night. In the evening they ate their sandwiches of smoked sausage on rye bread and drank *Seltzer* from a common bottle. They slept in jerks, sitting up, staring at the signs as they rode through dimly-lit stations and sleeping towns. They rode groggily on and on into the next dawn, the next morning—their last day together.

"Such a long trip spoils the grand finale of our drama, doesn't it?" Alma remarked, brushing the creases out of her suit. "Flattens everything and you get so you only stare at yourself from far away and wonder where you're going and where you'll get off."

"I know."

"There are things I still must speak to you about, things we never settled, but they'll have to be left unpronounced. We—you and I—need space to talk so the words can go out, not turn under, like snails pulling into their houses."

"True." Milda reached for Alma's hand. She took it eagerly, catching all of it in her larger palm that sweated. "Oh, you're bringing such a lot to that unworthy man, my darling," she said softly sighing.

"Unworthy?" Milda turned as much as she could, pulling her hand away. "Why suddenly unworthy? It is I who feel unworthy and dishonest—so small and uncertain next to him, always wanting to crowd him with my emotions—the bad poetry of my flesh and soul. The invalid, on the other hand, makes me feel—I don't know—like a queen, an angel, an impossible dream. Unreal, yet. . . ." She was whimpering again, and Alma repossessed her hand.

"Now don't talk nonsense and blot that man from your thoughts. I meant nothing as grand as what you are suggesting. All I meant to say was that most men are unworthy of the women who reach for the stars. At least those I've met, and," she paused, then went on softly speaking, "there have been so many—more than the fingers on my hands."

"Many?" Milda echoed. "What are you saying? Are you really. . ."

"Yes. — No, not really, not in my heart. I'm saying, confessing, admitting—whatever—that I have been the happy or unhappy companion of many men. We needed all of them to survive, to drag our bodies through our bleak exile. We needed to eat, to keep you decent so you can now cross that big sea like Jesus with clean, dry feet, which—I realize, are neither clean nor dry. Or, if you like a gentler comparison, so you can rise out of the shell like Aphrodite and go to him—white like foam, but you had to spoil it for me. You had let that shell fill up with muck."

"Oh, please! I never asked you to sacrifice yourself for me." Milda looked bewildered. "Why did you do it? We had our rations. We had. . ."

"Nothing!" Alma said through clenched teeth. "Not enough. Don't be such a silly romantic! It irritates me, and I don't want to be irritated with you on this day." Alma leaned back and closed her eyes. The train rambled on. The people around them kept looking and listening and pretending not to see the incomprehensible, extraordinary drama being enacted before them. *The Great Fatherland is full of foreigners. Who can understand them?—Thank God they are leaving, going away, as they should.*

"I did what I had to do," Alma continued. "Everyone who had any ambition traded and made deals, even he." She waved her hand in the direction where the preacher and his family were confined. "Some of our prettier young ladies worked on ships, others on airplanes and picked up surplus candy, cigarettes, and who knows what else and sold them to dealers, who sold them further. Some of those boys, you'll see, will end up millionaires once they get to America."

"I had no idea."

"Of course, you didn't and don't. I let you live in your dream world, protected you from all evil. . . . Yes, I worked. I entertained at an American club in Stuttgart, and they provided a little room for me. That's where I went when I wasn't with you. So I had a secret place, and I dealt with secrets. So, at least everything was safely concealed. And this part was exciting, like living in a spy or detective novel. I liked my job and the little extra jobs that followed and rewarded my efforts. On the whole, the men were interesting, and I became caught up in their jobs, impatient to know how each would end, who would get caught, who would go off free, who'd fall for whom and so on. I looked for clues when they made love to me. Oh, I was good, it all came naturally. After all the old, steady profession and the knowledge must be in women's blood, for no one teaches us. We just know. You know it also, and no one taught you!"

"Don't!"

"Well, no. My apologies, princess! But don't judge me too harshly. I was not just for money, oh no! Not I! In time I actually grew fond of the men I was with. They helped me forget my real love." Alma rested from her words, looking out. "Those I did not like," she continued, "I dropped quickly, losing nothing, gaining nothing. But whoever they were, they took me away from the feeling of exile and from our unbearably tight, claustrophobic room and the dusty stage that would make me sneeze without warning. Often I went to Stuttgart to relax, to stay in my room or be with one man and play at housekeeping and marriage. I liked that best. . . . He treated me quite like a wife, leaving me alone, when I was tired, making coffee for us, talking and comforting. . . . But, when I performed at the cabaret, all the men loved me. They waited for me with chocolates and oranges and highballs—it's a drink—strong, the kind I needed for my acts, for my songs and dance. They paid well. They brought in velvet and satin and nylon stockings. They dressed you up."

"Oh—"

"Yes! It's nice to remember that the men loved and adored me. They knew that with me, unlike other whores, they could be free and satisfied. With me there never was a threat that they would have to sacrifice anything. I was clean. The doctor examined me regularly, and I kept his evaluation handy, requesting same from anybody who propositioned. So we were selective. They all had wives and houses in America. Every one showed me his family portrait. . . . Now most of them have gone home." She paused, a flirtatious smile tugging at the corners of her red lips. "I wonder how they are. Do they remember me? Do they confess, and are they absolved, while they mown their lawns and make legitimate babies? However, some of the men stayed behind as long as I did. They would not finish up until I set my date—until this very date. Silly fools! Americans are so naive! I think it is because they always assume to win—by right—as if the world owed it to them. They don't bother to probe too deeply, search for the hand of fate, like we do. They live as though everything were a cocktail party, where no one gets drunk. They are good at fixing and organizing things but only as long as it's painless. They took me like Europe—without any pain and I, meanwhile, forgot mine. So it was good both ways—*all around the mulberry bush,* as they sang—good for all of us, even you. The last few months I had my favorite man, who has left some little scars. He is a Chicago journalist. He brought me breakfast in bed, and we talked a lot. He was interested in the Baltic States and because of me in Latvia especially. He had been in Riga and Kiev, Petrograd and Tallinn. He said he was collecting material for a book." Alma smiled again. "Imagine what all I must have contributed to a book I'll never read."

Milda said nothing. Hot tears seeped through her closed eyes and fell on her folded hands.

"Oh, don't my sweet, don't cry," Alma soothed, wiping the hands. "It all made the time pass quicker, and it made a better actress out of me. I cannot help that I was born for love. And when I go home, which I surely will, I shall return to my real and only one. I will then know how to love him supremely. Love, you know, is a real art."

"But you are not going home to him. You are going to be married to another, a man named Vilis, who sent you a hundred red roses and all sorts of weeds and things."

"All of which I discarded—with your help, remember? Anyway, he, Vilis is only a means to my real end. Through him I shall find my way back to Viktors, my Faust, my Mephistopheles, to everything that matters. Yes, even to Life! I'll take all that I am—with all the world that I have gathered, to him for a wedding present. I would go, have gone, to such great lengths for him and no one else. Let the world call me what it will! Its terms of morality do not apply to me. I believe that I explained it to you already." Alma's voice jumped a pitch higher, getting irritated, defensive. She did not say anything more until the train had crossed several fields and valleys and was now walled by thick woods.

"When I am back in Latvia," she resumed, "we will skip over everything. Cut out the superfluous scenes like in a play, stop the bad film from rolling on: *Roll it back to Scene One,* I'll command. . . . And we see Latvia rolling on from, say May 15, 1934. Standing under our banners the President smiles and waves with his big hand. . . . We fast-forward. *Cut out the deportations, the blood, the escapes. Cut it all out! . . . Let's stop for a drink, let's go to the cafe, let's sing!* We're all young and gay. Hey, why are those idiotic Germans glaring at me? Alma's face is a white mask. "What's the matter, why are you glaring at me like that? On whose side are you on anyway?"

"You scare me. It scares me, when you talk like that."

"Scares you? Well, it scares me too, this marriage that is about to strangle me. It scares me quite a little, but then I always have stage fright, always shake a bit before the curtain rises. You see how I tremble now, but it's to be expected." She laughs too loudly. The people stare. "It is a new, strange act I am about to perform," she says, looking straight at them all, speaking in loud Latvian. "To hell with all of you!" Alma says to the other passengers and looks out and away.

"I want you to come to America," Milda says composed. "I will sponsor you as soon as I get settled. I'll talk to Miss Fern. She will help. I feel so horrid leaving you right at the edge of the sea, while I sail away. I will never forgive myself. Never!"

"Now you stop that nonsense!" Alma shouts in a harsh whisper. "Stop treating me like a helpless old woman, and here I am barely over thirty, still kilometers away from forty—the age from which the wise, ancient Greeks only began to count Life." They rode on in oppressive silence, their minds bursting with pain and outrage, struggling with the huge hand of fate that pushed them like those old black and red checker discs.

"Has it ever occurred to you," Alma started up, "that I might want to be free of you? Ha?" She turned to her niece harshly, her eyes flashing mad warning signals. "I want to carry out the idea of my life, too, don't you see? I don't want to meddle with you and that stiff Kārlis boy. I must leave you alone to mold and make him, to turn him into a man—if that's possible. And there will be babies, lots of them. Well, would you make a nurse out of me? Would I have to rock them and tell them little moral tales and watch you grow fat and nervous? We would not be free to be what we are, as we have been and would need to be. He would always be there spying around corners—he and his eternal mother, who can fill a house all by herself. Oh, I don't think America would be big enough for all of us, not to mention your tempting Vanags, who, true to his name would circle around your nest in patient, eagle-eye swoops, waiting for his chance to plunder your nest. Actually, on the other hand, it would be very interesting, but I'll pass on that."

Milda wept silently leaning against the windowpane, pulling the corner of the blanket up to her chin.

"It's out of the question," Alma finished. She dug deeply into her bag and brought out a package of *Lucky Strikes*. She opened it slowly and pulled out a cigarette. Milda stared at her hand holding on to the white nicotine post, from which, she had assumed, Alma was free. Then she saw the impatient hand shake and Alma rise and, hitting her feet against other feet, go out into the corridor to smoke, to in-and exhale. Milda stared blankly at the blue back framed in gray fumes, and then she turned her head away to watch the sliding landscape until she fell asleep.

She jerked awake at a station. They were crossing into the British Zone. Alma was sitting again beside her, cool and far away. There was the tedious border check with barking men taking the passports, glaring at them suspiciously and then passing on with a polite *Danke*. The passengers glanced at each other and mindlessly watched people get off and on. Those who stayed put, acknowledged their new fellow travelers with polite nods and promptly ignored them. And then the train, leaving yet another German town, rode at full speed over the flattened and hazed landscape.

Around noon they unwrapped their sandwiches, the apples and grapes and the bottle of lukewarm, flat *Seltzer* and ate their last meal together, at times swallowing hard, at times choking, not saying any words, hardly looking sideways at each other. To distract herself, Milda offered an apple to a little girl, who took it eagerly. "You have such pretty blue eyes," she said and the child, grinning, bit into the red fruit.

"I'm hot," Alma said, and they stepped over the newly arrived German feet and went out into the corridor. Alma lit up and pulled the fire into her lungs in long, hungry draws. Gray-blue stinging smoke came out of her dilated nostrils. Her lips puckered, eager for the next draw that left a red ring around the moist end of the diminishing cigarette.

"You are not actually planning to go back to Latvia, are you?" Milda asked cautiously.

"Oh no, no, no," Alma heaved, shaking her head violently, blowing smoke like an engine. "Not now, not yet. But I might later, when it's safe, when he calls me. I know the time will come. It always does. I'll trust my intuition that guides me better than a map. Stalin won't live forever, and when he does finally meet his maker in hell, things will change. There will be a great shaking up. There always is. But I would not go back unless Latvia was acceptably free. I won't go unless I can come out again, unless I can open and close my own doors. I will never be locked up, you know that."

"Yes."

"But I will stay close by. Close to the Baltic Sea, close to his call—like a lonely seagull."

"Do you really believe that he is still alive?"

"Yes."

"But why hasn't he written? He could have."

"Don't be stupid! For the same reason no one writes, for the same reason we're all here going every which way. Who knows what's going on behind those bars? These years must be really bad. Even the Americans admitted to it, but they had no specific information. No hard evidence. Only the silence of a slaughter house after all the animals have been stunned. The *Amis*, of course, don't care all that much. They were allied with Russia, and they don't want to rattle the Bear's cage. He's inside the Iron curtain, and what happens there, is his *internal affair*. The idea that the Americans would now go and fight Russia, as some of our politicians expected and hoped, is absurd. All the men I knew could not wait to get home to their wives and gardens. Even my journalist. See no evil, report no evil, especially about the Allies. It's bad foreign policy, bad public relations, they all told me." She smoked another cigarette quietly, looking into the eastern horizon as if probing its tight edge. Her face was very pale where the powder had worn off, and her hand shook slightly, dropping ashes.

"I know he lives. Don't ask me how. I simply know." She finished the cigarette and put her hand over Milda's as it held on to the slightly opened window. "You will find out soon enough, if you haven't already, about a woman's intuition. I won't be telling you things anymore. You will have to learn by yourself what it means to be a real woman, to know things, yet be helpless and never have peace because you don't have the freedom not to know. Men don't know things the way women do. It's just the way it is, and that is why we must struggle so much. Soon, when you are married, you will know that I am telling the truth."

"I think I know that already."

They went back into the compartment, back to their seats, back into their separate silences. The train raced on. Milda stirred. "When we reach our destinations," she said, "when we cross the Sea and the Ocean and you are in Sweden and I in America, will we then—in good time, of course—will we be at home? Will we ever find a home and be like normal people? Will this feeling of exile ever be over?"

Alma shook her head and shrugged her shoulders. "You ask hard questions, my dear girl." She took Milda's hand and warmed it in both of hers. "I don't think it will ever end, not as long as we haven't our land under our feet and our air in our lungs." She played with Milda's fingers, turning the diamond ring so it might catch the sun. "I am afraid it will always go on, and by the time we do get back, we'll have lived in exile so long that it will have become our home, though mobile, and what was once home, will be a strange place, full of strange people, unknown laws, changed ways of life, but meanwhile we'll be like animals in a zoo. No matter how well it goes with us, we'll always be out of place. If it goes too well, we'll become fat monkeys that couldn't run through trees even if suddenly the whole jungle were brought to them. If it goes badly, we'll drown in our own tears, and the world will laugh at us. The world has no sympathy for prolonged weakness or mourning. It wants laughing and dancing monkeys, not manic depressives." She breathed deeply; she was out of breath, tired from so many long sentences, but she forced herself to go on: "So, my darling, be sure you find the right face to wear, when you get to America. Smile. They smile a lot. I've seen no serious face in any photographs they showed me. And don't be too deep. I learned that also from my friends and lovers. They like people to be happy—the quicker the better. Instantly is best, and smiling. . . . Your smile is so beautiful! It will serve you better than your passport. It'll get you places. *You have what it takes.* A phrase I learned from the *Amis.* Just take care of yourself, especially your teeth."

Milda smiled.

"And don't, all of you *free Latvians* lock yourselves up behind the golden bars of sweet nationalism," Alma spoke on. "Bars are bars. They close over the mind also, and the mind becomes scarred, uncertain. It cannot fly, it cannot sail, and soon it cannot talk except in dull imprisoned, hacked out phrases. It has started to happen already, this dull unity. I felt it happening to the people who lived all bunched up on the other side of the river. The actors couldn't be creative but looked constantly to each other for approval, and together they sought the approval of the directors, who looked back to our poor, deported President. Only he isn't there anymore. The old ideal is gone, and everyone is afraid to chisel out a new one, one that would work in our ever-changing world. So our confused leaders of Exile regurgitate the old norms and fix them into a code of sorts: *This is the right way. The real Latvian way.* You heard it also in school pounded into you, didn't you? You memorized. We all did, but it killed something inside you and set you back a few notches. And so it was also with the theater, and if you broke the codes, if you kissed on stage or off, in your own way, different from the way the figurines of the director's mind kissed, you were suspect—especially if you're already suspect because you live on the other side, where bridges had to be crossed."

Alma rested, drinking the Seltzer, then went on bitterly: "Some of them hated me, I could tell, for knowing German and English, for going and coming at my own speed. As they clustered in bunches, they envied me because I lived in a real house, in a real room with walls and doors, not discarded army blankets, and because I would not let anyone see our room. And when they could not get at me—because I always knew my lines—every line, every emotion behind the lines and words and could project so the people could feel the drama—they went after you."

"What are you talking about?" Milda roused herself, sitting up straight, turning to face her aunt, whose words had bubbled on and on like an unruly fountain of bitter water.

"Listen," Alma said, holding her down. "That trial of yours, I am certain, happened because they had enough of us. They could not stand our being separate and free, yet, at the same time, they saw that we were loyal Latvians, only not like they. Wasn't I the best tragic heroine and you the rising Miss Exile Latvia?"

"Well. . . So?"

"Yes, and it was when they could not rule over our lives, our spirits, our decisions, they threw us out, burned us like witches in the marketplace of Medieval Riga."

"It all sounds too well made, too worked out, like a play, my dear Aunt, a play you have created in your fertile mind." Milda said, shaking her head, showing her disbelief, wanting to point out that Alma might see things in others that were not there but only phantoms of her own mind, teetering between madness and enlightenment. But any crossing of her mind's path would only result in angry contradictions. But Alma was serious; her eyes shone full of spite and flames.

"But why do you say *us*? . . . Only I was on trial, and for a very specific act. I did not behave properly. They were right, of course, actually. I deserved to be disciplined, for order must be maintained, even when I did not like it, because I should not have left the girls alone. I should never have jumped over the fire. There were other ways to escape from him, but I was not thinking; I made a scene. I should never have provoked Mr. Vanags." Milda's voice lowered, her fingers interlocked. Only saying the name made her blood pump flashing blushes to her face. But Alma didn't notice.

"Exactly," she said. "But you did, and that's that, and it isn't over yet. But that is your problem which you will have to solve. However, they didn't know all that, didn't know why you acted the way you did. They didn't know that you were terrified of being raped. And why didn't they go after him? Why didn't someone look into that?"

"I don't know."

"I'll tell you why! Because he is a man and an invalid and therefore infallible, and because you are different—too beautiful, too smart. Because they couldn't control you. And—you lived with me—such a bad, bad influence. . . . Oh, had we lived on as we did, I would have come under attack soon enough." Alma paused again, her brow wrinkled, thinking, pondering. "They had nothing on me. No proof. I never confided in anyone; never went sunning on their rooftop. I had to keep my trips secret, and the men I worked for helped me. Secrecy was their business. *The secrecy of Cold War,* they said, trying to explain that new phrase to me as best they could, not really understanding it themselves. "If you speak, we'll dismiss you, and you and any dependent will lose forever the chance to enter the United States of America". So I swore to keep their mystifying secrets; I am still sworn to that secrecy, still afraid of punishment, for they could find anyone anywhere. So now you understand why I had to keep my trips hidden even from you so that you would not have to carry my secrets and my burdens. But, in time, you can be sure, they would have been discovered. Secrets always are, and then I would have been thrown out of enchanting *Esslingen am Neckar* and perhaps turned over to the Soviets with a free ride East. And so, naturally, I was afraid, still am. . . . There would have been no place to go, nowhere to hide. . . . Nothing to eat, no way to take care of you. Anything could have happened if those who ruled our lives in out beautiful oasis had real power."

"But they didn't have that power and still don't."

"Thank God for that. But still, they can spoil your mind, your name, your belief in your own goodness. Power is the most dangerous weapon man has, especially over women, especially talented and beautiful women. So, take your old Aunt's advice, my child, always find your little attic room and keep your hand on the door handle. Don't let the zealots ever find the handle to your weakness. It will become the leverage of their power. They will band together and the force will be devastating."

"Oh. . ." She thought Alma was getting too carried away by her wild imagination.

They rode on, resting their minds. The day was slipping into late afternoon. The sun shone in their faces, squinting and distorting the lines. Someone pulled down the drab shade. Looking at the half sky, Milda thought about the future, which Alma presented to her more like a battlefield than a promising construction site. But she was too tired to listen and didn't want to think about conflicts and winning or losing. She thought about Miss Fern's house and her prepared room, which would be roomy and on the first floor. That house has no attic rooms. Everything is low and accessible. From the back door she will step right into the lily garden. It will be so easy! She will have a house like that after she and Kārlis are married—after only another year. She will always avoid hot attics and cold, damp cellars; she will have her parlor and kitchen and dining room, with a large table and chairs, on the ground floor, her bedrooms and nursery on the second, the way she had seen layouts in American magazines. She would not go any higher, except, perhaps to store things. She knew that high places are hard to keep clean, and she has had enough of carrying buckets up and down stairs. She imagined herself spending many happy hours in the kitchen, cooking and baking. She will like that, especially if her babies sit close by in high chairs. Oh, it will be all so lovely! She will forget the pains of these years, even this trip, this final agony and that afternoon with Vanags. *Why, oh why did I do it? What was the matter with me?* She swore to forget all that and be the best wife and mother.

"I'll have many children," she sayed. "It will make up for all those I am leaving behind—Anna, Lilia, Zelda. . . Zelda.—We also rode a train together once, just like this, planning to meet again. . . . She waited for me. Perhaps she is still waiting. Anyway, that is where I see her—always waiting on the platform next to a gigantic black locomotive that blows out clouds of steam. I see her lost in the steam, like in a cloud. Same as Mamma. Simply lost in steam. . . . How could I ever find them in steam clouds?" Milda wept, bent over, looking at the sun that was turning red. She blinked into it and saw lots of rings—red, green, purple, black, all floating in the dark caves of her mind like helium balloons.

"Stop!" Alma put her hand over the wide eyes. "Don't look at the sun, you'll turn blind." She pulled Milda to her, close to her heart and let her finish crying. Against the heart the orphaned child whispered in heaving phrases, "Thank you, Aunty, for saving my life. I must make it worth your sacrifice. I owe such a huge debt to you and everyone, and most of all to Latvia for giving me this—my life. Now I'm turning my back to it also, leaving it behind, just when, God knows, it needs me—all of us—very much." She rested, and closed her eyes, feeling Alma's breasts like comforting pillows, so soft and fragrant, remembering. . . remembering that they are not alone in this train that races to the ends of their world. She sat up and saw beads of sweat on Alma's forehead and upper lip. Tiny drops making pin-size rainbows. "I must give birth to many children and take them all back to Latvia, that is how I'll pay back for your sacrifice, for your saving and keeping me in nylons and velvets."

"Good luck, my beautiful dreamer," Alma said yawning. "Only don't take on too much. I absolve you from any obligations toward me, but I won't forgive you if you don't write to me."

"Of course I'll write!" Milda lightens up. "Pages and volumes, whole books. We are very good at letters. We have lived and breathed through ink. We have interred our souls in sheets of lined paper."

"Yes. True."

The train is near Bremen. Houses appear. People stir, get up, stretch, and reach for their luggage. Milda's blood begins to race, working havoc throughout her pulses. A short while, and they will be forever separated, buried in opposing continents, across roaring waters.

The sun peaks from below the shade, scorching the obstructed horizon with its brilliant flames. Milda rises, grabbing for her things, but Alma holds her fast to the seat, close to her. "You saved my life also," she says. "So we are even. Our scales are balanced."

"Oh, you mean, when I was thirsty at the time the bombs fell?" Milda asks, clutching the blanket that faintly smells of mold.

"I almost forgot that," Alma answers. "But, yes, of course," she says, running her fingers gently over the woven design of the old relic. "Then most of all—most clearly, that is." She shades her face from the sun, saying, "I was thinking of the other time. When I was sick. In Oeslau. I really did want to kill myself on that Walpurgis night, the same when, by sheer coincidence and unbeknown to any of us, Hitler killed himself. I would have if it hadn't been for you. Never did I want to die as much as then, as when the Iron Curtain fell on us—also at the time unbeknown to you and me. But, actually, we must go back to the very beginning. If you hadn't been with me, I would never have left Latvia, and they surely would have deported me.

"Lots of things would have happened differently if I had not lost the checker game. But you would still have escaped with Zelda. She might be here, going to America and not I. Oh!" Milda choked up again, "How will I ever be free?"

"Hush," Alma pulls her tightly to herself. "All our past is behind us like this country we have traveled through and across. It is not our fault that we are dead or alive, innocent or guilty. Other hands rolled the real gigantic dice right over our land and people—before we even had learned how to count and measure. So don't cry for me or them, but live for all of us." Alma swallows hard, trying to keep her voice from breaking. "Yes, live deeply and splendidly!"

The people around them are moving out into the corridor. Time has almost run out. "There was something I still want to ask you." Milda turns her face so she would see Alma's eyes.

"What?"

"Children. Babies. How is it that you never had any—even accidentally?"

Alma lets out a bitter sigh and reaches for her purse, for her *Lucky Strikes*. "Yes. You must know about that too," she says, playing with the half empty package. "So be it.—Well, I closed myself up. Had an operation. You need not know when and how. She took a deep breath and whispered, "This has been my darkest secret, and now it, too, comes to light. Well, all right. . . . I am an actress above all, and I had no husband but men who had wives or girlfriends. So—I could not, nor would risk any chances. It's all right. I didn't want to bring children into this world. And what could have come out of my flesh? What language would I teach her? In what accents? And how would she or he answer me? How could we talk to each other?"

Slow tears flood Alma's eyes. "The War, damn it! War is a monster that swallows even the unborn. It is a hydra that never has enough. . . . But I saved you. You are my child. My sister's precious, her jewel she was so proud to show off, whenever we walked pushing your stroller on the boulevards of Riga; when we sunbathed on our white beaches and you crawled up to where the water glazes the sand. You tried to catch the foam. . . . Poor Zelda, the ugly duckling, she dove into the water, head first. I pulled her out, and she didn't even cry. She laughed and dove again. . . . Ah. . . . I wonder where she is now. What's become of her? She was the clod, you the pearl, and I saved you. Pulled you out of the mouth of the hydra. I saved you so that you could carry our blood and culture to the New World and plant the best of us there. You are right in wanting children. You are so right! And you will know what to do with them. One day, you will bring them to Latvia. I see that day." She stares at the vanishing sun. "You were right in choosing Kārlis Arājs. So right. He will protect you from the invalid and any other silly temptations. He will fence you off good and keep you busy."

"Please! Don't talk about him! Don't make me remember! It gives me the shivers. See?"

"I see. It doesn't go away so easily—the desire, the forbidden longing—so be always careful. Keep the hawk out of the hen house!"

The train is braking, slowing down. The landscape, too, slows down. Milda watches the sharp contours of the fields, trees, houses. The houses of Bremen come to meet them. The journey is over. Only seconds, and they will be in the station. Milda pulls down her handbag and holds on to the blanket.

"Your magic mantle," Alma says stroking the frayed edges. "It is all that I can bequeath to you. It will protect you from harm, as always, so hold on to it! In times of trouble, cover yourself with it and I'll be there. We'll all be together again."

Milda smiles sadly.

The train is inside the station. It stops, and they fall forward and then into each other's arms. They hold on tightly, for dear life, and for all the love in the world. They stay locked, glued together, for precious second the length of eternity, and then they separate slowly as if they would bleed if they pulled apart too quickly and carelessly. They don't mind that their compartment is almost empty. They don't hear the warning whistle. . . . A hard knock on their window makes them jump. They pull out of each other and for a moment mirror themselves in each other's tear-flooded eyes. Then Milda picks up her things, leaving all the wilted flowers on the rack, and without any final kiss hurries off the train.

She runs to stand below their window, which Alma pushes open. Alma leans out, down, down, to reach the tips of Milda's outstretched fingers. They touch as the whistle blows its shrill scream. The doors slam shut. The train is moving, and Milda, still reaching, runs beside it and then falls behind. Alma tosses a heap of flowers out the window. They fall on the platform and in the train cavity, and then she waves a white wrinkled handkerchief, and Milda lifts up her tear-soaked, lace-trimmed one. As the train curves out of the station, Alma leans further, but all that can be seen from the platform is the white hanky, like a feather, fluttering against the blackness of the train. And then it, too, vanishes in the smog and the twilight.

Last Screening and Benediction

A warm, strong hand pulls Milda away from the mammoth tail of the train and the gleaming tracks. A smaller, cooler hand takes hers, and she moves mindlessly, wrapped in an old, odd blanket. She is swept along by the crowd that hurries she knows not where. She fixes her eyes on the back of the preacher, who seems to know where they should go. He walks quickly, at times glancing back at his wife and children who lag behind, tangled up in the mob, waiting for Milda to get around those people who come between them. They go down stairs, through an under path and up again. Mrs. Gramzda stops to catch her breath. She is flushed, holding on to a railing. No one sees her heart, only a pained face, red, then pale. Vizma waits with her like a nurse, tenderly. Little Aija holds her mother's skirt with both hands. Helga, tight by Milda, stops. Jānis runs back and asks what's wrong. He is dragged down by his large accordion case and shifts his grip. But the preacher has hurried on. He must be there on time because no one will wait for them. No one. The world will not stop and wait for the heart to catch up. The bus will not wait, neither will the ship.

The bus takes them to the clearing camp. The bus is full of tired people who look out the windows at a darkening sky which wears a bright orange band all around its edge. The bus rides through dark pine forests, down a sand-dune road until it reaches the camp—some camouflaged, useless army site. The people get off. Uniformed Englishmen show them their assigned spots in the barracks. They put their things on bunks and gradually, like falling dominos, fall asleep.

They endure a week at this camp. More shots, more questions, DDT, deep breathing, peeing in bottles, eating thin, pale soup and black bread that has no taste. They get bananas, the first ever. They eat and are disappointed. It's neither fruit nor vegetable. Fruit should have juice, but bananas have none. They are more like potatoes without gravy, mushy and strange in the mouth. Aija spits them out and will not eat. She cries and holds her mother's skirt most of the week.

Refugees of other nations are there also, sitting in small, segregated groups during the long evenings, talking in their own languages and singing their folk songs. Poles, Hungarians, Lithuanians, Estonians, Romanians, Jews. . . Each finds his own spot; each makes a campfire. There are only a handful of Latvians, but they pull together, close to the fire and tell their stories, which are all the same, one like the other: deportations, burning, war, refugee camps, and now—the dream of America. All the same. Jānis plays his accordion, softly so as not to disturb the others. They sing in muffled but clear melodies, and when they are done, the preacher says a few words—a prayer or fitting Biblical lines, and then they all go to their bunks. Thus they wait impatiently for the day of departure.

"Tomorrow," at last they tell each other excitedly. "It will be over. We're off to America!"

The last day on Europe's shore dawns normally. The sun breaks through the darkness and haze and shines down on the earth, shines on the children of the earth—the homeless and the housed, the hungry and the satisfied, the just and the unjust. It shines because it is the sun that must burn and in burning give life.

*

Milda turns her face to the sun. The wind blows back her hair and skirt. She is out walking alone through the dune paths, up the hills growing with small wind-twisted pines. She walks to the edge of the land and sees the sea—shimmering, blue, and vast. She cannot go down to the sea because a tall wire fence is in the way. She is inside the fence; has been all week, like a prisoner on probation, eating thin soup and tasteless bread. She remembers that beyond the fence and the water waits her bridegroom. She looks at her diamond. It shines out its bright promise. It sparkles, and she is happy. It will soon be over, this waiting, this bleak exile.

She walks along the fence, wondering who has walked in these dunes before her. Who were those people standing here, their fingers woven through the tight wire tatting, looking at the sea? Were they prisoners of war? Boys like her cousin Juris drafted and handed a gun, buried alive in a trench like a grave? Yes, boys reaching out through this same fence, waiting for letters, waiting for freedom, waiting for ships to sail.— And who were they who built the fence? Who gave the commands? Who rules the world?

But no one answers her, nor is she seeking any real historical facts. She only tries to read the sand, where no footsteps have remained. She turns to look back and sees her own small footsteps quickly blown away. "I am not here, I never was," she whispers, feeling the wind blow at all things.

She sees the seagulls flying, circling all around. They are lean and free scavengers, their silver wings shining. They fly in flocks and in small units—in threes and twos, darting, white, white in the blue sky. They seem, through her blurring tears, like white torn handkerchiefs tossed and flopping in the wind and the spray of the sea. She watches three gulls flying close together, winging straight into the sun toward the harbor, where the ships rock, but a strong wind pulls them apart, and they separate in three directions. One flies high, the other circles around, lost in another flock, while the third plummets into the sea. . . . In the twinkling of her eye, Milda loses all of them. She cannot tell one from another. There are so many, so many waiting for the ships to come in and go out. They circle all around, free but bound by fate forever to the edge of land and sea, their white, silvery wings shining, shining in the sun.

*

That evening the refugees gather again around their separate bonfires. Again they sing their folk songs and talk softly, the men poking the fire, the women cradling their sleeping, whining children. They share the last pieces of bread. They pass around bottles of drink and then sing again—louder, with hope and fear in their voices, the way Gypsies sing on strange hills.

Milda sits on her blanket, one corner around her shoulders, the other around Helga. They sit tightly against each other, like sisters. On the next blanket sits Mrs. Gramzda with Aija, her head on her mother's lap, looking at the fire, her hands reaching for the sparks that fly up to the stars. Vizma sits close to her mother, ever watchful, ever helpful. With one foot on a piece of driftwood, stands Jānis and plays the accordion. The small, congealed group sings as one—all the verses, all the variations. Everyone knows the words by heart, and the words go from heart to heart, slowly, mournfully. Suddenly, Jānis spreads out the pleats of his instrument wide open, pushes them back together and sings, *"Oh, give me a home, where the buffalo roam. . ."* He sings the whole ballad easily, in his new-born baritone. *"Home, home on the range, where the deer and the antelope play. . ."* Vizma hums along and nudges Milda to join. The trio sounds good. Helga joins in and sings loudly, here and there going off tune, but she knows all the words and thinks it's a very appropriate song. People from other camps gather around and are welcomed. When this and other American songs are finished, the preacher asks his son to play a hymn, something that all would know. Jānis presses down the full opening chords of *A Mighty Fortress is our God.*

After the first bars, all the people—from every nation—sing in the German language, in a united chorus. After the *Amen*, the preacher stands up and, by the light from his flashlight, reads from the Bible in heavily accented English, hoping that all would hear and understand:

O give thanks unto the Lord, for he is good, for his mercy endures forever.

Let the redeemed of the Lord say so, whom he hath redeemed from the hand of the enemy and gathered them out of the lands, from the east and from the west; from the north and from the south.

They wandered in the wilderness in a solitary way; they found no city to dwell in.

Hungry and thirsty, their soul fainted within them.

Then they cried unto the Lord in their trouble, and he delivered them out of their distresses.

And he led them forth by the right way that they might go to a city of habitation.

Oh, that men would praise the Lord for his goodness and for his wonderful works to the children of men!

For he satisfies the longing soul and fills the hungry soul with goodness. Amen.

Amen, say the people. *Amen.* And slowly, having put out their fires, they walk the sandy paths to their barracks, where they will sleep.

But Milda cannot sleep. The preacher does not sleep either; he reads the Bible by flashlight. The others toss about their bunks. From her top bunk, through a small window, Milda watches the stars shining brilliantly. She would see such stars over Europe, her Europe, for the last time, she is certain, because she knows that the Atlantic Ocean is very wide and deep and those who go to America hardly ever return. . . . She knows that Alma talked about returning only to make her feel better. She allowed that.—

The sky is full of stars, but Milda can see only those framed in her window. She names them, as she and Alma had often done. It's a game. She gives each star a name until she runs out of the names of her loved ones, all those who now are as far away from her as the most distant star. She calls that star Zelda. . . . The star in Orion's belt is her father, and the cluster of the Seven Sisters—well, these are naturally: Katerina, Matilde, Alma. . . The brightest is Alma. . . . And beyond them the nameless, the Milky Way, the masses of people, her people— now scattered all over the universe like grains of sand, like seeds, like stardust.

"Pastor, what are reading?" Milda asks softly.

"The Book of Revelation, my dear, trying to read in English, to memorize it," he answers. "But you should be sleeping. It's very late."

"I can't, so please read to me, read so I can hear," she asks. But they all hear her. No one is able to fall asleep. Even the children raise their heads and listen:

> *After this I beheld, and, lo, a great multitude, which no man could number, of all nations, and kindred, and people, and tongues, stood before the throne and before the Lamb, clothed with white robes, and palms in their hands.*

> *And they cried with a loud voice, saying, "Salvation to our God, which sitteth upon the throne, and unto the Lamb."*

And all the angels stood round about the throne, and about the elders and the four beasts, and fell before the throne on their faces, and worshipped God, saying, "Amen: Blessing and glory, and wisdom, and thanksgiving, and honor, and power, and might, be unto our God for ever and ever. Amen."

After echoes of whispered *Amen,* a silence settles over all. The preacher turns off his flashlight.

"Thank you," Milda says, looking out the window. She says good night to the stars, then pulls her blanket up to her chin and soon falls asleep. In the glassy harbor, gently rocks a white, anchored ship. The sea gulls sleep.

The End

CPSIA information can be obtained
at www.ICGtesting.com
Printed in the USA
LVOW12s1150120516
487912LV00001B/1/P